Gullible

by

Rosemary Kubli

Gullible

Cover Art by *Jennifer Greeff*

The Wild Rose Press, Inc.
PO Box 708
Adams Basin, NY 14410-0708
Visit us at www.thewildrosepress.com

Publishing History
First Edition, 2023
Trade Paperback ISBN 978-1-5092-4851-3
Digital ISBN 978-1-5092-4852-0

Published in the United States of America

Tiptoeing back to her suitcase, Marie was unexpectedly consumed with guilt. She'd fretted for weeks over not being able to obtain the necklace. Now that it was in her hands, she questioned whether she could go through with the job.

A month ago, when she and Gus concocted their scheme, she hadn't anticipated falling in love with her target. Since meeting Jonathan, she'd shed the hard-hearted, deceitful persona she hid behind in order to perform the deeds required of an expert con artist. Jonathan had awakened her conscience and made her realize it was time to right her wrongs.

So, what are you going to do? Follow your heart and sacrifice the job in deference to the man you love, or stick with the plan out of loyalty to Gus?

Marie had lingered in the dressing room long enough for her absence to be noticed. "Marie? Are you all right?" Jonathan's groggy voice called out.

"Yes, I'm fine," she replied. Time had run out and she had to make a choice.

Dedication

To Tim, for your love, encouragement and, above all, your patience.

Chapter 1

Siena
Summer 2021

Siena Ricci tossed back her head and burst into a raucous laugh befitting the tipsy, devil-may-care party girl she was pretending to be. Faking a proper English accent, she said, "Bloody hell, Parker! That was the funniest joke I've ever heard!"

Nestled inside a luxury limo with the handsome and playful Parker Dupree, she was posing as Candace Carmichael, a feisty Brit hell-bent on carousing her way through a carefree holiday in the States. Lurking underneath the stilettos and skimpy, skintight dress, however, was a devious woman whose intuition was attuned to every detail of her surroundings. She sat back against the cool leather seat and calculated the timing of her next move. The con was in its final stage and, although she'd never yet (to coin a phrase) been caught in the act, even the smallest misstep could result in her being exposed for who and, more disastrously, *what* she truly was.

She sipped her champagne, just enough to wet her glossy dark red lips, and studied Parker as he refilled his drink while crooning along to Milo Everett's soulful tune, *Slide By*. She had to admit, Parker really was adorable. But, despite her fondness for him, she was too savvy to ever let her emotions interfere with business. Besides, by the end of the evening this job would be history, and Parker Dupree would be just another name on the long list of men she'd successfully deceived.

"To us!" Parker toasted. He pinged his flute against hers, then downed half his glassful in one swig.

A thirty-year-old attorney with political ambitions, Parker enjoyed inherited wealth that afforded him any indulgence he fancied. This evening, he and the woman he believed to be Candace Carmichael were celebrating his good fortune amid ambient lighting and soft music as their limousine inched its way through the congested traffic on Fifth Avenue. While she'd been sipping her champagne sparingly, Parker's glass had been bottomless. He was just shy of being three sheets to the wind which was right where she wanted him.

The time was right to put Parker to The Test. She rested her arm on the seatback and caressed the nape of his neck with her fingertips. When he didn't resist her touch, she slid her fingers upward and toyed with his thick, dark hair. Parker hunched his shoulders. A low moan purred in his throat.

Her gesture was subtle, but his response played an integral part in the web she was spinning. Over the years, she'd used numerous men as guinea pigs and had formulated a theory. If her target didn't object to being touched in such a tender spot, she'd gained his trust. When the man trusted her, he let his guard down. And, when his guard was down, he became putty in her hands.

Parker finished off the remainder of the champagne in his glass. Lifting the nearly empty bottle from its bed of ice, he asked, "Sweetness, can I pour y'all a smidge more?" His normally suppressed Southern drawl oozed out in full flourish when he had too much to drink.

Raising her flute, she replied, "Far be it from me to refuse bubbly when it's offered!"

Just then, the limousine jerked to a stop. The cold champagne shot from the bottle, missed her flute, and hit the center of her chest instead. Gasping with surprise, she and Parker stared with wide eyes at her well-exposed, alcohol-drenched cleavage. She snickered, then giggled. One glance at Parker sent them both into fits of laughter.

"I'm so terribly sorry, sweetness," Parker said, slipping into his quirky habit of speaking as though he were a genteel southern belle. "Will y'all ever find the kindness in your heart to forgive me?"

"Darling, what is there to forgive?" she asked after catching her breath. "Until now, I never experienced the pleasure of champagne being splashed on my—what do you call them?—tatas."

"Well, still," Parker said, "dowsin' y'all with bubbly was not my finest moment. At least let me offer to clean y'all up." Affecting a crazed expression, he flicked his tongue, lowered his face to her chest, and proceeded to lap up the liquid from her skin.

"Oh, Parker, you're daft!" Although she was willing to let Parker do whatever he desired, she questioned how long he'd carry out the farce. Parker was adept at playing the ladies' man in public, but in their private moments they'd shared only a few dispassionate kisses. Which was fine with her. Their platonic relationship was a welcome break from the bedroom antics she'd engaged in during many of her previous con jobs. "Mm…this feels wonderful. You know, darling, I wouldn't mind if you poured the rest of the champagne on some other parts of my body as well."

Springing up like a jack-in-the-box, Parker glanced at her sheepishly, as if he had something to hide but suspected she was already privy to his secret. He downed the remaining champagne straight from the bottle, then wiped his mouth with the back of his hand. "My daddy taught me to never let good champagne go to waste."

Until that moment, she'd given Parker the benefit of the doubt, but she was now certain he was making a conscious attempt to conceal his homosexuality. His reluctance to come out was understandable. His ultra-conservative family would surely disown him, and his political dreams might go down the tubes if he were to openly admit his preference for men. He was trapped, and for that reason she empathized with him. Like Parker, she also masked her true self and longed for the day she could discard the pretense once and for all.

She had targeted Parker a few weeks earlier when he attended an event at the renowned Willow's Auction House where she was legitimately employed. With a little digging, she learned Parker was in New York to work on a political campaign, but he'd begun his career at the family law firm's UK office where he was often spotted gadding about with fair-haired, party-hearty English women. Donning a strawberry blonde wig, a pair of hazel-colored contact lenses, and a British accent, she captivated Parker's attention one evening at a cocktail lounge where he was having drinks with friends, introducing herself as Candace Carmichael, a single thirty-something vacationing in the States. They began seeing each other on a regular basis, although their friendship remained casual. Still, sex or no sex, Parker proved to be a pushover.

Her next step was to interest Parker in the vintage

Valdière perfume bottle listed in her employer's catalogue. To ensure he would win the item, she'd accompanied Parker to the auction event held earlier that evening. A less skillful chameleon might have been recognized at her place of employment, but her performance as Candace Carmichael had duped even the colleagues with whom she'd worked side-by-side for ten years. With her expert assistance, Parker offered the winning bid and obtained the perfume bottle at the bargain price of $20,000. Parker was unaware, however, the birthday gift he'd soon present to his mother would be a worthless copy of the genuine Valdière. The switch she was about to make would see to that.

The limousine stopped in front of the legendary Baldwin Hotel where Parker had reserved a suite for the duration of his stay in New York. The hotel valet opened the back door and pleasantly greeted Parker by name. "Good evening, Mr. Dupree."

Stepping out of the limo, Parker proclaimed, "The evening is more than good, Jesse. It's spectacular!"

"How's our favorite candidate doing in the polls today?" Jesse inquired.

Fueled by the alcohol, Parker jumped onto his soapbox. While he spewed his long-winded campaign rhetoric, she seized her moment of opportunity. She stealthily repositioned the bag containing the gift-wrapped Valdière to a spot beside her oversized handbag. Concealed inside her purse was a credible copy of the crystal and diamond studded perfume bottle, identically wrapped to match the original. In the shadows, she exchanged the expensive antique for the worthless replica. She zippered her handbag, scooted across the leather seat, and held out the bag from the auction house. Pretending she was surprised by his forgetfulness, she said, "Parker, darling, don't forget the gift you bought for your mum."

Parker swiveled around to face her. "Now, wouldn't I just forget my head? Sweetness, I swear y'all are my saving grace." Passing off the bag containing the fake Valdière, she accepted Parker's free hand for assistance as she emerged from the limo one long, shapely leg at a time.

Jesse ogled her with the same lust-filled gaze she'd ignited in countless men before him. "Ms. Carmichael," he said in greeting, his voice deep, his tone suggestive, his eyes in no hurry to reach her face. After thanking Parker for his tip, Jesse bid the couple a good evening.

"Have a good night yourself, Jesse," Parker replied. "I'll be sure to give Senator Wilkins your best regards." Strolling into the hotel lobby, Parker presented her with an option. "Shall we have dinner now, or another glass of champagne first?"

"More bubbly, of course," she giggled. "But, darling, I need to freshen up. Order for us, why don't you, while I dash into the ladies' room."

"All right, Candy honey," Parker cooed. "Don't be long now."

As Parker stepped away, he collided with a man of comparable age, well-dressed, and extremely handsome. She couldn't help but notice the heat that passed between the men as they exchanged apologies. The stranger continued into the lounge with Parker staring after him, burning desire lingering in his eyes.

She grasped Parker's arm and regained his attention. "Go for it, darling," she said. "You deserve to be happy." Parker's smile and the delight in his eyes confirmed that he understood her meaning and was grateful for her encouragement. She gave him a tender kiss, her way of bidding him good-bye.

In the ladies' room, she entered the stall at the far end of the row. She removed her wig and combed out her blonde hair. Wriggling out of her miniscule dress, she changed into the street clothes she'd hidden in the bottom of her handbag. She replaced the contact lenses with a pair of framed glasses, then wiped off her dark lipstick. Lastly, she placed the gift-wrapped Valdière in a shopping bag which she affixed to the hook on the back of the stall door.

She exited the stall and made eye contact with the younger woman approaching her. The nod she gave the woman was almost imperceptible, but it conveyed her message. The woman, fulfilling her part in the sting, would obtain the shopping bag from the stall and deliver the goods to the man who headed their operation.

Passing through the hotel lobby, she glimpsed into the lounge and eyed Parker with his back leaning against the bar. One full champagne glass, presumably hers, sat near his elbow awaiting her return. She was pleased to find Parker sipping from his own glass while conversing with the man he'd bumped into just a short while ago. Their body language gave the impression they were interested in sharing more than drinks and cocktail munchies. *Perfect!* Parker's new fixation would help him forget all about Candace Carmichael and her mysterious disappearance.

****

From the privacy of her apartment, she called her accomplice. "It's done."

"Excellent," he replied. "Tomorrow evening?"

"I'll meet you at seven." She'd known the man her entire life and understood his cryptic speech. Tomorrow, their black-market buyer would receive delivery of the Valdière. In the evening, over dinner, they would celebrate the tidy profit they'd made on their latest scam.

She whispered a final farewell to Parker Dupree as she tossed her champagne-dampened dress into the trash. Her cunning mind was already running down a list of potential marks for her next con. She considered one of her newer clients, a charming widower who taught English literature at a university near Boston. She made it a rule to never target clients she personally assisted (doing so was simply too risky), but she saw no harm in making this one exception. Although they were acquainted only by phone, this particular gentleman was always receptive to her flirtatious comments, even bantered back with his own subtle insinuations. Plus, despite the fact he was nearly twice her age, they'd formed a strong connection over their similar likes and dislikes on everything from sports and politics to music and fine wines.

Funny how sometimes personalities just click.

Her one concern was the logistics of running a long-distance con. Then again, she'd always thrived on a good challenge. She would test the waters during their next phone conversation. Something about the professor from Massachusetts led her to believe he'd be worth the extra effort.

Chapter 2

Jonathan

Dr. Jonathan Woodward had chosen the wrong time to sink his teeth into Tyler Winslow's latest best-selling legal thriller. For two years, he'd eagerly awaited the release of this newest volume in the ongoing series, but even Winslow's suspenseful writing couldn't keep him from repeatedly glancing at his cell phone and wondering how much longer his call with Willow's Auction House would remain on hold. When his eyes skimmed over the same paragraph for the third time, Jonathan removed his reading glasses, massaged the bridge of his nose, and questioned why he'd bothered to open the book in the first place.

The irony that he, an honored professor of literature, would have difficulty concentrating on a contemporary work of fiction was laughable. Perhaps he should have listened last semester to his graduate students who, in their efforts to talk him out of retiring, had teased that his brain would go to mush the moment he stopped teaching. Jonathan chuckled; he knew better. His mind was merely preoccupied by the impending auction. He closed the book's cover with a snap and tossed the novel onto the top of his antique mahogany desk. He'd wait to enjoy the best-seller, along with a relaxing glass of wine, at a more fitting time.

Out of curiosity, Jonathan lifted his cell phone to check the timer on the screen. His call with Willow's had been on hold for twenty-six minutes. Grunting with exasperation, he rose from the chair and raised his arms to stretch out his back. As he did so, the classical music emanating from the phone's speaker was interrupted (for what Jonathan swore was the tenth time) by a recorded message that offered an apology for the delay, thanked Jonathan for his patience, and assured him his call was important and would be answered shortly.

"Hah!" he grumbled, as if ridiculing an actual person. "Twenty-six minutes is not exactly my definition of *shortly*."

Normally, Jonathan would not have tolerated such an idle use of his time, but the item he was about to bid on was worth his perseverance. In a few minutes, he would participate via phone in an auction event being held that evening at Willow's gallery in Manhattan. To be fair, when his liaison at Willow's placed the call on hold, she'd forewarned Jonathan the wait could be lengthy. To Jonathan's dismay, she hadn't been exaggerating.

Jonathan scanned his library for something to focus on other than the upcoming auction. Stepping over to the glass showcase built into the wall adjacent to his desk, he picked up his twelfth century Chinese porcelain vase and admired its beauty and remarkable history. Procured from a private collector in San Francisco, the vase was the most recent addition to Jonathan's collection of antique trinkets. What had begun forty years ago with his late wife's impulsive purchase of a bejeweled Coudriet cigarette case while on honeymoon in Vienna became a hobby the couple had indulged in during the years they were married. After his wife's passing, Jonathan expected to lose interest, but his desire to comb the world for historical relics had never waned. Whether scouring through a centuries-old shop in a remote European village or working with a retail dealer in the States, the hunt for unusual artifacts continued to be one of his favorite pastimes.

In recent years, Jonathan had developed a close relationship with Willow's. He enjoyed the luxury of participating in their auctions by phoning in his bids to their gallery in Manhattan from the comfort of his home on the outskirts of Boston. Willow's didn't ordinarily keep his calls on hold for such an extended time, but the auctioneers were running behind schedule this evening. Fortunately, Jonathan was a determined man who let nothing stand in the way of getting what he wanted. He'd waited many years for the chance to obtain the item that the prestigious auction house was about to sell to the highest bidder; a few minutes more made no difference.

At last, Marie Lacroix's voice replaced the music loop. "Are you still with me, Dr. Woodward?"

"Yes, I'm still here," he responded.

With great care, Jonathan replaced the vase on the glass shelf, then rushed to take his seat. He opened his laptop to view the live feed being transmitted from Willow's gallery in Manhattan. From the podium, the auctioneer was speaking with his assistants as they prepared to commence bidding on the Singing Bird Pistol, the rare piece that had captured Jonathan's interest.

The Singing Bird Pistol, although appearing to be a real weapon, was instead a miniature replica of a nineteenth century revolver. Encrusted with jewels, the intricately designed ornament was valued for its uniqueness and for the quality of its craftsmanship. Jonathan had coveted the Singing Bird Pistol for most of his adult life. However, the relic had been privately owned and off the market for decades. He was thrilled to discover the *objet de vertu* in the latest catalogue published by the auction house, and the timing couldn't have been better. He'd been searching for a special birthday gift for his daughter-in-law, Catherine, and knew she'd be delighted to receive such a valuable present. With Catherine's happiness in mind, he would let nothing prevent him from winning the upcoming auction.

The bidding was about to begin. As the auctioneer commenced the proceedings, he commanded the attention of everyone inside the gallery. "Ladies and gentlemen, our final item this evening is the Singing Bird Pistol, Lot 12. This is an exquisite work of art, circa 1820, from the famous Swiss watchmaker, Jean-Pierre Barbier."

Jonathan removed a pad of paper and a pen from his desk drawer to keep track of the bidding. Marie had disclosed he'd be going up against some heavy hitters, but Jonathan was not the type to shy away from stiff competition. He was mentally and emotionally prepared for the challenge and, with his inherited wealth to back him, his pockets were deep.

The fervor among the competitors was understandable. The renowned jeweler, Jean-Pierre Barbier, had utilized his skill at crafting timepieces to create lavish *boîte à oiseau chanteur*, singing bird boxes, at the beginning of the nineteenth century. Similar in size to a snuff box, the watchmaker's bird boxes were ornate devices made of shining gold or sterling silver and adorned with a variety of jewels and *guilloché* enamel. Each box was equipped with a key used to prime the mechanism just as one would wind a clock. Then, by triggering a button, the lid opened, and a tiny bird covered with the iridescent feathers of a hummingbird popped out. While opening and closing its beak, twisting back and forth, and flapping its wings, the bird sang for its audience before falling back into the case, the lid closing over it. A singing bird box was admired for the opulence of its jewel-adorned exterior as well as for the precision of its internal workings.

Viewed as a novelty, the popularity of singing bird boxes grew quickly among imperial rulers. Presenting one as a gift to royalty and foreign dignitaries became a custom of the times. Competition between the designers was intense, as was the demand for unique ideas.

One of the most famous creations was a pair of pistols fashioned for the pleasure of the Emperor of China. The pistols were small enough to fit into the palm of the emperor's hand. Their translucent scarlet enamel handles were embellished with emeralds, rubies, and diamonds. The sides were decorated with gold plates depicting exotic animals, and the hammers were gold-matted tiger heads each capped with a single diamond. Blue enamel covered the double barrels which were decorated with golden filigree. When the hammers were triggered, the birds emerged at the barrels' ends as if being shot from the pistols.

Over the centuries, the two pistols were separated and, in the continuous possession of private owners, were seldom offered for sale to the public. Individually, they were valued at close to $1 million. Experts speculated that, if ever reunited, the pair could fetch as much as ten times that figure.

"We will begin the bidding at $250,000," the auctioneer continued. He pointed his gavel at one of the gallery attendees to acknowledge his acceptance of the initial bid. "Do I hear three hundred?" Another paddle was raised.

"Bidding opened at two-fifty, Dr. Woodward," Marie Lacroix said into the phone, her hand concealing the mouthpiece and blocking out the noise inside the gallery. "The price immediately rose to three hundred. Do you want to offer three-fifty?"

"No, not yet." Jonathan had learned to be patient and to rely on Marie's expertise. He muted the volume on his laptop and took his cell off speaker. Holding the phone to his ear, he focused all his attention on Marie's voice as she kept him apprised of the action taking place inside the gallery.

Jonathan would have preferred to attend the auction in person, but a mandatory board meeting at his club late that afternoon had left him with insufficient time to travel into Manhattan. Instead, he left the handiwork to Marie, his liaison at the auction house. Jonathan had worked with Marie in the past, and he trusted her judgment and advice. Not only did she act on his behalf during the live auctions, she also notified him of pieces taken into inventory which she believed would be to Jonathan's liking.

As their professional relationship developed, Jonathan and Marie had also become familiar on a personal level. Jonathan was intrigued by Marie's candor, intelligence, and sharp wit, and he wasn't embarrassed to admit he found the slight accent in her speech to be just a tad sexy. Although he hadn't yet gotten around to asking Marie about her upbringing, considering her name, he assumed she'd spent her childhood in France, or was perhaps French Canadian.

Jonathan was also unsure of Marie's age. Based on the sound of her voice and a few clues he'd gathered during their phone conversations, he made an educated guess she was in her mid-thirties. He was certain Marie was aware he was considerably older than her, but she didn't seem to mind the difference in their ages. Unless he'd allowed his imagination to run wild, he took her coquettish innuendos as indication she was interested in him as more than just a client. Having remained a widower by choice for the past twenty-one years, Jonathan was no stranger to alluring women. Still, his ego was flattered by the enticement he detected in Marie's voice, and he rationalized that perhaps she preferred older men. Regardless, he would schedule a trip to Manhattan soon so he and Marie could meet face to face and explore where their friendship might lead them.

"I'm offered three hundred-fifty thousand," the auctioneer announced. "Do I hear four?"

"I advise you to make an offer, Dr. Woodward." Marie's voice was but a whisper through the phone.

"I agree. Place a bid."

Marie raised her paddle.

"I have four-fifty on the phones. Do I hear five?"

A woman in the audience held up her paddle.

"Five in the house. Do I hear five-fifty?"

An offer in the gallery was immediately raised, then raised again.

"Bidding is at six-fifty," Marie informed Jonathan.

"What would you like me to do?"

"I'll bid six-fifty." Jonathan jotted the figure down on his notepad. The pen still in hand, he fretfully stroked his brow with his fingertips. If he didn't play his cards right, the fast-paced action could result in him losing the bid.

"I have six-fifty. Do I hear seven-fifty?"

Several seconds passed without another offer. Jonathan held his breath as he waited for the auctioneer to continue.

"I have six-fifty. Do I hear seven?"

A pause. A paddle was raised.

"Seven hundred thousand, Dr. Woodward. Do you want to offer seven-fifty?" Jonathan could almost feel the moisture from Marie's breath in his ear. Before he responded, a paddle was raised. "Too late. Someone beat you to it."

Jonathan could wait no longer for the Singing Bird Pistol to be his. As the auctioneer asked for the next bid, he made an impulsive decision. "Offer nine-fifty."

"Are you sure?"

"Yes," he responded sharply. "Make the offer."

Marie raised her paddle and called out, "Nine hundred-fifty thousand!"

A hushed murmur permeated the gallery as those present reacted to the jump in bidding.

The auctioneer challenged the audience. "I have nine hundred-fifty thousand on the phones. Do I hear one million?" He waited several moments but received no response. "Nine hundred-fifty thousand going once…going twice…" He took a moment to scan the gallery before striking his gavel. "Sold to bidder AL75 for $950,000!"

Jonathan gasped and pounded his fist on the desk. "Yes!" he shouted. Both he and Marie laughed with pleasure.

"You got it, Dr. Woodward. Congratulations!"

"Thank you, Marie," Jonathan said. "You have no idea how much this means to me."

"You must be incredibly pleased. I know you've waited many years for the Singing Bird Pistol to be offered on the market."

Tears stung Jonathan's eyes. "It's more than merely adding another trinket to my collection." Taking Marie into his confidence, Jonathan gave himself permission to share with her his family's dismal situation. "Since we last spoke, our family received tragic news. My daughter-in-law, Catherine, has been diagnosed with brain cancer."

"Oh, no!" Marie's voice caught. A moment passed before she whispered, "I'm so sorry."

"Thank you. We're hoping for the best," Jonathan confessed with a heavy sigh, "and she is under the care of the top cancer specialists in the country. But, in all honesty, it doesn't appear hopeful. She and I are close and have shared an affinity for antiques ever since she helped me select the Coudriet snuff box I gave my son, Patrick, when he graduated from medical school. Catherine's birthday is next month. It may be the last birthday she'll ever share with us, so I'm giving her the Singing Bird Pistol as a gift." His voice choked with emotion. He was unable to continue.

Marie's response was soft with empathy. "That's a beautiful gesture. I hope your daughter-in-law knows how lucky she is to have your love and support."

Jonathan took a deep breath and cleared his throat.

"No, I'm the one who's lucky. Catherine and Patrick have been together since their freshman year in college. Three years ago, they had their first baby, a boy they named Oliver. Oliver is such a sweet child. I can't bear the idea of him growing up without his mother if Catherine doesn't survive this disease."

"That's heartbreaking. *Pauvre petit!*"

Jonathan appreciated Marie's sophistication. Only she would express sympathy for the poor little one by means of a French idiom that may be familiar to her but was uncommon in American conversation. However, he'd gotten off track. Marie certainly had other matters that required her attention.

"Marie, I've taken up enough of your time. Can you please see to it that my payment is processed, and have the Bird Pistol shipped to my home?"

Marie was back to being the consummate professional. "I'll be happy to do that for you, Dr. Woodward. On behalf of Willow's Auction House, I'd like to thank you for your patronage and for your valued loyalty."

"Thank *you*, Marie. Without your assistance, I may not have been so fortunate this evening. I'm sure we'll be speaking again soon."

"Yes, I'm sure we will." Marie's voice took on a softer, more personal tone. "But, you know, as much as I enjoy our phone calls, I've been thinking…maybe it's time we chatted in person. Over drinks."

Jonathan smiled, pleased to have confirmation that he and Marie were of the same mind. "I would enjoy that," he told her.

"Good. Let's plan to meet soon. Until then, take care, Jonathan."

Jonathan tossed his phone onto the desk and sat back to savor the evening's outcome. After years of attempting to track down its whereabouts, he was elated that he'd at last taken possession of the Singing Bird Pistol. And he was convinced Marie's flirtatious suggestion just now—*Face it, Jonathan, she was being downright seductive*—was a subtle but bold hint that she, too, was eager for them to become more intimate. Jonathan's instincts warned him to buckle up. A relationship with Marie Lacroix was bound to take him on one hell of a provocative ride.

Chapter 3

Patrick
Summer 2022

Dr. Patrick Woodward refilled his wine glass, excused himself from the dinner table, and retreated to his study. Sitting motionless in his easy chair, his fingers idly traced the spiraled stem of the goblet while he stared into the gloomy shadows. Patrick welcomed the fading light. Under its blanket of darkness, he could hide from the world and express his sorrow without the scrutiny of his well-meaning family and friends.

This room had once been Patrick's favorite space. After a long day, he and Catherine would gravitate to the study where they'd discuss current events, plan for their future, or simply enjoy the comfortable silence while engrossed in their latest novels. Patrick only entered the room these days when he wanted to be surrounded by Catherine's spirit. He was foolish to assume that, by now, he would have overcome her loss. Although he put on a good front for the outside world, the pain and void were always with him. This Thursday, the seventeenth, would mark eight months since her passing. Two hundred forty-five days. Not that he was counting.

Toward the end of her life, when they admitted her cancer was winning the battle, Catherine had been more concerned for her husband and son than she was about her own mortality. Her wish was for Patrick to open his heart to another woman so he and Oliver would have someone to care for them. At the time, Patrick was willing to promise Catherine anything just to put her mind at ease, but he doubted he'd ever replace the woman who'd been his everything. He simply couldn't be that lucky twice in a lifetime.

As a teenager, Patrick was a straight-up geek, the overachieving class valedictorian who always had his nose in a book. Being a head taller than the other boys in his class, unmuscular, and painfully thin, he considered himself unattractive. However, he soon realized the girls in his social circle were willing to overlook a man's physical attributes if his bank account was well-funded. Unfortunately for Patrick, most of his competition was both wealthy *and* handsome. Succeeding in the romance department was not so easy when the odds were stacked against him.

Patrick had always been at home in the classroom, but he was uncomfortable in social situations. Frankly, girls scared him. He avoided school dances and refrained from joining organizations composed of mostly female students. He entered his freshman year at Harvard convinced he was the only boy in his class who had never been on a date, nor had ever been kissed.

All that changed after he met Catherine. At the beginning of his second semester, they were partnered in Organic Chemistry and soon discovered they were two peas in a pod. Patrick, the guy who worried he'd forever be a bachelor, was thrilled to have found his perfect match. From that day on, he never glanced twice at another woman.

His devotion to Catherine, however, didn't stop

other women from flirting with him. As he matured, Patrick blossomed into a man with boyish good looks, and his frequent trips to the gym added muscle to his trim frame. At social events, he'd noticed more women going out of their way to engage him in conversation. He was fairly certain he'd even received one or two indecent proposals.

After Catherine's death, his sister, Veronica, advised him to be cautious. "You've got everything a woman wants, Patrick. You're an attractive doctor from a prominent family who is suddenly eligible again. Divorcees will throw themselves at you, as will the married women who are bored with their husbands. I know how gullible you can be. Please be discerning."

"Don't worry, Veronica," he'd assured his sister. "Oliver and my practice are my only focus now. It will be a long time, if ever, before I have any interest in dating."

Patrick had taken a two-month sabbatical following Catherine's funeral. He needed the time to grieve and to interview nannies for his three-year-old son. Settling on someone who was good with Oliver, reliable, and willing to work around a physician's erratic schedule presented a challenge Patrick had not foreseen. He was at his wit's end when one of the nurses in his practice arranged for him to interview her neighbor, a retired kindergarten teacher who was widowed and had no children of her own.

Louise Grainger was the answer to Patrick's prayers. She was delighted to accept the position and fell in step with Patrick and Oliver as though she'd known them for years. Patrick paid Louise handsomely to accommodate the unpredictable demands of his profession, and in turn she worked above and beyond the call of duty. In addition to her responsibilities as Oliver's nanny, she managed the household for Patrick, prepared dinner for them every evening, and often stayed to share the meal with them. She was almost too good to be true, and Patrick lived in fear that one day Louise would inform him she could no longer continue their arrangement.

Louise had been especially accommodating that evening. Patrick had returned home after a grueling day at the hospital and wanted nothing more than to be alone. While he sulked in his study after dinner, Louise had cleaned up the kitchen, then bathed Oliver and put him to bed. When Patrick emerged from his cocoon and found Louise folding laundry in the kitchen, a pit formed in his stomach. Louise never stayed so late into the evening unless Patrick was on call. He worried she'd hung around to say she couldn't take one more second of his moping and was giving her two weeks' notice. His brow furrowed as he approached her.

"Can't the laundry wait until tomorrow? This has been an awfully long day for you."

"Oh, I don't mind," Louise replied somberly as she folded Oliver's pajamas.

From the wine cooler, Patrick removed the same bottle of Chardonnay he'd opened at dinner. "Would you care to join me?" he asked.

"I would if I didn't have to drive home. Thank you anyway."

He took a seat at the island and faced Louise. "Why do I have the feeling there's something weighing on your mind?"

Louise placed the last of Oliver's T-shirts in the

basket. She set her palms on the countertop and gazed into Patrick's eyes. For once, she appeared to be at a loss for words. Her cheeks flushed, and she blinked back tears.

"You know, Tom and I were so young when we got married. We faced all of life's challenges together, the good and the bad. He was my whole world and when he passed away, I suffered through a period of grief from which I was certain I'd never recover."

She paused. Patrick kept his head down and stared blankly at the countertop. In his mind, he compared Louise's situation to his own.

"What I'm trying to say is, I've been where you are, and I understand what you're going through. You're making a valiant effort to mask your grief but, in all honesty, it's not working. And the one who's affected the most is your son. Do you know what Oliver said to me today?"

Patrick's eyes met hers as he prepared for her words to pierce his heart.

"He told me his daddy is sad because his mommy left him to go to heaven. He may only be three, Patrick, but he can sense your grief is distancing you from him. When you spend time with Oliver, are you giving him all your attention, or are you thinking about your wife the whole time?"

Patrick took a gulp of wine and lowered his head. He didn't need to respond.

"Believe me, Patrick, you'll always feel the pain of Catherine's death, but you've got to get on with your life. If I may offer a suggestion, what got me back on track was the grief counseling group I joined."

Patrick smirked. "Now you sound like my medical

partners. They've wanted to intervene, too, and I've stonewalled them each time. Sorry, Louise, but I can't see myself doing something like that."

"I initially rejected the idea, too," Louise confided. "I'll admit, it took every bit of nerve I could muster to drag myself to that first session, but honestly, Patrick, I couldn't have given myself a better gift. Being around other people who had suffered a loss, who could empathize with my situation, helped more than I ever could have imagined. I still drop by on occasion when depression starts to overwhelm me. You see, grief never entirely goes away."

Patrick took a moment to mull over Louise's advice. He had to admit, she presented a persuasive argument. "How often did you attend the sessions?"

"Twice a week for three months. I didn't need to go that often, but I kind of became addicted."

Patrick shook his head. "I don't know…"

"Well, you need to consider that I had the freedom to attend whenever I wanted. That's not a realistic schedule for you. However, the nice thing is, you're free to show up whenever it's convenient. If it helps you, great. If you don't click with it, well, at least you tried."

After Louise left for home, Patrick returned to his study where he asked Catherine for her guidance. A realist would have insisted his imagination was playing tricks on him, but Patrick ardently believed Catherine's spirit spoke to him and encouraged him to follow Louise's advice. He left the study, placed his empty wine glass in the kitchen sink, then read through the grief counseling pamphlets Louise left on the counter. Unless his schedule changed, he was free to attend the next Monday evening's meeting. He noticed the group met in a church hall. *If nothing else*, he chuckled to himself, *at least the venue is a good omen.* Patrick made up his mind. He'd take Louise up on her offer to stay with Oliver while he gave the group a try.

Chapter 4

Marie

Daybreak shot past the edge of the window blind, hitting Marie Lacroix square in the eye. Marie hated mornings like this when she woke before the alarm sounded. Now she was forced to decide whether to linger in bed, or to get her ass in gear and seize the morning. With her face partially buried in the pillow, she raised one eyelid to check the time. She had ten minutes to play with which, she rationalized as she threw off the covers, was not worth the debate. Besides, the empty space next to her was a sorry reminder that, in her mid-thirties, she still lacked a special someone with whom she could have spent the extra time engaged in a more pleasurable start to the day.

When her feet hit the bare hardwood floor, she reminded herself (as she did every morning) that she needed to invest in an area rug. Although she'd lived in her one-bedroom Manhattan apartment for several years, Marie had never bothered to give the place a homey appearance. She was too busy with more important matters to waste her time shopping for wall hangings and window treatments. What's more, her decorations would be unappreciated as she was seldom at home and never entertained guests there. She viewed the apartment as nothing more than a way station. If her plan played out as expected, within the next few years, she'd be living on a Caribbean Island, a far cry from New York City.

After showering, Marie wrapped herself in a plush towel and entered the bedroom to select an outfit suitable for the auction she was scheduled to participate in that afternoon. Willow's had instructed its employees to wear muted colors while inside the gallery to avoid drawing attention away from the items going up for bid. With that in mind, Marie chose a simple gray dress and matching jacket.

"That policy is a joke when it comes to Marie," Sara, *one of her colleagues at Willow's, had once said to Nan, another colleague, not realizing Marie was also in the restroom.*

"I know," Nan had replied. *"As if that black suit will stop* anyone *in the gallery from staring at her through the entire auction."*

Sara's and Nan's stinging comments had opened Marie's eyes to the fact that her attempt to pass herself off as a Plain Jane during work hours had been an exercise in futility. At five feet nine inches, Marie had been blessed with a perfectly proportioned figure, a flawless complexion, enviable silky hair that cascaded to her shoulders in soft waves and curls, and a face Da Vinci would have begged to immortalize. Around the age of fifteen, she became aware of the stir she caused when she entered a room. As she matured, she grew accustomed to—and secretly enjoyed—sparking a lull in dinner conversations; to women staring, their eyes filled with a mixture of envy and hatred; to men gawking at her with unbridled desire. Her co-workers were correct. Despite her drab wardrobe, minimal use of cosmetics, and hair tugged tightly into a bun, Marie's mere presence in a room created a distraction.

Still, staying under the radar at her day job was essential to the success of her nighttime ventures. To that end, she made a practice of not participating in water cooler discussions, nor did she accept her colleagues' invitations to join them for lunch and after work get togethers. Rather than becoming invisible around the office, however, her aloofness only made her mysterious personal life that much more intriguing. *Why is such a gorgeous woman still single? Has she ever even dated anyone seriously?* Marie had overheard the conversations on many occasions and was amused by the chatter. She so badly wanted to send out a company-wide email to satisfy their curiosity:

Dear Colleagues,
I'm still single because I've not yet met a man
who excites all my senses.

Although Marie firmly believed her ideal match was out there just waiting to be found, she'd ruined the possibility of ever having that head-over-heels-in-love type of relationship she'd dreamed of as a young woman. No decent, self-respecting man would want anything to do with her after learning of her sordid after-hour activities. And if she couldn't be with the man of her dreams, Marie preferred to be alone.

Her burner phone buzzed.

"Good morning," she said. She didn't need to question who was calling. Only Gus communicated with Marie on the burner.

"Hey, doll," Gus's husky voice replied. "Sorry for the early call. I wanted to catch you before you left for work."

"Why? What's up?"

Their habit was to avoid using names and mentioning details. They couldn't risk being overhead by the wrong people.

"I think I've got something big. Can you stop by?"

"I'll be at work until around six. Meet me for dinner?"

"That works. Our regular place?"

"Yes. If I'm late, wait for me."

Had Jonathan Woodward been listening to Marie's side of the conversation, he would have wondered why her normal speaking voice held no trace of a sexy foreign accent.

Chapter 5

Patrick

Patrick finalized a phone call with a consulting physician, then stepped out of his office to resume his afternoon schedule. Strolling down the hall, he opened his laptop to review his next appointment's post-op report.

"Mrs. McElroy is in Room 3," his nurse, Maggie, informed him. "We're running a check on her pacemaker, then she'll be ready for you."

"Thanks," Patrick replied, his eyes never leaving the laptop screen. "I'll be right in."

A moment later, an overheated discussion, which Patrick speculated was more scripted than spontaneous, drew his attention away from Mrs. McElroy's bloodwork results. The flat screen television mounted on the wall in the clinic's waiting room was tuned to a reality TV courtroom drama. A tenant was suing the landlord for not refunding his security deposit. The landlord claimed damage had been done to the apartment.

Judge Sylvie raised her voice as she reprimanded the tenant. "Don't interrupt me while I'm speaking!"

Patrick recognized the voices of Mrs. Evans and Mr. Morales, two of his better-natured patients, as they commented on the action taking place in the mock courtroom.

"Oh, he's in big trouble now," Trudy Evans commented, her eyes glued to the TV screen.

Julian Morales agreed. "You got that right. Nobody gets away with talking to Judge Sylvie like that. No way."

"Good afternoon," Patrick said in greeting as he entered the waiting room.

"Hey, Dr. Woodward!" When Mr. Morales smiled, his entire face lit up. Despite his serious health issues, he was a pleasantly optimistic man.

Mrs. Evans didn't respond. In addition to being absorbed in the courtroom drama, she was acutely hard of hearing. Her son, Warren, who always accompanied his mother to her appointments, gently touched her arm. "Mom, Dr. Woodward is talking to you."

"What?" Mrs. Evans shouted as she swiveled in her seat. "Oh, hi, Dr. Woodward. Judge Sylvie is about to throw this man out of her courtroom."

"That's not good," Patrick shouted back. What he wouldn't do for his patients. "Do you think she'll throw him in jail?"

"She might. And it wouldn't be the first time she's done that either."

"Well, perhaps the judge will show some mercy with these folks," Patrick suggested, feigning interest in the judge's decision. "Maggie will escort you both to your exam rooms in a few minutes." Only Mr. Morales and Warren acknowledged Patrick. Mrs. Evans's attention was again fixed on the television screen.

Forty minutes later, Patrick wrapped up his final examination of the day. "Everything's fine, Mrs. Evans. My only suggestion is that you continue doing whatever is keeping you in such good health. Remember what I always say—I'm counting on dancing with you at your one hundredth birthday party."

Mrs. Evans let out a hoot. What ninety-three-year-old wouldn't be delighted with such a glowing report? "And what do I always tell you, Dr. Woodward? You'll have to wait in line!"

"I'd stand in line all day to dance with you, Mrs. Evans." Patrick assisted his frail patient as she wiggled off the exam table, then shook Warren's hand and wished them a good evening. While opening the door to the hallway, Patrick noticed Warren rush to his mother's side to help her with her jacket and handbag.

Back in his office, the tenderness displayed between Mrs. Evans and her concerned son prompted a fantasy to play out in Patrick's mind. The image of Warren was replaced with a middle-aged Oliver, and Mrs. Evans's face was that of an elderly Catherine. He quickly swiveled his chair to face the wall. Heaven forbid one of the staff should barge in and witness the tears flooding into his eyes.

What had the grief counselor suggested? Instead of focusing on what you've lost, pour your energy into appreciating what you have. Taking a deep breath, he spun his chair back around and gazed at the photo of Oliver and Catherine sitting on the corner of his desk. His adorable son, a true blessing, was a striking combination of his parents, having inherited Patrick's soft brown eyes and dimpled checks (a Woodward family trait) and Catherine's curly auburn hair. He then glanced at the other photo he kept on his desk of himself as a toddler posing with his mother in the garden on their family's estate.

The two most important women in his life, gone forever. As it turned out, the grief counseling sessions were not only helping Patrick learn how to cope with Catherine's death, they also opened his eyes to the fact that he'd never come to terms with the other great tragedy of his life. Keeping his mother's image before him, gazing at her joyful face throughout the day, kept Patricia Woodward alive, at least in Patrick's mind and heart.

Patrick was fourteen when his mother died. He still clearly recalled being summoned from class to the headmaster's office where Uncle Burton, his father's older brother, was waiting for him. Because Uncle Burt was not the type to drive out to Patrick's boarding school for a casual visit, Patrick's intuition instantly warned him that something awful had happened. The headmaster asked Patrick to take a seat and, with Uncle Burt's assistance, sympathetically broke the news: Patrick's mother had gone into cardiac arrest that morning. She could not be revived.

The days following her death were a blur. Patrick had a vague recollection of the drive home, the never-ending string of condolences, of his mother's casket being placed in the mausoleum. His most vivid memory was of the day following his mother's funeral. He was desperate for his family's company, to be reassured they weren't going to desert him as his mother had. Veronica, three years his senior, was about to graduate and make the transition to college. She could not accept the fact that her mother wouldn't be present to witness either of those important events in her life. She was in her bedroom sobbing inconsolably when Patrick rapped on the door and asked if he could enter her room. Instead of welcoming him in, she'd thrown her shoe at the door and screamed for him to leave her alone.

Dejected, Patrick went in search of his father. He entered Jonathan Woodward's office and caught sight of his father through the paned glass of the French doors that opened onto a private terrace. Jonathan was standing in the middle of the backyard, his arms at his sides, his head straight, his eyes staring into the woods that bordered their property.

Patrick remained inside the room and waited for his father to return. After a few minutes, he became alarmed when he noticed Jonathan had clenched his hands and raised his face to the sky. With his forehead pressed against the cold glass, Patrick witnessed the startling release of his father's pent-up grief and pain and anger as Jonathan's jaw opened wide and, dropping to his knees, a tormented scream erupted from deep inside him.

The concerned teenager yearned to go to his father, to console him, but his immaturity stood in the way. He couldn't put his own feelings into words let alone understand what his father was experiencing. Instead, he ran to his bedroom, slammed the door shut, and buried his face in a pillow. At last, he shed the tears he'd been suppressing for days until, exhausted, he fell asleep.

Twenty-two years later, Patrick at last understood why his father had needed to express his emotions in such a primal manner. He didn't believe he himself would benefit from going into the woods and screaming as his father had, but with his group's help he was learning to work through the sorrow of losing Catherine in his own way.

What's more, the group had opened Patrick's eyes to the possibility that he may have specialized in cardiology for a reason. Each time he performed a procedure that extended the life of one of his patients, he was giving their loved ones the gift of time he himself had so cruelly been denied.

Chapter 6

Marie

Marie entered the crowded restaurant at half past six. She spotted Gus sitting at the isolated table against the back wall, their usual spot.

"Welcome to Maestro. Do you have a reservation?" The young hostess was new and didn't recognize Marie as a frequent patron of the establishment.

"Actually, I'm meeting someone," Marie explained as she brushed past the girl. More than a few heads turned when Marie entered the dining area, and the chatter dropped a decibel or two as she wound her way across the room. Her lips curled into a sly grin. Nice to know she hadn't yet lost her touch.

Gus stood as Marie approached the table. "Hey, doll," he said, his endearment accompanied by a light kiss on her cheek.

Gus, whose full name was Wendell Ferguson, hated the fact he'd been named after his father, a hulking brute who drank too much and treated his family as though they were an inconvenient burden. As early as elementary school, Wendell insisted on being addressed only by his last name. One of the boys in his class declared Ferguson took too much effort to pronounce, so he shaved off a few letters at the beginning and end of the name. From that day on, Wendell Ferguson was known simply as Gus.

"Sorry I'm late," she said. "The auction ran longer than expected."

"Not a problem." Gus spoke with an accent that had been cultivated in the Bronx and a voice that was damaged by too many cigarettes. "I ordered you an Old Fashioned." He slid the whiskey glass in her direction.

"Thanks. Why am I not surprised to find a drink waiting for me?" Marie smiled affectionately at Gus as she swirled the liquor around the ice cube to blend the flavors.

"I enjoy spoiling you. Always have."

They clinked their glasses together. "*Salute!*"

A confirmed bachelor in his late fifties, Gus's light brown hair was thinning and graying at the temples, but he could still win over the ladies with his rugged good looks and smooth mannerisms. He and Marie's father, Dominic Ricci, grew up in the same neighborhood and were often mistaken for brothers. When Marie and her sister were born, Gus was the only person Dominic considered to fulfill the role of godfather to his daughters. Marie adored Gus and, in Dominic's absence, relied on him for counsel and guidance. Their inherent bond had also proved to be a good foundation for their mutual business dealings.

The waiter set a plate of piping hot calamari with a side of marinara sauce on their table.

"Thanks, Manny." Gus winked at the waiter, a gesture Marie recognized as his customary way of conveying his gratitude.

"That was quick," Marie commented.

"I told Manny to serve the appetizer as soon as you arrived." Gus placed a few calamari on Marie's plate before serving himself.

Marie dipped a piece into the marinara. "I'm starving," she said, taking her first bite. "I skipped lunch today. Too busy."

"My guess is you probably skipped breakfast, too." Gus swallowed his food before continuing. "You can't survive on coffee alone, doll. You're thin enough as it is."

"You know my motto. A woman can never be too thin, too beautiful, nor too wealthy."

"Well, you've got the first two covered," Gus declared as he took a sip of his scotch. "And, I may have a plan to help you with the third."

****

Dominic
Fall 1980

When Dominic Ricci and Wendell Ferguson were teenagers, they dreamed of making the kind of money that would afford them a one-way ticket out of the Bronx. How they'd achieve such a lofty goal was a mystery, though, as neither was inclined to pursue a formal education. For that matter, even the likelihood they'd complete their senior year of high school was questionable. Fate, however, was on their side. An opportune meeting in a neighborhood bar led them to realize monetary success could be gained in ways that were far from conventional.

At seventeen, both boys were maturely handsome and could pass as young men in their early twenties. Dominic had a connection with a guy who was an expert at forging IDs, and overnight their worlds changed. During the day, he and Gus were disinterested high school students. At night, their fake drivers' licenses transformed them into working-class men with easy access to over-21 bars. They drank alcohol without being questioned and met women who were more than willing to hook up with the virile teenagers in any space that was convenient for five minutes tops. Dominic and Gus soon had a steady stream of eligible young ladies to satisfy their youthful libidos.

One evening, the two were making good headway with a couple of secretaries at The Blind Spot, one of their favorite haunts. The crowded tavern was dingy, and the air was hazy from cigarette smoke, but the drinks were cheap and the clientele consisted largely of single young women on the prowl. Dominic stepped up to the bar to refresh his drink when a stranger struck up a conversation.

"Hey, kid. How's it going?" The man leaned across the bar and flicked the end of his cigarette into an ash tray. He appeared to be in his early forties, around the same age as Dominic's father. His unaccented speech gave Dominic the impression he was from anywhere but the Bronx.

"I'm good. How you doin'?" Dominic, a friendly type, was always open to making a new acquaintance.

The bartender poured Dominic's whiskey and soda. "That'll be three bucks. Am I putting this on your tab?"

Before Dominic could answer, the stranger leaned forward and handed the bartender a ten-dollar bill. "Here. This will cover my beer and his drink. Keep the change."

"Thanks, man!" the bartender said as he snatched the bill out of the stranger's hand.

The transaction happened before Dominic had a chance to react. He was grateful for the stranger's generosity, but leery of his intentions. "Whoa, whoa, wait a minute," he said, holding his hands up in front of him. "I appreciate you buyin' me a drink, but if you want somethin' in return, you should know I ain't into that kinda shit."

The stranger grinned and shook his head. "Oh, no, it's nothing like that. Hey, I'm straight, too. I am in the market for a guy to do some work for me, though. I wondered if we could discuss a business proposition. Do you have a few minutes?" He took a drag from his cigarette.

"Yeah, sure." Dominic, currently unemployed, was open to anyone who had a solid lead on a job.

"Good. Let's talk where it's more private." With his beer in hand, he slid off the bar stool and headed toward a secluded table in the shadowy back corner.

As Dominic crossed the room, he eyed Gus who appeared to be dazzling the two working girls with his charm and witty sense of humor. Dominic was certain, if he didn't rejoin their company soon, Gus would be nailing both girls before the night was over.

At the same time, Gus glanced over at Dominic. A frown and a nod of his head in the stranger's direction indicated Gus's curiosity about what was going on. Dominic responded by shrugging his shoulders. He had no idea what he was getting into, but he could at least spare a few minutes of his time to listen to what his new acquaintance had to say.

"This table is good," the stranger announced. He slid out a chair for Dominic. "By the way, my name is Joe."

Dominic seated himself and placed his whiskey on the table. "Nice to meet ya, Joe. I'm Dominic." He accepted Joe's handshake as Joe sat in the chair across from him.

"So, tell me, Dominic, how old are you?"

An alarm triggered inside Dominic's head. This guy didn't appear to be a cop, but sometimes those undercover guys were hard to spot. Now unsure of what he'd gotten himself into, Dominic hesitated before responding. He glanced across the room and, unconvincingly, replied, "Twenty-four."

Joe took a drag on his cigarette. He exhaled and studied Dominic through the cloud of smoke. "Yeah, right. How old are you *really*?"

Dominic stuck to his guns. This time, he faced Joe's scrutinizing smirk head on. "I told you, man. I'm twenty-four."

Joe continued to stare his drinking companion straight in the eye. Dominic had the chance to come clean if he wanted to, but he didn't falter. His unwavering glare proved to Joe, and more importantly to himself, just how good a liar he could be.

Joe shrugged and moved on. "You working anywhere?"

"Oh, ya know, I'm between jobs right now." Dominic put forth his best effort to sound like the badass he aspired to be one day.

"What's your background? What kind of work are you interested in?"

At his young age, Dominic's entire resume could fit on one line. He'd worked for a year flipping burgers at a fast-food restaurant but quit the job just last month. He had learned, however, to put a spin on his background to make a good impression.

"Well, ya know, I've used my talents mostly in the restaurant business, but I'd like to find somethin' that pays a lot more. Somethin' where I don't come home every night smellin' like a grease ball. Ya know what I'm talkin' about?"

Joe nodded his head. "Sure do. I had those kinds of jobs myself, way back when. Once I got out of the kitchen, there was no turning back."

"Yeah, that's exactly where I'm at," Dominic concurred. He sipped his drink, bolstered by the knowledge that he and his new acquaintance had much in common.

Joe took one last drag, then stubbed out his cigarette in the table's ashtray. "How do you feel about getting into a line of work that involves a bit of, shall we say, adventure?"

Dominic sat up straighter, now at full attention. The little bit of money he'd managed to save over the last year was dwindling fast. Taking this guy up on a job offer was a lot more appealing than searching through the want ads. He smiled happily when he replied. "Sure, ya know, why not? I'm an adventurous kinda guy. What's the job?"

Joe raised his beer bottle and took a long swallow. He glanced around the bar before settling his piercing gaze on Dominic. Placing the beer bottle and his elbows on the table, he leaned forward. "I need someone to make a delivery," he said as if sharing a secret.

Dominic's head nervously bobbed up and down as he waited for Joe to elaborate. After several seconds, he grew tired of waiting. "Okay, so, ya know, what kinda delivery? Do you need me to drive a truck over to Jersey or somethin'?"

"No, no, it's not that big a job. The package is small enough for you to carry. I need someone to hand deliver it to a guy locally, that's all. It should take you, at most, an hour."

Dominic's head continued to nod up and down, this time in agreement. "Sounds easy enough. When are we talkin' about?"

"Tomorrow night, around this time. Does that work for you?"

"Well, ya know, I'm busy later tomorrow night, but around this time should be okay." The reality was, Dominic had nothing on his schedule for as far as the eye could see, but he didn't want Joe to think he was completely without purpose.

"Good." Joe retrieved a small, sealed envelope from the breast pocket of his jacket and slid it across the table. "There's the key to a box at the post office on Rhodes Avenue in this envelope. The box number is eighteen. You'll find a wrapped package inside the box. On top of the package will be a piece of paper with an address written on it. All you need to do is deliver the package to that address between eight-thirty and nine o'clock tomorrow night. Nothing more, nothing less. Can I trust you to do that?"

Dominic shrugged his shoulders. "Sounds easy enough. But, ya know, it all depends on how much the job pays." After all, his time was valuable.

"How's one hundred dollars sound?"

Dominic's eyes shot wide open, and his jaw dropped. He'd barely cleared that much in a month working at the burger joint. "Are you shittin' me?" he blurted out, a little too aggressively.

Joe shushed him. "Keep your voice down, kid. We don't want the whole world to know. This deal is just between you and me. Do you understand?"

Joe's serious tone and menacing glare gave Dominic the willies. The package he'd agreed to deliver was obviously important—and maybe just a little shady. "Sorry, Joe. I didn't mean to get carried away. But that's some serious moolah for such an easy job. A *hundred* bucks?"

"Twenty-five up front," Joe confirmed, "seventy-five when you complete the delivery. Cash under the table. Are you up for it?"

"Hell yeah!" Dominic remembered to keep his voice low so he didn't anger Joe again and blow this incredible opportunity. He was already dreaming about the basketball-style sneakers his father refused to buy for him unless Dominic could foot half the bill.

"Just a couple of things to remember. Don't get curious and open the package. What's under the wrapping is none of your business. And don't make any stops along the way. You go straight from the post office to the address you're given. Understand?"

"Yeah, I got it."

"Good. One last thing. Like I said before, this job is just between you and me. You can't tell anyone about it. You hear me?"

Dominic didn't like the last condition. The best part of this job, aside from the fast cash he'd make, would be bragging about it to Gus. *Guess what I'll be doin' tonight while you're bangin' some bimbo in the back room?* Although he seldom hid anything from his best friend, Dominic got the message loud and clear that Joe's demands were non-negotiable. He'd need to come up with a clever excuse for why he couldn't meet Gus at the bar until later in the evening.

"Yeah, I hear ya," Dominic reluctantly agreed.

Joe extended his hand. "Do we have a deal?"

"Yeah, we got a deal," Dominic said, accepting the handshake.

Joe again dug into his breast pocket and removed another envelope. This one was unsealed. "Here's twenty-five. Like I said, you'll receive the balance upon delivery."

Dominic peeked into the envelope to confirm its contents, then tucked it into the pocket of his jeans along with the one holding the post office key. "Thanks, Joe."

"You're welcome, kid."

Dominic glanced over at Gus who had his arm around the bleached blonde's shoulders as he whispered what Dominic imagined was his latest come-on line into her ear. Dominic wondered how pissed Gus would be that Joe hadn't offered this job to him. As he took a drink of whiskey, Dominic scanned the faces of the other guys in the bar and grew curious.

"Hey, Joe, can I ask you somethin'?"

Joe took a swig of his beer. He stared at Dominic with narrowed eyes, giving Dominic the impression he shouldn't ask too many questions. Setting his beer on the table, Joe said, "Depends. What's on your mind?"

"Why me? Out of all the guys in this bar, why'd you pick me for this job?"

Joe grinned. "You're the only one who knows Jersey Pete, that's why."

Jersey Pete, a relative of Dominic's mother, was an influential figure in the Ricci family. Pete had taken Dominic under his wing at an early age. He'd schooled the young boy in *moorah*, a mandatory game at all the family gatherings, and had slipped him bottles of beer when his parents weren't watching. Jersey Pete was also the forger who'd made the fake IDs for Dominic and Gus. In Dominic's eyes, Jersey Pete was an idol.

Dominic rested both forearms on the table and held his drink between his hands. "Jersey Pete? He told you about me? What'd he say?"

Joe nodded his response. "He told me you're a trustworthy kid who's interested in making some serious money. He vouched for you, and that was a good enough recommendation for me."

"I can't believe it," Dominic chuckled. "Ya know, he's a *goomba* on my mom's side of the family. Damn, I'll have to go see him. To thank him, ya know?"

"You do that," Joe said. "Can I trust Pete's judgment? Are you interested in making something of yourself?"

Truthfully, Dominic was seldom serious about anything. But when presented with the chance to make some decent money, he put all joking aside. "Let me tell you somethin', Joe. I have ambition, ya know? One of these days, I'm gonna have enough money to get outta the Bronx. I'm gonna have a big apartment facin' Central Park, maybe even a house on Long Island. I'm just waitin' for the right line of work to get into, ya know, and then my career is gonna take off."

"Well, your enthusiasm is a good sign," Joe replied. "My partner and I need someone to make regular deliveries. Being a runner is what you might call an 'entry level' position. If you don't screw things up tomorrow night, we could talk about other possibilities for let's say 'job growth' down the road."

Dominic wanted to pinch himself to make sure he wasn't dreaming. This could be the break he'd been hoping for. He studied the man sitting across from him and noticed in detail his expensive Italian loafers and leather jacket, his perfect haircut, and his manicured fingernails. Joe spoke with confidence and without a Bronx accent. Dominic wanted to be just like him.

"Yeah, ya know, that's sounds great to me. I'm definitely interested in improvin' myself."

"I like you, kid," Joe confided with tenderness in his voice. "You remind me of myself when I was your age." He removed a packet of cigarettes and a gold lighter from the inside pocket of his jacket. Shaking two cigarettes loose from the pack, he drew one out with his lips, then offered the other to Dominic.

"No, thanks. I don't smoke."

"Good. Don't ever start," Joe advised, the cigarette bouncing between his lips like a pointed finger scolding a warning. He snapped open the lighter and struck the flame. The tobacco crackled as he took the first drag to start the burn. Smoke billowed from his mouth as he spoke. "If you're serious about making something of yourself, may I offer a suggestion? Clean up your grammar. Stop saying 'yeah' and 'ya know' so often and start pronouncing the 'g' at the end of your words." He returned the cigarettes and lighter to his pocket and rose from the chair. "Don't disappoint me. If I like how you handle yourself, I'll be in touch."

Dominic stared after his new mentor with awe as Joe crossed the bar and disappeared through the dimly lit doorway.

Chapter 7

Marie
Summer 2022

"When was the last time you spoke with your sister?" Gus questioned Marie during a lull in their dinner conversation.

"A few days ago," Marie answered between bites of grilled salmon. She wasn't in the mood to discuss personal matters, but Gus asked anyway.

"You haven't mentioned her in a while. What's she been up to?"

"Basking in the Caribbean sunshine, as usual." She paused while Manny, their waiter, refilled their water glasses. "You didn't ask me to meet you here to talk about the family."

Gus finished chewing his food before getting to the point. "I remember you mentioning Jonathan Woodward's name a time or two. Wasn't he one of your clients at the auction house?"

"Still is." Marie patted her mouth with her napkin. What interest would Gus have in Jonathan Woodward? "Why?" she asked. "What about him?"

"I understand he currently owns the Somerset Necklace." Gus popped another chunk of ribeye into his mouth. He raised his left eyebrow and gazed expectantly at Marie as he gnawed on the juicy piece of steak.

Marie waited for Gus to continue, although she was certain he wouldn't elaborate just yet. Gus was playing his favorite game, the one in which he baited Marie with a one-liner, then allowed the suspense to build while he waited for her response. After finally conceding she was unfamiliar with the topic, he would feign surprise at her ignorance and then expound on his knowledge of the subject, oftentimes going into more detail than Marie deemed necessary.

In some dysfunctional way, this silly game inflated Gus's ego. Although he'd never admit it, Marie was convinced Gus considered himself intellectually inferior because she was well-educated, and he was a high school dropout. So, she played his game, even though it annoyed her. She loved Gus and would do anything to make him happy.

Marie grew tired of their staring contest and reluctantly threw in the towel. "And what, may I ask, is the Somerset Necklace?"

Gus cocked his head as his eyes grew wide. "You don't know what the Somerset Necklace is? Well, I guess they didn't teach you everything at that high-priced college you graduated from."

And there it was. The same reaction every time, always the derogatory dig about her schooling. Did Gus have any idea how often he'd repeated those identical words over the past thirteen years? Marie had stopped counting a long time ago.

"No, I don't know what the Somerset Necklace is, so fire away and tell me all about it."

Gus wiped his napkin across his mouth and placed his forearms on the table. "I'm guessing you're familiar with the Somerset family."

"Come on, Gus. Everyone knows who the Somersets are. They've practically ruled commerce and politics in this country for the last two centuries."

"Yeah, so, in the early 1900s, Clarence Somerset had an extramarital affair with some dancehall floozy."

"Her name was Daisy Monaghan. Their scandalous story is famous and has been the subject of several documentaries. The affair lasted for decades."

Gus swilled down the last of his scotch. "Sure, it's common knowledge now, but at the time, their affair was hush-hush. Old man Somerset provided a lush lifestyle for his secret girlfriend—a nice apartment, cars, furs—anything she wanted, she got, and then some. Over the years, he adorned her pretty little body with beautiful pieces of jewelry. Real unique stuff he had designed especially for her."

"Yes, I've read about his generosity. I'm sure Daisy had to put up with a lot of his shit in exchange. From what I understand, Clarence Somerset was a real tyrant."

"So the story goes." Gus was back to cutting his steak and talking around the food in his mouth. "No doubt he expected a lot in return. I've known plenty of women who would have agreed to anything to be set up the way Daisy Monaghan was. It's all about living for the moment and not worrying about tomorrow."

"And who are we to disagree?"

"Are you done with your dinner, ma'am?" Manny asked as he passed by their table.

"Yes." Marie sat back while the waiter cleared her plate and silverware from the table, then resumed her conversation with Gus. "Seems to me, Daisy was a big girl. She chose the way she wanted to live."

"You're right, as usual." Gus wiped his mouth a

final time and dropped his napkin onto the empty plate.

"Will you be having dessert this evening?" Manny was back to clear the final plates from their table.

Gus spoke for them both. "No, but we'll have coffee. And put a shot of whiskey in mine."

"Yes, sir. Skim milk for your coffee, as usual, ma'am?"

"Yes. Thank you." She stared at Gus. Where was he going with this history lesson? "So, all this talk of the Somersets has been fascinating, but how does Jonathan Woodward fit into the conversation?"

"First, we have to finish the story of Daisy Monaghan." Gus brushed away a few crumbs and rested his elbows on the table. "Daisy was living the life of Reilly until Clarence Somerset croaked. Without her sugar daddy, she had no source of income, and by then she was old, used goods. No other millionaire would have her. To pay the bills, Daisy started selling off the gifts Clarence had given her."

Gus sat back while Manny served their coffee. He thanked Manny with a wink, then leaned forward again and continued his narrative.

"In 1947, Daisy unloaded much of her jewelry for bargain prices. The most admired of the lot, and the most expensive, was a diamond and sapphire necklace set in platinum. Jonathan Woodward's grandfather, Ashton, had been pals with Clarence Somerset, and was the lucky guy who took the necklace off Daisy's hands. Ashton Woodward bought the necklace as a gift for his wife. When their grandson, Jonathan, got married, Old Grandma Woodward gave the necklace to Jonathan's bride on their wedding day to wear as her *something blue*." Gus paused to take a drink of his coffee.

Skeptical, Marie squinted her eyes. "How do you know all this?"

Gus frowned, appearing surprised Marie wasn't aware of the family's notoriety. "The Woodwards are big news in Boston. Details of the wedding were in all the papers at the time."

"Huh," Marie grunted. For some reason, she couldn't imagine the Jonathan Woodward she was acquainted with as having once made the headlines on the society pages. But then, his marriage happened a long time ago, even before Marie was born. A lot can change in forty years. "The obvious question is, how is this relevant to me?"

"When Clarence Somerset commissioned the jeweler to design the necklace for Daisy, he also had a bracelet and earrings made to match. Daisy only sold the necklace. What she did with the other two pieces has been a mystery ever since. That's why the necklace is infamously called the Somerset Necklace. It's the only piece known to have survived from the set. Recently, however, the bracelet and earrings surfaced on the black market."

Marie raised an eyebrow. The story had all at once become much more intriguing. "Let me guess. You have a buyer who wants all three pieces."

"Bingo."

Marie's pulse quickened. She leaned forward and asked, "How much is your buyer willing to pay?"

"For the entire set…" Gus drew close until his face was mere inches away from Marie's. He finished his sentence in barely more than a whisper. "Two million dollars."

Marie allowed the dollar amount to sink in as she

eased back in her chair. She held Gus's gaze and pondered the possibilities. As a team, the two had flourished in their careers as con artists. A few of their previous transactions had come close to seven figures, but they'd not yet hit the million-dollar mark. The idea of raking in twice that much was heady indeed. Marie's body tingled with excitement at the prospect.

"You're certain you can obtain the bracelet and earrings?"

"The deal's as good as done," Gus assured her.

"And you're positive the necklace is still owned by Jonathan Woodward?"

"Either by him or someone in his immediate family. There's no knowledge of it changing hands since Woodward's wedding."

"What about a copy of the necklace?" she asked. "Do you have one I can take with me?"

"Not now, but I'm working on it," Gus informed her. "I can have it to you in the next few days."

Although Marie and Gus were both legitimately employed, Marie at Willow's Auction House and Gus as the proprietor of an antique store, their day jobs were merely fronts behind which they operated their more lucrative business of stealing from the rich and selling to discriminating buyers who knew better than to ask questions. Marie selected most of the men they swindled from the clientele at Willow's. While she lured in the unsuspecting target with her beauty and seductive persuasions, Gus worked behind the scenes to create the forgery she'd swap for the genuine article. Marie then handed the piece over to Gus who sold the goods on the black market. Fake invoices and receipts were created, and the profit was laundered through the antique store as a valid sale.

Jonathan Woodward had been at the top of Marie's list of potential targets since she'd begun assisting him with his auction bids. However, other than the call she'd made to express her condolences following his daughter-in-law's death, she had not spoken with Jonathan in several months. With the prospect of obtaining the Somerset Necklace from him, her decision to not pursue Jonathan for the time being had worked to her benefit.

For a moment, Marie considered taking a pass on this job. She found Jonathan to be thoughtful and courteous, a true gentleman, and she'd developed a genuine fondness for him. From what he'd told her of himself, she gathered he was an intellectual who used his wealth and notoriety in altruistic pursuits, and she wasn't convinced she wanted to perform such a devious act on such a likable man. However, Marie had her own benevolent reasons for doing what she did, and she reminded herself that her take of a $2 million deal would have a dramatic impact on her personal goals.

Marie placed a muzzle over her conscience. How could she pass over a job with such an enormous profit? As she formulated a game plan in her mind, a cunning grin crept onto her face.

"I've been leading Jonathan Woodward along for some time and have him convinced I'm interested in pursuing a relationship with him. I think, at last, the time has arrived for Marie Lacroix to fit a trip to Boston into her schedule."

Chapter 8

Dominic
Fall 1980

Dominic Ricci entered the post office on Rhodes Avenue to tackle the first of what he hoped would be many assignments for his new idol, Joe. He'd allowed himself forty-five minutes, plenty of time by his estimate, to gather the package from the post office box and make Joe's delivery deadline. Stopping a few feet inside the door, he gave the place a quick once-over. Surprisingly, at that late hour, the place was bustling with activity.

So, where do I find Box 18? Dodging two women as they passed by, Dominic stepped to his right and peered through a set of double glass doors. The lobby area inside was dark. A tug on the handles confirmed the doors were locked.

"You need help finding something?" the stranger who came up behind him asked.

Startled, Dominic swung around and glanced at the man long enough to notice his left eye drooped and was laden with scar tissue, as if the skin at his temple had healed poorly after a severe burn. He opened his mouth to respond just as a movement over the stranger's right shoulder caught his eye. A glass door opened across the way, and out stepped a man carrying several large envelopes. Dominic took a leap of faith that he'd found the room containing the post office boxes.

"No, thanks," Dominic told the scarred man as he stepped around him.

Dominic breathed a sigh of relief when he opened the glass door. Inside the room, the walls were covered with row after row of inlaid doors in varying sizes, each with its own number and keyhole. He slid his hand into the pocket of his jeans and withdrew the key Joe had given him. Locating Box 18, he inserted the key into the lock and opened the door.

The package was small, maybe four inches square, weighed a couple of pounds and was covered in plain brown parcel wrap. As promised, a folded piece of paper lay on top of the package. Dominic removed both items, then relocked the door and put the key back into his pocket. Written on the paper was an address on East Truman Avenue. Glancing at his wristwatch, Dominic figured he could arrive at the designated address well before the deadline. He tucked the package inside his jacket, drew the zipper up to his neck, and sauntered out to the street.

From the post office, he strolled south for eight blocks until he reached East Truman. He'd foolishly assumed his destination would be nearby, but the numbers on the buildings in front of him weren't even close to the address printed on the piece of paper in his hand. He shouted a string of curse words, not caring if he offended the people around him, and picked up his pace.

Dominic checked his watch at every new corner and noticed the minutes were passing by faster than the cross streets. As he neared the 3300 block on Truman, he broke into a sprint. With five minutes to spare, he crossed the last intersection and arrived at the prescribed address just under the wire. As he burst through the doorway, a bell tinkled overhead to announce his entrance. Dominic took a moment to catch his breath. He wanted to appear cool and competent when he turned over the goods.

While he waited for someone to greet him, he took in his surroundings. The place was an antique store, small and crammed full of old lamps, rugs, and odd pieces of furniture. Inside the glass display case before him were vintage jewelry items and beaded evening bags. Dominic wrinkled his nose, displeased with the musty odors emitted by fabrics that were desperate to spend some much-needed time in the fresh air.

Another minute of unnerving quietness passed. Dominic was starting to get the creeps. "Hello!" he called out. "Anybody here?"

Finally, the sound of a toilet flushing followed by a door closing, then footsteps approaching. He wasn't alone after all. Focusing his attention on the curtained doorway that partitioned the showroom from the back section of the store, Dominic anxiously waited for the person to make his appearance. When the curtains parted, he was surprised to find himself again face to face with the scarred man from the post office.

"Hey, kid," the geezer said from behind the display case. "It's about time you got here."

"You…you're," a tongue-tied Dominic blurted out, not sure what he was trying to say. "The post office. You're the guy I spoke to at the post office."

"Gee, kid, you're a regular genius. How'd you recognize me?" The man's sinister grin taunted Dominic at his own expense.

"But, why?" Dominic asked, still confused. "Why

were you there, and now you're here?"

The scarred man sneered. "Just keeping an eye on you, kid."

Dominic didn't know why he should be annoyed, but he was. His grimacing face conveyed his irritation.

"What? You think we'd trust a green kid like you not to screw things up? Or change your mind halfway here and decide to keep the goods for yourself? I didn't just fall off the turnip truck yesterday, kid. I followed you here from the post office to make sure you did what you were told."

Dominic could have raised all kinds of indignant hell over the sneaky treatment he'd been given, but he reminded himself how much he wanted this job. If this man was the business partner Joe had referred to, Dominic needed to play nice.

"Yeah, so, how'd I do?"

"Hey, I have to say, not bad. Except for being a little late getting here, you did good."

"The address threw me," Dominic admitted. "I didn't expect your store to be this far from the post office."

"Live and learn, kid. Live and learn." An uncomfortable moment passed as Dominic glanced around at the items on display. How much longer was he expected to chitchat with the old guy before they got down to business? At last, the man spoke. "So, can I have my package?"

"What? Oh! Yeah, sorry," Dominic apologized as he unzipped his jacket. He'd nervously forgotten his reason for being there. "I've got it right here." He withdrew the package from inside his jacket and set it on the display case.

The man raised an eyebrow and stared expectantly at Dominic. Hunching his tense shoulders, Dominic shoved his hands into the back pockets of his jeans. His eyes darted around as his mind raced. Was there something else expected of him? Had he neglected part of Joe's instructions?

"The key, kid," the geezer said impatiently. "I need the key to the post office box."

"Oh! Sorry, again." Dominic dug into the pocket of his jeans and dropped the key into the man's outstretched hand.

"I'm gonna assume you didn't switch out the goods since I had my eyes on you pretty much the entire way over here," the man said, tossing the key into the breast pocket of his shirt.

"Oh, hey! Ya know, I wouldn't do somethin' like that, ya know." Since Joe had commented on his poor grammar, Dominic had made a concerted effort to speak better English. The man's accusation unnerved him, however, causing Dominic to revert to his old habits.

"Stop worrying, kid." The man obviously enjoyed putting the teenager behind the eight ball. "I ain't accusing you of anything. I'm just yanking your chain a little."

Dominic's continuing uneasiness caused his head to bob up and down like a tic he couldn't control. He remained silent and hoped the man would pay him soon so he could be on his way. He couldn't take the musty smell, let alone the uncomfortable conversation, much longer. Instead, the man teased him with another question.

"So, you wanna see what's so important inside this package?"

In all honesty, Dominic was curious about the item he was being paid so handsomely to deliver. "Yeah, sure," he replied.

The man picked up a scissors and cut away the wrapping. As he did so, Dominic wondered why he hadn't yet introduced himself by name. This guy was as odd a person as Dominic had ever met.

"Go ahead, kid." The man slid the cardboard box across the glass counter in Dominic's direction. "Open it up."

Dominic took a step closer, unfolded the top flaps on the box, and lifted out a wad of crumpled newspaper. He grinned with the anticipation of finding the treasure hidden within, but his smile was quickly replaced with a frown of confusion when he removed the paper and uncovered nothing more than a small bag of marbles. Raising his head, Dominic glared with irritation at the nameless man whose face was filled with amusement.

"Marbles?" Dominic asked resentfully. "Joe had me come all this way to deliver a bag of marbles?"

The man threw his head back as a sadistic guffaw exploded from his wide-opened mouth. Dominic wanted to throw a punch and knock out every one of the man's crooked teeth with their shiny silver fillings.

"Your reaction was priceless, kid," the man said when he was finished laughing. "Did you really think we'd let a rookie like you handle goods that were worth something?"

"So…what? You guys just tricked me?" Dominic was careful with his choice of words and to keep his anger in check, but he was beginning to despise this insufferable jerk. He was also reconsidering his allegiance to Joe.

"No, kid, we didn't trick you. We wouldn't waste our time doing something like that. We were conducting a test."

"A test?" Dominic repeated, his tone demanding further explanation.

"Sure. We needed to see how well you follow instructions, and if you'd try to rip us off." Unexpectedly, the man showed his tender side. He patted Dominic's cheek as he said, "We weren't being mean, kid. We just needed to make sure we could trust you."

Dominic understood the necessity of the hoax they'd played on him. He guessed he'd have done the same thing if he were the person in charge of the operation. His temper faded away as quickly as it had flared. Out of curiosity, he asked, "And, if I had ripped you off, what would have happened?"

"That, kid, is something you don't even wanna think about."

Dominic took the man's response as a firm warning rather than a statement of fact.

"If this was for real, if this job wasn't a test, like you said, what would have been wrapped up in this box?" Since he was asking questions, Dominic figured he may as well ask the most important one.

The man stared at Dominic, his eyes threatening. "What's that famous quote—'If I told you, I'd have to kill you'? Stop asking so many questions, kid." He opened a drawer in the wall behind him and removed an envelope. "Here's the balance of the money we owe you. If we need you to do any other jobs, we know where to find you."

"Thanks." Dominic recognized when he was being dismissed. He checked inside the envelope to confirm it contained the seventy-five dollars he'd been promised, then headed for the exit. Realizing his future might be at stake, that he might be competing against others for the job, he decided to stand up for himself to prove he wasn't just another face in the crowd. With his hand on the doorknob, he glanced over his shoulder and stared the geezer straight in the eye. "By the way," he said, "my name isn't *kid*. It's Dominic Ricci. Do yourself a favor and remember it."

The man's mouth curled into a lop-sided grin, his head nodding as if in approval. Dominic closed the door behind him, confident Joe would be tracking him down to carry out his first real job before long.

Chapter 9

Marie
Summer 2022

Marie stared at Jonathan Woodward's number on her cell phone, hesitant to make the call. She and Jonathan hadn't spoken with each other in nearly a year, and she worried their rapport, which she'd worked so hard to nurture, might not have withstood the test of time. She berated herself for not considering this possibility *before* agreeing to Gus's Somerset Necklace scheme. *Well, there's only one way to find out if Jonathan is still under my spell.* She took a deep breath, touched the screen, and listened as the call rang once…twice…

"Marie! What a welcome surprise!"

Jonathan sounded happy to hear from her, an encouraging sign. "Hello, Jonathan," she said in her sultry voice, the one that usually hooked her unwitting target within seconds. "Am I catching you at a bad time?"

"No, not at all," he replied, his tone soft and intimate. She'd successfully set the mood. "We haven't been in touch for a while. How are you?"

"I'm well, thank you. I wanted to call you before now, but I hated to intrude on your privacy."

"I appreciate your consideration. My family has had a rough year, but I think we're finally on the mend."

Marie understood loss. The sadness in Jonathan's voice elicited memories and emotions she preferred to keep buried. When she responded, her empathy was sincere. "It takes a while to recover from such a tragedy."

"Yes, longer than we imagine, unfortunately." Jonathan sighed heavily. "So, what prompted this call? Is something interesting going on the auction block?"

Marie giggled coyly. "Oh, I'm sure I can always find some little trinket for you to add to your collection. But this isn't a work-related call. I just made plans to spend this weekend in Boston. You live near there, don't you?"

"Yes, in Burgess, just west of the city. Why are you traveling up this way?"

To keep things casual, so she didn't appear to be aggressively pursuing him, Marie fed Jonathan a tall tale about a weekend reunion. "A couple of friends from college invited me to join them for a girls' getaway. I'll be in Boston Friday night through Sunday afternoon."

Dead silence. Then, "That's nice. It's always fun to get together with old friends."

The disappointment in Jonathan's voice came across loud and clear. He'd probably assumed Marie was traveling to Boston to meet him in person as they'd discussed the last time they spoke, then realized she was instead calling to ask for recommendations on restaurants and sightseeing venues.

"Yes, I'll be happy to see them. It's been a long time since we were last together."

"Well, if you need my input about places to go or things to do, don't hesitate to call."

Okay, time to get to the point. "Thank you for the offer. But Jonathan…gosh, I hope I'm not being too forward." She paused to give the impression she was worried he'd reject her suggestion. "I was hoping we could get together while I'm in town."

Again, silence. *Uh-oh.* Had she misread the playful insinuations he'd made during their previous phone conversations? Or perhaps, in the months since they'd last spoken, he'd become involved with someone and was no longer interested in pursuing a relationship with her.

At last, he said, "I'll need to rearrange my schedule. How's Saturday, mid-afternoon?"

Relieved, she breathed easily again. "Saturday afternoon works for me, but I don't want to interfere with your commitments. Perhaps I could make a trip to Boston another time."

"No, no," he said hastily. "We've waited long enough to meet as it is. Text me the name and address of your hotel. I'll find a café close by where we can spend the afternoon getting better acquainted."

"That sounds wonderful. I can't wait to meet you."

"Same here. I'm afraid I need to go for now, but I'll call you Saturday morning to finalize the details. Take care, Marie."

Marie grinned with satisfaction as she strolled over to her closet to select her wardrobe for the upcoming weekend. Her plan was moving along perfectly. As a matter of fact, Jonathan was playing right into her hands.

****

Jonathan

Jonathan Woodward refused to label himself a Senior Citizen. On the brink of entering his golden years, the retired college professor was committed to aging as gracefully as possible. His healthy lifestyle kept him physically strong, and his exuberant spirit kept him young at heart. New acquaintances mistook him for being years younger than his true age and assumed his still full head of dark brown hair must be graying prematurely. Although he admitted to his friends at the club that the waistbands on his trousers had gotten a little tighter in the last few years, he'd managed to maintain an athletic physique throughout his adult life.

Failure had never been an option for Jonathan, so his ability to control the aging process came as no surprise to those who knew him well. Within his inner circle, Jonathan was considered the golden boy, both admired and envied by his peers. From childhood on, he'd excelled in academics, sports, leadership—virtually any endeavor he pursued. He possessed the confidence and determination that would have ensured his success despite the advantages afforded him as a member of one of Boston's wealthiest and most prominent families.

One of his fraternity brothers liked to razz Jonathan about always being the most popular man in the room, an observation not far from the truth. Old friends and new acquaintances alike were naturally drawn to Jonathan's congenial personality, keen intelligence, and urbane sense of humor. Physically, he was tall, just a hair over six feet, well-groomed, and handsome in a dashing, silver screen secret agent sort of way. With so much going for him, one would imagine Jonathan to be insufferably self-centered, but he firmly believed humility and compassion were the foundations of a strong character. The adversity he witnessed firsthand through his community involvement was a constant reminder of his own good fortune, and the personal losses he and his family had experienced taught him that tragedy doesn't care how much money you have.

That didn't mean, however, he was apologetic for his privileged lifestyle. Jonathan was accustomed to, and enjoyed, indulging his whims and desires, but he did so without calling attention to himself. For this reason, few people realized that underneath his kind, tenderhearted exterior was a shrewd man who wisely and discreetly used the resources at his disposal to satisfy his cravings.

In short, what Jonathan wanted, Jonathan got.

With his academic career now behind him, Jonathan was free to assume some new responsibilities. In addition to directing The Patricia Woodward Memorial Scholarship Foundation, a tuition assistance fund he'd established in memory of his late wife, he'd recently been appointed to the Board of Trustees at Burgess University. He'd also taken a more active role in his family's charitable foundations. Along with his older brother, Burton, and a few of their cousins, he'd served for many years on the administrative side of these organizations. Since retirement, he'd been working hands-on with housing rehabs, an after-school tutoring program, and an inner-city soup kitchen.

When not in a meeting or volunteering, Jonathan spent much of his free time at his club. Depending on the harsh and oftentimes unpredictable New England weather, most mornings began with either a round of golf or indoor pickleball. Following lunch with his friends, he fit in an afternoon swim whenever possible. Regardless of his activities, however, Jonathan's children were his top priority. Nothing interfered with the time he spent with his daughter, Veronica, and her family who lived nearby, or with his frequent trips to Connecticut to visit his son, Patrick, and grandson, Oliver.

Jonathan's life, by his own admission, was

remarkably fulfilling. His only regret was that he'd never remarried after Patricia's death. Although his children claimed that, married or single, his happiness was all they cared about, he was convinced Veronica relished her role as the family matriarch and would never agreeably take a back seat to a stepmother. Still, he was more than willing to take the plunge a second time. He'd come close once or twice, but he hadn't yet found that one woman who could completely captivate both his mind and his heart.

So, his search for a new Mrs. Jonathan Woodward continued. He was amused by the fact that, as he'd matured, the traits he found appealing in women had gone from one end of the spectrum to the other. While he'd always downplayed the label, Jonathan had a reputation as a playboy before he met Patricia. Of course, marriage put an end to his philandering, and by the time he became a widower his desires were driven more by intellect than instinct. He was now drawn to a woman who intrigued him with her sophistication, wit, and adventurous spirit, as well as her allure. Marie Lacroix had checked all those boxes during their phone conversations. He was curious to discover if she'd be just as engaging in person.

When searching for a relaxing place where he and Marie could while away the afternoon, Jonathan settled on The Tea Party, a quaint café located in a historic building in Cambridge. The Tea Party was a popular haunt for Harvard students and faculty during the regular academic year but was less crowded with the school currently in summer session. In close proximity to Marie's hotel, the café offered a cozy patio where they could enjoy the warm weather and a picturesque view of the Charles River.

Jonathan took a seat at an outside table well ahead of the time he and Marie had agreed to meet. He ordered a cappuccino while he waited for her with growing anticipation. Fifteen minutes past the time she was expected, his drink gone cold, Jonathan worried Marie had a change of plans. He was about to call her when a taxi drove up and stopped at the curb.

The back door opened and a tall, blonde woman matching the description Marie had given of herself stepped out. The woman, outfitted in a form-fitting top and above-the-knee skirt, passed under the wrought iron archway and followed the stone path to the café's entrance. Jonathan spent a few seconds admiring her willowy figure and amazing legs before approaching her.

"Excuse me," he said.

She cocked her head and regarded him quizzically. "Yes?"

"Would you happen to be Marie Lacroix?"

Her smile was hesitant, but her eyes were filled with hopeful anticipation. "Jonathan?"

A smile spread across Jonathan's face. "Well, Marie, it appears we've found each other."

"So we have!" Marie offered her hand in greeting. "Jonathan, it's wonderful to finally meet you."

"My thoughts exactly," Jonathan said, holding her delicate hand between his. "I only wish we hadn't waited so long to make this moment happen."

Jonathan had expected to be pleased, maybe even thrilled, to meet Marie, but he never imagined he'd be so…so…*Go ahead, Jonathan, admit it*…so enamored. Marie's disarming personality had already charmed him during their phone conversations. Now that she was, at last, standing before him, he was captivated by her physical appearance as well—her large, expressive eyes; her dainty nose and full lips; her long, silky hair; her sensuous figure. And those legs! She was the most ravishing woman Jonathan had ever laid his eyes on.

"Please forgive me for being late. I hope you haven't been waiting long."

Jonathan brushed off her apology. "No, not at all. Do you mind if we sit here on the patio?"

"I prefer to be outside. It would be a sin not to enjoy this gorgeous weather."

Jonathan guided Marie to their table. "I picked a shady spot for us. Since it's such a warm day, I thought you'd want to avoid the sun." He held the chair for her as she sat.

"Thank you. Yes, shade, please, since I didn't think to apply sun protection. I'm a firm believer in covering every inch of my exposed skin with sunscreen when I know I'm going to be outside, especially at the beach."

"Oh, I completely agree." Jonathan grinned as he envisioned Marie lying on a beach towel in a scant bikini. Then his lewd imagination planted a *Private Beach—Swimwear Optional* sign in the sand. In his fantasy, Marie's bikini vanished. Jonathan's grin widened. "Would you like something to drink?" He signaled the waiter to their table.

"Yes, please."

"Good afternoon," the waiter said in greeting. "What can I get for you folks?"

"We'd both like a cup of your house brew," Jonathan ordered, "one black, and one with a shot of skim milk."

"You got it. I'll bring those coffees right out to you."

"How did you know what to order for me?" Marie asked. She scooted her chair closer to Jonathan's.

"You once mentioned you're a caffeine addict," Jonathan reminded her, "and that you drink your coffee with just a splash of skim milk." From her tender smile and the delight Jonathan detected in her eyes, he inferred Marie was pleasantly surprised he'd remember such a minute detail.

"You have a remarkable memory." Marie sat back in her chair and gazed at the scenery. Jonathan stole the moment to soak in her incredible beauty. "How nice to watch the boaters on the lake and just enjoy the afternoon," she mused. "This isn't at all my typical Saturday."

"If you weren't in Boston, what would you be doing at home right now?"

"Running errands, no doubt. There's always so much to do on the weekends, I barely have time to relax."

Jonathan agreed. "I understand. I don't get to New York often, but when I am there I'm in constant motion. Have you lived in the city all your life?" He asked the question, although the answer was obvious. Her accent hadn't been nurtured anywhere in the United States.

"No, not always," Marie replied. "I grew up just outside of Paris. Have you been to France?"

"Yes, I have on a few occasions. I traveled through Europe with my parents when I was young, and I was in France a couple of times as an adult. I guessed from your accent that you'd been born abroad."

"Ah, my accent. It always gives me away. Yes, my mother was French. Our family lived in Versailles."

The waiter was back with their order. "Here you go, folks. Two coffees, one black and one with skim milk.

My name is Marcus. Flag me down if you need anything else."

"Thank you, Marcus," Jonathan said, then continued their conversation. "Tell me how you made the transition from the scenic countryside of France to the hustle and bustle of New York City."

"Oh, it's not that interesting," Marie answered demurely. "My father was from upstate New York. His parents dealt in antiques and, when they retired, he took over their business and relocated the shop, and our family, to Manhattan. That was when I was around ten years old. So, although I've lived most of my life in New York, I never completely lost my accent."

Intrigued, Jonathan raised an eyebrow. "I wasn't aware your family owns an antique store. I'd love to stop in the next time I'm in New York."

"Well, I'm sorry to say the shop closed after my parents passed away."

Jonathan offered his sympathy. "I'm sorry, Marie. Your parents must have been awfully young."

"Yes, losing them was devastating." Marie searched in her bag and removed a pair of sunglasses.

Jonathan wondered if the glasses were needed to guard against the bright sunlight, or if she was using them to conceal her teary eyes. Based on his own experience with the loss of loved ones, he instinctively understood this was not the time to question her for any further details about her parents' demise. "Is that how you got into the auction business? Did you inherit your family's love of antiques?"

"I did." Marie smiled at the mention of her family legacy. "I spent my childhood in my father's shop. As soon as I was old enough, he put me on the sales floor and made me his assistant. Then I was off to the university where I studied Art History and Business Management." She paused to sip her coffee. "This coffee is excellent, by the way. I'm glad you suggested we meet here. So, now let *me* ask the questions. Have you always lived in Burgess?"

"Actually, I grew up in Boston and lived just a few blocks from this café while I attended Harvard."

"I remember you retired not too long ago. Is Harvard also where you taught?"

Jonathan shook his head. "Harvard offered me a position, but I realized I'd found my niche after my first interview at Burgess University. And, as fate would have it, joining the faculty at Burgess was the best decision I ever made." He stopped, caught up in his own memories.

Marie frowned inquisitively. "Why do you say that?"

"A year into my tenure, the university hired a new professor, coincidentally to teach Art History. Her name was Patricia. She and I started dating and, after a brief engagement, she became my wife." Jonathan had steered the conversation in the wrong direction. He was there to become better acquainted with the provocative woman sitting beside him, not to dredge up irrelevant stories from his past. "Anyway, we found a home near the university, and I've lived in Burgess ever since."

"Have you lived in the same house all these years?"

"Oh, heavens, no. My first house was a twelve thousand square foot home on five acres of land. A tad large for one person, don't you think?"

"My goodness, Jonathan, that wasn't a home. You lived on an estate!"

"You could call it that," Jonathan chuckled.

"Without sounding like a braggart, the home was a wedding gift from my parents." He imagined Marie was aware of his personal net worth since she managed his account at Willow's; otherwise, he wouldn't have divulged this little-known fact. When she didn't dwell on the subject of his finances, his suspicion was confirmed.

Marie leaned closer and rested her chin in the palm of her hand. "So, where do you live now?"

"When my daughter married, I followed the family tradition and gave the property to her and her husband as a wedding gift. I then built a home with access to Lake Burgess."

"Oh, Jonathan," she said, placing her hand on his forearm, "how generous of you to gift your home to your daughter." Jonathan made a mental note that Marie enjoyed sentiment almost as much as he enjoyed the sensation of her fingers caressing his skin.

"Well, it's a historic home, and we wanted to keep it in the family."

"Was that her *something old*?" Marie asked. "Don't brides usually wear a piece of jewelry to fill that portion of the adage? Or am I confusing that with *something borrowed*, like an heirloom necklace the bride wears on her wedding day?"

Jonathan chuckled. "If Veronica followed that tradition, she certainly wouldn't have involved me." While on the subject of weddings, Jonathan ventured to ask Marie about her own love life. "Speaking of marriage, you told me you're single now, but were you ever married?"

"No. I was serious with someone for a while." She sighed. "It didn't work out. Since then, I've remained focused on my career."

Jonathan was delighted Marie wasn't seeing anyone but, at the same time, bewildered. "How does a woman as attractive as you not have a hundred men beating down your door?"

"Oh, I've had my share of romances," Marie admitted. She discarded her sunglasses and gazed intently into Jonathan's eyes. "Perhaps I'm just waiting for the right man to come along."

Jonathan leaned forward. In an intimate voice, he told Marie, "You and I are alike in that respect. We don't settle for second best."

When he met Patricia, Jonathan was convinced he'd rewritten the definition of love at first sight. In the twenty-two years since her death, he'd convinced himself he'd never come close to having that same experience with any other woman. He was willing to admit he'd been wrong.

Their eyes danced over each other's faces for several seconds, both spellbound. Marie was the first to break the silence. "Tell me about your son. Does he also live nearby?"

Jonathan cleared his throat and brought himself back down to earth. "No. Patrick lives in Old Greenwich, Connecticut. I make the trip to see him and Oliver about once a month. I'll be visiting again soon to celebrate Oliver's fourth birthday." Jonathan smiled proudly. "It's beyond me how he's that old already."

"I'll bet he's adorable. Children are so lovable at that age."

"I won't argue about that. Oliver is a joy."

Marie spoke softly and with tenderness as she broached her next question. "If I'm not being too forward, may I ask how your son is coping since his wife's passing?"

"Poor Patrick." Jonathan lowered his head, embarrassed to expose his raw emotional response whenever the topic of Catherine's death was raised. "He's gone through some difficult times the past couple of years. But he joined a grief counseling group a few weeks ago. I'm praying the therapy will help." He was relieved when Marie changed the subject, as if she intuitively understood he needed to have the mood lightened.

"And what about your daughter and her husband? Do they have children?"

"Yes, Veronica and Brian have two daughters. Teenagers. Need I say more?"

"Jonathan, you exaggerate." Marie sat forward and rested her elbow on the table. "I bet your granddaughters are not as difficult as you make them out to be."

Taking her lead, Jonathan inched forward in his chair. "You're right. They are good girls. Just a little temperamental at times."

"It's a difficult age. No doubt they adore their grandfather."

"That's true. I've always had a close relationship with both girls. I'm afraid I spoil them a little too much," he confessed.

"You can't help yourself." She ran her fingertips along the top of his hand, then intertwined her fingers with his. "Being kind and generous is in your nature. Those are your most endearing qualities, and just two of the reasons why I'm attracted to you."

Jonathan's instincts had told him from their first phone conversation that he and Marie had an inherent chemistry. Now, sitting so close together, the air between them was charged with electricity. Jonathan couldn't remember the last time a woman had captivated his attention the way Marie did. He admired her candidness, sincerity, and compassion. But, above all, she excited him. Being with her was like stepping into the Garden of Eden. He was consumed with the temptation to reach out, to touch the forbidden fruit.

As if on cue, a light breeze infused with Marie's fragrance of vanilla and fresh flowers encircled Jonathan. He suddenly ached to be alone with her, to draw her into his arms and brush back the wavy lock of hair that fell across her forehead, to nuzzle his face against her neck, to get drunk on her intoxicating scent. Then, starting with her soft lips, he'd explore her body with his eyes, his hands, his mouth. From the enticement he read in Marie's eyes, he knew she shared the same desires.

He could have suggested they drive over to her hotel right then and there, but he chose to wait. He wanted her passion to simmer. For now, they'd spend the afternoon enjoying each other's company. Before the day ended, however, he would be alone with her.

What Jonathan wanted, Jonathan got.

The afternoon passed too quickly. As the shadows deepened, Marie grabbed her phone to check the time. "Goodness, it's getting late," she announced. "I need to get back to the hotel."

"What are you doing?" Jonathan asked.

"I'm calling for a taxi."

Jonathan took the phone from her hands and placed it on the table. "Don't be silly. My car is here. I'll drive you. Just give me a moment to pay the bill." He motioned the waiter to their table.

"Jonathan, I hate to make you go out of your way." She again picked up her phone. "Besides, you have your own engagement to attend tonight."

"I'm just having dinner not far from here with some of my fraternity brothers. I insist on driving you so we can spend a little more time together. This afternoon was too short, and now all I can think about is when we'll be able to see each other again." As they strolled to his car, Jonathan shared an observation. "I have to say I'm surprised to see you have blonde hair and blue eyes. For some reason, I always imagined you with darker features."

Chapter 10

Marie

Back in her hotel room, Marie called Gus. "It's me."

"How's it going?"

"I'm right on target." She perched on the edge of the bed and kicked off her sandals. "He's practically eating out of my hand."

"Good, because the heat's been cranked up on my end. We need to wrap things up as soon as possible. Are you able to do that?"

"When have I ever disappointed you?"

"Never."

"Then you have nothing to worry about. I'll take care of it."

"Meet me for dinner tomorrow night?"

"Sure. I'll call you when I'm back in town."

Marie ended the call and tossed the phone onto the bed. She removed a bottle of water from the mini-fridge and poured the liquid into a glass she selected from the bar. Standing at the window, she surveyed the Boston skyline while she reviewed the progress of her plan thus far.

She'd been truthful with Gus. Her afternoon with the enthralling and strikingly handsome professor had gone as well as she'd expected. She didn't like to brag but she was, above all else, a master of planning and manipulation. Staying on top of her game and always being one step ahead of her target was her forte.

Marie was delighted with Jonathan's responses to the teasers she'd thrown at him. His facial reaction when she described how she protected her skin while sunbathing was priceless. She could almost visualize the scene he'd created in his mind of her rubbing her nearly naked body with sunscreen lotion. She'd stroked his ego by praising his choice of venue for their leisurely afternoon, his devotion to his family, his attention to her needs. She'd tantalized him with the occasional touch of her bare skin against his, sparking his desire for more *please*. She'd even gone so far as to intimate he might be the man she'd been searching for all her life. Her confidence in the job grew stronger as Jonathan fell for her charades one after the other.

Most men were tongue-tied by the time she'd finished enticing them. Depending on the circumstances, they'd take the opportunity to grope her on the spot. Jonathan, however, had remained a gentleman and showered her with compliments, which she found both charming and refreshing. Perhaps he'd been a widower for too many years and had grown accustomed to a life of abstinence. If the pleasure of her company was all he craved, that was fine with Marie. She was willing to be whatever Jonathan wanted as long as the ploy granted her access to the Somerset Necklace.

Marie made a modest attempt to work in the subject of jewelry, but Jonathan hadn't taken the bait. She'd need to find other subtle ways to wedge the topic into their conversation. When he eventually admitted ownership, she'd plead with him to let her see the necklace. A small distraction, spilling a glass of wine for instance, would occupy Jonathan's attention while Marie deftly switched the necklace for the fake replica Gus had crafted. By the time Jonathan discovered he no longer possessed the original piece of jewelry, Marie Lacroix would be long gone.

She sipped the water and pondered how to use the remainder of the weekend to her best advantage. A plan developed in her mind, one she was certain would work. After rehearsing the lure she would use to reel Jonathan in, Marie next gauged when to make her move. She placed the phone call around the time she estimated he and his friends would be finishing dinner.

"Marie?" While his greeting was subdued, Marie detected the pleasure in his tone.

"Hello, Jonathan." Marie noticed other men talking in the background which meant Jonathan was still at the restaurant and close to her hotel. Good timing. "Can you talk?"

"Hold on. Let me find a place that's more private." Jonathan's voice was muffled as he excused himself from the table. A few moments later, he resumed their conversation. "Sorry. My frat brothers have a tendency to eavesdrop, and then the teasing begins. Sometimes, I wonder if they'll ever grow up."

"I understand," she told him. "I returned to my room for the same reasons."

"We're about to finish dinner. I was going to call when I got to my car and ask if you have anything planned for the rest of the evening. Is everything all right?"

"Oh, yes, everything's fine," she assured him, then added a tinge of anguish to her voice. "But ever since we left the café, a comment you made has been haunting me."

Jonathan sounded concerned when he asked, "Why? What did I say?"

"You questioned when we'd see each other again. I've been thinking all evening about how soon I'd be able to make another trip to Boston, or when you'd be free to meet me in the city. Over dinner with my girlfriends, I realized how little I have in common with them these days, and how much I'd rather spend the remainder of this weekend with you." *Shame on me for throwing my imaginary friends under the bus!*

Jonathan chuckled. "Funny. I've spent my entire evening mulling over that same dilemma."

Marie made her response sound as though she were swooning. "Oh, Jonathan! I'm so happy to hear you say that. I gave my girlfriends *(Sorry again, ladies!)* the excuse of needing to cut the weekend short and returned to my room to call you." She took a breath before continuing. "When you leave the restaurant, would you like to meet me for a nightcap? There's a lounge in my hotel that's open late. Or, if you prefer, I can have a bottle delivered to my room."

"We could do that," Jonathan replied, "but I had something else in mind." He paused, as if waiting for her reaction.

"What is it?"

"Why don't you check out of the hotel? I'll pick you up, and we can spend the night at my home instead."

Marie congratulated herself on a job well done. Placing herself inside Jonathan's home had been her goal all along. "How soon can you be here?"

She caught the smile in his voice when he said, "I'll meet you in your hotel lobby in forty-five minutes."

"My suitcase and I will be waiting for you."

Grinning, Marie disconnected the call and sat back in the chair. Mission accomplished.

Forty-five minutes, however, did not give her much time to prepare for the evening ahead. Humming one of her favorite tunes, Marie hastened to the bathroom and stripped off her clothes. She was honestly looking forward to the time she'd spend with Jonathan over the course of this job. She wasn't surprised she enjoyed his company. He'd been fun to converse with during their many phone calls, and she'd anticipated he'd be equally as amiable in person. What she hadn't expected, though, was how much she liked being with him. She'd never met a more provocative man, nor one who asked all the right questions and was so attentive to her responses. Little nuances, like the fact he remembered how she preferred her coffee, certainly gave him a checkmark in the plus column.

Also, she had to admit, Jonathan was damned sexy. She'd known from the get-go that, to complete this job, she'd need to wheedle her way inside his home which meant she'd most likely end up in his bed. Unlike her experiences with most of her other targets, however, she presumed she'd actually *enjoy* having sex with Jonathan. Keeping her emotions distanced during this job might require her most concerted efforts.

Following a quick shower, Marie slipped into a long, strapless dress and sprayed on the perfume Jonathan had complimented earlier that day. Before leaving the room, she scrutinized her appearance in the mirror one last time. Smoothing her hair in place, she recalled Jonathan's astute observation that he'd imagined she'd have darker features. She wondered if he'd be as infatuated with her if he discovered her eyes were blue due to tinted contact lenses, or that blonde was not her natural hair color.

Or that Marie Lacroix was not her real name.

Chapter 11

Marie

For the remainder of the evening, Marie put her need to bring up the subject of the Somerset Necklace on the back burner. Instead, she sat back and let Jonathan do most of the talking. Being a good listener was a key component in building the trust of the unwary target, and Marie's primary goal was to establish a strong rapport with Jonathan as quickly as possible.

When they arrived at his home, Jonathan opened a bottle of wine and invited Marie onto the terrace. They sat close together on a cushioned settee and conversed as smooth jazz played softly through the outdoor speakers. Marie listened intently as Jonathan described his involvement in his home's construction. Who knew talk of blueprints, excavation, and brick laying could be so captivating?

"So, you almost doubled the square footage of the house," she commented.

"Yes. The original design…" As Jonathan's voice trailed off, Marie recognized the yearning in his eyes. The warm-up "let's get to know each other first" act was being ushered off stage to make way for the main event. He took Marie's wine glass from her hand and set it next to his on the table. Then, gently placing his hand on the back of Marie's neck, he leaned in and kissed her.

The instant Jonathan's lips touched hers, the world around Marie crumbled away. Gone were the murmured strains of the soprano saxophone, the crickets chirping in the nearby woods, the scent of lemongrass drifting in from the garden. All that mattered was the touch of Jonathan's fingers caressing her skin, the taste of his mouth, and the smoldering lust in his eyes. A moan of desire rose from deep inside her.

Jonathan stood and held out his hand. "Dance with me," he said.

Marie rather liked that his invitation was more a command than a request. She placed her hand in his and willingly complied.

As they swayed to the music, Marie detected Jonathan's hunger for her in his firm but tender embrace. She closed her eyes and was overcome with a blissful contentment she'd never before experienced. *What is happening to me?*

"I'm glad you chose to spend tonight with me," he whispered in her ear.

Marie gazed longingly into his eyes. "I can't image wanting to be anywhere else but here with you." Although she'd meant for her response to be contrived, the words flowed naturally from her heart.

Jonathan kissed her again, longer and more passionately this time. When the kiss ended, Marie said, "It's getting chilly. Why don't we go inside?"

Later on, the grandfather clock in the foyer struck midnight. Under the comfort of a feather duvet, the melodic chime ticked off the hour as Marie, cuddled in Jonathan's arms, drifted into a tranquil slumber.

****

Marie rose just before daybreak. Taking care not to

disturb Jonathan's sleep, she left the warmth of his bed, wrapped herself in his thick terrycloth robe she found hanging in the bathroom, and slipped away. Navigating her way through the house, she recalled her initial reaction to the home's pleasant ambience when Jonathan welcomed her in the previous evening.

The house was, simply put, spacious. She estimated her entire apartment could fit inside the kitchen. Compared to the pretentious homes owned by men she'd scammed in the past, however, Marie was impressed Jonathan had managed to create a cozy, hospitable atmosphere. The high-tech systems and electronics were cleverly blended into the design of an old-fashioned country cottage. The furnishings were expensive, yet she was certain Jonathan wouldn't think twice about inviting his guests to put their feet up and chill. Just as Marie had been relaxed with Jonathan from their first conversation, she was equally as comfortable in his home.

She opened the door that led to the backyard terrace and ventured outside to delight in the sunrise. A low wall, which Jonathan informed her had been built from repurposed fieldstone excavated during construction, created a border along the perimeter of the paved terrace. A wrought iron gate fitted into a section of the wall granted passage to a path that led to a garden lush with hybrid, exotic, and wildflowers on one side and a vegetable and herb garden on the other. Beyond the gardens, a manicured lawn extended to Jonathan's boat dock on Lake Burgess.

Resting one knee on the stone wall, Marie drew the robe closer to guard against the morning chill and soaked in the dawn of a new day. A thin mist clung low to the grass, daring the sun to rise and burn away the haze.

Mama birds chirped as they swooped from their nests to gather food for their chicks. Closing her eyes, Marie breathed in the garden scents of rose and honeysuckle while she recalled the remarkably pleasurable intimacy she and Jonathan had shared during the night.

When was the last time I woke in such a good mood?

Although the harried big-city bustle she faced every morning was an adrenaline rush that got her juices flowing, Marie envied those who awakened to this kind of quiet serenity. She longed for the day she could escape the concrete and pollution of New York and the unsavory memories the city held for her, but she first had a goal to meet. Until her coffers were funded to her satisfaction, she'd continue to work one con after the other and invest the profits into her offshore accounts. Once her objective was met, she'd flee from Manhattan and join her family in the secluded tropical paradise they called home.

Tomorrow, she'd wake again to reality. So, today, why not indulge in a little fun? Marie imagined a world in which she was the mistress of this sumptuous property and these glorious mornings were hers to enjoy as she fancied. She pictured herself and Jonathan (*Seriously, how can I leave him out of my fantasy? This* is *his home, after all!*) enjoying their morning coffee while discussing how they'd spend their day. Perhaps they'd go antique shopping, take the boat out on the lake, prepare dinner using fresh vegetables from their garden. Sadly, her pie-in-the-sky pipe dream might not have been such a farfetched notion if not for one horrid twist of fate.

Once upon a time, Marie was a zealous college graduate eager to create a name for herself in the world of international finance. Too soon, an unexpected family crisis interfered with her plans. Rather than asserting her independence and forging her own path, she was suddenly responsible for supporting herself as well as the other members of her family. To that end, she needed an immediate and dramatic increase to her income.

She considered enrolling in graduate school but obtaining a higher degree would delay a promotion for at least a couple of years. Besides, of the many junior execs in her office who boasted an MBA in their credentials, few were skyrocketing their way to the top. Marie, however, recognized the one distinct advantage she had over her colleagues. With her exceptional good looks, she was propositioned more often than she cared to admit by high-level executives of both sexes. She could easily have slept her way to the top but not without risking serious repercussions. Acknowledging that corporate America could not resolve her dilemma, she investigated other options.

The fashion world was her next consideration. Yvette Marchand, Marie's mother, had been a successful runway and catalogue model. Her career began in Paris and, after her marriage to Dominic Ricci, continued in New York City. Marie toyed with the idea of using her mother's old contacts to launch her own career in the fashion industry. With her natural beauty and ideal figure, she was certain she could have gotten agency representation, but what would she do when youth was no longer on her side? She'd witnessed firsthand her mother's bouts of depression as the modeling assignments dwindled with each passing year.

Marie preferred to avoid the painful memories of her mother's mental illness and its effect on their family. A normal day for Marie and her sister, Jacqueline, included a return home from middle school to find their mother still in bed with the curtains drawn. There were periods when Yvette refused to venture outside their apartment for weeks at a time. Marie's Grandmother Ricci, repulsed by a behavior she viewed as intolerable, muttered insults in her native Italian while she managed the household for her self-absorbed daughter-in-law. Marie and Jacqueline could do nothing to prevent the domestic tension that licked around them like wildfire.

Dominic's patience with his wife's despondency grew short. One day, at the end of his rope and in a fit of anger, he gave Yvette an ultimatum: either shape up or ship out. His words backfired when Yvette did both. She reconnected with her fashion world friends and, at a party hosted by an *haute couture* designer, she met a successful real estate developer from Los Angeles. Shortly afterward, Yvette divorced Dominic, married her new beau, and moved to the West Coast. Marie was twelve years old at the time. Still haunted by the many nights she and Jacqueline cried themselves to sleep, Marie soured on the idea of seeking a career in modeling.

So, in her early-twenties and needing to make a radical decision, she sought Gus's counsel. She asked his honest opinion of her idea to turn to what was familiar to her, the world of thievery her father had exposed her to, and which, for most of her upbringing, she'd viewed as a normal way of life. Did Gus think she had the essential ability to convincingly fool an innocent target? Had she inherited her father's nerves of steel and his talent for talking his way out of a compromising situation?

Gus reminded her that, since she was a child, she'd been obsessed with an unflinching determination to succeed. She wasn't satisfied unless she was the star performer in her dance class, got the highest grades in school, gained admission to the best colleges. He was convinced she could accomplish anything if she wanted it badly enough. Gus's confidence in her was all the encouragement she needed. With Gus as her mentor, she learned the intricacies of the business he and her father had embraced as teenagers. In no time at all, Gus taught her to be a skilled con artist.

For her own protection, Gus insisted that she create a new identity. Overnight, Siena Ricci, the ambitious young woman from New York who'd been raised among thieves and con men, became Marie Lacroix, the cultured girl from France whose father had schooled her in the world of fine antiques. Having learned French from her mother, Italian from her grandmother, and Spanish from her college professors, she incorporated a cosmopolitan background into her contrived history. Through Gus's connections, she obtained all the necessary paperwork to make her fake identity legitimate.

Armed with her looks, her gift of persuasion, and her stellar (albeit fake) resume, Marie found employment at the Manhattan gallery of Willow's Auction House, the renowned buyers and sellers of the world's finest *objets d'art*. She set her sights on becoming a professional in the industry and an expert on the clientele. In a short while, she was using the knowledge she'd gained to prey on her targets.

With thousands of vulnerable men in a city the size of New York, Marie's supply of victims was plentiful and her game plan was simple. She sought men who had plenty of discretionary funds and freely flaunted their wealth. Regardless of their age or profession, whether they personally attended the auctions or phoned in their offers, they met her criteria if they didn't flinch while placing a multi-figure bid. She then had one of Gus's associates follow the client she'd selected to get a feel for his activities. Where did he live? Which clubs and restaurants did he favor? What were his social commitments? Once the information was gathered, Marie created an appropriate alter ego and a physical disguise to match.

Men, she quickly discovered, could be so malleable when a beautiful, seductive woman gave them her undivided attention peppered with the hint of a little naughty excitement. Pretending her spiked heels caused her to lose balance and twist her ankle, the corporate executive passing by on the sidewalk caught her in his arms and offered her the first of many clandestine rides in his town car. During a fund-raising event, she "clumsily" spilled her drink on a well-heeled senator, then began a brief fling when she insisted on going to his apartment the next day to personally take his tux to be cleaned. And, she'd never forget dear Parker Dupree, her sweet Southern lawyer whom she'd encouraged to embrace his sexuality.

After meeting the target, Marie searched the upcoming auctions for an appropriately expensive item, then convinced the target to bid on the piece she'd chosen. Following the auction, she would invent a clever way to swap the forgery Gus had crafted for the genuine article. As soon as the switch was completed, Marie's alter ego vanished into thin air, leaving the mark bewildered and unaware he'd been victimized.

If Marie should happen to have an accidental meeting with any of her marks afterward, she could not leave herself open to the possibility of being recognized.

For that reason, she never used the same name, the same way of speaking, nor the same change in her appearance twice. She had no birthmarks, tattoos, nor any other identifying marks on her body. She was a chameleon and was confident the men she scammed couldn't track her down, no matter what means they used.

Before entering her life of crime, Marie had to face the fact that she might need to use her body to accomplish her objective. Although she admitted being intimate with men for whom she had no feelings was demoralizing, she viewed sex as a necessary part of the job, a means to an end. She convinced the men she targeted that she was in love with them, but she never allowed herself to develop an emotional attachment. In truth, Marie found most of her marks to be overbearing buffoons with falsely inflated egos, certainly not the type of men who could stir her affections.

The con she was playing on Jonathan Woodward was not her standard modus operandi. This job required her to obtain a family heirloom, a commodity already in the target's possession. She'd had to change her tactics in order to manipulate Jonathan, which was fine with Marie. She welcomed the opportunity to use a fresh approach and was primed for the challenge of persuading Jonathan to give her a peek at the Somerset Necklace. She had Gus's imitation necklace in her bag, ready to swap with the authentic piece when the situation presented itself.

Also, for the first time, she was completing the con as Marie Lacroix instead of creating a unique persona for the job. She'd need to be on high alert if Jonathan were to realize she'd swapped the Somerset Necklace for an identical fake. Should such an unlikely event occur,

Marie Lacroix would become dust in the wind with the quick removal of her blue contact lenses and a return to her natural brown hair color. She'd be untraceable as only a handful of people still remembered her as the person she used to be.

Chapter 12

Marie

Marie blamed the morning's serenity for her reflective mood, for leading her to fantasize about what might have been her reality if only she'd made different choices. Then again, maybe she still had a chance to live out her dream. During the time she and Jonathan had spent getting to know each other, he'd given her the distinct impression he was searching for a woman who, like himself, was serious about committing to a long-term relationship. Despite the difference in their ages, she and Jonathan connected on all levels. Last night, they'd definitely passed the intimacy test. Marie's intuition told her that, if she were so inclined, she could easily become the next Mrs. Jonathan Woodward.

With the sun now crested over the horizon, Marie snapped back to reality. Why was she allowing herself to entertain such frivolous ideas? She was sorely aware her sordid past prevented her from sharing her life with Jonathan Woodward, or with any man of his caliber for that matter. The years ahead will be filled with spectacular sunrises, she consoled herself, but where she'd view them *from* and who she'd view them *with* remained the questions.

Behind her, Jonathan stepped out to the terrace dressed in sleep pants and a T-shirt. He wrapped his arms around Marie and kissed the side of her neck. "Good morning," he said, his voice still gravelly with sleep.

Marie leaned her head back against his shoulder. "Good morning. I tried not to disturb you. Since we were awake half the night, I thought you might want to sleep a while longer." A quiver of pleasure coursed through her body as she recalled the various techniques Jonathan had used to titillate her throughout the night. An impish grin crept onto her face. For once, her intuition had been wrong—sex with Jonathan was *far* more pleasurable than she'd anticipated.

"We didn't get much sleep, did we? Not that I'm complaining." Jonathan squeezed her tighter. "When I woke up alone, I wondered where you'd wandered off to."

Marie moaned with contentment. She'd quickly grown fond of being enveloped in Jonathan's arms. Although she'd never allow him to control her heart, she didn't see any harm indulging in a few feel-good moments while she carried out the con. "I came outside to watch the sunrise," she told him. "Isn't it beautiful?"

"Yes." He kissed her neck. "But not nearly (*kiss*) as beautiful (*kiss*) as you (*long kiss*)."

As much as she was enjoying the moment, Marie had work to do. She swiveled around to face Jonathan and, resting her arms on his shoulders, slid her fingers up the nape of his neck and into his pillow-tousled hair. Normally, she didn't put a mark to The Test this early in the game, but she'd spend limited time with Jonathan and needed to know if she'd earned his trust. Not only did Jonathan pass her test with flying colors, the glint in his eyes confirmed he'd already fallen in love with her. The weekend was progressing just as she'd planned.

"Shall we go back to bed?" she asked.

Jonathan grinned mischievously, showing off his adorable dimples. "Last night wasn't enough for you?" He kissed her, then said, "Normally, I wouldn't pass up such an enticing offer, but I'm starving. Let's go into the kitchen, and I'll whip up a delicious breakfast for us."

Marie blinked several times to make sure she was awake. *Did Jonathan just offer to cook breakfast for me?* She was accustomed to men who were only interested in using her for their own pleasure and expected Jonathan to want an early-morning romp in the hay, then to send her packing. Not only did she find his suggestion to be pleasantly refreshing, she also anticipated having a better chance of working the Somerset Necklace into the conversation while they chatted over toast and coffee.

"All right, but only if you let me help." *Geez, I'm genuinely excited to cook. With food. In a kitchen! Who am I?*

Jonathan took her hand and led her toward the house. "I'll go easy on you. You can make the coffee while I prepare the eggs. What vegetables would you like in your omelet?"

****

"Breakfast was delicious, Jonathan. Thank you."

"I'm glad you liked it." He dropped another pod into the coffee maker and brewed a fresh cup. "A lot of people skip breakfast, but I can't face the day without it."

Marie had assumed a man of Jonathan's stature would have a chef on his payroll, just as he had told her of his gardener, housekeeper, and personal assistant. She liked the normalcy of him puttering around in the kitchen. "Is cooking another one of your hobbies?"

Jonathan returned to his seat at the kitchen island

and placed the mug of coffee by her plate. He sat sideways, facing Marie as he spoke. "You might say so. I eat lunch most days at my club, have a dinner date once or twice a week with my daughter, Veronica, at her husband's local restaurant, and schedule an occasional dinner party with friends. Otherwise, I'm right here making home-cooked meals for myself." He smiled lovingly at Marie. "We partner up pretty well in the kitchen. I could easily get used to this." Marie welcomed Jonathan's affection as he leaned over and kissed her, but she refrained from encouraging his notion of them becoming a normal couple. "Speaking of food reminds me, I wanted to ask what type of cuisine you prefer."

"I'm not picky, although I tend to eat a lot of seafood." She lifted the mug and blew on the coffee before taking a test sip.

"Then you'll love Arianna's. That's Brian's, my son-in-law's, steak and seafood restaurant, although the menu is varied. When my son and I go there, Patrick always orders a pasta dish." Jonathan chuckled. "I've never known anyone who likes Italian food more than Patrick. Anyway, Arianna's has a quiet atmosphere with live piano music in the evening. The next time you venture up this way, I'll take you there for a romantic, candlelit dinner."

"I'd love that!" Marie said with delight even though she didn't intend to be around long enough for the dinner date to ever take place. The turn in conversation, however, did provide her with a lead-in to the Somerset Necklace. "I'm already thinking about what I'll wear." While sipping her coffee again, she squinted her eyes, giving the impression she was visualizing her wardrobe. "Oh, my grandmother's necklace! Such an elegant restaurant would give me an excuse to wear it. But, Jonathan, I want to make sure I wear things that please you. Do you like vintage jewelry?"

Jonathan frowned and glanced at her curiously as he gathered their dishes together. "Don't worry about me. Wear whatever you think is appropriate." He took the plates to the sink and rinsed them.

Well, that didn't play out as I'd hoped it would. Fortunately, she had more than one trick up her sleeve. "Speaking of jewelry, I wanted to mention that many of my clients have asked me to notify them when fine or rare pieces become available. Can I provide the same service to you? Do you own any antique jewelry?"

Jonathan appeared pensive while he loaded the dirty plates and utensils into the dishwasher. After a few moments, he replied. "I would have to say that jewelry does not hold an interest for me. I wear only a wristwatch, and I can assure you my daughter and her girls would not wear anything that was previously owned."

Marie put every ounce of willpower she had into controlling her inherent Italian temper. Why couldn't she get Jonathan to engage in a conversation about the Somerset Necklace? Frustrated and out of ideas, she gulped her coffee, counted to four, and mulled over what to say next.

Jonathan closed the dishwasher and dried his hands with a towel. "Now that I think about it, I have always wanted a pocket watch. My grandfather used to wear one, and I remember, as a boy, being intrigued by it. I'd appreciate your help in finding one I could add to my collection."

Although the conversation had not steered in the

direction she'd intended, Marie didn't mind doing Jonathan a favor. His fond memory of his grandfather was reminiscent of her affection for her Grandmother Ricci. "I'd be happy to scout out a pocket watch for you," she told him while, at the same time, wishing he'd stop being so damned likeable.

Returning to his seat, Jonathan said, "Speaking of items I've acquired with your assistance, I'd like to show you the display case where I keep my collectibles."

"Yes, please," she replied. "I'd love to see them."

Taking Marie's hand in his, Jonathan guided her past the dining room, the great room, the foyer, and a first-floor bedroom, then down a hallway to the far side of the house. Along the way, he explained his proclivity for privacy. "Most people I know couldn't care less about antiques, so I've always kept my acquisitions tucked away where I can enjoy them in private."

Jonathan opened the door and welcomed Marie into his library. Marie examined the room closely, taking in every detail. To her left was a wall of built-in bookshelves crammed full with hard- and paperbacked editions. Paned windows on the adjacent wall granted a picturesque view of Jonathan's garden and the lake beyond. The wall behind Jonathan's desk was covered with family photos that captured several generations of Woodwards. The fourth wall was bare except for an ornate antique wall clock.

The walls, coffered ceiling, and floor were all made of the same rich mahogany. A large Oriental rug in deep reds, greens and tans lent color and warmth to the room. An oversized upholstered chair with matching ottoman sat in the corner between the bookcases and the windows. A table holding a lamp with a stained-glass shade in the Mission design was placed by its side.

The room spoke to her of intellect and wisdom, of masculinity and comfort, of permanence. What a stark contrast to her own barebones apartment which was devoid of personal touches and occupied by a woman who must always be prepared to skip town at a moment's notice. She loved that Jonathan had designed his home with great care and attention. As a result, his essence permeated every nook and cranny. Marie wished she could lock herself inside these walls and never find a reason to leave.

Add another item to my growing list of reasons why I like Jonathan Woodward.

Marie wandered through the library, touching the spines of the books as she read the titles. An assortment of high-brow and contemporary novels in a wide range of genres—just what she'd expect of an English professor. She gazed at the scenery outside the window, then examined each of the portraits hanging on the wall behind Jonathan's desk.

"Jonathan, your home is beautiful," she told him, "but this room is by far my favorite. Are these photos of your ancestors?"

From behind the desk, Jonathan said, "Yes. I'll explain how I'm related to each of them later. First, let me show you my collection."

Jonathan lowered his right hand to a spot underneath the center of his desk. As he did so, Marie detected a faint whirring sound. She stared with curiosity as the panel on which the antique clock was hung broke away and slowly descended. Inch by inch, Jonathan's showcase was revealed. Several glass shelves were mounted behind the protection of a thick glass door. Canned spotlights concealed in the ceiling automatically switched on as the panel stopped and the whirring ceased.

Marie's pulse quickened. She'd been so focused on getting Jonathan to reveal the Somerset Necklace, she hadn't considered all the other antiques he'd purchased over the years. His collection was of significant value, which was why, Marie assumed, he'd created this secret hiding place. Maybe she'd get lucky and find the Somerset Necklace displayed among his treasures.

"What a clever security system!" she commented, crossing the room to stand in front of the showcase.

"Well, it may be a little over the top," Jonathan said as he stepped beside her, "but of course I worry about theft. A burglar would have no idea there's a secret panel in this wall. Few people outside my family even know I own these antiques."

"But you've chosen to share them with me?" Marie asked, hoping she didn't sound too theatrical. "Jonathan, I'm honored." Taking a cursory glance at the items in the case, she did not notice the Somerset Necklace on any of the shelves. This wasn't her lucky day after all.

"Would I bore you too much if I bragged about a few of my favorites?"

"No, not at all." Sharing Jonathan's interests was part of gaining his trust. Besides, from a professional and personal standpoint, she was genuinely fascinated by his antiques.

Jonathan placed his right thumb on a small pad imbedded in the frame. Slowly, the glass doors broke away from the center and disappeared into the walls on either side of the case.

"Wow!" Marie exclaimed, pretending to be

enthralled with his abracadabra magic show. "You've installed safeguard after safeguard."

"I don't believe in taking chances," he explained. "The device under the desk and on this panel open only if my thumbprint is detected. The glass doors are shatter proof."

"First-rate security is a must," Marie told him, "if for no other reason than for your own peace of mind." What she didn't say, however, was that she'd seen similar systems before, and she could easily break into his showcase by asking Gus's tech guy to circumvent the safety features. "Everyone has a special piece that initially sparked their interest. Tell me which of these trinkets got you hooked."

Jonathan gently lifted the piece that held the center position on the top shelf. "I don't need to think hard for that answer," he replied. "This Coudriet cigarette case was my first find." He passed the case to Marie as if he were handing her a newborn baby.

"It's beautiful!" Marie examined the cigarette case from every angle. She had extensive experience with Coudriet pieces, so she truly appreciated its history and value. "When and where did you acquire it?"

"Patricia and I toured Europe on our honeymoon," he explained. "We stopped into a little antique shop in Vienna, and this cigarette case caught her eye. An impulsive purchase marked the beginning of our addiction."

"You also made a wise investment," Marie remarked. "I won't ask what you paid for this case, but similar items have sold recently for $50,000 at auction. If you're ever interested in selling, I have a few clients who would be happy to take this piece off your hands."

Jonathan smiled as he took the cigarette case from her and returned it to its designated space. "Sorry, but this little beauty isn't going anywhere." He lifted a book from its wooden easel. "Being a professor of literature, this treasure is closest to my heart."

Marie raised her eyebrows, intrigued. "Why? What is it?"

"This is a first edition print of Hemingway's *To Have and Have Not*." He opened the cover and handed the novel to Marie. "It's signed by the author himself."

Marie held the book carefully and admired Hemingway's inscription and signature. She found the excitement in Jonathan's expression to be contagious. "Oh, Jonathan!" she exclaimed. "This truly is special. Hemingway's note is written to someone named Artie. Do you know who that is?"

"Artie was my Granddad Collier, my mother's father," Jonathan explained. "My grandparents used to spend the winters in the Keys where they met and became friends with Hemingway. During that time, Hemingway wrote the novel and, when the book was published, he gave a signed copy to my grandfather. When I was sixteen, Granddad became gravely ill. He and I had always shared an interest in literature, so before he passed away, he handed the novel down to me. I still consider this book one of the best gifts I've ever received."

"What an amazing story!" Marie told him sincerely. "As we spend more time together, I want you to share the history behind every piece in your collection."

"It will be my pleasure."

Marie could tell from Jonathan's smile he delighted she'd implied they had a future together as a couple. As Jonathan placed the novel back in its cradle, Marie examined the shelves again, this time with more care, and frowned with disappointment when she confirmed the Somerset Necklace was not among Jonathan's trinkets. However, in the next instant, her attention was drawn to the object on the shelf directly below the Coudriet cigarette case.

"Jonathan, you have the Singing Bird Pistol. Didn't you purchase it as a birthday gift for your daughter-in-law? Why did you keep it for yourself?"

"I did give Catherine the Bird Pistol you helped me obtain at auction last year," he explained as he removed the sparkling piece from its case. "This one had been in my mother's family for several generations. My parents passed it on to Patricia and me in recognition of our passion for antiques. That was the main reason I wanted to purchase its mate for Catherine. She always admired mine, and I was thrilled to give her the matching piece. I just wish she could have lived to enjoy it." Marie recognized the pain in Jonathan's eyes. Her heart ached for him, and she tenderly caressed his back. The somber moment passed, and he returned to being playful. "Have you ever seen the bird in action?"

Jonathan wound the mechanism and triggered the bird to pop out and tweet for their enjoyment. Marie stared at the relic with wide eyes and a gaping mouth, astonished to have unraveled the decades-old mystery regarding the whereabouts of the second Singing Bird Pistol. Jonathan's sentimental rambling was touching, but did he realize the value both pieces garnered as a pair? He must, she reasoned, or he wouldn't have been so eager to pay close to a million dollars last year for the mate to the Bird Pistol in his hand.

This unexpected discovery had just made the con she was pulling on Jonathan much more interesting, and her potential profit from the job substantially more lucrative.

Chapter 13

Dominic
Winter 1981

At the age of seventeen, Dominic Ricci was living the dream. He had a nice income from the jobs Joe was throwing his way, a believable fake ID, and a steady stream of liquor and loose women. As he and Gus strolled home from school one dreary January afternoon, Dominic whistled a tune from his all-time favorite movie. Stepping in time to the beat and swinging his arms like pendulums at his sides, Dominic imagined himself as the main character in the story, a good-looking guy of Italian heritage who lived for the nightlife and dreamed of an exciting future.

"You going to tell me what you've been up to?" Gus asked.

"What do you mean?" Shaken out of his daydream, Dominic was confused. The last thing he remembered, he and Gus had been arguing over their differing opinions on which pro football team would win the championship game next Sunday.

"Come on, Dominic. Don't act dumb with me. I've known you my whole life. I can tell when you're hiding something."

"Sorry, Gus, but I don't know what you're talking about." Although Dominic understood his friend perfectly, he was still under strict orders from Joe to keep his mouth shut.

"Okay, dumbass. I guess I've got to spell it out for you. In the last couple of months, you meet me at the bars instead of first coming to my house. Then you show up late with some lame excuse about having to help your father, like that's ever happened before. You always have a pocket full of cash, and you're starting to talk different. All those signs point to the fact that something's changed, and I want to know what's going on."

"All right, I'll come clean. The truth is, I've been sort of, you know, *servicing* Mrs. Jenkins." Dominic had anticipated Gus would eventually ask him to explain where his current stream of money was coming from and had prepared a response in advance. However, he didn't realize how unbelievable his story sounded until he said it out loud.

Gus stopped dead in his tracks. "You're talking about my neighbor? The hot redhead with the size forty-double-Ds who wears the clingy sweaters and tight pants. *That* Mrs. Jenkins?"

"Yeah, *that* Mrs. Jenkins." Dominic himself wasn't convinced by his yarn, yet he continued to dig deeper into his lie. "She asks me to come over when her husband isn't home. We fool around, and she gives me a little money to show her appreciation."

Gus stared at Dominic with suspicious eyes for a few seconds, then burst out laughing.

"What's so funny?" Dominic was insulted by Gus's caustic reaction. He didn't consider his fib to be that farfetched.

"Do you really expect me to fall for that ridiculous

story?" Gus asked between fits of laughter. "Dominic, there is no way in hell you're banging the luscious Mrs. Jenkins. And, even if you were, she damn sure wouldn't pay you for it!"

"Okay, so I made it up. You can stop laughing any time now." Feeling sheepish over being caught in a lie, Dominic dismissed his friend's comment and continued trudging down the street.

"Then come clean and tell me what you've really been up to," Gus demanded as he caught up and fell in step with Dominic.

Dominic lowered his head to hide the scowl on his face. From day one, he'd been dying to tell his best friend every detail of his assignments, but Joe's dire warnings had scared the crap out of him. Then again, he rationalized, what harm was there in leaking just enough information to put an end to Gus's curiosity?

"I got a new part-time job," Dominic confessed. "The work isn't much, but the pay is good. And that's as much as I can tell you, so don't ask me any more questions." Dominic was proud of what he perceived as a spot-on imitation of Joe and assumed his threatening, tough guy demeanor had struck fear in Gus. He was wrong.

"Does your new career have anything to do with the older guy you were talking with at The Blind Spot a couple of months ago?" Gus asked.

"Come on, man. I'm serious," Dominic whined. "I can't tell you anything else."

"Okay, I won't bug you about it. But just tell me two things—how'd you get the job, and can you get me in?" Gus had a job on the weekends making deliveries for a local furniture store. Like Dominic, he was always searching for something better.

"I was recommended for the job by my mom's cousin, and I'll ask." Dominic was confident his response didn't cross any lines. Anyway, the idea to ask Joe about welcoming Gus into their circle had crossed his mind, so he was glad to find out Gus was interested.

"Thanks, buddy. We have each other's backs, right? You know I'd do the same for you if I was ever offered a sweet gig." Gus squeezed Dominic's shoulder. Best buds forever. "Are we going to The Blind Spot tonight? I've been working on sweet Kimmy, you know, the one with the big blue eyes. This might be the night she finally gives it up."

Since he had no work for Joe to tend to that evening, Dominic agreed to the plan. "Yeah, sure. I'll be by your house at seven."

****

Dominic Ricci and Wendell Ferguson were inseparable from the age of four. As boys, they played kickball in an empty neighborhood lot. As adolescents, they struggled through the angst of puberty together. When one dropped out of high school, the other followed suit. As adults, they found prosperity working side by side in the underbelly world of black-market transactions.

After Dominic proved his worthiness, Joe groomed him in the art of flimflam. Dominic's new career introduced him to social circles into which he never dreamed he'd be admitted. He learned that a well-cut suit and a visit to a stylish Park Avenue salon could convince anyone he hailed from the best part of town. His good looks and suave personality led him to rub elbows with New York and Long Island socialites. Businessmen offered him high-salaried positions; their bored wives offered him clandestine pleasure.

Gus, on the other hand, was better suited to the back end of the business. Having a creative eye and an artistic hand, he worked with Tommy DeLong, the man with the scarred eye, behind closed doors in the basement of the antique store on Truman Avenue. Tommy schooled Gus in the creation of forgeries, a skill for which Gus proved to have a natural talent.

Soon, the boys from the Bronx were living out their fantasies. They each found a nice apartment in Manhattan and worked hard to disguise their working-class upbringing and lack of a high school diploma. Reinventing themselves was not as difficult as they'd expected, and those who didn't know their histories were none the wiser.

Dominic's apartment was large enough to house his mother when his father passed away. If Carmella Ricci suspected her son's unusual rise in social status stemmed from illegal activities, she didn't let on. She'd been raised in the Old Country where women were taught to not ask questions. Her simple wish was to share her only child's company and to bask in his success.

At one of the many parties Dominic attended, he was introduced to Yvette Marchand, a gorgeous French fashion model. From the first smile Yvette flashed his way, Dominic wanted no other woman. Yvette, much to Dominic's pleasure, had eyes for no other man. The couple tied the knot shortly after they met.

Soon, Dominic was searching for a larger living space to accommodate the addition of his wife and their two adorable daughters. Dominic could have rented a separate apartment for his mother, but Yvette was used to the European traditions and insisted Carmella Ricci remain in their home. Not only did Yvette want to keep the family together, she also appreciated the convenience of having her mother-in-law around to help with the girls while she continued her modelling career.

Gus never sought the type of family life his friend desired. He was content to live vicariously through Dominic, being godfather to his daughters and joining the family for Sunday dinners. Over the years, he'd had his share of long-term relationships, but none of his female companions ever convinced him to make the trip down the aisle.

Regardless of what happened in their individual lives, Dominic and Gus always had each other's backs. Gus was there for Dominic throughout Yvette's bouts with depression and their contentious divorce. They took over the business after Joe died of lung cancer and Tommy's advancing dementia left him incapable of managing the antique shop. When Gus slipped on a patch of ice and broke his leg, he slept on Dominic's couch and allowed Mama Carmella to care for him until he could function again on his own.

If Dominic had to depend on anyone in the world to come to his rescue in a dire situation, he had no doubt that person was Gus. Their loyalty was put to the test one evening when Dominic was shot multiple times and left for dead by the jealous husband of a woman he'd been conning. Bleeding out and unable to help himself, Dominic managed to grab ahold of his cell phone and place an SOS call to Gus before fading into blackness.

Chapter 14

Marie
Summer 2022

The antique store was closed for business on Sundays, but in the basement bright overhead lights illuminated Gus's workshop. A radio, the volume set low, was tuned to the afternoon baseball game. Gus sat at his worktable, hunched over in deep concentration as he maneuvered the delicate instruments in his hands. He'd spent most the day replicating a ring that Marie needed for a con she was running on an overbearing corporate executive, a job she worried was dragging on too long and was anxious to wrap up as quickly as possible. Gus preferred to spend his Sundays away from the shop, but if he had to give up a few hours of his free time to finish forging this ring for Marie, then so be it.

Marie let herself into the store through the back entrance. She opened the basement door and called out to Gus as she descended the stairs. With her hobo purse slung over her shoulder and a paper shopping bag in her hand, she stepped over to the workbench and greeted Gus with a kiss on his cheek.

"Hey, sweetie," he said. "I didn't think you'd be here this early."

"What are you talking about, Gus?" Marie teased. "It's six o'clock."

Gus's eyes widened when he glanced at his wristwatch. "So it is. I let the afternoon get away from me."

"I figured as much," Marie said as she set the shopping bag on the counter, "so I stopped by Max's Deli and picked up dinner for us."

"I swear to God you know how to read my mind," Gus told her, his face beaming. "I've been hankering for a pastrami sandwich from Max's for the last two days."

"Well, guess what? That's exactly what I ordered for you." She nodded in the direction of the radio. "Sounds like that game is almost over."

"Yep. Ninth inning."

"Is our team winning?"

Gus gave Marie a thumb's up. "You bet. Five to one."

Marie peeked over Gus's shoulder at the materials in his hands. "What are you working on?"

"It's the diamond ring for your Wall Street bigwig. I'm almost done." He handed the work in progress to Marie. "What do you think?"

Marie examined the ring from every angle under the work lamp. "This is beautiful. I don't see a flaw anywhere. Let me see the photos I gave you."

Gus handed Marie the folder she'd borrowed from Willow's. "These pictures helped me create a damned good replica, if you don't mind my bragging."

Marie compared the counterfeit ring to the photos of the original. "I honestly can't see the difference. And, if I can't tell it's a fake, it's sure to fool Richard Leister." She handed the ring back to Gus. "Will I be able to wrap up this job by the end of the week?"

"Absolutely," Gus assured her. "I'll have this piece

finished before you leave tonight."

"Good. I want Richard out of my hair so I can devote all my attention to Jonathan Woodward." She removed the food from the shopping bag and set up places for them to eat on a clean area of the worktable.

"From that comment, I take it you weren't successful in getting your hands on the Somerset Necklace," Gus said before he bit into his sandwich. With his mouth stuffed with pastrami and rye bread, he managed to mumble, "Mm-mm, this is good!"

"I asked them to go heavy on the pastrami, so don't accuse me of never doing anything nice for you," Marie told him as she removed a bottle of water from Gus's mini fridge. "Do you want anything?"

"Yeah, grab me a beer while you're in there. Thanks."

"Back to the topic of the necklace, no, things did not go as I'd hoped." She used the bottle opener sitting on top of the fridge to pop off the cap, then handed the cold beer to Gus. "I ran out of ways to work the necklace into the conversation. I couldn't get Jonathan to even talk about it, let alone get my hands on the damned thing. We may need to consider the possibility he doesn't own the necklace any longer."

Gus shook his head in disagreement. "He must still have it. Christopher did some research for me and didn't find any record of the necklace changing ownership."

"Yeah, well, maybe not *outside* the Woodward family," Marie said as she stabbed a fork into her Chef's Salad. "Jonathan impresses me as being a generous person. After his wife died, he may not have wanted to keep the necklace and handed it over to one of his relatives. If that happened, there wouldn't be a record of the transaction."

Gus frowned. "You're not saying you're giving up on this job, are you?"

"Of course not." Marie was insulted Gus would suggest she could be defeated so easily. "If I need to ransack Jonathan's home, I will. I'm just letting you know this job may take longer than we expected."

"I'll let the buyer know we may need to push out the delivery date, but he's not going to be happy," Gus replied.

"I hear you. I promise I'll wrap up the job as soon as possible. But, more importantly, I discovered Jonathan Woodward owns something of much greater value than the Somerset Necklace."

Gus took a swig of beer and washed down his food. "What would that be?" he asked.

"Are you familiar with the Singing Bird Pistols from the nineteenth century?"

"Yeah, sure. I researched them last year when you told me you helped Woodward buy one at auction. They're remarkable pieces, no doubt, but their real value is in keeping them together as a pair. Separately, they're not that easy to fence. Woodward owns one of the Bird Pistols, but no one knows the whereabouts of the second one." He took another bite of his sandwich.

"Oh, but you see, I do." Marie tingled with excitement, as if she were about to tell Gus he held the winning ticket in last night's lottery drawing. "The second Bird Pistol is in Jonathan Woodward's library."

Gus swallowed hard. He stared at Marie without blinking. "He owns both pistols?"

"Yes."

"You're certain?"

"Gus, I wouldn't lie about something like this," she said indignantly. "He keeps it in his glass showcase. I viewed it with my own eyes and held it in my hand." Marie described the showcase Jonathan kept hidden behind the sliding wall in his home library.

"But you didn't see both pistols in the case?"

"No. The second pistol is at his son's home in Connecticut."

Gus sat back in his chair. "This is incredible. Last year, after you told me about the bird pistols, I sent out some feelers. One of my Asian buyers told me, if we ever located both pistols, he would be extremely interested in obtaining them. He loves anything having to do with his country's history and said he'd be willing to pay upwards of $10 million for the pair."

Marie's breath caught. Ten *million* dollars! Splitting a purse of that size with Gus would have a huge impact on their futures. Anticipating Gus would be all-in on the job, she'd already fleshed out a plan to acquire both Singing Bird Pistols.

"The fact that you have an interested buyer means we have no choice but to take advantage of this opportunity. There can't be any chance of messing this up, Gus. A sale of this size means we can both retire from the business. I know I'm ready to call it quits, and I think you are, too."

Gus gazed at her with sadness in his eyes. "I'd miss it, for sure. It's been my life. But my fingers aren't as nimble as they used to be, and the strain on my eyes is becoming a problem. I've been thinking about turning the operation over to the younger guys for a while now."

Marie made the decision for them both. "Then, let's do it!" She opened her purse and removed a manila envelope. "I stopped at the office on my way over and picked up all the information Willow's has on file for the pistols. Here are detailed photos, dimensions, the specific jewels and techniques that were used. This should be everything you need to make the forgeries."

"The detail is intricate, but the pistols are small." Gus wiped his hands on a napkin, then reviewed the pages Marie presented to him. "It shouldn't take me long to make them. I'll get Christopher to help. The only detail I won't be able to duplicate is the interior mechanism that makes the bird pop out and sing. That would require watchmaking skills I don't possess. Even if I did, it would take too much time to build that function into the pistols."

"Don't worry about the bird. Jonathan gave me a demonstration this morning, but he normally just admires the pistol from where it sits inside his display case. To make the swap, you only need to duplicate the exterior."

Gus grinned as he glanced at the photos another time. "Not a problem, then. I'll start working on them tomorrow. Now, let's talk about your role in this job. How is this going to play out when the men who own these Bird Pistols live in two different cities?"

"It'll be tricky," Marie conceded, "but let me fill you in on the plan I have in mind."

Chapter 15

Patrick

The community room on the second floor of the First Unitarian Church in Old Greenwich was designed for informal gatherings. Furnished with high-backed upholstered chairs, thick carpeting, soft lighting, and a gas fireplace, the space exemplified comfort and privacy. When not in use by the church members, the room was offered as a resource to the public. Patrick Woodward's grief counseling group met there every Monday and Thursday evening at six-thirty.

Patrick had joined the group several weeks earlier but had so far only managed to attend three sessions. His initial awkwardness was true to form. He was uneasy being candid in a group of strangers and, at his first session, he spoke just long enough to introduce himself. Tracy, the group leader, assured him he was okay to sit back and observe. He'd know when he was ready to share the circumstances of his own loss with the others.

Weighing the pros and cons of attending a second meeting was torture but, at the last minute, he made the decision to return. Just as he reminded his patients that recovering from major surgery doesn't happen overnight, Patrick understood his emotional wounds wouldn't heal after just one session. In the end, he was pleased he'd stuck with the program. By the third session, he'd gelled with the other members of the group and opened up in a way that surprised no one more than himself.

However, as he parked his car in the church's back lot, Patrick wondered if he should have skipped this particular Thursday evening. He'd rushed home from the clinic, taken a quick shower, and lumbered through a combative dinner with Oliver who was unusually out of sorts. Although Louise had prepared Oliver's favorite meal of spaghetti and meatballs, he refused to eat, preferring instead to whine and cling to his father. Louise managed to distract Oliver long enough for Patrick to slip away without being noticed.

By the time Patrick arrived at the church hall, he was several minutes late for the session. He sprinted from the parking lot and entered the building through the back door. Hurrying from the entrance to the stairwell that led to the second-floor meeting room, he collided with a woman as she stepped out of a darkened classroom.

"I'm so sorry," Patrick apologized. He stooped down to pick up the notebook he'd knocked out of her arm. "Please, excuse me."

"No, really, it's my fault." While lifting the strap of her purse back onto her shoulder, she admitted, "I'm completely lost and honestly didn't see you."

"Maybe I can help. Are you here for a meeting?" Patrick had noticed more cars in the parking lot than usual and assumed a church committee was meeting in one of the other gathering rooms.

"Yes, I am. I recently joined this church and volunteered to serve on the Finance Committee. They're holding a meeting on the second floor, but I've never been in this part of the building and don't know where the staircase is."

"Then you're in luck. I'm headed upstairs myself, so you can follow me."

"Thank you so much. You're a lifesaver." As she fell in step with Patrick, she asked, "Are you also on the Finance Committee?"

"No," Patrick explained, "I attend a grief counseling session that meets here twice a week."

"Grief counseling? I wasn't aware the church offered that type of support group."

"It's my understanding the group isn't affiliated with the church. We're just given the privilege of using the space for our meetings."

They took the last step and stood face to face on the landing of the second floor. The woman cocked her head and smiled beguilingly. "Well, thank you for your help."

Patrick spent a moment soaking in the woman's stunning beauty before responding. Her eyes reminded him of rich chocolate. Her long, dark hair cascaded past her shoulders in soft waves and curls. Even under the harsh fluorescent lighting, the olive complexion on her perfectly sculpted face was flawless. The tan on her bare, well-toned arms hinted of a woman who enjoyed outdoor activities. Her skirt revealed just enough leg for him to imagine the rest of her body was equally as pleasing. Her gaze drew him in and erased the uncomfortable misgivings of the socially awkward boy still lurking in his psyche.

"My pleasure," he managed to say, "but I'm sure you would have found your way upstairs on your own."

"Oh, I don't know," she said as though teasing him. "Maybe our bumping into each other was more than just chance." She glanced down the hallway. "It appears the meeting started without me. Thanks again for your help."

"You're welcome," Patrick said. "Have a good evening."

As the woman sauntered away, Patrick ogled her fabulous legs one last time before entering the room where his counseling group's session was already under way.

Patrick took the last empty chair in the circle and listened as the others in his group shared the highs and lows of their week. Occasionally, he interjected a comment or question, but his mind kept wandering back to his encounter with the beautiful stranger he'd met in the hallway. Why was he so thoroughly captivated by her? Had he misinterpreted her comments? Misread her friendliness as flirtation? He wished now he'd paid more attention to her hands and the rings she was—or was not—wearing.

Tracy directed her next question to Patrick and startled him out of his daydream. "Patrick, how have you been since you were last with us?"

"Better." Patrick cleared his throat and sat up straighter in his chair. "I've made an honest effort to spend more quality time with Oliver, my son, and to keep in touch more often with Catherine's parents. Oliver and I drove to Philly last weekend to visit them, and they were thrilled to have us there. On one hand, being together was difficult on all of us. Catherine's absence was like the elephant in the room nobody wanted to address. There were tears, especially from Mary Jo, my mother-in-law, but the result is that we're bonded together now in a way we never were before."

After the others shared similar experiences and offered Patrick their words of encouragement, Tracy wrapped up the session. "Well, everyone, our hour is up. We'll meet again next Monday evening. I hope you all have a good weekend."

Tracy was in a hurry to leave, so Patrick offered to stay and set the room back in order. While he relocated the chairs and tossed the empty coffee cups, he wondered if the Finance Committee might, by chance, also be wrapping up their meeting. If so, he might have the opportunity to continue his conversation with the beautiful stranger. At the doorway, he glanced hopefully down the hall, but all the rooms were dark. He lowered his head and grimaced with disappointment. Some things, he guessed, were not meant to be. After closing the meeting room lights, he trudged toward the staircase. Just then, the door to the ladies' room opened and the woman he couldn't erase from his thoughts stepped out.

"Well, hello," she said.

"Hi, yourself." Patrick hoped his excitement wasn't shamelessly bubbling over.

"We meet again." Her smile gave Patrick the impression she was also pleased their paths had crossed a second time. "Another strange coincidence? Or were you purposely waiting around for me this time?"

"I'll let you think that," he joked as they took the stairs to the main floor, "but you should know my mind isn't that cunning. After my group left, I stayed behind to straighten the room, or else I wouldn't still be here."

"My committee disbanded a while ago. I wouldn't still be here either except I stopped to use the ladies' room and made the mistake of glancing at my phone. Twenty minutes and eight texts later, here I am meeting you once again in the hallway."

"Business or pleasure?" Patrick asked as he held the

outside door open for her. When she passed by, carrying her notebook in her left arm, he noticed the absence of a ring on her finger.

"Pardon me?"

"Your text messages. Were they for business or pleasure?"

"Oh!" she exclaimed, then laughed out loud. Patrick was not surprised that her laugh, along with everything else about her, was enchanting. "Sorry, I wasn't following you. I'd like to say the messages were from friends, but they were all business related."

"Since I'm being nosy, what type of business are you in?" Patrick worried he'd ventured beyond the border of polite interest. She, however, didn't seem to mind his bold curiosity.

"I'm a licensed realtor," she answered matter-of-factly. "The calls and texts never end."

Patrick chuckled. "I know exactly what you mean. I face the same situation in my profession."

"And what would that be?"

"I'm an electrophysiologist," he answered.

"Pardon my stupidity," she apologized with a light giggle. "What is an electro…"

Patrick stepped in to assist her. "…physiologist. That means I'm a cardiologist who specializes in correcting the electrical impulses in patients with heart conditions such as arrhythmia." Patrick stopped himself, embarrassed that he sounded like he was reciting an article from a medical journal.

"You lost me at cardiologist," she replied. Although she appeared confused, her smile gave Patrick the impression she considered his rambling to be endearing. "So, I'm guessing you were the smartest kid in your class."

"Yep, that's me, 'The Class Nerd'." Patrick attempted to sound flip, as though the title held the same prestige as "Class President" or "King of the Prom." In truth, from the age of twelve, his classmates had taunted him with that label. Would the embarrassment that consumed him at the utterance of those three words ever diminish? Hoping the revelation of his derogatory nickname wouldn't scare her away, he quickly changed the subject. "Where is your car parked?"

"This is me right here." She pressed the key fob in her hand. Her car's headlights blinked at them.

"Another coincidence. I'm parked right next to you." Patrick copied her action and unlocked his own car with a touch of his fob. "By the way, my name is Patrick Woodward."

"It's nice to meet you, Patrick. I'm Kelsey Adams." She offered a handshake.

"Kelsey," Patrick said almost in a whisper. As he held her hand in his, he was mesmerized by her alluring smile. "A beautiful name that suits you well."

"What a nice compliment. Thank you."

Embarrassed by his forwardness, Patrick released her hand and glanced away. He didn't want their time together to end but couldn't find the words to continue the conversation.

After an uncomfortable moment of silence, Kelsey spoke up. "You know, you've been so nice to me, and to be honest I enjoy talking with you. Can I buy you a cup of coffee, a glass of wine…a shot of hard liquor? You pick."

Patrick recalled the time his college chemistry partner, who later became his wife, coerced him into meeting her for coffee. He'd resisted at first, but Catherine wouldn't take no for an answer. If not for her persistence, Patrick would never have gotten to know the love of his life. As he read the hopeful anticipation on Kelsey's face, the old phrase about history repeating itself popped into his mind.

"I'm sorry, Kelsey. I'd really like to, but I can't tonight. I need to get home to my son and relieve his nanny."

"Your son and his nanny?" She was obviously confused, then appeared to put two and two together. "Oh, my gosh! Are you a widower? Is that why you attended the grief counseling meeting?"

"Yes," Patrick replied, "to both questions."

"How could I be so stupid?" She placed her hand gently on his arm. "Please forgive my cluelessness and accept my sincere condolence."

"Thank you." Patrick was proud of himself for overcoming a big hurdle. For the first time since Catherine's passing, he could make eye contact while accepting someone's concern over the death of his wife. Was this breakthrough a result of the counseling sessions, or did Kelsey have magically curative powers? "And please don't misinterpret my excuse. I would like nothing more than to join you for a drink, but tonight doesn't work for me. Can I take a rain check?"

Kelsey let out a sigh, as though she were relieved she hadn't insulted Patrick. She smiled when she said, "Since I've made such a fool of myself, please let me make it up to you over dinner. Do you like Italian? Giorgio's on Third Avenue is my favorite restaurant."

"How did you know? Italian is also my favorite cuisine. I haven't eaten at Giorgio's in a long time so, yes, I'd like to have dinner there with you." Patrick checked the calendar on his cell phone. His next free evening was Monday. Although he would need to skip his counseling session that night, his intuition told him dinner with Kelsey might be a more helpful therapy. "How's next Monday at six o'clock?"

"The nice thing about being in business for myself is that I control my own schedule," Kelsey said as she entered the time into her cell phone. "I have no appointments scheduled on Monday evening. Six o'clock is perfect."

"Great," Patrick replied. "Let's swap phone numbers in case one or both of us has a schedule change between now and then."

****

Later that night, Patrick sat in bed reading through some professional literature when the buzz of his cell phone announced a text from his fourteen-year-old niece, Phoebe. Patrick regretted that he lived too far away from Boston to attend Phoebe's tennis matches and made her promise to keep him posted on her team's progress. She'd sent a photo of herself with her teammates and texted that they'd made it to their divisional tournaments. Her announcement was followed by many exclamation marks and several emojis. Patrick texted his congratulations. Feeling silly but wanting to relate to Phoebe on her level, he added a few of his own emojis to express his enthusiasm.

After the text was sent, Patrick scrolled through his list of contacts until he reached Kelsey's name. His thumb hovered over the screen as he toyed with the idea of hitting the call button. He wanted to tell her again how much he enjoyed talking with her, and that he was glad they'd scheduled a dinner date for Monday. *No!* Using the word "date" was too presumptuous. He'd just say he was happy they'd made plans to have dinner and avoid implying they were getting together as anything more than casual acquaintances. He glanced at the time. The hour was still early enough that she wouldn't consider him rude for calling.

As his thumb was about to touch the screen, Patrick stopped himself. A more confident man would have had the guts to be so forward with a woman he'd just met, but Patrick's cowardice got the better of him. He suddenly second-guessed Kelsey's intentions and surmised her dinner invitation was merely a polite way of returning Patrick's kindness.

Why can't I get this woman off my mind? Well, the reasons were obvious. She was outgoing, beautiful, and beguiling, and he couldn't deny they'd had a bit of chemistry. Still, as much as he wanted to, he couldn't bring himself to place the phone call. Monday was just four days away. He had a busy schedule of surgeries tomorrow and was committed to a father-son weekend with Oliver. His dinner with Kelsey would be here before he knew it. He set his cell phone on the nightstand and returned to his reading. Dreams of Kelsey were officially relegated to the back of his mind until the next time they met.

****

On Saturday, the warm and breezy weather conditions were ideal for Oliver to experience kite flying for the first time. In an open field at the park near their home, Oliver was squealing with delight as his kite, designed to resemble a Tyrannosaurus Rex, caught the wind and soared high above them. Patrick was instructing his son to keep the kite clear of the trees when he became aware of someone calling out his name. He scanned the area the voice came from and noticed a woman waving to him from the running path nearly eighty feet away.

From that distance and with the sun in his eyes, Patrick couldn't see the woman's face well enough to distinguish who she was. As she sprinted toward them, Patrick recognized her.

"Kelsey?" he questioned in a way that suggested she was the last person he expected to see at the community park. "We seem to bump into each other in the strangest places." He reeled in the kite so they could converse without interruption.

"We do, don't we?" she agreed while catching her breath. "The kite caught my eye, and then I realized you were the person holding the string." She stood with her hands on her hips and drew in several deep breaths. Her hair was drawn up into a ponytail, and she was dressed in tights and a cropped tank top. Her skin glistened with sweat and her tight-fitting running gear clung to her as though it had been painted on. As a physician, Patrick had seen hundreds of bodies, but he was positive he'd never seen one as well-toned and perfectly shaped as Kelsey's. He told his eyes not to stare. They refused to listen.

"So, you're a runner." He was aware the comment was dumb, but he needed to say something to redirect his attention to Kelsey's face.

"Yes, and I like the running path in this park. I come here every day when the weather's good. I'll bet we've seen each other here a dozen times without realizing."

"We probably have." Although Patrick agreed with

Kelsey, he was positive he'd remember a body like hers if he'd seen her running in the park at any time in the past.

"Who's this little guy?" she asked, bending at the knees to be at eye level with Oliver.

"This is my son, Oliver," Patrick replied.

Oliver, who was well-trained in Stranger Danger, grabbed onto Patrick's leg for security.

"Oliver, it's okay," Patrick assured his little boy. He pried Oliver's arms from his leg and bent down to his son's level as well. He put a protective arm around Oliver. "This is my friend, Kelsey. Can you say hello?"

"Hello," Oliver said as instructed, although he continued to glare at Kelsey as though he still wasn't convinced she was safe.

"Hi, Oliver," Kelsey said sweetly. "I'm pleased to meet you. Gosh, you're a handsome boy. How old are you?"

When Oliver didn't answer, Patrick prompted him. "Go on, Oliver. Your birthday is in a few weeks. Tell Kelsey how old you'll be."

Oliver responded by holding up four fingers.

Kelsey's eyes widened and her voice sounded incredulous. "No way! Four? Wow, that's awesome. Can you give me a high five?" She held her hand up to Oliver, and he slapped her palm hard with his own hand. "All right! That was a good one! By the way, that's an awesome kite. Something tells me you like dinosaurs."

Oliver nodded his head with enthusiasm. "It's a Tyrannosaurus Rex!" he shouted.

Kelsey laughed. "Well, you taught me something new today. Your daddy told me what a smart boy you are, and you know what? I think he's right."

Oliver giggled. Kelsey had broken the ice. Patrick recognized the same trait in Kelsey that he detected in Louise. They both had a natural kinship with children.

The adults straightened their legs and stood facing each other once again.

"He's adorable, Patrick."

"Thanks. He's a great kid." Oliver had resumed his grasp on Patrick's leg. Patrick smoothed his hand over the top of Oliver's head, reassuring him all was well.

"So, are we still on for dinner Monday night?" Kelsey asked Patrick.

"I'm counting on it," he confirmed. Patrick carefully considered his next words as he wasn't sure how Kelsey would respond. "You know, you've been on my mind a lot since we met on Thursday. A couple of times, I was tempted to call you."

Kelsey raised an eyebrow. "What stopped you?" she asked.

"I don't know," Patrick replied. He shrugged his shoulders and glanced away, embarrassed to meet Kelsey's inquisitive eyes when he confessed the truth. "Nerves, I guess. Fear of rejection."

"Can I tell you a secret?" she asked coyly. Patrick's eyes darted back and his gaze locked with hers. "I stopped myself from calling you for the same reasons."

As it turned out, Patrick was glad he'd been honest with Kelsey but at the same time was caught off guard. He was too tongue-tied to give an appropriate response. Thankfully, Oliver saved him from embarrassment.

"Da-addy," Oliver whined while tugging on Patrick's hand.

Patrick bent down and lifted his son into his arms. "Okay, buddy. I know you want to fly your kite some more." He mouthed a silent apology to Kelsey.

"It's okay. I need to get going anyway." She lightly rubbed Oliver's back. "Have fun flying your kite, Oliver." She wagged her index finger at Patrick. "No excuses now. I'll be waiting tonight for your phone call."

Kelsey returned to the running path, her pace quickening once she hit her stride. Patrick's eyes were glued to her until she was out of sight.

****

Patrick called Kelsey that evening as soon as Oliver was put to bed. On Sunday, she hosted an open house, then spent the remainder of the day at Patrick's home. During their dinner at Giorgio's on Monday, Patrick invited Kelsey to stop by for an after-dinner drink on Tuesday evening. By the time they said their goodnights on Wednesday, they were officially seeing each other on a regular basis.

Chapter 16

Marie

The short route from New York to Nantucket was routine for the pilots in command of the chartered flight, but the attention they paid their sole passenger was far from ordinary. Buckled into one of the plush seats in the cabin of the aircraft, Marie enjoyed the interaction she'd created between the robust aviators. From the moment the pilots assisted her onto the plane, they'd been acting like a couple of prizefighters sparring for her favor.

Rather than ignore the men, Marie encouraged their behavior. She admired their stories of derring-do, although she was certain their tales had been exaggerated for her benefit. By the end of the flight, Marie was confident that one of the men, if not both, would request her phone number or suggest they meet for a drink when she returned to Manhattan.

The plane touched down with ease and taxied to a stop. Marie unbuckled her seat belt and gathered her handbag while the co-pilot unlocked the cabin door. Donning a pair of sunglasses, she passed through the open doorway into the bright sunlight, descended the stairs, and stepped onto the tarmac. She glanced in the direction of the hangar where Jonathan told her he would be waiting. True to his word, Jonathan had arrived ahead of schedule. He was leaning against the side of his red convertible sports car, arms folded across his chest, one foot crossed in front of the other. He waved at Marie and headed in her direction.

Although they now had daily phone conversations, Marie and Jonathan hadn't seen each other since her jaunt to Boston two weekends ago. Jonathan was willing to travel to New York, but Marie had nixed that idea in the bud. She was still in the process of swapping rings and ending her fling with Richard, her obnoxious Wall Street exec. And, in her spare time since she'd discovered the Woodwards possessed both Singing Bird Pistols, she was masterminding the scheme in Connecticut against Patrick Woodward. As much as she would have welcomed his company, she simply couldn't cram a visit with Jonathan into her already jam-packed schedule.

The co-pilot approached Marie with her suitcase in tow. "It's been a pleasure having you as a passenger, Ms. Lacroix."

Anticipating he was about to take advantage of the few moments they'd have alone while the pilot was stuck inside the cockpit finalizing the flight details, Marie couldn't stop herself from flirting just a little to give him a smidgeon of hope. "Thank you for an enjoyable trip. I've never flown in a plane this small, and I'll admit I was afraid at first, but listening to your adventurous stories helped to calm my nerves." *Such a big, fat lie! I'm surprised my nose isn't growing.*

"It's all part of our service," he replied, his voice full of bravado. "I was hoping we could meet for dinner when you return to New York. I promise not to spend the entire evening talking about my flying experiences."

Once again, Marie's feminine wiles did not

disappoint. However, she was too busy to waste her time on a man who could provide her with nothing more than stimulating dinner conversation. "Thank you for the invitation," she said as the pilot emerged from the cabin door, "but I'm afraid I'm not available."

"Marie, you've finally arrived," Jonathan called out. "My God, it's good to see you." He drew Marie into his arms and, despite the presence of the two gawking pilots, welcomed her with a passionate kiss.

Marie had convinced herself her sole purpose for accepting Jonathan's invitation to join him for a long weekend at his Nantucket home was to pursue her agenda. However, being with him again sparked a desire that was no longer a contrived part of the role she was playing. The mere touch of Jonathan's hand on her bare arm made every nerve in her body tingle. When their kiss ended, she told him sincerely, "I could hardly wait to get here."

Jonathan took a moment to shake hands with the two pilots. "Thank you, gentlemen. I hope you have a safe return flight." Smiling at Marie, he said, "Shall we go?"

"Yes," she replied. "I'm ready."

Jonathan rolled Marie's suitcase along while they strolled to his car, their arms wrapped around each other's backs. Marie waved and shouted a final thank you to the pilots. Their woeful expressions did not slip past Jonathan's notice.

"What's that sound?" He tilted his head as if straining to hone in on a faint noise. "Ah, just as I suspected. It's the resonating crack of the two pilots' hearts breaking." His grin revealed he was only joking.

"Oh, Jonathan, that was cruel." Marie poked him in the ribs, pretending to be shocked by his statement.

"Perhaps." He opened the trunk and placed Marie's suitcase inside. "But I'd venture to guess you have that effect on most men."

"You don't honestly believe that, do you?" *Well, fiddle-dee-dee!* Marie was well aware of the hearts she'd been breaking since she was a teenager, and of the ways she had used her beauty and guile to her own advantage. However, she wanted to correct Jonathan. She hadn't broken the two pilots' hearts as much as she'd spoiled their dreams of engaging her in a bit of hanky-panky. That sentiment summed up the degree of interest most men had ever shown in her. Then again, she hadn't spent quality time with any man who wasn't the subject of one of her cons in over ten years.

"Oh, I'm certain you've broken many hearts." Closing the trunk lid, he stepped to the side of the car and opened the passenger door.

Marie removed her sunglasses. She faced Jonathan before taking her seat. "I hope you don't think I was flirting with those two pilots," she replied with mock innocence.

"I'm not accusing you of anything." Jonathan's intense gaze conveyed his seriousness. "I'm merely stating a fact. You capture every man's heart, just as you've captured mine." Placing his arm around her waist, he held her close and kissed her again.

Marie's heart raced as she grappled with the myriad of conflicting emotions Jonathan ignited inside her. She didn't want to be attracted to him but, at the same time, treating him with indifference had turned into a nearly impossible task. Although Marie was reluctant to admit it, Jonathan Woodward was proving to be the man of her dreams. When their kiss ended, she avoided his gaze and slid into her seat. For the first time in her life, a witty response eluded her.

If Jonathan noticed her uneasiness, he didn't mention it. As he got in on the driver's side and started the engine, he ran down the evening's agenda. "We have a dinner reservation for seven o'clock. That gives you plenty of time to unpack and freshen up before we go into town."

"Sounds great." She'd managed to calm herself and placed her sights back on the target. "Can we sit outside during dinner and watch the sunset?"

"That's the plan." He stopped the car before driving out onto the road. Manually shifting the car into first gear, he stole a moment to gaze adoringly into Marie's eyes. "Since we've watched the sun rise together, we need to enjoy a sunset as well."

During their journey to the Cliff neighborhood where Jonathan's home was located, he provided an entertaining narrative to embellish the scenic drive. Marie enjoyed his accounts of his childhood vacations on the island. She could almost visualize him with his brother and cousins playing tag football in the fields and riding bikes along the then deserted country lanes. She also cursed him. Just as she was managing to squelch her fondness for him, Jonathan had won her over again with his heartwarming stories.

Jonathan circled off the main road and steered the car toward a decorative iron gate mounted between two large stone pillars. When the security device detected the car, the gates swung open long enough to allow Jonathan to drive through. The property was at a slight elevation, and Marie was treated to a stunning view of Nantucket Sound and the main harbor. As the drive curved, the view of the water was blocked by the homes that composed the Woodward compound.

"Here we are," Jonathan announced. While he lifted Marie's suitcase from the trunk, she stepped out of the car and took in the scenery.

"Jonathan, is this all your property?"

"Every square foot of it. What do you think?"

Jonathan's homes, three in all, sat on four acres of prime Nantucket real estate. On the left side of the property sat the largest of the three structures, a two-story home styled in the traditional Nantucket gray clapboard with white doors and window shutters. The center portion of the home ran parallel with the shoreline below, while the sections at either end of the house angled inward toward the water. The front entrance was protected by a covered porch large enough to accommodate a hanging swing and four high-backed rocking chairs, all painted white to match the trim on the house.

To the right side of the property were two identical three-story cottages. Both matched the design and color of the main home. The cottages were angled toward each other so that, combined with the garage wing of the main house, the three formed a protective alcove for the swimming pool area. A black wrought iron fence ran along the property line and tall hedges provided privacy from the neighboring homes.

Marie was no stranger to beachside estates. Many of her former marks had taken her to their vacation homes on Long Island or along the Jersey Shore to dazzle her with their nouveau riche lifestyle. She found all of them to be, like their owners, pretentious. Jonathan's property, however, was not designed to impress his visitors. There were no pillared façades, no towering rooflines, no marble foyers. Like his home in Burgess, this property spoke of an owner who enjoyed providing a comfortable haven for family and friends. Marie, the born and bred big city girl, would leave Manhattan in a heartbeat in exchange for the peacefulness afforded on either of Jonathan's properties.

"The views are breathtaking." Marie paused to appreciate the entire landscape. "Is this where your family vacationed when you were growing up?"

"Well, yes and no," Jonathan told her. "My father bought the property in the 1940s when few people considered it fashionable to live on Nantucket. He built one large home and our entire family—grandparents, aunts, uncles, cousins—spent a good portion of our summers here. My brother and his wife prefer the Cape, so, after our parents passed, I bought Burt out of his share of the inheritance. For many years, I was too busy to come here as often as I should have and the house started to need a lot of TLC. Then, almost overnight, the island became popular. Compared to the new homes in the neighborhood, my house was an outdated eyesore. Rather than remodel, I tore down the old place and designed something more conducive to my family's needs. Veronica, Patrick, and I had the idea of building a main house plus two guest cottages. That was about six years ago. Now, I come here a lot more often. Veronica and Patrick sometimes join me; occasionally, they come here on their own."

"Have you ever considered living here year-round?" Marie asked as she retrieved her bag from the car and closed the passenger door.

"Sometimes I stay longer than just the weekend,"

Jonathan explained as they approached the front entrance of the main house, "and I'll invite friends to join me. But being here is too far removed from Boston and everything that's most important to me."

The inside of the home was brightened by a wall of windows and sliding glass doors that overlooked the cliffs and the beach in the distance. The floors were light hardwood, and the furniture was upholstered in tans and corals with splashes of turquoise that reflected the colors of the seascape. The only dark piece in the room was a black baby grand piano which sat in the far corner by the windows.

"Oh, Jonathan, this is stunning," she remarked.

"Thank you." His bright smile was evidence of his pride in the home. "I have my daughter, Veronica, who inherited her mother's creative genes, to thank for the décor. Veronica worked with a local decorator to furnish all three houses." Jonathan led Marie into the great room. "Let me give you a quick tour so you'll know your way around. This, of course, is the main living area. I asked the architect to design the ceiling in this room to be open to the second story to give the illusion of being outdoors. The spiral staircase leads to the loft which is pretty much a game room for the kids. We furnished it with a billiard table, a home theater system, and video games. I also insisted the children have a library, so there are bookcases and a reading nook as well."

"Are you sure the area is just for your grandchildren?" Marie teased.

"Okay, I'll admit to spending a lot of time up there with them. It's true what they say, there's a bit of kid in all of us."

"Did Veronica paint this picture?" Marie inquired

about the landscape hanging above the stone fireplace.

"No. Veronica may be creative, but she's not artistic." Jonathan gazed reminiscently at the painting as he continued. "Patricia painted this picture. She loved to wander around the island and capture her favorite scenes on canvas. You'll see a few of her smaller pieces throughout all three houses." Jonathan's attention lingered on the painting for a few moments before he resumed the tour. "So, the kitchen is this way."

Marie followed Jonathan through the dining room and into the kitchen where a staircase led to three mini-suites on the second floor. At the far end of the kitchen, French doors opened onto the patio and the pool area. Returning to the great room, Jonathan grabbed Marie's suitcase and wheeled it down a hallway to the opposite side of the house.

"And your tour ends," he announced as they stepped through a set of double doors, "in my suite."

Marie gave her approval as she circled around and took in the details. "I like the strong, masculine touch. Your daughter, I assume, had nothing to do with decorating this room."

"You're right," Jonathan confessed. "I insisted on choosing the furnishings for my own personal space. Although this room is designed to my tastes, I think you'll find it comfortable."

As they gazed into each other's eyes, a message of mutual desire passed between them.

"Jonathan," Marie said seductively, "I've missed you these past two weeks." She placed her hands on his shoulders. "Have you missed me?"

"You know I have." He folded his arms around her and enveloped her in his embrace.

"Then we need to make up for lost time."

****

At twenty minutes past seven, the restaurant declared the Woodward party of two a no show. Their table reservation was given to the next couple on the waiting list.

Chapter 17

Marie

Marie awoke with a jolt, startled out of a dream that was with her for a second, then vaporized into oblivion. Still foggy, her eyes darted around, confused by the unfamiliar surroundings. *Where the hell am I?...Jonathan...Nantucket...Mm, Jonathan.* She rolled over to wrap her arm around Jonathan, but caressed only the cold, vacant sheet. *Piano music?* Leaving the bed, she grabbed a robe from her suitcase and fastened it around her while she strolled toward the great room.

Jonathan was seated at the piano, deep in concentration as he played a classical piece from memory. Not wanting to disrupt him, Marie tiptoed across the room and stood to his side behind the piano bench. After a few moments, Jonathan became aware of her presence. He grabbed her hand and drew her onto the bench to sit beside him.

"Good morning, sleepyhead." He greeted her with a kiss.

"Good morning. I didn't know you play. Debussy?"

"Yes," he answered, sounding both surprised and pleased she'd recognized the piece. "Do you like classical music?"

"Mais oui," she replied in French. "I attend live performances as often as I can."

"Well, we've just found another common interest. Perhaps I'll make it into the city and accompany you to the symphony."

"I'd enjoy that," Marie said, her smile sincere. "Please, continue."

As Jonathan's fingers caressed the piano keys, Marie closed her eyes and soaked in every nuance of his performance. At the end of the piece, she commended his talent. "Jonathan, that was beautiful. You must have started taking lessons at an early age."

"I did. My mother was a devoted supporter of the arts and insisted my brother and I learn to play at least one instrument. Burt chose the violin, which he gave up the second he was no longer under our parents' rule. He was never musically inclined, so being forced to take lessons was pure torture for him."

"Oh, *pauvre petit*," Marie responded, using one of her favorite French sayings.

"That would have been a perfect description for Burt at his recitals, as well as for those of us who were obligated to endure his scratchy performances. I, on the other hand, chose the piano and demonstrated a proficiency for music. I still set aside one hour every day. It's relaxing and, dare I say, therapeutic. Plus, I genuinely enjoy playing."

"You're lucky to have such a natural talent."

"Well, a little talent plus a *lot* of practice," Jonathan said with humility. "So, since we missed dinner last night, I woke up with a huge appetite. Let's go into town and grab some breakfast. Then we can take the bikes out on the trails, and I'll give you a tour of the island."

"That sounds like fun, but I'm afraid I didn't pack my athletic shoes."

"Not a problem. We'll visit one of the shops in town and buy you a pair. Now, quick, go get dressed. My stomach's growling."

****

By noon, Jonathan and Marie were back at the house to enjoy a light lunch, a relaxing swim, and an afternoon of lounging on the cushioned poolside chairs. Jonathan's playful spirit and boundless energy resolved a question that had often perplexed Marie—how a younger woman like herself could be attracted to a much older man. Age, she now understood, really is just a number. What truly mattered were Jonathan's tender affections, his desire to please her, and their honest enjoyment of each other's company.

Marie adjusted the back of her chair to a comfortable position for sunbathing. While Jonathan patted his skin dry with a beach towel, she ogled his buff physique from the shade of her sunhat and imagined them as a normal couple enjoying a weekend getaway at their cozy Nantucket retreat. Their backstory went something like this: She'd mustered all her courage and come clean with Jonathan about her identity and her past. He'd been horrified to learn of the deplorable deeds she'd committed during her career as a thief, but he'd gotten over the initial shock and was willing to forgive and forget. They would live happily ever after—

Stop it! her conscience screamed. *Stop courting the notion that this make-believe world you like to lose yourself in is magically going to become real. Just erase those absurd ideas from your mind right now and be content to enjoy your time with Jonathan while it lasts.* She blinked away the fantasy and lowered her gaze.

"Are you all right?" Jonathan asked, his brow

furrowed with concern.

Marie slapped on the smile of a person who didn't have a care in the world. "I'm fine. Why?"

He shrugged his shoulders. "You looked a little forlorn for a moment."

"I'm just exhausted. You're wearing me out today."

Jonathan stepped between their chairs, leaned down, and kissed her. "How about I go into the kitchen and make us a pitcher of margaritas?"

"Mm…frozen margaritas?"

"If that's what you want." He pecked another kiss on her lips. "I'll be back in a jif."

Marie ogled Jonathan once more, his broad shoulders and muscular legs this time, as he sauntered away and entered the house. Tilting her wide-brimmed hat forward to shade her face, she slipped in her earbuds and was lightly dozing off when she became aware of an overshadowing presence. Lifting the brim of her hat, she was startled to find a woman standing at the foot of the lounge chair with her fists placed warningly on her hips. Two teen-aged girls stood at the woman's side.

"Excuse me," the woman barked, "but who exactly are you?"

Removing her earbuds, Marie was about to ask the woman the same question when Jonathan rushed from the house.

"Veronica? What are you doing here?"

"Granddad!" the teenagers shouted as they ran to Jonathan.

"Hello, my sweets." Jonathan wrapped his arms around the girls and kissed the tops of their heads. "I'm surprise to see you."

"I might ask you the same," Veronica said,

answering her father's question. "Didn't you say you had a board thing, or an event at the club, or *something* you had to take care of this weekend that required you to stay in town?"

"I did, but the meeting was rescheduled," he explained. "I told you I was spending the weekend on Nantucket."

"You most certainly did not," Veronica corrected her father. She folded her arms as if daring him to defy her.

Jonathan apologized but held his ground. "I'm sorry. I could have sworn I informed you of my change in plans."

"Well, I guess you had your mind on other things," Veronica scoffed as she stared down her nose at Marie. "Thank God you are here. I was worried we'd found a squatter on the property and was about to call the police."

Jonathan reprimanded his daughter as he stepped closer to Marie's lounge chair. "Veronica, you're being rude. Marie is my guest."

"Oh, so the tart does have a name," Veronica snapped in response.

Marie was amused by the terse interaction between Jonathan and his daughter. At the same time, she couldn't ignore her inner alarm. Conning Jonathan was one thing; fooling his children was another. So much for her plan to spend a relaxing weekend gaining Jonathan's trust as well as information about the Somerset Necklace.

"Veronica, that's enough!" Jonathan reprimanded his daughter. "Marie, please forgive my poor manners and my daughter's rudeness. This is not the way I intended to introduce you to my family. As you've gathered by now, this is my daughter, Veronica, and these two young ladies are my granddaughters, Gwen and Phoebe. Girls, this is my friend, Marie Lacroix."

Gwen and Phoebe politely greeted Marie. Veronica, on the other hand, stood with her arms folded defensively as she glared at her father's guest. To even out the playing field, Marie rose from her chair to be at eye level with the others and to flaunt her well-toned, bikini-clad body in front of Veronica's flat chest and wide hips. Marie normally got along with everyone, but Veronica's viciousness unleashed her vengeful streak.

"Hello," Marie said with her most pleasant smile. "I'm delighted to meet you."

"Really?" Veronica sneered with contempt. She grabbed Marie's cover-up from the foot of the lounge chair and threw it at her. "You might want to put this on before I *do* call the police and have you arrested for indecent exposure." She then snapped an order at her daughters. "Girls, carry your bags into the waterfront cottage. I think it's best we leave the main house to Granddad and *Marie*." Veronica's voice dripped with disdain when she spoke Marie's name.

When Jonathan said nothing, merely sighed and shook his head, Marie surmised Veronica had a history of temperamental behavior, and they'd played out similar scenes many times before. Marie stood quietly by his side as Veronica stomped away like a spoiled child and disappeared inside the cottage situated nearest the harbor with her obedient daughters close behind.

Marie, acting like an innocent victim, placed her hand on Jonathan's chest. "Jonathan, I'm afraid I've created an uncomfortable situation. Perhaps I should leave."

"You're not going anywhere," Jonathan insisted, raising her palm to his lips for a kiss. "Veronica is a control freak. She didn't like the fact she wasn't told in advance you were going to be here. Her dour mood will blow over soon enough."

"And your granddaughters? Aren't they a little young to see us together like this?"

Jonathan lowered his head as if ashamed he hadn't considered how the young girls might view the affair their grandfather was having with a woman who was closer to their age than she was to his own. "I'll speak with them." Gazing into her eyes, he confirmed the place Marie held in both his heart and his life. "But what's happened is no reason for you to leave. I want to be with you, and my children will just have to accept that."

Congratulations! You've ingrained yourself in Jonathan's life in record-breaking time. Marie put her arms around Jonathan's waist. "All right, *mon cher*," she said submissively. "I'll stay if it pleases you. And I'll make every effort to win Veronica's approval this weekend."

"I'm sure she'll find you as charming as I do before long," Jonathan replied, giving Marie a light kiss. "Come inside and help me finish making those margaritas."

They ambled toward the house, their arms around each other's backs. Feeling Veronica's eyes boring a hole in her, Marie took cruel pleasure in stoking the fire. She blatantly slid her hand down Jonathan's back, slipped it under the waistband of his swim trunks, and gave his derriere a squeeze. Marie could almost hear Veronica's head explode inside the cottage when Jonathan let out a yelp, then took Marie into his arms. He kissed her at length before drawing her into the house.

****

Veronica may have been difficult to warm up to, but her daughters were a different story. Gwen and Phoebe continuously vied for Marie's attention, seeking her advice on everything from clothing and hair styles to career choices and dating. Marie devised a strategy: she'd use her rapport with Gwen and Phoebe to break the ice with Veronica. However, regardless of Marie's numerous attempts to befriend her, Veronica remained aloof.

On Saturday afternoon, Gwen and Phoebe were anxious to take Marie shopping in town. Happy to oblige them, Marie dashed into the bedroom to change her clothes and grab her purse. On her way back through the house, she overheard Jonathan and Veronica talking in the kitchen. Suspecting their conversation was about her, Marie hid by the dining room doorway and eavesdropped.

"Yes, I care what you think," Jonathan said, "but why can't you understand how I feel? Marie makes me happier than I've been in a long time."

"Oh, I'm sure she does. Such as when she slipped her hand inside the back of your swim trunks yesterday afternoon? I don't even want to imagine the kind of happiness she's giving you."

Jonathan's response was stern. "Veronica, don't be crude. I'm not referring to our intimacy—"

"Please, don't go any further!" Veronica cautioned.

"I'm talking about how comfortable we are with each other. She's the kindred spirit I've been searching for since we lost your mother."

Veronica sounded exhausted with the subject. "Daddy, she's younger than me, for God's sake. Have you bothered to question why she's become so chummy with you? Don't you think, just maybe, she's using you as her sugar daddy?"

"Of course, that possibility has crossed my mind. I'm not a fool! But, despite the difference in our ages, have you considered that it's equally as possible Marie's interested in me for who I am, not because of my wealth?" A long pause followed, during which Veronica did not respond. "I care for Marie more than you can imagine," Jonathan admitted. He spoke so softly, Marie strained to understand him. "I'm not sure what the future holds, but I want to at least give us a try. So, can you please take pleasure in my happiness instead of being intent on destroying it?"

Veronica let out a heavy sigh. "Yes, I suppose I can be more open-minded. I'm sorry, Daddy. You'd never mentioned her to me, and I was unnerved to have her thrown in my face. I guess I'm having a hard time getting over the shock."

Marie detected footsteps, then Veronica's muffled speech. She assumed Veronica was hugging her father as she said, "Can you forgive my ill-mannered behavior?"

"You know I can," Jonathan replied. "And I'm sorry for keeping my relationship with Marie a secret. I wanted to be sure of my feelings first. I'll fill Patrick in when I visit him and Oliver next week."

Marie had listened long enough to gather the information she needed. Jonathan had pacified Veronica, at least long enough for Marie to proceed with her con. She burst into the kitchen and pretended to be surprised by their presence.

"Oh, I'm sorry," Marie said, acting embarrassed to have interrupted them. "I didn't realize anyone else was in the house. But I'm glad you're both here. I'm going shopping in town with Gwen and Phoebe. We'll be back in plenty of time for dinner." She gave Jonathan a light good-bye kiss.

"Have fun," Jonathan told her.

"Thanks for taking the girls off my hands for a few hours," Veronica said, her attitude much friendlier now. "Make sure they have their bank cards with them. And please don't allow them to buy anything ridiculous. They like to test their boundaries."

"I'll try my best," Marie promised. "See you later!"

****

Veronica

Alone inside the carriage house, Veronica placed a call to her husband.

"How's it going?" Brian asked. Veronica had spoken to him at length the previous evening and made him aware of the situation into which she and their girls had inadvertently stumbled.

"Well, our daughters are enthralled with the little tramp," Veronica told him. "They're shopping with her in town as we speak. I promised Daddy I'd give her a chance, but that was only to pacify him. You know, all these years, I've accused Patrick of being gullible. Now I can see he inherited that trait from my father. Brian, I wish you could hear the way Daddy speaks about this woman. I'm afraid he's fallen head over heels in love with her!"

"Is she really that hot?"

"Hot? I'm surprised she didn't start a fire yesterday with that itsy-bitsy bikini she was wearing."

"Damn!" Brian teased. "Of all the weekends I couldn't get away. Can you at least take a picture of her and send it to me?"

"Aren't you just so funny?" Veronica replied sarcastically. She was not in the mood to banter with her husband. "Do me a favor. Find the business card we have in the office for Lou Biondi and text me his phone number."

Brian questioned the benefits of contacting Lou, a frequent customer at their Boston restaurant, but he was wasting his breath. Once Veronica was dead set on completing a mission, her family understood they'd best stay out of her way.

"Fine. I'll be home in a little while. I'll look for his card when I get there."

Thirty minutes later, Veronica was reading by the pool when her phone chimed to announce a text from Brian. Marie and the girls were still in town, and Daddy was on a bike ride. As no one was within earshot, Veronica placed the call to Lou Biondi from where she sat.

"Lou, it's Veronica Lambert...I'm well. How are you?...Good. How's Becky?...Oh, I'm sorry you're not seeing her any longer...No, she didn't!...And she appeared to be such a nice person...Well, then, you had no choice but to end things with her...I absolutely agree... So, Lou, I'd like to hire you to do a background investigation on a woman who's trying to weasel her way into my family...Well, I know little about her, but I'll tell you as much as I can...Yes. Do you have a pen?...For starters, her name is Marie Lacroix, and she works for Willow's Auction House in Manhattan."

Chapter 18

Marie

While Veronica was conspiring to prove her father's newfound love was a charlatan, Marie was in town winning over the hearts of Veronica's daughters. Gwen and Phoebe were at an impressionable age and, to advance her own agenda, Marie took advantage of the girls' naiveté. So far, she'd been unsuccessful in learning the whereabouts of the Somerset Necklace from Jonathan. With a little coercion, his granddaughters might be more forthcoming.

Marie had forgotten the frenzy with which teenaged girls could attack a clothing store. Seemingly in competition to outdo each other, Gwen and Phoebe plucked garments off the racks at record-breaking speed. They then rushed off to the fitting rooms where they modeled their selections and asked Marie for her expert advice. *Is this skirt too long? Tuck the shirt in or leave it out? Are hats still a thing?*

While dishing out compliments and suggestions, Marie was entertained by the girls' liveliness. Gwen and Phoebe were the personification of Marie and her sister, Jacqueline, at that age, so lighthearted and carefree. What she wouldn't give to be an adolescent again, to discover the woman she might have become had she made different choices. But would she be content as a suburban housewife and mother? Or was it in her DNA to crave danger? Perhaps becoming a con artist had been her fate from birth.

Marie couldn't deny that, as soon as she was old enough to notice the stir she caused just by entering a room, she'd used her physical appearance to her advantage. At sixteen, drawing attention to herself was a novelty. As she matured, she learned to misuse her beauty as a weapon. She'd needed quick access to a large sum of money to support her family following her father's shooting, and wealthy men could so readily be swayed by a gorgeous, seductive woman.

Her first few jobs were carried out with trepidation. She was, after all, committing a crime. But the risks were thrilling, and the successes were hers for the taking. Without even noticing the transformation, she'd become a habitual thief who had convinced herself the end justified the means.

Recently, however, her conscience had been nudging her with an increasing urgency to readjust her moral compass. She'd come full circle, and the reality of her unscrupulous behavior had smacked her in the face. Although she and Gus had a brief discussion about retiring from the business, they hadn't yet made a final commitment. Marie, however, was getting ever so close to making that decision. Out of respect for Gus, she'd finish the jobs they had in progress. Then, she'd let him know that, perhaps, the time had come to call it quits.

Gwen and Phoebe approached the check-out counter with more clothing than they could possibly ever get around to wearing. Despite her promise to Veronica, Marie took cruel pleasure in talking the girls into a few additional accessories. If Veronica and her husband didn't approve of their daughters spoiling themselves, Marie reasoned, they shouldn't give the girls access to bank cards with unlimited buying power.

While the store clerk scanned the electronic reader over price tag after price tag, Phoebe asked, "Marie, aren't you buying anything for yourself?"

"No, I'll pass. My suitcase is already too full."

"Then don't pack so much the next time you come to Nantucket with us," Gwen, the older of the two sisters, told Marie with an air of superiority, as though she couldn't believe Marie wouldn't have grasped this concept on her own.

"That's good advice, Gwen. Thank you." Marie glanced away, annoyed with herself for leading Gwen along. But what choice did she have? Tell Gwen and Phoebe this was the one and only time they'd ever be on Nantucket together? Reveal her true reason for being with their beloved grandfather? She hated the necessity of entangling these innocent girls into her lie.

As they left the clothing store, Marie noticed a jeweler two doors down. Imaging she could strike up a conversation about family heirloom jewelry while they perused the counters, she asked, "Girls, do you mind if we pop into the jewelry store?"

"Sure, if you want," Gwen replied, although she appeared bored by the idea.

"Gwen, let's pick out a ring for Granddad to give Marie," Phoebe suggested, her expressive face lit up with excitement.

Confused, but also amused, Marie frowned and smiled at the same. "Phoebe, why would your grandfather buy me a ring?"

"He's going to marry you, isn't he?" Phoebe

sounded as though an impending marriage between Marie and Jonathan was common knowledge.

"Phoebe, don't be such a dolt," Gwen said with a loud tsk. "Why would they get married already when they just started dating?"

Phoebe's eyes were wide with innocence. "But, when Granddad spoke to us last night, he told us he loves Marie. I'll bet he's going to ask her to marry him soon."

"God, Phoebe," Gwen said, rolling her eyes, "you do realize Marie's right next to you and can hear everything you're saying."

Marie took a moment to absorb Phoebe's statement: *Granddad told us he loves Marie.* Although Jonathan had not yet spoken those words to her, his affection was conveyed through his endearments and lingering gazes. Marie was pleased to have her suspicion confirmed but saddened by the reality that soon she would unintentionally break Jonathan's heart. Phoebe's comment, however, gave Marie butterflies in her stomach. Was it possible she cared for Jonathan just as deeply as he cared for her?

When they entered the jewelry store, an eager salesman whose name tag identified him as *Roy S.* greeted them. Marie asked Roy to direct her to the store's display of necklaces. Rather than follow her, Gwen and Phoebe instead wandered over to the case containing the diamond rings. Marie chatted up Roy for a while, hoping the girls would lose interest in the rings and wander her way. After a few minutes, she determined she needed to coax them into action.

"Excuse me, but I'd better see what my young friends are up to," she told Roy. While crossing the store, Marie glanced into another display case and spotted a beautiful pair of sapphire and diamond earrings. "Roy, it looks like I will need your assistance after all."

Marie speculated the earrings might assist her in gaining access to the Somerset Necklace and made an impulsive decision to purchase them. As she was finalizing the sale, Gwen and Phoebe called for her to join them at the ring counter.

"Marie, come and see the rings we picked out," Phoebe demanded.

"What are you girls up to?" Marie asked as she approached them.

"We did Granddad the favor of picking out some engagement rings," Phoebe explained. "What do you think about this one…" she asked as she pointed to one of the rings in the case, "…and this one…and those two on the left side in the bottom row?"

Marie admitted the rings were indeed to her liking. Phoebe insisted she try on their choices and called Roy over to retrieve them from the case. Although she cringed on the inside, Marie played along and humored Phoebe's enthusiasm. She'd been the recipient of several rings in the past, rings she'd conned her victims into purchasing and then stole from them. However, when Roy removed her favorite of the lot from the display case and she slipped the ring onto her finger, her breath caught. This cluster of diamonds held a much different connotation than the others which had previously adorned her finger. This ring could represent Jonathan's promise to her of his endless love and devotion.

Suddenly, Marie admitted to herself that, while tricking Jonathan into falling in love with her, she'd broken her cardinal rule and had recklessly fallen in love with him. As she envisioned Jonathan presenting her with this ring and asking for her hand in marriage, she was unexpectedly overwhelmed with sadness. She could carry on this illusion of being the dream woman Jonathan had spent years searching for until she was blue in the face, but in truth she was nothing but a lying thief running an insidious charade against a kind, loving man and his innocent family. So, no, a blissful future with Jonathan was not in her cards, no matter how much she wanted to pretend otherwise. Tears spilled from her eyes and careened down her cheeks.

"Marie, are you all right?" Gwen asked, the disdain in her voice and her scornful face expressing how appalled she was by Marie's behavior.

Attentive to his customer's every need, Roy slid a box of tissues toward Marie. Marie sniffled and mumbled an embarrassed thank you. She dabbed her eyes and glanced over at the girls. At least Phoebe appeared to be concerned.

"Sorry," she said. "I didn't expect to become so emotional. I guess we found ourselves a winner." She handed the ring to Roy. "Thank you, but I don't think I'm in the mood to try on any of the others." As Roy replaced the ring and locked the display case, Marie did a 180 and pretended that awkward moment had not just happened. She removed the earrings she'd purchased from her shopping bag, and said, "Well, girls, I treated myself after all. Do you like the earrings I bought?"

"Oh, they're so pretty!" Phoebe exclaimed.

"They are awfully nice," Gwen agreed. She took them from Marie and, swiveling the mirror on the countertop in her direction, held them up to her ears. "Is your birthday in September?"

"No. Why?"

"Sapphire is the September birthstone," Gwen told her as she handed the earrings back to Marie. "My birthday is in September. One day, when we were at Granddad's, he showed me this old necklace that's made of sapphires and diamonds. He said he plans to give it to me when I get married."

Marie's lips curled with gratification. Her ploy had worked. Unless Jonathan owned multiple old sapphire and diamond necklaces, Gwen must have been referring to the Somerset Necklace. A little more digging may unearth the information she needed. She placed the earrings back into the shopping bag and, following the girls, exited the store.

"How sentimental of your grandfather to want to give you such a cherished gift on your wedding day," Marie told Gwen with the hope of weaseling more information out of her. "A vintage necklace can be valuable, especially if it has a history attached to it."

"What kind of history?" Phoebe asked, appearing to be more interested in the subject than her older sister.

"For example, a famous former owner can increase the value of the jewelry. I've seen that happen several times at the auction house where I work."

"Cool," Phoebe commented. "Marie, how can we find out if Grandad's necklace used to belong to a famous person?"

"Oh, I imagine your grandfather is already aware of who the previous owner was. But, if not, that's when you hire a person like me who deals in antiques to do the research for you."

"Well, famous former owner or not," Gwen announced, "I don't want the necklace. It's old fashioned and ugly. I'd never wear it."

"Tell Granddad to give it to me, then," Phoebe told her sister. "I think it's awesome to own something with a famous history."

"No way." Gwen's aloof response demonstrated how closely her personality resembled her mother's. "I plan to sell it as soon as Granddad dies."

Marie lowered her head to hide her disgust. Now, foreseeing the fate of the Somerset Necklace, she didn't feel the slightest bit of remorse over the knowledge that at the time Gwen would attempt to sell her grandfather's heirloom wedding gift, she'd be shocked to learn the piece was worthless. By then, Gwen most likely wouldn't remember the woman her grandfather once had a fleeting affair with, nor would she put two and two together and realize her grandfather's much younger mistress had stolen the necklace years earlier and left a cheap replica in its place.

Phoebe was more like Jonathan, concerned for others and interested in holding onto items for their sentimental rather than their monetary value. Again comparing Gwen and Phoebe to her own family, she recalled how she and Jacqueline were also as different as night and day. Jacqueline's personality was much like Phoebe's. She had always been sensitive and caring, concerned for people's wellbeing and unable to make those tough decisions. Marie was the more pragmatic sister who could handle saying no when necessary and be willing to deal with the consequences. Hence, Marie had stayed in New York and committed herself to doing whatever was required to support Jacqueline when she relocated with the rest of the family to their Caribbean hideaway.

All at once, Marie was overcome with a deep

longing to be with her sister. With the objective of moving to the Caribbean before her fortieth birthday, she remained focused on her goal of sufficiently funding her bank accounts to make her dream possible. She reminded herself that, thanks to Jacqueline stepping in to help with this job, a reunion with her family would be just around the corner.

****

Jonathan followed Marie into the bedroom when she and the girls returned from their shopping trip. "How did you get along with Gwen and Phoebe?" he asked eagerly.

"We had a wonderful afternoon," Marie told him truthfully. "They're sweet girls. I can understand why you're so proud of them."

"They are good girls," Jonathan replied. He sat on the cushioned window seat as Marie kicked off her sandals and tossed her purse and shopping bag onto the bed. "I'm relieved that you get along well with them."

Marie was amused by his comment. "Why were you so nervous? Have I given you reason to believe I'd eat them alive?"

Jonathan's grin revealed his slight embarrassment. "No, of course not. I knew you'd be wonderful with them. But I was concerned the girls might treat you rudely, considering how their mother has been behaving."

Marie retrieved the case containing her earrings from the shopping bag and sat beside Jonathan. "They were fine. And Veronica will be fine. Stop worrying." She held up the jewelry box and asked, "Would you like to see what I purchased this afternoon?"

"Hmm...looks like you bought yourself something special."

"I did!" Marie replied as she opened the box. "We were browsing, and these earrings caught my eye. Do you like them?"

"I'm not sure," Jonathan teased. "Model them for me."

Marie fastened on the earrings, then hooked her hair behind her ears. "There. How do they look?"

"They're beautiful." He leaned closer and said softly, "You're beautiful," before he kissed her.

Marie's heart fluttered as once again Jonathan mystified her with his power to elicit new and exciting emotions she'd never before experienced. She couldn't face him for fear her eyes would betray her guilty conscience. She lowered her head and replied, "You're too sweet."

"Do you know what I think?"

Marie forced herself to meet his gaze. "No, tell me."

"I think you need to attend a dressy occasion to show off your new earrings."

Marie grinned. Could Jonathan have just provided a reason to bring the Somerset Necklace into the conversation? "What sort of dressy occasion do you have in mind?"

"The summer gala at my club is later this month. Tuxedos and evening gowns are required attire. Will you be my date?" He raised an eyebrow and waited for Marie's response.

Marie smiled with delight. Jonathan had indeed provided her with the ideal excuse to broach the subject of the Somerset Necklace. Her new sapphire earrings would require a necklace to complement them, wouldn't they? And Gwen had given Marie the perfect lead-in.

However, she worried about her availability. The

ring swap she was in the process of completing on Richard, her Wall Street exec, had been put on hold. The overweight Richard, who had abused his health for years, had been rushed to the hospital. Following an emergency procedure to open a blocked artery, he was ordered to remain at home for several days of rest. Based on the calls he'd made during the few private moments his wife granted him, Marie deduced Richard was extremely restless to see her. He was waiting for permission from his wife (apparently, she had him under lock and key) to leave the house on his own in the upcoming week. With his accessibility being so restricted, finalizing the job on Richard took priority over Jonathan's social event.

"Jonathan," Marie said, playfully giggling and shivering her shoulders with excitement, "I feel like you've just invited me to your high school prom!" She stepped over to the bed and removed her cell phone from her purse. "I'd love to attend the gala with you. When is it?"

"It's on July thirtieth, two weeks from tonight," Jonathan informed her.

Certain the con she was pulling on Richard would be finalized by then, Marie opened the calendar feature on her phone and said happily, "What do you know? I just happened to be free that weekend."

"Wonderful!" Jonathan replied. "I can't wait to introduce you to my friends at the club. I've been bragging about you for weeks, and they're all dying to meet you."

"And I can't wait to meet them. As soon as I get back to New York, I'll begin shopping for a dress to match my new earrings." She retook her place next to Jonathan. Sitting close, her thigh pressed against his, she said in a voice shaky with bashfulness, "Jonathan, while we were in the jewelry store this afternoon, Gwen mentioned you own a sapphire and diamond necklace." She paused to wait for his response.

"Giving away our family secrets, is she?" Jonathan frowned. "What about the necklace?"

Jonathan's suddenly serious tone gave Marie the impression she was treading on thin ice. She proceeded with caution. "Gwen said the necklace would be a perfect match to my new earrings, and I don't own any jewelry appropriate for an event as elegant as your club's summer gala. Do you think…I mean, may I…" She purposely stumbled over her words to appear nervous about asking for a favor.

Jonathan finished Marie's question for her. "Do you want to wear the necklace to the gala?"

"If you wouldn't mind." She gazed imploringly into his eyes as she took his hand and entwined her fingers with his.

"Sweetheart, you don't realize how gaudy that necklace is," Jonathan explained. "But if truly want to, you're welcome to borrow it that evening."

Marie's eyes sparkled with delight. Finally, confirmation she'd soon have the Somerset Necklace in her possession. She caressed Jonathan's cheek and told him honestly, "You have no idea how happy you make me."

Chapter 19

Jonathan

"Oliver," Jonathan called out, "come here and let Granddad push you on the swing." Oliver skillfully climbed backwards down the rope ladder on his backyard playset and ran to his grandfather. Jonathan grunted, pretending to have difficulty lifting the boy's thirty-four-pound body onto the seat. "I swear you grow in leaps and bounds between my visits!" When Oliver giggled at his playfulness, Jonathan's grandfatherly love gushed from every pore on his body.

"Careful not to hurt Granddad's back now, Oliver," Patrick joked. "So, Dad, what will you be doing while you're in Alaska?"

"Oh, this vacation will be adventurous," Jonathan replied as he set Oliver's swing in motion. "Burt signed us up for zip lining and salmon fishing. Another day, we'll fly over the wilderness by seaplane, so I expect to come home with some spectacular photos. But the highlight of the trip will be our helicopter ride to a dog sled camp where we'll spend the afternoon mushing over the glacier."

Travel was another of Jonathan's passionate indulgences. His journeys had taken him across Europe and Australia, and to parts of Asia, Africa, South America, and the Middle East. On the heels of his

Nantucket weekend, he was embarking on a cruise to Alaska with Burt and Jane, his brother and sister-in-law. With Brenda, his personal assistant, handling the arrangements, Jonathan had the luxury of visiting Patrick and Oliver prior to departing for the cruise.

"That sounds awesome," Patrick said. "Pretty soon, Oliver will be old enough to go on trips like the ones I used to take with you and Grandad. I can't wait to go hiking with Oliver, as well as teaching him to sail and snorkel and ski. Just so you know, I'm counting on you being right there with us."

Jonathan smiled at his son's selective memory. Since Patrick had never been athletically inclined, what Jonathan remembered of those trips was Patrick's whining when he couldn't keep up with his father and grandfather on the hiking trails. Ski resorts, in Patrick's opinion, were for sipping hot chocolate and reading by the fire, not for traversing the slopes. And, although Patrick was a decent swimmer, he'd never gotten the hang of coordinating his breathing in order to snorkel properly. Sailing was, as far as Jonathan knew, the only sport Patrick ever truly excelled at and enjoyed.

Not that these minivacations had been a total ruin, but Jonathan had tolerated an excessive amount of pouting followed by Patrick begging to go home to his mommy. Although Patricia had been a wonderful mother, Jonathan had often accused her of excessively coddling Patrick. She'd even nursed Patrick well into his toddler years, a practice Jonathan didn't agree with, but he'd known enough to keep his mouth shut. Following her demise, Jonathan made it his mission to toughen up his son, and his efforts had paid off. Today, Patrick was the product of both parenting styles, a nurturing and compassionate man with a strong, resilient character.

However, unless Patrick had turned into a triathlete behind everyone's back, Jonathan would need to step in and rescue poor Oliver from certain disaster. "Don't even think of taking Oliver anywhere without me tagging along," he replied. There. The warning had been issued.

"Getting back to Alaska," Patrick said, "I'm surprised Marie isn't going on the cruise with you. Didn't you want to invite her along?"

Ah, Marie. Jonathan's heart erupted like Mount Vesuvius at the mere mention of her name. "I'd like nothing better than for Marie to join us. I asked her several times, but she said she couldn't get away from work on such short notice. And maybe it's for the better. I don't know if Veronica could handle Marie going on vacation with me quite yet. Over the weekend, we had a few heated discussions about my current lifestyle."

"I know all about it," Patrick informed his father. "Veronica already called and chewed my ear off. Don't worry. She'll be fine once she gets used to sharing your attention."

"I hope you're right," Jonathan said.

"When will I have the opportunity to meet Marie?" Patrick asked.

"If it's all right with you, I'd like to invite her to join us in a few weeks when we're all here to celebrate Oliver's birthday."

"That's a great idea," Patrick replied. "But, what about Veronica? Do you foresee a problem with her and Marie being under the same roof for a few days?"

"No, I'm sure Veronica will soon put this past weekend behind her," Jonathan responded confidently. "She and I are having dinner before I leave for the cruise.

I plan to smooth things over with her then."

"Good luck."

"Granddad, stop swinging," Oliver commanded. As soon the swing was stilled, he hopped off the seat and ran to the sliding tube.

"You know, Dad," Patrick said, "I don't mean to sound judgmental—I know you've dated women much younger than yourself in the past—but was Veronica exaggerating when she told me just how young Marie is?"

Jonathan grinned, amused that his love life had caused so much family controversy. "Patrick, I'll be honest. Yes, Marie is thirty years younger than me, but the difference in our ages is not an issue for either of us, and I frankly don't care what anyone else thinks about it. When you finally meet that one person who's your perfect match, nothing else matters. I love everything about Marie. She's intelligent, cultured, funny, athletic— the list is lengthy, so I won't go on. Plus, she's ravishingly beautiful, but that's simply icing on the cake."

"She sounds wonderful, Dad." Patrick paused, then continued hesitantly. "There's, uh, there's something I've been meaning to tell you. I've also been seeing someone."

"You have? Patrick, that's fantastic news! I know you're still devastated by Catherine's loss, but you deserve to find companionship again."

"Well, don't put the cart before the horse," Patrick replied, his cheeks turning a pale crimson. "I'm still not ready to rush into anything. Kelsey and I are simply friends right now, although that could change down the road. But do you know what's odd? From what Phoebe told me of Marie," he chuckled, "—you know how Phoebe can go into great detail about a person's appearance—I could have sworn she was describing my friend, Kelsey. I'm curious to see if Kelsey and Marie really do look that similar when we see them together."

While the men were comparing notes on the new women in their lives, Oliver was just a few feet away taking mischievous advantage of their inattentiveness. Patrick glanced over at the playset and discovered his son in a precarious position on top of the sliding tube.

"Oliver, come down from there before you fall!" Patrick shouted with alarm.

As he rushed to Oliver's rescue, Patrick's foot slipped on a muddy spot in the grass. In an instant, his feet were in the air, and he landed flat on his back.

"Patrick, are you hurt?" Jonathan asked while lifting Oliver down from the playset.

Patrick winced as he eased into a sitting position. "No, I don't think so."

Oliver ran to his father. "Daddy, did you get a boo-boo?"

"I'm okay, Oliver," Patrick assured his son. With Jonathan kneeling by his side, he said, "Although my ankle is a little sore. I may have twisted it."

While Jonathan helped Patrick examine his ankle for injuries, Oliver threw his arms around Patrick's neck and said with great sympathy, "*Pauvre petit!*"

The medical jargon spewing from Patrick's mouth became a buzz in Jonathan's ears. Certainly, he'd misunderstood his grandson. After all, Oliver's face *was* buried in Patrick's neck, and his words *had* been muffled. However, as much as Jonathan wanted to believe otherwise, the phrase was too uncommon to sound like any other.

His heart filled with dread, Jonathan raised his head in slow motion and stared with bewildered eyes at his grandson. "Oliver, what did you say?" The question was blurted out in such a sharp tone, he knew at once he'd scared Oliver. When Oliver hugged his father even tighter, Jonathan softened his voice. "It's okay, Oliver. Granddad is just amazed by how smart you are. Did you say '*pauvre petit*'?"

Oliver nodded.

"That's such an unusual expression." Jonathan swallowed hard before posing his next question. "Can you tell me how you learned to say it?"

Oliver, now emboldened, raised his head and responded proudly. "I learned it from Kelsey. She says it a lot!"

Chapter 20

Marie

Marie first spotted the man at the coffee shop on Thursday morning. While waiting for the barista to fill her order, she stood to the side of the counter and savored one of her favorite aromas—roasted Arabica beans blended with vanilla, cinnamon, and, yes, a subtle hint of hazelnut. *Mm...* The man normally wouldn't have warranted her interest when he strolled in but, unlike the rest of the clientele, she noticed he wasn't in a hurry to place an order and rush back to his office. Instead, he sat at a table near the door and unfolded the newspaper he'd carried in. Holding the paper just high enough to give the impression he was reading, his eyes scanned the room as if he were searching for someone. His gaze ultimately settled on Marie.

Accustomed to attracting attention, Marie ignored his uncomfortable stare, writing him off as just another person admiring her from a distance. The barista called her name and slid her order across the counter. With coffee in hand, Marie elbowed her way across the store. As she stepped sideways to bypass a group of people loitering near the doorway, the man holding the newspaper crossed his legs. Marie instinctively glanced down to avoid bumping his foot and, in an instant, her emotions flew into a tailspin.

Made of black leather, the stranger's tasseled loafers had been a favorite style of Marie's father, Dominic Ricci. Out of the blue, Marie was hit with a flashback of the evening she'd arrived at the hospital where her wounded father was being treated. While she and Gus consoled each other in the surgical waiting room, a harried staff member had thrust a clear plastic bag at Marie. Inside the package were her father's blood-stained clothing and shoes. She was so deeply disturbed by the episode that, years later, just glancing at a comparable pair of loafers worn by a stranger in a coffee shop sent shudders through her body. She burst out of the store, desperate to escape the unwelcome memory.

By mid-morning, Marie had all but forgotten the eerie encounter. She was too busy contacting clients in preparation for an upcoming auction to think about much of anything else. At lunch, she took some quiet time to prepare for her date that evening with Richard Leister, her Wall Street exec. Tonight, she would accept the diamond ring Richard had purchased for her, then she'd gently break the news that she was ending their relationship. She would return the ring to Richard, but only after she'd swapped it for the replica Gus had forged.

At six o'clock, Marie left Willow's and hailed a taxi. Traffic was slow moving, but Marie had allowed herself sufficient time to alter her appearance prior to meeting Richard. Finally arriving at her destination, she paid the driver and dashed inside. She'd worked several con jobs at the Wedgewood Hotel and was well acquainted with the building's layout. As she headed toward the ladies' room off the reception area, a family of four stepped in front of her. The younger daughter's suitcase toppled over and blocked Marie's path.

"Mommyyyyyyy…." The little girl whined.

"Riley, here, let Mommy help you," the mother said as she rushed to the rescue. In a second, she had the suitcase back on its wheels. "There you go," she told her daughter, then apologized to Marie. "Kids," she said, shrugging her shoulders. "I'm sorry."

"Don't worry about it." Hopefully, the phony smile she'd plastered on her face concealed her annoyance. Marie didn't have much experience with young children and considered them too troublesome for her liking.

On the plus side, had the incident not happened Marie wouldn't have glanced down as she stepped around the little girl, and she wouldn't have noticed the pair of Italian loafers on the feet of the man passing by. Raising her head, Marie was shocked to again be face to face with the gawker from the coffee shop. He quickly pivoted away, as if hoping she hadn't recognized him. *Now, what are the chances I'd cross paths with the same man twice in one day, especially in a city the size of New York?* The chilling vibe she'd gotten from him in the coffee shop that morning suddenly made sense. The stranger, she was certain, was following her.

Who was this man, and why was he suddenly everywhere she went? If he was stalking her, she had a real problem on her hands, although her instincts told her he was more likely a private investigator. The question then was, who had employed his services? As Marie crossed the lobby and slinked into the ladies' room, she shoved this troubling situation aside. Right now, she needed to focus her efforts on obtaining the diamond ring from Richard.

Marie latched herself inside the spacious ladies'

room stall with its full-length door and began her transformation. Her hobo bag was large enough to hold a dress, a pair of strappy sandals, a wig, and a cosmetic bag. Within minutes, the blonde-haired, blue-eyed woman dressed in professional attire would disappear and a woman fitting an entirely different description would take her place.

She changed her clothing and popped out the blue contact lenses. Hanging a makeup mirror from the hook on the stall door, she applied false eyelashes, black eyebrow pencil, a smoky shade of eye shadow, and darker blush and lipstick. Lastly, she attached a wig over her pinned-up hair and styled the short ebony locks with her fingers. Reversing the hobo bag to show the black leather on the outside, she placed the mirror, cosmetics, and her workday clothing into the bag. She exited the stall as the black-haired, brown-eyed Paige Carson, outfitted for an evening engagement.

Marie, now Paige, strolled out of the ladies' room and surveyed the hotel lobby. The man in the Italian loafers was sitting under a potted palm tree near the elevators with his cell phone held to his ear. This time, she paid closer attention to the details of his appearance—average height and weight; a clean-shaven, uninteresting face; a short, non-descript hair style. She noticed his skin was devoid of any visible tattoos and piercings and he wore no jewelry, not even a wedding ring. Dressed in jeans, a black collarless knit shirt, and a dark sport coat, he'd put considerable effort into making himself appear as inconspicuous as possible. In fact, if not for his shoes, she wouldn't have given him a second thought.

In turn, he gave Marie a cursory glance then

returned his watchful gaze to the door of the ladies' room. She grinned as she strolled past him. Her ability to hide in plain sight never failed.

She located Richard sitting in a curved booth at the back of the lounge. As she approached, he rose to greet her but refrained from displaying any sign of affection. Marie understood his wariness when they met in public. Richard couldn't risk being seen by anyone who would report a questionable embrace to his wife, children, or business associates. She also noticed his movements were slower and more labored since she'd last seen him. His recent health issue had taken its toll.

"Hello, Paige. It's good to see you."

"Sorry I kept you waiting." Sliding into the booth, she sat close beside him. As Paige, Marie spoke with a flat, Midwestern accent and in a pitch that was higher than her natural voice.

"Here, I ordered a martini for you." His lingering stare gave her the impression he was committing her face to memory. Be my guest, she wanted to tell him, for she was certain they'd never see each other after this evening.

"Thank you," she said. "I've been so worried about you. How are you feeling?"

"It's a hell of a thing to go through." His voice quivered and his eyes watered. Would he ever again be the same capable executive who'd romanced her just a few weeks ago? "Like everyone my age who begins to experience health issues, I regret not taking better care of myself when I was younger. I'd give anything to go back thirty years and have it to do all over again. I'd eat better, get regular exercise, do more to relieve stress. But it's too late now. I feel like I'm a walking time bomb."

"Oh, my darling," Marie cooed with feigned affection. "I hate for you to speak that way." Her sympathetic comment masked her disdain. Richard's brush with death had been a cathartic experience that had transformed him into a softer, more contemplative person—for now. Knowing how brash his personality had been before his health scare, she doubted this new version of Richard would last. His decadent lifestyle was an addiction. She was certain he'd relapse to his old habits before long.

Jonathan, always present in Marie's thoughts these days, was the antithesis of Richard. Although both men were of comparable age, Jonathan had kept his body and his health in excellent condition, a tribute to having lived in a fashion that the flabby, overweight Richard now wished he'd followed. Not only were the two men light years apart physically, their personalities also couldn't be more different. She ached for Jonathan and wished she were cozied up in the booth this evening with him instead of Richard.

"It's the truth, Paige, and it's made me reevaluate my life." Lowering his head, he stared down at the tabletop. "I had a lot of time to think while I was recuperating from surgery." He paused and fidgeted with the edge of his cocktail napkin.

"To think about what?" Where was this conversation headed? Was it possible that, while she had prepared a good-bye speech, Richard would instead be the one to end their affair?

"About my wife and my family," he continued, "and my loyalty to them. And about us." At last, he looked her in the eye. "Paige, you're a gorgeous woman and the times we spent together were incredible, but I realize now how precious my family is to me. I regret all the things I've done over the years that almost destroyed what I have with them. My infidelity needs to end right now. I'm sorry, but I can't continue to see you any longer."

Marie stared at Richard in disbelief, her eyebrow raised, her mouth agape. This dolt was presumptuous enough to think he was breaking her heart, but he had just made her job a whole lot easier. How typical that his ego would sway him to imagine she was in love with him, and that *his* departure would destroy *her*. He had no idea the number of times she'd questioned how his wife could have tolerated his arrogance for so many years. She would need to unleash her finest acting skills to convince Richard that he'd just dealt her a crushing blow.

Then, the reality of the situation dawned on her. If she were no longer Richard's main squeeze, he wouldn't be obliged to present her with the diamond ring she'd convinced him to purchase from the auction house. The ring he'd bought specifically for her. The ring he said he couldn't wait to see adorning her manicured finger. In the privacy of a suite on the tenth floor of this hotel, he had kissed that finger, and she'd giggled enticingly as his kisses crept up her arm to her neck and on to any other parts of her body he wished to explore. She'd tolerated those intimate moments as a necessary part of the job. Now, thinking about their sexual interludes made her sick to her stomach.

She took a deep breath and kept her temper at bay. Had she just wasted the last two months working a con on this clown only to have nothing to show for her efforts? Gus would be furious, as would his buyer who had been promised delivery of the ring by the end the week. She had never blown a job before and wasn't sure how she would explain to Gus why she couldn't salvage this one. Crossing her fingers, she proceeded with her gut instincts.

"Richard," she began, her voice trembling, "please don't tell me I'll never see you again. After everything we've meant to each other, I don't know what I'll do without you." Contrived tears filled her eyes.

Obviously, Richard had not expected her to have such an emotional reaction. He glanced furtively around the lounge before continuing in a low voice. "Paige, I didn't arrive at this decision rashly. I've given our relationship a lot of consideration over the last two weeks, and I think this is what's best for everyone involved."

"But it's not what's best for me! Don't you care at all about my feelings?" She spoke loudly enough to attract the interest of those sitting close by. Marie's Paige was not going down without a fight. Tears spilled from her eyes. She was just that heartbroken.

Richard nudged his body in such a way that the others in the lounge saw more of his back and less of his face. "Look, Paige, I said I'm sorry."

Marie had spent enough time around men like Richard to know he was used to being the boss. His word was final with his underlings in the office and, probably, with his family at home. With such an overbearing personality, she imagined no one had ever dared to challenge him. In his eyes, the apology he'd given was beyond what he even owed her. Marie had found his Achilles heel, and the time had come to exploit it.

"Well, being sorry isn't enough for me!" The

volume in her voice had risen a notch. A few more people craned their necks to stare at the couple in the booth at the back of the lounge. "What about all those promises you made?"

"Paige, please, keep your voice down," he muttered. Beads of sweat appeared on his brow and his cheeks flushed. He rested his elbow on the table and placed his open hand against the side of his face, thus concealing his identity to everyone but her. "People are beginning to stare."

"I don't care what other people think," she said, still loud enough to carry to the tables around them. "Like you, all I care about is myself. You promised to leave your wife for me and said we'd be together forever. You even bought me a ring, or did you lie about that, too?"

Richard's agitation was becoming more apparent by the second. "This was a mistake. I should have gotten a room and done this in private."

"Don't change the subject, Richard." She had him backed into a corner now and was not going to relent. "I want to know where my ring is!"

"Damn it, Paige," he said angrily through gritted teeth. He patted the side of his jacket. "It's right here in my pocket. I was going to be a nice guy and give it to you as a parting gift, but you're being such a bitch, I've changed my mind."

Marie needed to confirm Richard did indeed have the ring with him. If he did, she still had an opportunity to switch it for the forgery secreted in her bag.

"I don't believe you." She sneered as she baited him. "I don't believe you ever intended to give me that ring. You know what I think? I think it's not in your pocket at all because you already gave it to your lousy wife."

Richard's face was red. His body shook with anger. He thrust his hand into his pocket and removed a ring box. "How dare you call me a liar! You don't believe me? Well, here's your damned proof!"

Just as he was about to open the ring box, Richard's face contorted. He panted for air and clutched his chest. As he slumped over, his bulging eyes conveyed a desperate plea for help. By the time his head landed in Marie's lap, he'd lost consciousness.

Marie gasped loudly enough to draw stares from the few people who weren't already glaring at the scene taking place at the back of the lounge. For a moment, her mind and body were frozen with the horror of realizing that, by goading Richard, she'd caused him to have a heart attack. Reacting on pure instinct, she screamed out, "Richard! Oh, my God! Richard!"

Then, just as quickly, she regained her wits. She gently raised Richard by the shoulders and slid out from under him. By the time she rested his head on the cushioned seat, several people had rushed over to help. Two men lifted Richard and laid him prone on the floor next to their booth. A woman stepped forward and announced she was a doctor. Kneeling beside Richard, she checked for a pulse.

Marie's emotions were torn. She was concerned for Richard's condition, but she had to escape from the hotel before she was dragged into the drama. Also, she needed to consider the consequences she would face if she left the hotel without the diamond ring which she assumed was still clenched in Richard's fist. Weighing her options, she decided that delivering the ring was the lesser of her priorities. She needed to disappear into the crowd without being noticed.

Glancing around to make sure all eyes were focused on the CPR being performed on Richard, she slyly slid across the booth. When she lifted her purse, a small object on the seat caught her eye. *Is that...?* Marie raised the ring box into the light. She was struck with guilt over her good fortune, considering Richard's dire situation, but she couldn't look a gift horse in the mouth. She opened the lid to confirm the ring was enclosed. Extracting an identical box from her purse, she dropped the authentic piece into her bag and placed the forgery on the table.

Keeping her head down, Marie slinked past the hotel manager as he rushed into the lounge and announced the EMTs were on their way. Several guests in the lobby had sauntered over to the doorway to see what had caused the commotion in the lounge. Thankfully, the disturbance had also captured the interest of the man in the Italian loafers who was not aware the woman he'd successfully followed that day had just eluded him. The valet assisted Marie into a taxi, and she vanished from the scene as if she'd never been there.

****

In the bedroom of her apartment, Marie stripped off all her clothes and slipped into a T-shirt and lounge pants. She poured a glass of wine, downed it, poured another, and flopped onto the sofa. Leaning her head back, she closed her eyes and attempted to wish away the entire day. However, as much as she wanted to pretend the events at the Wedgewood Hotel had never happened, she couldn't prevent the harrowing evening from replaying in her mind.

She was fraught with worry for Richard and tormented by guilt over the tragedy she'd caused. She hadn't intended for their argument to end in such a disastrous manner. In the past, Marie had performed some regrettable acts to get the job done, but tonight her behavior had sunken to a new low. Although she didn't want to think about the repercussions she'd have faced had she not obtained the ring for Gus's buyer, the price Richard was paying to make sure her ass was saved was unconscionable. Tomorrow, she would discreetly ask around the office or call every hospital in New York, if need be, to learn of Richard's fate. She would never forgive herself if she discovered she'd caused his demise.

This day couldn't have been much worse. Covering her face with her hands, the image of her father's bloodied shoes filled the darkness behind her eyelids. How she detested the stranger in the coffee shop for resurrecting memories she preferred to keep locked away, reminders that she, more than anyone, shouldered the blame for her father's gruesome assault all those years ago.

As a young girl, she had romanticized her father's business dealings, even admired his ability to con people. But, as she matured, she developed a clearer understanding of his activities. The risks he took were dangerous, not to mention illegal. She worried he and Gus would one day end up in jail or, worse, the morgue. She and Jacqueline had already been deserted by their mother; they couldn't bear to lose their father as well.

The night before the fateful shooting, she and her father had gotten into yet another argument over his profession, and she'd allowed her temper to get the better of her. She'd stormed out of his apartment vowing to never speak to him again if he didn't change his lifestyle.

In the hospital the next evening, while she sobbed on Gus's shoulder and prayed for her father's survival, she blamed herself for his life-or-death situation. She was convinced he would have been astute to his surroundings and avoided the enraged husband with the loaded gun if he hadn't still been distracted by her contentious behavior.

Dominic was in surgery for several hours. When the doctors entered the waiting room in the wee hours of the night, they informed the family that their medical team had successfully saved his life. The family rejoiced. Then came the bad news: Dominic's injuries had left him permanently disabled. He would never again walk. The family didn't care. Dominic was alive, and that was all that mattered. They'd learn to cope. They'd gladly attend to his every need.

Love, devotion, and a hefty dose of remorse were what motivated her to saddle the financial support of the Ricci family and, ironically, what led her to follow in her father's footsteps when she needed an additional source of income. Now, as she relived the nightmare from all those years ago, she wondered if she had a death wish, for here she was flirting with the same danger she'd once warned her father against. She needed to stop ignoring the writing on the wall and put an end to her precarious sideline ventures before she ended up like her father, in a situation from which she was unable to escape.

Marie opened her eyes as her thoughts wandered to the stranger who'd been tailing her throughout the day. She thanked her lucky stars for the crazy fluke of identifying him by his choice of shoes. Was he still sitting in that same chair by the hotel elevator? At what point would he admit he'd lost track of her and abandon his surveillance? And, most importantly, who would he submit his report of her activities to in the morning?

Marie's cell phone rang. She dragged herself off the couch, shuffled into her bedroom, and dug the phone out of her purse. Jonathan was calling from the cruise ship off the shore of Alaska. During their weekend on Nantucket, he had begged Marie to join him on the journey, but she'd declined. Nothing would have made her happier than to escape reality for a week with sweet Jonathan, but such dreams were simply not possible. Not now—she blinked back tears—and not ever.

Marie let the call go to voice mail. She couldn't fake being upbeat right then. Gulping down the rest of the wine, she fell onto her bed and curled into a fetal position. With any luck, sleep would numb her senses and she would wake to a better tomorrow.

Chapter 21

Marie

The next morning, Marie forced herself to smile as she approached the cubicle of one of her colleagues. "Good morning, Steph," she said cheerily.

Stephanie placed the receiver of her office phone on its cradle and swiveled her chair around. "Hi, Marie. How's your morning going?"

"Good, so far. Am I interrupting?"

"No, I was listening to phone messages. Nothing crucial, just a few clients to call back. God, they can be so needy," she proclaimed, eyes rolling. "So, what's up?"

"I overheard something about a client who I think works with you. Haven't you assisted Richard Leister a time or two?" Marie was already aware of Stephanie's association with Richard. Otherwise, she wouldn't have dared to strike up a conversation with the woman known around the office as the Gossip Monger.

"Yeah, sure," Stephanie replied. "I've helped Rich with several purchases. Jewelry mostly. Matter of fact, he bought a *gorgeous* diamond ring from us not too long ago. Top of the line, real expensive piece. And I don't think he bought it for his wife, if you get my drift." Stephanie said her last tidbit in a loud whisper, as though she were sharing a secret. Marie imagined she was chomping at the bit to start a tale that would make its way around the office and back to Marie's ears by the end of the day.

Marie raised an eyebrow to appear intrigued by the rumor. Wouldn't Stephanie just love to learn Richard's secret paramour was standing before her and that the ring she referred to was currently stashed inside an empty oatmeal canister on the top shelf of Marie's kitchen cupboard?

"Anyway," Chatty Stephanie continued, "I know Rich has had some health problems recently. What did you hear?"

"I was listening to a few people talking in the elevator on my way in," Marie explained, although her story was a complete fabrication. "All I was able to gather was that Mr. Leister collapsed in a hotel lounge last night. I wanted to make sure you knew."

"Shit!" Stephanie exclaimed. Marie glanced around to make sure no one close by had perked up to listen in on their conversation. "I hope he's okay. If he croaked, my commissions are going to take a big hit. So, that was all you found out?"

"Yes. Sorry. I wish I could tell you more."

"Huh," Stephanie grunted. She frowned and gnawed on her lower lip.

Marie attempted to nudge Stephanie into action without appearing too anxious about Richard's situation. "Is there anyone you can contact to ask about his condition…so you can put your mind at ease?"

"I guess I could start with his assistant," Stephanie replied. She opened her laptop and typed in her password.

"If you don't mind, would you let me know what

you find out?"

Stephanie glanced up at Marie with squinted eyes. "What's with the big concern over Rich Leister?"

Marie should have guessed there was no hoodwinking Stephanie. She covered her tracks by explaining, "I met him at one of our auctions. He seemed like a nice man, and I'd just like to know if he's okay."

Stephanie shrugged. "Yeah, sure. I'll give you a buzz after I talk to his staff."

"Thanks. I'd appreciate it."

"No problem. And, hey, some of us are going out for drinks after work. TGIF! You're welcome to join us."

"Thanks. I may just do that." She'd need a few drinks if she learned Richard was in the morgue instead of recovering in a hospital bed.

After returning to her cubicle, Marie cleared her mind of all other thoughts and focused on work. New acquisitions had come in that week, and she hadn't yet taken the time to view them. She rode the elevator downstairs to the galleries on the lower floors of their building and spent most of the morning inspecting the new *objets d'art*, collectibles, and jewelry. She identified certain pieces which might be of interest to her clients and took notes as she gathered information about them from the gallery specialists. Normally, she would have singled out a few of the pricier items for use in potential scams but, with last night's events still so fresh, she couldn't wrap her mind around starting another con game just yet. *Um, excuse me,* her conscience prodded, *weren't you planning to end your illicit activities for good after the Woodward jobs were completed?* Yes, well…

She wandered over to a display of watches and

recalled Jonathan's request that she scout out a pocket watch for him. Dear, sweet Jonathan. What part of Alaska would he be exploring today? While she dressed for work that morning, she'd played the phone message he'd left her last evening over and over again, each time closing her eyes and envisioning him being right there with her. He missed her terribly and couldn't wait to get home so they could be together. She hated to imagine what his opinion of her would be if he discovered the despicable deed she'd been carrying out last night while he was admiring the magnificent Alaskan scenery from his balcony and pining for her.

Marie's concern for Richard was still foremost on her mind. She needed to get back to her desk and check her phone for a message from Stephanie. As she was leaving the gallery, she stopped dead in her tracks. Standing at a jewelry display near the entrance was the non-descript man from yesterday. She'd changed her routine and not stopped for coffee that morning in hopes of throwing him off her scent, but that obviously hadn't done the trick. Perhaps her best tactic was to go on the offensive. She approached the man as if he were a potential client, not indicating she recognized him from the day before.

"Good morning," she said with a welcoming smile. "The bracelet that's caught your eye was just acquired as part of an estate sale. I'd be happy to assist you if you're interested in learning its history."

"No, thanks," he replied, his tone gruff. "I'm just browsing."

Marie could tell she'd made him uncomfortable. She imagined the last thing he wanted was to be recognized. What fun she was about to have making him squirm.

"Is this your first visit to Willow's?" Marie asked, purposely keeping him trapped in conversation.

"Yes. I'm in town on business, so I stopped by to kill a little time until my next appointment." While he spoke, he angled his body and directly faced Marie.

"Let me guess," Marie said, tilting her head flirtatiously. "You're from Boston." She needed the stranger to confirm her suspicion. Pinpointing him to the Boston area would most likely narrow his employer to someone in the Woodward family.

"Did my accent give me away?" Sadly, his attempt to be charming came off as anything but. "Happens every time. And your accent is from…?"

"I was born in France. My family relocated here when I was a child, but I never completely lost my accent."

"Wow, this is a first for me," he said with a lecherous grin. "I've never met anyone from France before."

Marie had caught yet another man in her snare, and this one in record time. How was it that men were so easily duped? A beguiling smile, a forced blush, and a few bats of the old eyelashes had any man eating out of her hand within minutes. She imagined the person who'd employed him wouldn't be pleased to learn that, rather than digging up some dirt, he was hitting on her.

"Well, thank you for choosing Willow's as one of your stops while you're in New York. Just so you know, our galleries are open until six o'clock."

"Thanks, but I think I've seen enough antiques." He inched closer. "However, I wouldn't mind getting a cup of coffee at that nice place across the street. Why don't you join me? You can turn me on with your accent while you tell me all about your childhood in France."

If Marie could shoot daggers from her eyes, the man would have been dead within seconds. Did he not pay attention to the news? Know anything about the Me Too movement? *Honestly.* Dipping her fingers into her jacket pocket, she handed him her business card.

"My name is Marie Lacroix. Feel free to call me if you're interested in discussing any of the pieces in our galleries. Have a good day and a safe trip back to Boston."

Before exiting the gallery, Marie glanced back and was not surprised to find the man still leering at her. She gave him a wave of her hand, as if affirming this was their final good-bye, before disappearing into the hallway. Hopefully, their conversation had satisfied his curiosity, and the report to his client would state he observed nothing unusual about her activities. Still, to be on the safe side, Marie would continue to keep her radar up over the next several days until she was certain he, and anyone he might be working with, was off her tail.

When Marie returned to her desk, the message light on her phone was illuminated. She dialed into her voice mailbox and listened to Stephanie's update. Richard, thank God, had survived his heart attack last evening and was currently in the Cardiac Intensive Care Unit where his progress was being closely monitored. "Oh, and FYI—I just found out Amanda from Accounting is having an affair with John from Marketing. Shocker!" Marie shook her head (*Enough with the gossip, PLEASE!*), and spoke one single word into the mouthpiece: "Delete."

Relief. She could now place last night's events, and Richard Leister, behind her once and for all. Richard was alive and under excellent care which placed him in the category of being just another job completed, the same as every mark she'd worked before him.

However, none of her other marks had ever collapsed into her lap because she'd provoked them into a near-fatal episode of cardiac arrest.

So, now I have that bit of guilt to add to my nagging conscience.

As if she didn't have enough to worry about, Marie had not yet delivered Richard's ring to the antique shop. She'd already ignored three calls from Gus and dreaded their next conversation. Knowing Gus as well as she did, she anticipated he'd be prickly if not downright angry. She waited to call him until everyone around her had gone to lunch.

"It's me," Marie said into her burner phone.

Gus, as expected, was pissed. "What's going on? I've been trying to get in touch with you all morning. Should I be worried?"

"No, there's no need to worry. It's just…things didn't go as expected last night and my morning hasn't been much better. This is the first chance I've had to call you, so don't give me any grief, okay?"

Several seconds passed before Gus responded. "Did you get the job done?"

"Yes, of course."

"Then we need to finish this right now. The buyer is angry. He's demanded delivery by four o'clock this afternoon. Can you get the ring to me within the hour?"

"No. You'll need to send someone to my apartment to get it."

Gus heaved an exasperated sigh. "Why? What's the problem?"

Marie checked around to make sure no one was close by. She lowered her head and replied in a near whisper, "I'm being followed."

"Jesus," Gus muttered. "All right, I'll send one of the runners. Where is it?"

Marie described where she'd hidden the ring in her apartment. "I need to talk to you. Can I stop by your place tonight?" she asked.

"Sure, doll. I'll order in dinner." He was back to being her concerned godfather. "Be careful, you hear me?"

"Aren't I always?"

Chapter 22

Marie

Wearing sunglasses and a baseball cap, Marie kept her face downcast as she traveled across town to Gus's apartment. She may have been overreacting to her experience with the private investigator, but she'd rather be safe than sorry. The last thing she wanted was to lead the P.I. to Gus.

Gus welcomed Marie into his apartment with a bear hug that took her breath away.

"What's this about?" she asked, squeezing him equally as hard. On Marie's regrettably short list of people she cared about deeply, Gus held a prominent position near the top. He was a second father, and she relished his shows of affection.

"We had words earlier today. I'm sorry."

"You had every right to be upset. I let my lousy mood interfere with finishing the job. So, I'm sorry, too."

"We're good then?" Gus asked with a hesitant grin.

"Water under the bridge."

Gus lifted off her hat and tossed it onto the sofa. He kissed her on the forehead and gave her one final hug. "Let's eat. I ordered in Italian."

"It smells wonderful," Marie admitted as she followed him to the dining table, "but you know I don't do carbs."

"Make me happy and go crazy for once," Gus said, holding a chair out for her.

As she took her seat, Marie was struck with a twinge of melancholy. "Gus, the aroma reminds me of my Nonna Ricci's Sunday dinners."

Gus smiled tenderly. "Those family dinners were some of the best times of my life." He filled a plate with pasta and chicken parmesan and set it in front of Marie. "Let's hope this food tastes as good as Mama Carmella's cooking. *Mangia!*"

Marie politely waited for Gus to fill his own plate and take his place across the table from her before digging in. After one bite, her willpower was broken. "This is delicious," she declared as she prepared another forkful of pasta.

"What about your diet?" Gus teased.

"I guess I'll have to work out harder at the gym tomorrow."

Gus picked up the bottle of wine and offered to pour her a glass.

"Only a little," she insisted. "I had drinks after work with some people from the office. I've already hit my limit of wine for one day." Gus, ignoring her instruction, filled her glass to the brim. "You don't listen well, do you?" she scolded, although his cagey grin told Marie her reprimand had fallen on deaf ears.

"You had drinks with the people from work? That's not like you."

"You're right. I don't normally socialize with my co-workers, but I want the person who's following me to think I'm just a normal working girl."

Gus's eyebrows furrowed. "Tell me more about this tail you picked up on."

Marie filled him in, from the time she noticed the Italian loafers at the coffee shop yesterday morning to her conversation with the man in Willow's gallery earlier that day.

"Who do you think he's working for?"

"When he said he was from Boston, the first person I suspected was Jonathan's daughter, Veronica. She put on a good front last weekend, but I know she distrusts me."

"The daughter, huh? You don't think Woodward himself wants to make sure you're legit?"

"Jonathan? No!" Marie blurted out, perhaps protesting a little too emphatically. "He would never hire someone to investigate me."

Gus set his fork on his plate and stared at Marie unflinchingly. "What makes you so sure?"

"I know him too well." As she spoke of Jonathan, Marie's eyes sparkled and her smile grew wide. A bad tell. "He's in love with me, a fact that was confirmed by his granddaughters. And you should have heard the way he defended me against Veronica's insults. Besides, he's such a gentle and trusting soul, I can't imagine him being suspicious of anyone, especially not me." Gus's doubtful eyes stopped her from blubbering on. "Why are you staring at me like that?"

"Looks to me like you've fallen in love with this guy."

"What?" Marie scoffed. "That's crazy. What on earth gave you that idea?" She focused on her wine glass as she guided it to her lips and took a large gulp. If she avoided eye contact with Gus, he might not notice she was lying.

Gus was frank with her. "You almost never have a

nice thing to say about the blowhards you trap into your schemes, but you sure light up when you sing the praises of this Woodward fellow. You may not realize it, but I can tell you've gotten too involved with him."

Marie angrily sliced into her chicken parmesan. "You've got it all wrong. Getting close to Jonathan is just my way of gaining his confidence. I'm behaving the same way with him as I have with all my other marks."

Gus returned to the ritual of twirling his spaghetti. He shook his head as if he weren't entirely satisfied with her explanation. "Okay, doll. I trust you know what you're doing."

"Thank you," Marie snapped. Angry with herself, she idly pushed the food around on her plate. Gus was right; she was in love with Jonathan. She could protest all she wanted but, without meaning to, she'd shown her heart to Gus. Now he would never be convinced otherwise.

"Just remember our cardinal rule," Gus reminded her. "Don't get emotionally involved. That's when you let your guard down and end up getting into trouble."

"All right! Can we please change the subject?" Marie put on a noble act but, deep down, Gus's warning rang true. She'd already stepped out of her role a few times by allowing her affection for Jonathan to take priority over the job. From now on, she needed to keep her head on straight before she made an unwise decision she'd later regret.

They ate in silence. Gus washed down his food with a drink of wine, then asked, "When will you complete the Somerset Necklace job? My buyer is getting impatient."

"Soon," Marie promised.

Gus raised an eyebrow. "Can you be more specific?"

Marie rolled her eyes and heaved a sigh. "In the next couple of weeks, okay?" She was irritated by the pressure Gus was placing on her. They'd had buyers in the past who were insistent, even threatening, and Marie had needed to be inventive to complete the job in a rush. She'd never had an issue with meeting their demands, but she was being unusually sensitive about this job. Although she couldn't admit it to Gus, she was pleased she hadn't had the opportunity to swap out the necklaces. She didn't want the job, nor her time with Jonathan, to come to an end. Not just yet. "Jonathan has invited me to a party at his club next weekend, and he's promised to let me wear the necklace to the event. I'll make the switch that evening."

Gus nodded. "Sounds like a solid plan. And what about those other things, the…uh…"

"The Singing Bird Pistols."

"Yeah, the pistols. What's going on with that job?"

"It's coming together nicely." She turned the tables to remind Gus she wasn't the only one holding up the job. "When will *you* have the forgeries ready?"

"Sometime next week," Gus assured her while he buttered another slice of bread.

"Good." Thankful the interrogation had ended, Marie took a bite of chicken parmesan and contemplated what she was about to say. "Gus, you know how we've been tossing around the idea of getting out of the business? Well, I've made up my mind. As soon as this double job with Jonathan Woodward is completed, I'm done. For good." She justified her decision by telling Gus what had happened the previous evening in the hotel lounge. "I played really dirty last night, and now Richard

Leister's life is on the line because of me. This was a warning, Gus. I need to stop before something even worse happens."

"I'm sorry you got trapped in that situation," Gus said, his gaze pensive. "You're right. We were getting close to our retirement goal, and this Woodward job will put us over the top. I agree with you. Matter of fact, Christopher's been wanting to take over the business. I've already drawn up a purchase agreement to legally transfer the antique shop into his name. It's time for us to leave New York and enjoy the Caribbean sunshine." He raised his wine glass. "To our retirement."

"To retirement!" she echoed as they clinked their glasses together.

"Are you going to Boston again this weekend?" Gus asked.

"No, Jonathan is in Alaska for the next week. While he's gone, we've got to focus on getting deeper inside Patrick Woodward's home. I know the second Singing Bird Pistol is there but, so far, it's nowhere to be found."

Gus's brow knitted and his lips pursed. After a moment, he said with concern, "You've been juggling a lot of balls lately. How are you managing?"

"To be honest, I'm starting to feel the stress," Marie admitted while helping herself to a bit more pasta. "Running a long-distance con is harder than I'd anticipated. To get this job done, I need to free up my time, so I'm going to ask for a month's leave of absence from work. I hate to use my French grandmother this way, but I'll say she's nearing the end and I need to be with her. What Willow's won't know is that, by the time I'm due back from my leave, this job on the Woodwards will be finished. I will be in another country by then, but

I won't be anywhere near France."

Chapter 23

Patrick

Patrick stood at his patio doors and stared at the torrential downpour pummeling his backyard. He took a sip of coffee and glanced down at the radar image on the screen of his cell phone. The dark green blob blanketing the east coast hadn't budged in the last half hour. Patrick, however, was convinced the hammer of raindrops on the patio's canvas awning had eased up a little. Or maybe he was just having a bout of wishful thinking. Either way, he anticipated a dicey Monday morning commute.

At least the weekend had been warm and dry. *Thank you, Mother Nature.* Kelsey had freed up her schedule and spent most of Saturday and Sunday with him and Oliver. Patrick was delighted that Oliver had bonded so easily with the affectionate and kind-hearted Kelsey. And, just maybe, her magical personality had also done a number on him.

Louise was at the kitchen stove preparing Oliver's breakfast. Oliver, still in his pajamas, sat at the breakfast table running a miniature toy car back and forth across the placemat, his lips vibrating as he replicated the sound of a revved-up engine.

"Was the rain coming down like this on your drive over?" Patrick asked Louise.

"No, it's raining much harder now." Louise ladled

oatmeal into a bowl, stirred in a touch of cinnamon and milk, then set the bowl on the breakfast table in front of Oliver. "Here you go, sweetie."

When Oliver didn't respond, Patrick reminded his son of his manners. "What do you say, Oliver?"

Oliver continued to maneuver his toy car with one hand while eating his oatmeal with the other. The kid had great dexterity for his age. "Thank you," he politely told Louise just before shoveling a spoonful of warm cereal into his mouth.

"You're welcome," she replied, giving Oliver's back a gentle rub.

Patrick took one last gulp of coffee before placing his mug in the sink. Regardless of the rain, he couldn't postpone his commute any longer. "I need to be on my way." He grabbed his car keys and laptop case from the desk in the kitchen. "Will you be venturing out today?" he asked Louise.

"Not if the rain keeps up like this," she replied while rinsing the breakfast dishes in the sink. "But, not to worry. I planned some fun indoor activities to keep us busy."

"Louise, I honestly don't know what we'd do without you." Patrick leaned down and kissed the top of Oliver's head. "I love you, buddy. See you tonight."

"'Bye, Daddy," Oliver said. "Daddy, is Kelsey coming over to play with me today?"

Patrick shot a glance at Louise. Her raised eyebrow and upturned chin needed only the question mark above her head to complete her thought.

"I think she might be planning on it, Oliver," Patrick replied. "Would you like her to?"

"Yes," Oliver shouted. "She's fun!"

To Louise, Patrick explained, "Kelsey is a woman I met a few weeks ago at the church where the grief therapy sessions are held. She's been here to the house a few times and has bonded really well with Oliver."

"I see. And when will *I* get to meet Kelsey?"

Patrick got the message loud and clear: Louise had been slighted, and he needed to make amends. Truthfully, he was eager for Louise, as well as his entire family, to meet the new woman in his life. "Soon. Maybe tonight at dinner if she's free."

"Well, then, I'll set an extra place at the table, just in case."

****

The normal start-of-the-week chaos at the clinic was compounded by the unrelenting weather. The staff spent the entire morning rescheduling appointments at the patients' requests, contacting no-shows to make sure they were safe and sound, juggling appointment times for those patients who did make it in but arrived late, and routing an above average number of messages to the appropriate physicians in the practice. Patrick, as a thank you to the staff for A) coming in on such a miserable day when they could have instead reported off and B) their efforts as a team to keep the office running like clockwork, personally arranged to have lunch catered in from a local restaurant.

With the crazy day behind him by late afternoon, Patrick at last had time to pay attention to his personal life. He'd earlier seen the two missed calls from Kelsey, which was not an unusual occurrence, but her frantic voice mail message caused concern. He returned her call immediately.

"Kelsey, what's wrong?"

Kelsey sounded out of breath and frustrated when she replied. "Oh, Patrick, I'm beside myself. This damned rain caused a flood in my condo."

"That's awful. How did it happen?"

"Apparently, the drainage system in my development couldn't handle the downpour. When I passed through my dining area this morning, I noticed the carpet was soaked. The rain had risen over the threshold of the patio doors and was seeping inside."

"How much damage was done?" Patrick asked.

"A lot! I called a damage recovery service right away, but by the time the crew got there the living and dining areas were soaked and the kitchen had about an inch of standing water."

"Were they able to stop the water from flooding in?"

"Yes, thankfully, but the damage was already done. I'm just sick over the pieces I had to throw out. I'm afraid I lost some family heirlooms I'll never be able to replace." Kelsey's last words were caught in a sob.

Patrick's heart went out to her. "Kelsey, I'm getting ready to leave the office. Give me your address. I'll drive over and help you."

"Oh, Patrick, I really appreciate your offer," she said, "but the recovery crew has everything under control. However, I can't live in my condo until they fix all the damage. I spent the afternoon showing houses to a couple who's moving into the area, and just now got back to my office. I'm going to relax for a few minutes, get some work done, then decide where I'm going to live for the next several days."

"It's almost dinnertime. Why don't you come over to my house? We'll have a nice meal and figure this out together." When she didn't answer, Patrick pressured her for a response. "Okay?"

"Oh, Patrick, you truly are my knight in shining armor." She started to cry again, but this time Patrick understood her tears to be ones of relief. "I appreciate your support, I really do, but I don't want to be a burden."

"Kelsey, don't be silly," he said, his voice filled with tenderness. "That's what friends are for."

****

Patrick greeted Kelsey at the back entrance of his home with a heartfelt hug. "Thank you for coming over. I couldn't stand the idea of you being alone tonight."

"It's me who owes *you* the thanks. At times like this, I really miss having my family close by."

"You know I'm always here for you." Patrick took her hand and led her toward the kitchen. "Come in. Louise is here, and she's dying to meet you."

When Kelsey entered the kitchen, Oliver jumped off his chair and ran to her. "Kelsey's here!" he called out. Kelsey bent down to catch him as he wrapped his arms around her neck.

"Hi, Oliver," she said, squeezing him into a hug. "Did you have a nice day?"

"Come see the picture I made," Oliver demanded. He grabbed her hand and dragged her toward his play desk.

"Oliver, you can show Kelsey your picture in a minute," Patrick said. He then reminded Oliver of his manners for the second time that day. "Louise has never met Kelsey, so you need to introduce them to each other."

Oliver spun around, his face unabashedly surprised, as if he'd forgotten Louise was in the room. "I'm sorry," he apologized. "Louise, this is my friend, Kelsey."

Kelsey extended her hand. "Hi, Louise. Patrick talks about you all the time. I'm happy to finally meet you."

Louise accepted Kelsey's handshake. "It's nice to meet you as well. I hope you're not a vegetarian. I made a chicken dish for dinner."

"Don't worry about me," Kelsey assured her with a chuckle. "I'm frequently referred to as a human garbage can. Can I help you?"

"Kelsey," Oliver whined, "come see my picture." He tugged on Kelsey's hand.

"Okay, Oliver, I'm coming. I'm sorry, Louise. I guess I'm not free to help you after all."

"That's all right. The table is set. I'll just put the food out and we'll be ready to eat."

"Oliver, show your picture to Kelsey, then wash your hands," Patrick instructed his son. "We're about to eat dinner."

Patrick and Louise transferred the food to the table while Kelsey helped Oliver wash his hands in the half bath. Throughout dinner, Louise battered Kelsey with questions. What city in Ohio was she from? How long had she lived in Stamford? Where was her condo? Patrick's face reddened with embarrassment. Kelsey, on the other hand, appeared undaunted as she dutifully answered Louise's questions.

"So," Kelsey explained, concluding her biography, "in my senior year at Ohio State, I met a guy who I believed was my one true love. After graduation, he took a job in Stamford, and I followed him here. Our relationship didn't last, but I really like living on the east coast and chose to stay. And that's me in a nutshell."

"Patrick told me about the flood in your condo. What are you going to do until your place is habitable again?"

Kelsey shrugged her shoulders as if in defeat. "I guess I'll check into a hotel for a few days. My parents are upset with that scenario, but what other options do I have?"

An alternate solution formed in Patrick's mind. He waited until Louise had left for home and Oliver had been put to bed before mentioning his idea to Kelsey.

"It's getting late, Patrick," Kelsey said. She rummaged through her purse for her car keys. "You need to get to bed, and I need to go home and pack my things so I can check into a hotel. Thanks again for dinner, and for helping to take my mind off my problems for a while."

"Kelsey, I have a suggestion, and I want you to hear me out before you turn it down."

"Okay." She shot Patrick a curious glance. "What is it?"

"Like your family, I hate the idea of you staying at a hotel, even if it's only for a few days. I want you to stay here instead." He clenched his jaw and waited for her response.

Kelsey frowned, as if she'd misunderstood. "Patrick, are you serious?"

"Absolutely."

"But...I can't do that." She shook her head in objection.

"Give me one good reason why not."

"Patrick, we've only known each other for a few weeks. I'm not sure if moving in here is, well, appropriate."

Patrick was quick to explain himself. "Kelsey, I'm not asking in the sense that we'd be living together. I have no intentions other than to offer you a place to stay while your condo is being repaired."

Still, Kelsey hesitated. "I don't know…"

Patrick placed his hands on her shoulders and gazed seriously into her eyes. "With eight thousand square feet and six bedrooms, there's plenty of room for you. Louise has claimed the suite on the first floor for nights she needs to sleep over while I'm at the hospital. You can have one of the empty bedrooms upstairs with its own private bath. No strings attached." He gave her a moment to let his offer sink in. "I'm all out of reasons to convince you. What do you say?"

"Well, you're right, it would be nicer than staying in a hotel…"

"And?"

"…and it would only be for a few days, right?"

"Only until you're ready to move back into your condo."

They stared into each other's eyes. "All right," Kelsey ultimately said, her face breaking into a huge smile. "You convinced me."

Patrick swept her into his arms. "Thank you, Kelsey. You'll be much more comfortable here than in a hotel. And much safer."

"To be honest, it will be nice to stay here with you and Oliver. Do I have time to run home and grab a few things, or do you need to get to bed right away?"

"I can stay up until you return," Patrick said. "I'm used to functioning on only a few hours of sleep."

Kelsey grabbed her purse. "Great. I promise to be back within the hour." Before she was halfway across the kitchen, Patrick stopped her.

"Wait," he said. Opening the cupboard above the

kitchen desk, he removed a garage door opener. "Take this opener and park in the bay at the far left when you return. I'll leave the door from the garage into the house unlocked."

"Thank you so much. I can't tell you how much I appreciate your hospitality."

"Don't mention it. I'm happy I can help. While you're gone, I'll put together a spare set of house keys for you."

"You're the absolute best," Kelsey said. She hugged Patrick and gave him a light kiss before leaving. "I'll be back in a bit."

Although Kelsey might consider herself lucky to have Patrick on her side, in Patrick's opinion, the opposite was true. Kelsey was amazing. With her looks and personality, she could have her pick of any man in the world. Patrick was amazed that she'd chosen to spend her time with him. The kiss she'd just given him was one of friendship, but Patrick interpreted her show of affection as a signal that a more intimate relationship was waiting in the wings.

At a time when he most needed them, Patrick neglected to recall his sister's strong words of advice. Veronica, who understood her little brother better than anyone, had warned him on several occasions to be wary of women who'd want to worm their way into his life for all the wrong reasons. She understood Patrick's experience with the opposite sex was limited and, when it involved matters of the heart, he could be incredibly gullible.

Chapter 24

Patrick

The next evening, Patrick kissed his sleeping son's forehead and switched the bedside lamp to its nightlight setting. At the doorway, he glanced back to make sure Oliver hadn't stirred. After a harrowing hour of negotiating and coaxing and, when all else failed, sternly threatening punishment, Patrick was relieved his combative son was at last settled in for the night. Catherine, no doubt, was in heaven having a good laugh right now at his clumsy parenting skills. He lowered his head and blinked back the tears. *Sorry, Cath. I'm doing my best without you.*

The change had happened without warning. A month ago, Oliver had been the sweetest child on earth. Then, seemingly overnight, he began pitching tantrums and wakening during the night with terrifying screams. Patrick agreed in part with Louise's theory that Oliver's behavior was associated with the addition of Kelsey to their routine, but he also knew the tantrums and night terrors were not uncommon in children of Oliver's age. Patrick was taking a wait-and-see attitude and praying his son would be back to his normal self soon.

In the back pocket of his jeans, Patrick's cell phone buzzed. He made a fast exit from the bedroom, leaving the door open a few inches. "Hi, Kelsey," he whispered into the phone.

"Patrick, I shouldn't have called. Did I wake Oliver?"

"No," Patrick assured her. "He's sleeping soundly. Where are you?'

"I'm driving up to your house. Can you meet me in the garage to help carry in my things?"

"I'm on my way."

Patrick had falsely assumed the paraphernalia Kelsey hauled in the previous evening was everything she'd require for a week's stay at his home, but apparently much more went into creating a woman of such incomparable beauty. When Patrick entered the garage, he found Kelsey hoisting a large suitcase from the trunk of her car.

"Let me get that for you," he said as he rushed toward her.

"Too late," Kelsey announced. "But you can carry this big bag in while I grab the smaller one."

Inside the house, Patrick carried the suitcase up the back stairway and down the hall to the bedroom Kelsey had selected. "Again, I'm sorry I can't offer you the larger suite downstairs."

"Are you kidding?" she replied while unpacking her personal items in the adjoining bathroom. "This room has plenty of space, and it's way better than a hotel."

"I just want to make sure you're comfortable." Patrick crossed his arms and leaned against the bathroom door frame. "So, how's the work on your condo coming along?"

She grunted —*Ugh!*— and rolled her eyes. "The project manager was there today. Now, there's a hold up getting the insurance adjuster to sign off on the repairs. I have a feeling this is going to take longer than I anticipated."

"All projects seem to take twice as long as expected. But please don't worry about overstaying your welcome. Our house is available as long as you need it."

"Thank you so much." Kelsey arranged the last of her makeup and closed the drawer, then leaned her back against the countertop. "Is Louise okay with me staying here for a few days? She wields a lot of authority, and I don't want to create any friction."

"Yes, she's fine with the arrangement." Kelsey tilted her head and frowned at Patrick skeptically. "Okay," Patrick admitted, "she wasn't crazy about the idea at first, but she likes you and understands the predicament you're in. She actually told me this evening she's pleased I offered to help you."

"Good. I'm glad you're both on the same page." Kelsey brushed past Patrick and entered the bedroom. "Before I forget, I need to tell you I won't be here over the weekend."

"No?" Patrick asked. He sat on the edge of the bed while she unpacked her suitcase. "Where are you going?"

"It's my dad's birthday, so I'm flying home to celebrate with the family."

"That's too bad. I'd kind of already made plans for us." Patrick couldn't conceal his disappointment. He had the weekend free and was looking forward to spending the time with Kelsey. He'd even entertained the idea of inviting her to the family compound on Nantucket.

"I'm sorry I couldn't tell you sooner," Kelsey apologized as she placed her lingerie in the dresser drawers. "With the disaster at my condo, I wasn't sure if

I'd be able to make the trip until today."

"I understand," he replied with a heavy sigh. "So, did you find any more items in your cupboards that needed to be pitched?"

"No, thank goodness. I'm really grateful all the collectibles my grandmother gave me weren't ruined."

"Why? Are they valuable?"

"Heavens, no! They're just ceramic and glass figurines. Some may be worth a few bucks, but it's their sentimental value that's important to me. As a little girl, I can remember admiring them when we visited my grandparents. If I promised to be careful, Grammy would take them from her china cabinet and let me see them up close. When she transitioned to assisted living, she graciously gave me the ones that were my favorites."

Patrick closed Kelsey's empty suitcase for her and placed it in the closet. "Your grandmother sounds like a wonderful lady."

"Oh, Grammy is a hoot," Kelsey said with a giggle. "She's been a great role model for me, aside from her tendency to be a packrat. You know, while we're on the subject of home decorations, I've been meaning to ask why you don't have any tchotchkes sitting around."

As Patrick lifted Kelsey's suitcase onto the closet shelf, he was overwhelmed with memories of moving into the house with Catherine. They'd been so excited to decorate the home they'd call theirs for years to come. Little had they known.

He leaned against the door frame with his back to Kelsey. "We have plenty of decorations. It's just…" He hesitated, wanting to hide his anguish, then remembered that sharing his feelings was part of the healing process. "They remind me of Catherine. After she passed, I couldn't bear the sight of them. One day, I boxed them all up and stashed them away in the attic. And to be honest, I don't care to ever see them again."

"I'm sorry," Kelsey apologized. She approached Patrick and gently touched his shoulder. "I didn't mean to upset you."

"That's okay." Patrick faced Kelsey with a rueful smile. "This was Catherine's home, too. I can't pretend she never existed." He lowered his gaze so Kelsey wouldn't see the pain he still found impossible to conceal.

"Patrick, remember what you told me you learned in grief counseling? It helps to talk about the ones we've lost." As Patrick raised his head, Kelsey caught his eye. "Tell me about Catherine's style of decorating."

Patrick took a moment to savor his memories before responding. "She liked old pieces and the history that's attached to them." He grinned as scenes of their shopping excursions grew more vivid in his mind. "I have my father to thank for that. Whenever those two were together, they could lose themselves in an antique shop for an entire day."

"How nice that they had a common interest, although collecting antiques can be an expensive hobby."

"You don't know my father. If something catches his eye, he doesn't worry about the price tag. He's made purchases almost everywhere he's travelled, and now he's enlisted the help of specialists in the field. In the last few years, he's been working closely with Willow's."

"The hoity-toity auction house in New York?" Kelsey asked, her eyes wide with surprise.

"That's the one." As far as Patrick knew, Kelsey was

unaware of his family's wealth. He imagined she attributed his plush surroundings to the income from his medical practice. She had no idea that his prestigious home had been a wedding present from his father, a Woodward family tradition.

"You're right. Your father does have expensive tastes. After so many years, he must have an awfully large collection. Where does he keep it all?"

"Don't worry," Patrick assured her, "he's not a hoarder. My father is a generous man. He's given many of his purchases away as gifts."

"But, if he gave you and Catherine such valuable gifts, why would you stow them in your attic?"

Patrick was quick to correct the false impression he'd given. "I didn't mean to say I boxed up everything. I still keep the valuable antiques on display."

"Then, why haven't I seen them?"

Patrick made an impulsive decision. He gripped Kelsey's hand and said, "Come with me."

"Where are we going?"

"To my study," he replied as he led her down the front staircase.

"But you said that room is off limits."

"Normally, I prefer to keep the door closed, but for you I'll make an exception." Patrick opened the door to his study and flipped the wall switch which illuminated the floor lamp between the armchairs. Stepping into the room, his gaze was instinctively drawn to Catherine's secretary desk. Her laptop, journal, favorite writing pen, and family photos still sat just where she'd left them. The day was coming, he anticipated, when he'd remove her personal affects, but for now he still couldn't let go.

"I love this room," Kelsey remarked, her eyes

scanning the space. Running her fingers along the edge of Patrick's desk, she asked, "Is the furniture as old as it appears?"

"Most of the furniture is antique. With my father's help, Catherine purchased everything from a local shop. If I'm not mistaken, her secretary desk is the oldest piece in the room. This curio," Patrick mentioned, calling Kelsey's attention to the antique cabinet in the corner of the study, "is where we display the collection of relics my father gave us, plus a few Catherine purchased on her own." The wood-framed curio was designed with a curved glass door and rounded leaded glass on either side. From behind the curio, Patrick flipped a switch and illuminated the inside of the cabinet.

"My goodness, what beautiful pieces!" Kelsey exclaimed, her eyes sparkling with delight. "My Grammy's knickknacks are nothing compared to these."

"Don't discount sentiment. I'm sure your grandmother prizes her collection every bit as much as I treasure mine."

"Ah, Patrick, you always have the perfect way of putting everything into perspective." Patrick enjoyed watching Kelsey's excited reactions as she oohed and aahed over his treasures. "Does each piece represent a special occasion?" she asked.

"Yes, mostly." He bent down to point out a piece on a lower shelf. "For instance, this is the Coudriet snuff box my father gave me when I graduated medical school. And this is a Borchardt figurine we picked up in Germany during a family vacation." He stopped when he noticed the astonished expression on Kelsey's face. "What's wrong?"

"Patrick," she said hesitantly, "I'm no expert, but I

know enough to recognize the names you're throwing around. Coudriet. Borchardt. These items must be worth hundreds of thousands of dollars."

"Yes, they are." Patrick didn't bother to correct Kelsey. The entire collection, in fact, was insured for several million.

Kelsey stared at Patrick, her mouth agape, as if she couldn't believe his nonchalance. "Aren't you afraid of theft? Anyone could break into the house and steal everything in this cabinet."

"Oh, no, that wouldn't happen. I mean, a thief could attempt to break in, but he'd first need to get past the house security system. Then, he'd set off another alarm if this case weren't opened properly." Patrick pointed to a small device mounted on the left side of the curio cabinet. "See this keypad? If the door to the curio is unlocked without first entering the security code into this pad, a silent alarm is set off. The same alarm is triggered if the glass is broken. The private security company and the police would respond within minutes."

"Well, that makes me feel better," Kelsey admitted. "But, Patrick, the key is missing."

"Don't worry. The key is in safe keeping. Just in case someone with the wrong intentions were to discover the security code, I wouldn't want them to also have the key at their disposal."

"Please don't tell me the key is hidden under the rug," she chided.

"No, silly! I keep it tucked away inside Catherine's desk."

"Oh, I see," Kelsey said, her brows furrowing into a confused frown. "So, let me get this straight. To open the curio without setting off the silent alarm, you need to first insert the key, then punch in the security code and, lastly, unlock the door with the key you keep in the secretary desk."

"You got it."

"Is the reverse true, then? Lock the cabinet door, enter the code, then remove the key?"

"Exactly. Are you sure you don't work for a home security firm?" he joked.

"Trust me," Kelsey replied with a sardonic grin. "I'm the last person you'd want working in security." She continued to peruse the antiques on the glass shelves. "So, did you show me these amazing trinkets just to tease me, or are you going to open the case and let me get a closer look?"

Patrick squinted his eyes and asked her lightheartedly, "Are you trying the same tactics on me that you used on your grandmother?"

"Well," Kelsey said with a giggle and a shrug of her shoulders, "I figured, if they worked on Grammy, they'd work on you. But I get it. Your pieces are expensive. You don't want to take the chance I'll break one of them."

"Don't be silly. I'll gladly open the case for you, but it's getting late, so not tonight."

"That's fine," she said. "Just one more question before you turn out the light. What is that interesting piece on the top shelf?"

"Which one?"

"The one covered with jewels that's shaped like a gun."

"Oh, that's the Singing Bird Pistol."

Kelsey cocked her head and stared at Patrick disbelievingly. "A Singing Bird Pistol? Are you sure that's what it's called?"

"I know it sounds odd, but I promise you, I'm not making up the name."

"Okay, I believe you," Kelsey told him although the expression on her face said otherwise. "Can you elaborate and explain why it's called a Singing Bird Pistol?"

"Sure. See that tiny winding key?"

"Uh-huh."

"The inside of the pistol is designed like a clock. When you insert the key into the handle and wind it, then cock the hammer and pull the trigger, a tiny bird shoots out of the barrel and sings a song. Hence, the name 'Singing Bird Pistol'. My father has its mate. He said they were made as a set about two hundred years ago, and they're the only ones of their kind in existence."

"So, that isn't a real pistol that shoots tiny bullets?"

"No, the designer just wanted to create a unique gift for a Chinese emperor."

"How intriguing!" Kelsey exclaimed, her eyes wide as she continued to stare at the Bird Pistol. "I'd love to see the bird pop out of the barrel."

Patrick recalled Catherine's last birthday when his father presented her with the special gift he'd purchased for his beloved daughter-in-law. Jonathan had demonstrated the pistol's mechanism, and Catherine had laughed with delight when the bird shot from the barrel. The memory almost brought Patrick to tears. He desperately needed to escape the room and, more so, the haunting remembrance.

"I promise to show you how it works, but another time," Patrick insisted as he switched off the lights on both the curio cabinet and the floor lamp. With the sun now set, the room was in total darkness except for the dim light peeking in from the foyer. "I have an early morning and need to call it a night."

Taking Kelsey by the hand, he led her out of the room and closed the door behind them. Patrick's mood was sullen as they climbed the staircase. In the upstairs hallway, he muttered a good-night and began the trek to his bedroom.

"Patrick, did I say something to upset you?"

"What?" He was so wallowed in sadness, he'd forgotten his manners. "Oh, no, I'm just…tired. I'll be gone before you wake up in the morning, so I'll see you tomorrow evening." He gave Kelsey a brief and impersonal good-night kiss on her cheek before continuing down the hall.

"Good night," Kelsey whispered to his back.

****

As he lay in bed waiting for the sleep that so often eluded him, Patrick dissected what had caused his sudden mood swing. By barricading the room where he'd shared all those quiet and comfortable hours with Catherine, he was compartmentalizing his feelings. Since her death, the study was where he'd grown accustomed to hiding and enveloping himself in his memories. Behind that closed door was also where he'd done most of his grieving.

This vicious cycle needed to end. Tomorrow, Patrick would leave the door to the study open and allow Catherine's spirit to roam freely about the house as it should have all these months since her passing. Catherine's final concern had been for his and Oliver's happiness. As an image of Kelsey's beautiful face floated into his thoughts, he decided the time had come to fulfill Catherine's wish.

Chapter 25

Veronica

Veronica leaned in closer to the lighted vanity mirror in her private bathroom and applied a dusting of translucent powder. "So, I understand my brother is now sheltering the homeless," she said, her comment dripping with cynicism. Bailey, the Lamberts' short-haired calico, rolled over on the countertop and batted at her mistress' arm, seeking attention. Veronica dropped the powder brush into her cosmetic drawer, then gently rubbed Bailey's chest.

Louise's response emanated through the speaker of Veronica's cell phone. "Now, now, you're being a little harsh, don't you think?" Her words carried the same tone she'd used with her kindergarteners when they needed a reminder that we should always be kind to each other.

Since Catherine's death, Veronica had assumed the role of Patrick's guardian. After all, *someone* needed to ensure he was behaving in a proper manner. Periodically, she contacted Louise to get her perspective on what was taking place inside her brother's home.

"Well, how would *you* suggest I react to Patrick's announcement?" Louise could keep that holier-than-thou attitude to herself. Veronica was not going to soften her opinion of Patrick's decision to invite a woman he barely knew to live in his home, even if the situation was meant to be temporary.

"I understand your concern, Veronica, I really do. But trust me when I say you're misinterpreting their relationship. Patrick is simply being a good friend. Please don't read anything more into it."

"I'm sorry, Louise," Veronica said. "I'm protective of Patrick, and my father, for good reason. Over the years, I've seen their vulnerable sides, and I'll do anything to keep them from being harmed by women whose sole intention is to take advantage of them."

"I don't blame you for having their best interests at heart, and they're certainly lucky to have you in their corner. But, Veronica, they're grown men. They both seem capable of looking out for themselves."

"Well, maybe," Veronica replied, still not in complete agreement that her brother was up to making wise relationship choices while still reeling from the loss of his wife. "What's your take on this woman? Is she as wonderful as Patrick makes her out to be?"

"Yes, she is," Louse admitted. "Like you, I was skeptical when I first met her. But the more time I spend with Kelsey, the more I like her. Instead of being suspicious, I think you should be happy Patrick has developed a close friendship and maybe even a budding romance with such a nice woman."

Veronica picked up Bailey and held the cat to her shoulder as if she were a baby. Absent-mindedly scratching Bailey's cheek, she finalized her conversation with Louise. "Okay, I trust your opinion. I guess the whole family will meet her when we're there for Oliver's birthday next week."

"Yes, you will. Patrick is excited to have everyone together. Veronica, please don't spoil that special family time for him."

"I'll try my best to welcome his new girlfriend with open arms," Veronica assured her. "I've got to go, Louise. Have a good day."

Veronica disconnected the call without waiting for Louise to say good-bye. She dropped Bailey to the floor and stepped into the bedroom. The cat sauntered after her, stopping to rub her cheek against the door frame, then skittered out of the bedroom as if she suddenly remembered a pressing matter of great urgency.

Brian was sitting in a corner armchair tying the laces on his Oxfords. "Who were you talking to?"

"Hmm? Oh, I gave Louise a quick call," she told him while staring distractedly out the bedroom window.

"Louise?" Brian rose from the chair and crossed the room to his dresser. Opening the top drawer, he selected a watch to match his attire. "Why? Is something wrong?"

"No, I just wanted to get her opinion of my brother's new girlfriend is all." Approaching her husband, Veronica folded her arms across her chest and prepared to defend herself. She was used to Brian accusing her of being a buttinski.

"Snooping around again, huh?"

"Brian, don't make it sound that way. When I learned Patrick had offered this woman shelter from the storm—"

"Literally," Brian interjected with a snicker.

Veronica rolled her eyes. "I wanted to make sure he wasn't doing anything foolish."

"And?" Receiving no response other than a cold stare, Brian prompted Veronica to provide more information. "Is he?"

"As far as Louise is concerned, no."

"Why do I feel like there's a 'but' at the end of your sentence?"

Veronica glared at her husband. "*But*," she said with emphasis, "this woman is practically a stranger, and I'm not convinced the living arrangement she's made with Patrick is altogether innocent. I'm considering placing another call to Lou Biondi."

Brian shook his head in disagreement while he fastened his watchband. "Veronica," he said, "your brother is an extremely intelligent man. Why can't you trust him to know what he's doing?"

"That's not what this is about."

"You trying to control his and your father's lives is what this is about." Brian stepped closer until they were face to face. "First Jon, now Pat. What do you think they'd say if they discovered you hired a private investigator to follow their lady friends?"

"I think they'd be grateful I stopped these women from taking them for a ride and leaving them in the dust."

"Uh-huh," Brian responded. "So, even after Lou reported your father's friend is a normal person who leads a normal life, you're still not convinced there are women who can love the men in your family for who they are instead of for what they're worth?"

They regarded each other unflinchingly for several seconds. When Veronica spoke, the tone of her voice begged Brian to understand her motivation.

"Brian, I just need to be sure Daddy and Patrick aren't going to be hurt."

"Okay, I get it. No matter what I say, I know you'll do what you want, but can you do me one favor? Can you postpone your call to Lou until *after* you've met Pat's friend? You should at least give her the benefit of the doubt before accusing her of having ulterior motives."

Veronica chewed on her lip as she mulled over Brian's request. "Fine. I'll wait until after we meet her."

"Thank you." Brian gave her a light kiss. "Will you be at Arianna's tonight?" He meandered over to his suit valet and took his jacket off the hanger.

"Yes. Daddy's meeting me for dinner along with Uncle Burt and Aunt Susan. They're eager to tell me about their cruise to Alaska."

"Great! I'll have Oscar reserve a table. If I can, I'll join you. I'd like to hear about their trip as well." Putting on his suit coat, he bid her good-bye as he exited the room. "See you then."

Lost in thought, Veronica returned to the window. "Enjoy your day!" she called out over her shoulder, although she was certain Brian was already out of earshot.

Staring into the woods at the back of their property, Veronica considered Brian's request for her to put any concern over her brother's recent lifestyle choices on the back burner. However, she needed to do what she believed was best, even if that meant breaking the promise she'd just made to give Patrick's new friend a fair chance. Although Veronica understood her husband's point of view, she still wasn't convinced that welcoming this woman—*What was her name again? Kelsey?*—into their lives with open arms was the most responsible course of action.

Chapter 26

Marie

Early Friday morning, Marie received a call from Gus. "The products you ordered are ready."

"And just in time," Marie replied. She understood Gus was referring to the forgeries of the Singing Bird Pistols he'd been working on 24/7 to have completed by the end of the week.

"When do you want them delivered?"

Marie glanced at the clock on her nightstand. "Delivery isn't necessary. I'll pick them up." She ended the call and was out of her apartment a second later.

Still early morning, the antique shop was closed to business when Marie arrived. She strode around the building to access the store through the rear entrance and encountered Roberto Lopez, one of Gus's top guys, smoking a cigarette by the back door.

Roberto greeted Marie with a kiss to both cheeks. "*Buenos dias, Señorita.*"

"*Buenos dias*, Roberto."

"Gus told me to be on the lookout for you." Roberto flicked his cigarette into the alley then opened the back door of the shop for Marie. "He is waiting for you in the office."

Although Marie and Roberto were close in age, they'd grown up in vastly different environments.

Whereas Marie's parents had indulged her every whim, Roberto's large family lived in poverty. Born and raised in San Juan, Puerto Rico, he took to the streets as a young boy out of desperation and preyed on the island's tourists to hone his skills as a grifter. A few years ago, while vacationing in New York City, a mutual acquaintance introduced him to Gus. By then, Roberto had refined his technique as well as his sophistication and grooming, and Gus was keen to take advantage of his potential. After a few business discussions, Roberto relocated to New York and joined Gus's operation.

"You must have woken in a good mood," Roberto commented while escorting Marie through the storage room. "I have never seen you looking so radiant."

Marie couldn't deny her physical attraction to Roberto. When Gus first introduced them, she'd toyed with the idea of starting a relationship, but the timing had never been on their side. In the long run, Marie was grateful they'd never hooked up. As they became better acquainted, she recognized the void beneath Roberto's steady stream of superficial compliments. Her only association with him recently was to request his occasional assistance with a job, and to refresh her proficiency in conversational Spanish. However, as she often reminded herself, her disreputable history limited her options for romance to scoundrels like Roberto.

Thinking of romance reminded her of Jonathan and the fact that their time together was disappearing fast. In two days, she would kiss him good-bye for the last time. But how could she possibly banish him from her mind and her heart forever? *Simply live in the moment,* she told herself, *and stop worrying about what's going to happen two days from now.*

Just as Roberto enjoyed dishing out empty compliments, Marie took pleasure in feeding his overly-inflated ego. "How is it that you always know how to melt my heart, Roberto? Are you working with me on my Boston job this weekend?"

"Yes. Gus told me to clear my schedule through Sunday. I'll crash the party at your boyfriend's club, so watch for me."

"I will. Just remember to wait until after we've finished dinner to make your entrance. I'm not sure how much time I'll need to carry out my portion of the job."

"Whatever you say. You're the boss."

Roberto kissed her again, as was his custom. Marie then entered the office where she found Gus sitting at his desk.

"Morning, doll," Gus said without rising from his chair.

"Good morning," Marie said cheerfully. "I have a lot to do before I leave for Boston, so I can't stay long. Can I see the Bird Pistols?"

Gus picked up the box that was sitting on his desk. Holding it in front of Marie, he lifted the lid to show her the two identical replicas of the Singing Bird Pistols he'd created.

"Oh, Gus! They're perfect!" Marie took the box from him and examined the pistols. "No one will be able to tell the difference between these and the originals. You've done some remarkable replicas in the past, but these pieces are outstanding."

"Thanks," he replied curtly.

Why was Gus being so cranky? Maybe he was exhausted from having worked around the clock to have the forgeries completed by this morning. "You even managed to recreate the original presentation box. I have to say, you've really outdone yourself on this one."

"This is a big job. We've got to make sure every detail is exact."

"Especially when we're tricking a man who's as savvy with antiques as Jonathan," Marie said as she closed the lid and placed the box in her bag.

"The party at Woodward's club will be held tomorrow night, right?"

"Yes."

"Are you're positive you'll have the Somerset Necklace by the end of the evening?"

"That's the plan." She couldn't bear his somber mood any longer. "What's the matter, Gus? You seem unusually tense."

Gus appeared reluctant to share whatever was bothering him. He rose from the chair and paced nervously across the floor. "I'm getting a lot of pressure from the man who's buying the Somerset jewels," he told her in a low voice. "He's demanded receipt by Sunday afternoon, and he doesn't tolerate people who don't follow his orders. We cannot let anything go wrong with this job. You do understand that, don't you?"

"It'll be fine, Gus," she assured him. "I'll wear the Somerset Necklace to the gala. While we're at Jonathan's club, I'll make the switch and hand off the necklace to Roberto who will hightail it back to New York. You'll have the necklace by midnight Saturday."

Marie had never seen Gus in such a fretful state. As he combed his fingers through his hair and stared at the wall, she could tell his mind was a million miles away. Despite her normal nerves of steel, Gus's anxiety was rubbing off on her. Finally, Gus landed back on earth and delivered a word of warning.

"I'm placing all my confidence in you to not screw this up."

"Stop worrying," she told him with a bright smile meant to cover up her own misgivings. "I'm a professional."

"And the Bird Pistols?" he asked.

"I'll switch the one Jonathan has while I'm at his house over the weekend as well. The second pistol, the one at his son's home, is a work in progress."

"Can you give me a completion date?"

"Another week, at most."

Marie's cell rang. She took the phone from her bag and held up her forefinger as a signal for Gus to give her a minute.

"Hello, Jonathan," she answered with her Marie Lacroix accent. "Yes, I'm almost packed…That sounds wonderful…And I can't wait to be with you…I'll see you in a few hours…*Au revoir, mon cher.*"

Gus regarded her with skeptical eyes. "That moonstruck grin is lingering on your face longer than it should," he commented.

"Okay, Gus, I admit it. I like Jonathan. That doesn't mean I'll let my feelings for him interfere with my work." She checked the time on the screen before dropping the phone back into her purse. "It's getting late, and I have a plane to catch."

Gus placed his hands onto Marie's shoulders and gazed solemnly into her eyes. An unspoken message of mutual trust passed between them, as did a hefty degree of concern. Should an unexpected event take the situation out of Marie's control, resulting in a breach of Gus's agreement with his client, she didn't want to imagine the repercussions they could face.

Marie folded her arms around Gus's neck and hugged him with all her strength. She kissed him on the cheek and said, "I love you, Gus."

"I love you, too, doll," he replied with his arms tightly wrapped around her. "We're going to have one hell of a celebration when this weekend is over."

"Plan something really special for us," she said with a bright smile meant to convince Gus he had nothing to worry about. "See you Sunday!" She grabbed her purse and hurried away.

****

Jonathan was waiting at the front door of his home when the SUV drove up and parked in his circular driveway. Marie threw open the back door and rushed into his arms.

Jonathan gazed longingly into her eyes. "I thought you'd never get here."

"I missed you so mu—" Jonathan's mouth covered Marie's, preventing her from finishing her sentence. No matter. Actions speak louder than words.

Nearly a minute later, the driver coughed. When that didn't work, he cleared his throat as if to say, *Hello, I'm still here.*

Marie and Jonathan eventually got the hint. However, when their kiss ended, Marie continued to cling to Jonathan, not wanting to let him go. To hell with the driver.

"Can I carry these bags into the house for you, Dr. Woodward?" the driver asked. He was persistent, Marie would give him that.

"Yes, thank you, Bill. You can leave them in the foyer."

Jonathan led Marie inside the house, tipped Bill, and closed the front door behind him. He again took Marie into his arms. "Sorry I couldn't meet you at the airport myself. I was needed at the club to finalize last-minute details for tomorrow's gala."

"Well, we're together now, so stop talking and kiss me."

Marie simply couldn't satisfy her craving for Jonathan's scent, the taste of his mouth, the sensation of his hands on her body. But did she really want him to rip her clothes off right there in the foyer? Jonathan's lips were exploring Marie's neck and his fingers were slinking around the waistband of her capris when she broke the mood. "I should hang my gown so it doesn't wrinkle."

"Party pooper," Jonathan whispered into her ear.

Carrying her suitcase and garment bag up the stairs, Jonathan said, "When Anita was in to clean this morning, she stocked the bathroom with your favorite body gels and lotions. Oh, and Brenda ordered coffee from that little shop on Nantucket, their Kona Blend you fell in love with."

"Jonathan, you spoil me," Marie said as she followed him to the bedroom. "Thank you."

"Just making sure you feel at home." As they entered the walk-in closet, a sensor automatically illuminated the overhead lights. Jonathan hung the garment bag, then lifted Marie's suitcase onto the wooden dresser unit built into the center of the closet. "What are my chances of getting a peek at your gown?"

Marie would gladly have shown Jonathan her gown but used the garment instead as a bargaining tool. She needed to view the Somerset Necklace to allay her nerves that the swap she planned for the following evening would be carried off without a hitch. She crossed over to the garment bag and pretended she was about to unzip it. "I'll show you my dress if you'll show me the necklace you promised to lend me for the evening," she teased.

"Oh, but that would spoil the surprise," Jonathan bantered back.

Although her ploy hadn't worked, Marie deftly hid her annoyance. Sauntering toward Jonathan, she replied playfully, "Then I guess we'll both have to wait until tomorrow evening for the big reveal."

"I guess we will," Jonathan agreed as he snatched Marie into his arms. His lips went directly to the tender spot on her neck just below her earlobe. He knew exactly how to make her knees buckle.

"Did I mention we're having dinner tonight at Arianna's?" he asked.

"Your son-in-law's restaurant?"

"Yes. I know I promised you a romantic dinner, but Phoebe and Gwen insisted on joining us." He gazed into her eyes. "I hope you don't mind."

"Not at all." Marie replied honestly. "I'd love to spend some time with the girls this weekend. Will Veronica and her husband be there as well?"

"No, they're on the Cape scouting locations for another restaurant. They won't be home until late tonight." He tilted his head and tickled the tender spot beneath her other earlobe with the tip of his tongue. Goosebumps erupted on Marie's arms. She giggled.

"So, we'll attend the gala tomorrow evening. What shall we do during the day?" Jonathan's hand had worked its way under Marie's shirt. Her pulse quickened as his fingers slid up her side, then provocatively traced the lace design on her bra.

"Veronica scheduled late morning appointments for you both at her spa. She also said something about lunch."

"That's nice of her," Marie commented, although she had good reason to be suspicious of Veronica's intentions.

"She really is trying to become friends with you."

Jonathan may have believed his statement, but he hadn't convinced Marie. She understood that, as Veronica's father, Jonathan would naturally want to trust that his daughter meant well. Marie, however, could see right through Veronica's charade.

"When will you show me the photos of your trip to Alaska?"

"Later." He brushed his lips lightly across hers. "We'll have lunch on the terrace first."

"Mm...and what shall we do until lunch?"

"You didn't really just ask me that, did you?" he asked as he lowered her to the floor.

Chapter 27

Marie

Marie and Veronica arrived at the spa Saturday morning right on time for their ten o'clock appointments. Massages, facials, pedicures, manicures, hair stylings—the works. Veronica, who was familiar with the entire staff, introduced Marie in her own unique way: "The woman who's captured my father's eye." "I've honestly never seen him this infatuated." "And we've become such good friends!"

Yeah, right.

Marie kept up the pretense of being delighted by their new kinship, all the while remaining suspicious of what Veronica was *really* up to.

After a few hours of pampering, which Marie admitted were enjoyable despite having to share them with the Wicked Witch of the Woodwards, she returned to Jonathan's home prepared to resume her mission. She opened the front door and was greeted by the muted melody of a famous Broadway show tune. The notes increased in volume as she strolled through the house and entered the den. Jonathan paused his playing and glanced up from the piano.

"You're back," he said, unsmiling and surprisingly sullen. "How was your visit to the spa?" In the past, Jonathan never seemed to mind when Marie interrupted his piano sessions. However, he obviously didn't welcome her company right then.

"We had a wonderful time." She leaned forward and rested her elbows on the rim of the piano. "Veronica was a perfect hostess."

"I'm glad you enjoyed yourself." He lowered his gaze and continuing playing.

For the first time, Marie was uncomfortable in Jonathan's presence. Her intuition told her something unfortunate had happened while she was at the spa. For a fleeting moment, she worried Jonathan had rifled through her luggage and discovered Gus's forgeries, although she was certain she'd done absolutely nothing to raise his suspicion. Whatever the reason, she needed to understand what had caused his sudden change in behavior before she could proceed with the con.

"Jonathan, has something happened to upset you?" she asked. Jonathan stopped playing and stared at her with eyes that appeared to be searching for answers to questions he was reluctant to ask. Her brow furrowed with worry. "*Mon cher*, what is it?"

In an instant, sourpuss Jonathan disappeared. Flashing a big smile, he said, "I'm sorry. I received some news earlier that unnerved me, but I refuse to let it ruin our day."

"Would you like to talk about it?"

"No," he replied with a shake of his head. "It's nothing for you to be concerned about. If you don't mind, though, I would like to be alone for a while." Without waiting for Marie to respond, Jonathan placed his fingers on the piano keys and resumed playing.

Marie quietly stepped away. Upstairs in the bedroom, she changed into casual clothes then transferred the box containing Gus's replica of the Singing Bird Pistol from the camouflaged compartment of her suitcase to her shoulder bag. At some point that afternoon, she planned to talk Jonathan into opening his showcase. While admiring his collection, she'd create an opportunity to make the swap.

As she descended the stairs, Marie found the house to be unnervingly still. When the grandfather clock in the foyer chimed the top of the hour, she nearly jumped out of her skin. She easily located Jonathan in the same position at the piano, his hands resting idly in his lap, his expression pensive as he gazed out the window. She paused in the doorway to the den and studied him, attempting to make sense of his uncustomary moodiness. He became aware of her presence and rose from the piano bench with, thank goodness, a bright smile on his face.

"The last time you were here, I promised to explain how I obtained the other antiques in my showcase. Let's go into the library. I have a few interesting stories to share with you."

Well, that's a strange coincidence. "Funny, I was about to suggest the same idea myself," she said as an odd premonition washed over her.

Marie followed Jonathan across the house and down the hallway to his library, neither of them speaking. While he completed the process of opening his showcase, Marie stepped over to the windows and set her shoulder bag on the ottoman by the reading chair. Compelled to say something to break the awkward silence, she commented, "The weather should be perfect for tonight's gala."

"Yes, we really lucked out."

As the glass doors of the showcase were sliding open, Jonathan removed his phone from his pocket. He glanced at the screen and announced, "It's Will Carlson from the club."

Marie frowned and cocked her head. *Why didn't I hear Jonathan's cell phone ring? Am I too far across the room? No. Maybe he silenced his phone, although it's not like him to do that. Hmm...* She listened with concern to the conversation. From what she could surmise, a situation had surfaced that required Jonathan's attention.

"All right, Will," Jonathan said, ending the conversation. "I'll be there in fifteen minutes."

"Jonathan, is there a problem?" Marie feared a disaster—the electricity went out or, worse, the clubhouse had burned to the ground—resulting in the gala being cancelled. She was already dreaming up other tactics to get her hands on the Somerset Necklace.

"The only problem is my memory. I completely forgot I was expected at the club around this time to pay for the floral arrangements which are being delivered as we speak. I'm sorry, but I need to drive over to the club to settle our account with the florist."

"I understand," she assured him, relieved the event was still taking place. "These things happen."

"So much for our relaxing afternoon. I promise I won't be gone long." He gave Marie a quick kiss and rushed from the room.

Marie stood in the center of the library, her eyebrows raised in surprise. In his haste to leave, Jonathan had left his showcase open and his antiques exposed. A thief could enter the room, she conjectured with amusement, and wipe the shelves clean. Was it possible he trusted her so implicitly that he'd leave her alone with his collection valued in the millions?

She expected Jonathan to realize his error and return within seconds. She listened for his approaching footsteps, but the only sound she detected was the opening and closing of the front door followed by his car's engine roaring to life. Stepping down the hallway to the foyer, she glanced out the front window and viewed the brake lights on Jonathan's car as he eased out of the circular drive. She was alone in the house.

Dashing back into the library, Marie carefully removed the box containing the Singing Bird Pistol from Jonathan's showcase. "You, my sweet ticket to paradise, are about to change my life."

While crossing the room, Marie lightly caressed the second pistol-shaped indentation in the box's satin lining. Meant to house the Bird Pistol's twin counterpart, the space had been vacant for decades. What a remarkable coincidence, Marie mused. Just as these magnificent trinkets had been torn apart, so had she and her identical twin, Jacqueline, been separated for too many years. Stealing the Singing Bird Pistols from Jonathan and his son was an act of criminal and moral injustice, and Marie took no pleasure in being a felon. However, she would do anything to be joined again with her sister, even if she had to commit grand larceny to make that dream come true.

Thick as thieves from birth and indistinguishable from each other unless standing side by side, she and Jacqueline had supported each other through every high and low life tossed their way. When their father was whisked off to the Caribbean following his violent attack, they immediately formed a game plan: Jacqueline, with her degree in nursing, stayed with their father and attended to his medical needs while Marie remained in the States and tended to their financial needs. Whereas Jacqueline's income from her part-time job at a local clinic was helpful, the money Marie garnered from her cons paid for most of the family's living expenses. Jacqueline, grateful to her twin for shouldering such a dangerous undertaking, had offered to assist Marie whenever her help was needed. The few times Marie had requested that she return to New York and lend a hand, Jacqueline had proved to be surprisingly skillful. Dominic Ricci would be pleased that both his daughters' apples hadn't fallen far from the tree.

Marie had kept her sister in mind as she was working out the particulars of the Singing Bird Pistol job. Although running the con single-handedly would have been her preference, she had to be practical. She'd be stretching herself too thin if she attempted to divide her time between New York, Boston, and Connecticut. Enlisting her sister's aid for the Patrick Woodward piece of the scheme struck her as an ideal solution. With her easy-going, compassionate personality, Jacqueline was the perfect woman to charm her way into Patrick's heart and his home.

Marie had sent out the SOS to Jacqueline on the same evening she met with Gus in his basement workshop and received his stamp of approval to proceed with the Singing Bird Pistol con. Jacqueline accepted the assignment without hesitation and arrived in New York the following evening. Under Marie's close tutelage, Jacqueline created the persona of Kelsey Adams. By the end of the week, Patrick was already falling under her spell. So far, the twins' combined efforts had kept the con running as smooth as silk.

Marie closed the lid over the Singing Bird Pistol. While leaning over the ottoman to open her shoulder bag and make the swap, she detected a movement in the library's doorway. Her breath caught. Her eyes grew wide with terror.

"What are you doing?" Jonathan asked in a low, distrustful voice.

The next few seconds were a test of Marie's ability to remain calm, react spontaneously, and charm her way of out of a ruinous predicament. She glanced into her purse and identified the two most useful items: the box holding the fake Bird Pistol, and her cell phone.

She let out a startled scream and pretended his sudden reappearance caused her to drop the box holding the Singing Bird Pistol into her purse. "Jonathan, you scared me! Oh, no! I dropped the Singing Bird Pistol! If it's damaged, I'll never forgive myself." She thrust her hand into the bag and clutched the box Gus had crafted rather than the original.

Crossing the room, Jonathan asked, "Why did you remove my Singing Bird Pistol from the shelf?" His disapproving, accusatory glare stabbed Marie's heart.

Marie handed him the box containing the counterfeit Bird Pistol while, with her other hand, she subtly closed the opening of her shoulder bag. "It's so silly," she said, her eyes begging his forgiveness. When had she developed such an intense desire to please him? "I was just getting my phone out to take a selfie of me holding the Bird Pistol. I promise, I wasn't going to share the picture with anyone. The box honestly just slipped from my hand." Her chin quivered, and tears welled in her eyes.

"Come on, now, don't cry." Jonathan's suddenly

compassionate tone soothed Marie's nerves. She hadn't expected her meltdown to convince him she was just innocently having a bit of fun but, considering his behavior since she'd returned from the spa, nothing he did right now would surprise her. Jonathan opened the box and said, "See, the Bird Pistol is fine. If it makes you feel better, I'll wind the mechanism and make the bird pop out to prove there's no damage."

Is Jonathan taunting me? She had the impression he knew that simply threatening to wind the Bird Pistol was enough to panic her. *No, I'm being silly. This eerie sensation is all in my imagination.* Calmly, she told him, "No, Jonathan, don't bother. You're wonderful for understanding. I'm just being a worrywart."

"Well, at least let me take the picture you wanted," Jonathan said as he stepped toward her handbag. "I'll get your cell phone."

"You don't need to do that." Marie grabbed her handbag and slung it over her shoulder. "What would I do with such a silly photo anyway? Please, just put the box back on the shelf, and let's pretend this whole incident never happened."

Jonathan wiped a tear from her cheek and smiled tenderly at her before placing what he believed was his treasured antique on the shelf where it belonged. "There," he said, "no harm was done."

While Jonathan's back was to her, Marie closed her eyes and took a long, reassuring breath. She'd successfully dodged another bullet. "Don't you need to drive over to the club after all?" she asked.

"Yes, I still do, but I left without the checkbook for the account we use to pay the vendors." He pressed his thumb against the device on the showcase frame, initiating the closing of the glass doors. "I was at the end of the driveway when I realized I'd dashed out of the house without it." He stepped behind his desk and touched the security device mounted on the underside.

"It's a good thing you remembered when you did." Marie strolled closer to Jonathan as the showcase whirred closed and disappeared behind the wall panel.

"I know! Can you imagine how the guys at the club would have ridiculed me?"

Marie paid close attention as Jonathan opened the top drawer on the left side of his antique desk. The drawer was shorter than the length of the desk and for good reason. By extracting a long, thin tongue of wood imbedded into the frame supporting the underside of the drawer, Jonathan revealed a second drawer. From that hidden compartment, he removed a key which he inserted into the bottom drawer of his desk. At last, he'd arrived at the space where the checkbook was kept.

Marie had seen furniture like Jonathan's desk before, pieces that were built prior to the creation of wall safes and bank vaults. One drawer led to a secret compartment that oftentimes led to a third hidden section. Another small button in the intricate design would trigger the release of a false panel and expose the hidey-holes behind it. The furniture had been built centuries ago by expert craftsmen for their wealthy clients who needed places to secret away their valuables, important documents, and private letters.

After piecing the desk back together, Jonathan embarked on the journey to his club for a second time. "Well, I'm off. How will you spend the time while I'm gone?"

"I think I'll sit on the terrace and read my novel until

you return."

First, though, Marie had more important matters to tend to, such as removing the Singing Bird Pistol from her purse and hiding it deep inside her luggage. Jonathan wasn't the only person who had secret compartments in unexpected places.

Chapter 28

Marie

As Marie slithered into her evening gown, she worried she'd lost control of her con. Throughout the afternoon, her subtle efforts to get her hands on the Woodward heirloom necklace had been unsuccessful. She pictured Gus pacing the floor of his workshop while he anxiously awaited Roberto's arrival with the goods in hand, unaware that Marie was not yet one hundred percent certain the jewelry Jonathan promised to lend her for the evening was indeed the Somerset Necklace.

Jonathan rapped on the bedroom door. "Marie, are you ready to leave?"

"Almost," she called from the dressing room.

Marie stepped into the bedroom sheathed in a form-fitting sapphire blue evening gown. Thin shoulder straps led to a sweetheart neckline cut low enough to be revealing but not indecent. The back was scooped to her waist and the straight skirt was slit off-center to mid-thigh. The gown's wow factor was its brilliant color and its glittery, flowing material. Not to mention, the fabric clung to Marie's body like a second skin.

Standing before the cheval mirror, Marie leaned close to the glass as she fastened her sapphire and diamond earrings. "Can you help with the zipper?"

Dressed in his black tuxedo, Jonathan stood behind

Marie and accommodated her request. "There, all zipped up." Placing his hands on her shoulders, he eyed her silhouette in the mirror.

"Thank you, *mon cher*." Marie wriggled and ran her hand over the fabric to smooth out the creases. At last satisfied with her appearance, she glanced at Jonathan's reflection. No man had ever gazed at her with such enchanted desire in his eyes.

"You're absolutely stunning," Jonathan remarked with a tenderness that melted Marie's heart. She took a deep breath and reminded herself she could not allow her affection for Jonathan to interfere with the job.

"Do you really think so?" As if she doubted her appearance! "I was so focused on finding a gown in the right color to match my jewelry, I didn't consider what the other women would be wearing. Is this dress too risqué?"

"The gown is perfect on you, and I'm certain everyone at the club will have the same opinion. Now, about the necklace you wanted to borrow." He stepped around to face Marie and removed a long, flat jewelry box from his jacket pocket. "I hope you like this."

Marie glanced down, nervous with anticipation. Jonathan opened the lid and revealed an exquisite necklace designed with a double row of sapphires flanking a single row of diamonds that peaked downward in the center in imitation of the neckline on her gown. The necklace was a gorgeous and, Marie assumed, pricey piece of jewelry. However, to her great chagrin, what Jonathan held in his hands was not the Somerset Necklace.

"Like it?" she asked, hoping her mounting anxiety wasn't too obvious. "Why wouldn't I?"

Jonathan removed the necklace and tossed the empty case onto the upholstered chair next to the mirror. "Well, for starters, I can tell you're disappointed it's not the necklace you were expecting, but when I told Veronica of my intentions, she pitched a fit. I couldn't take the chance she'd create a scene at the gala tonight if I defied her and allowed you to wear a family heirloom." Standing behind Marie, he placed the necklace on her and fastened the clasp. "I'll come clean and admit I was treading in unfamiliar waters when I entered the jewelry store. I relied heavily on the saleswoman's assistance before making this purchase."

The jewels glistened against Marie's skin and were a striking complement to her gown. However, rather than delighting in her appearance, she could only envision Gus's intimidating client and imagine the danger she'd gotten them into because of the now strong possibility she would not deliver the Somerset Necklace as promised. Then, as her eyes wandered from the sparkling jewels to Jonathan's adoring reflection in the mirror, her brain processed what he'd said.

"You bought this necklace for me?"

"Yes, my love," he said, kissing her cheek. "Happy first month anniversary."

Gus's warning to not become personally involved with her target was screaming inside Marie's head. Normally, she paid heed to her mentor's advice, but tonight she chose to turn a deaf ear. Despite her best efforts to remain indifferent to Jonathan's repeated displays of affection, she could no longer deny herself the pleasure of losing her heart to the only man she was certain she would ever truly love.

****

The members of the planning committee for the gala which Jonathan chaired had been holding their breath all week in hopes the gorgeous summer weather would continue through Saturday. Luckily, the evening was warm with gentle breezes that glided wispy clouds across an otherwise clear sky. As the sun set and the pink hues on the horizon faded into midnight blue, the full moon and twinkling stars provided a romantic canopy for the event.

At the wooden sign indicating the entrance to The Burwood Club, Jonathan steered his luxury sedan off the main road and onto a winding lane that guided them past the manicured golf course and colorful, pristine gardens. Gradually, the historic clubhouse came into view. Painted a bright white, the two-story building's flat façade was covered with long, paned windows flanked by black shutters. Dormer windows and brick chimneys poked out from the roofline. A cupola topped with a weathervane capped off the structure.

Under the awning at the main entrance, Jonathan handed his car over to the valet. Marie accepted Jonathan's arm as they entered the clubhouse and ascended the grand staircase to the second floor. At the top of the stairs, they crossed the hall and stepped into the Terrace Room where the party was just getting underway.

Inside the venue, multiple rows of round tables clad in white linen covered the length and width of the room, each decorated with tall floral centerpieces and flickering candles. Yards of ivory-colored silk panels embellished with strands of miniature lights were draped in waves across the ceiling, giving the illusion of stars twinkling inside billowing clouds. In the far corner of the room, a pianist provided the pre-dinner entertainment.

After a final check with his planning committee, Jonathan was able to relax for the remainder of the evening. He placed his arm around Marie's back and nodded toward the bar. "I could use a drink right about now," he admitted.

With wineglasses in hand, Jonathan introduced Marie to his friends as they made their way around the room. Marie turned on the charm and engaged each new acquaintance in lighthearted conversation. Based on his friends' comments, she gathered Jonathan had bragged about her and was intent on proving he hadn't been telling tall tales. The new woman in his life was not a figment of his imagination, and she was indeed as enthralling as he'd led them to believe.

"I see Veronica and Brian have arrived," Jonathan told Marie. "Let's make our way over to them." He took Marie's hand and led her across the crowded room.

"There he is!" Brian called out as they approached. "Jon, it's good to see you."

"Hello, Brian," Jonathan said as he shook hands with his son-in-law. "Did you and Veronica just arrive?"

"We've been here long enough to hit the bar at least once," Brian replied with a chuckle and a raise of his whiskey glass. Ogling Marie from head to toe, he said, "Let me guess. You must be Marie. Jon's been talking non-stop about you for the last month."

Brian did not fit Marie's vision of the man who would complement Veronica's stature nor her personality. His short, compact body put him at eye level with his wife which explained Veronica's custom of always wearing low-heeled shoes. His ruddy complexion made Marie question whether he was afflicted with high blood pressure or was merely overheated in his tuxedo. He sported a goatee that was speckled with gray and, aside from his eyebrows, was the only patch of hair on his head. Unlike the milquetoast Marie assumed would be married to a domineering woman like Veronica, Marie's immediate impression was that Brian was an expert schmoozer who enjoyed working the room.

Jonathan smiled adoringly at Marie. "I won't deny Brian's accusation, although he may be exaggerating a little."

"Oh, no, I'm not," Brian insisted. "You rarely speak about anything else these days, and now I can see why." He offered his hand as a gesture of greeting and Marie followed suit. Instead of the expected handshake, however, Brian raised Marie's hand to his lips.

Marie giggled demurely, as if she were unaccustomed to men flirting with her. When Brian held her hand longer than she considered appropriate, Marie suspected he'd hit the bar in his den a few times before leaving the house. Perhaps alcohol, after all, was the primary cause for his reddened complexion.

"It's nice to meet you, Brian," Marie said in greeting. "I'm sorry you and Veronica couldn't join us at Arianna's last night."

"We're sorry we had to miss it. I trust you enjoyed your dinner?"

"Yes," Marie assured him as she politely disengaged her hand from his, "the food and the service were both excellent."

Veronica, having excused herself from the ladies she'd been chatting with, spun around to join in their conversation. "Good evening, Daddy," she said as she gave her father a kiss on the cheek. She then grasped

Marie's hand. "Marie, I've been telling everyone how much I enjoyed treating you to the spa today. Did Daddy introduce you to my husband, Brian?" Veronica stepped close to Brian and wrapped her arm possessively around his.

"Marie and I have met, but we're still working on getting acquainted," Brian said, raising a suggestive eyebrow at Marie. Marie feared, if she stood too close, Brian might salivate on her.

"Marie, your gown is gorgeous," Veronica patronized. "May I ask who the designer is?"

Marie attempted to lash back at Veronica in the same condescending manner, but the words caught in her throat. She was too mesmerized by Veronica's attire to speak. Fastened around Veronica's neck was an oval-shaped sapphire pendant from which hung a larger diamond pendant, both of which were attached to a glistening strand of intertwined diamonds and sapphires.

Veronica was wearing the Somerset Necklace.

Chapter 29

Marie

So, here I am, finally face-to-face with the, as Jonathan aptly described it, gaudy Somerset Necklace. Relieved, yes, but now my dilemma is how to get the necklace out of Veronica's clutches. I'm guessing I'd have better luck breaking into the Tower of London and stealing the Crown Jewels.

Isn't it sooooo Veronica to behave like a three-year-old whose parent caved in to her demands after she threw a temper tantrum? Any second now, I expect her to say "So, there!" and defiantly stick out her tongue.

All right. If Veronica thinks we're in a competition to win Jonathan's favor, I'll play along and let her believe she's won her imaginary contest. But make no mistake, those jewels will *be adorning my neck before this evening is over. If there's one thing I thrive on, it's a good challenge, and Veronica has no idea how cunning I can be.*

"Bremen's," Marie responded with subtle vindictiveness. She grasped Jonathan's hand and pressed up against him. Her body language sent the message that she could sway Jonathan to side with her in ways Veronica, as his daughter, would never have at her disposal.

"Excuse me?" Veronica half laughed, as if she

thought maybe Marie was joking.

"Bremen's," Marie repeated, louder and with crisper enunciation this time. "You know, the department store. I bought this gown off the rack. If I remember correctly, it was even on sale!"

Marie took malicious pleasure insinuating that she, unlike Veronica, didn't need to spend a fortune to look fabulous. Veronica's gown, in Marie's opinion, was an unflattering frock by anyone's standards and not worth whatever price Veronica had shelled out for it. The design lacked originality and the cut was all wrong, especially when draped on Veronica's pear-shaped body. And the color? Yuk! Was there even a name for such a lackluster shade of orange?

Grinning, Marie gave Veronica a wink. *Take that, Toots!* Veronica's cold, dagger-filled stare confirmed Marie's insult had hit its intended mark.

Round one of the evening's cat fight ended when a server approached to announce dinner was about to be served. As they took their places, Marie was relieved to find her name placard four chairs removed from Veronica's. Hopefully, they'd have no additional confrontations during dinner. An hour into the party and she'd already had her fill of drama for the evening.

The setting sun created a whimsical atmosphere inside the Terrace Room. As the sunlight faded and the miniature lights twinkling inside the swaths of fabric attached to the ceiling became more apparent, a celestial scene gradually appeared overhead. The piano music continued as the wait staff served each course in turn.

Throughout dinner, the men at the table delighted in recounting several shared experiences from their more youthful days, particularly those which included

Jonathan. Marie enjoyed their tales, but she couldn't ignore the glances of boredom exchanged between their wives whom, she guessed, were trapped into listening to those same stories at every gathering. And perhaps they were just a little irritated by their husbands' gregarious attempts to capture Marie's attention.

Marie kept up with the table chatter, but in the back of her mind she was creating different scenarios of how she could finagle the Somerset Necklace from Veronica. Her original plan, the one in which she wore the necklace to the gala, would have been simple to execute. While secluded inside one of the stalls in the ladies' room, she would have switched the necklaces and then handed the goods off to Roberto. Now, thanks to Veronica, her perfect plan had gone up in flames. Marie, however, would not allow a minor setback to unnerve her. Her conniving mind had kicked into high gear and devised an alternate plan in which she would seductively play on Jonathan's sympathies.

While the dessert plates were being cleared, the piano player exited, and a local cover band took the stage. Their dinner group broke up, and Jonathan introduced Marie to another couple she hadn't yet met. Although she pretended to be engaged in their conversation, her eyes darted around the room in search of Roberto. Before long, she noticed him standing near the terrace entrance to the ballroom.

Marie waited for Jonathan to finish his sentence before whispering into his ear, "I need to use the little girls' room."

Excusing herself, she scurried between the tables to give the impression she was headed in the direction of the ladies' room. As she neared the hallway, she darted behind a few people who were conversing near the bar. Using the group for cover, she scoured the room in search of anyone who might be watching her. In the dim light, her view was compromised, but she located Jonathan still chatting with the Sherwood couple and spotted Veronica and Brian swaying to a tender ballad on the dance floor.

Keeping to the edge of the room, Marie slinked around the clusters of partiers. She stepped onto the terrace where a handful of people were using the outdoor space for an after-dinner smoking break, and glimpsed Roberto's back as he descended the staircase. Clutching the wrought iron railing, she held up the hem of her gown and carefully negotiated the stairs in her heels.

"Over here," Roberto called out. The moonlight helped Marie locate him hiding in the shadows. "Quick! Give me the necklace so I can get back to New York," he nervously demanded.

"I wish I could, but it's not that simple," Marie told him, making sure to keep her voice low. She explained how Jonathan had succumbed to his daughter's demands and ruined her chance to swap out the necklaces during the soiree.

"Gus will be angry if he does not have the goods by midnight as you promised."

"No shit, Sherlock," Marie blurted out.

"This is not good," Roberto muttered under his breath. He tossed back the edge of his tuxedo jacket. Placing one hand on his hip, he lowered his head and scratched the back of his neck with his other hand.

Marie narrowed her eyes. *Why isn't Roberto behaving in his usual suave, easy-going manner? Maybe he had somewhere else to be and is annoyed Gus assigned him to this job. If so, he isn't going to be happy with my next suggestion.*

"All right, I get it," she said with irritation. "Listen, I have an alternate plan, and I'm ninety-nine percent sure I'll have the necklace by tomorrow morning. But, in order to get the necklace to Gus, I need to know if you can stay in town overnight."

Roberto stared at the ground and sighed heavily. Marie wasn't sure how to read him. He appeared antsy, almost frightened, rather than just bothered by the last-minute change of plans. She was about to ask him what his problem was when he responded.

"Yes, I will, if I have to."

"Good. I'll call you by nine o'clock tomorrow morning and let you where we can meet for the hand off. And tell Gus not to worry. I've never let him down before, and I certainly don't intend to start now." Marie prayed no further unexpected situations would interfere with that promise. Assuming their conversation had ended, she started toward the staircase.

Roberto grabbed her arm. "Wait! Gus also told me to report back to him about the singing parakeet job."

Marie was familiar enough with Roberto to giggle over his misnomer. "I'm sorry. I shouldn't laugh. They're called Singing Bird Pistols, Roberto, and there are two of them. Tell Gus I'll turn over one of the Bird Pistols to him tomorrow. We should have the other by the end of the week."

"Are you sure you have this job under control?"

Marie frowned and cocked her head, her skepticism rising another notch. Roberto had never been so concerned about a job that didn't benefit him directly, but she couldn't waste her time worrying about it.

"Yes, Roberto, I'm handling things just fine. Now, let go of my arm so I can return to the party before I'm missed."

As Marie hurried up the concrete staircase, the smell of cigar smoke wafted in her direction and conjured up childhood memories of the many Ricci family gatherings at which her father and his male relatives would huddle around the table to share their bottles of wine and puff on their pungent stogies. Although she'd never acquired a fondness for the odorous tobacco, she always found their comradery to be endearing.

A few steps higher but still in the shadows she was within earshot of the cigar smokers' conversation. The men were speaking frankly about her, unaware Marie was standing on the stairs below them.

"Did you get a load of that delectable beauty old Jonny Woodward's with tonight?" one of the men asked. His question prompted a whistled response from another man in the group.

"Sweet Jesus," a different voice replied. "Talk about winning the lottery!"

"Is that the woman he's been talking about all summer?" another man asked.

"If her name's Marie, then she's the one."

"How about that French accent? Ooo, la-la!"

"No wonder he's been wearing that shit-eating grin lately," a voice that sounded like the first man's chimed in. "Can you imagine jumping into bed with that body tonight?"

Before their discussion became any cruder, Marie climbed the remaining steps. The repartee ended when a few of the men noticed her. Within seconds, every man in their circle appeared to have been caught with his hand in the cookie jar.

"Gentlemen," she said in greeting to the group as she smiled and sauntered past.

Even though her back was to them and she was several feet away, Marie overheard one of the men pose a question which she was certain was meant only for his friends' ears. "Do you think she's wearing anything underneath that dress?"

Marie lips curled into a sly grin. *Only Jonathan will ever know.* Distracted by her game of enticement, she didn't notice Veronica lurking in the shadows along the terrace railing.

"Marie!" Veronica called out.

The mere sound of Veronica's voice caused Marie's blood to boil. *Poor Brian, jilted by a wife who'd rather spy on my activities than enjoy a romantic dance with her husband. Well, here we go again!* She swiveled around to face her nemesis.

"Veronica, what are you doing out here all by yourself?" she asked pleasantly. She couldn't risk appearing suspicious, despite what Veronica may have witnessed or overheard while peering over the railing.

"Never mind what I'm doing. Who were you talking with on the lower patio?"

Marie should have known she couldn't escape Veronica's eagle eye as she slinked away to meet with Roberto. She was now certain the friendliness Veronica extended at the spa that morning was just an act. The witch had adopted the strategy of keeping her friends close and her enemies closer.

Marie shrugged her shoulders, sloughing off her meeting with Roberto. "Just a gentleman I've known for several years."

"Really? What a strange coincidence you'd know someone who's a member of a private club this far away from New York City."

"It's not that unusual. In my line of work, I assist people from all over the world."

"Where did your friend go? I'd like to meet him."

Marie needed to put an end to Veronica's inquisition. "Veronica, is there a reason you followed me out here?"

"I just wondered where you were going all by yourself." Veronica then transitioned to her next point of contention. "So, is that the necklace my father bought you? He's been fretting for days over whether you'd be pleased."

"Yes, he presented me with this necklace while I was dressing." Touching the necklace, Marie smiled contentedly as she recalled Jonathan's sentimental recognition of their first month as a couple. A few times in the past, she'd proclaimed she was in love, but she never understood what true love was until she met Jonathan. "Jonathan shouldn't have worried. I would cherish any gift from him, no matter what it was."

"My father does have excellent taste. But you must be disappointed that he'd promised you'd be wearing one of our most treasured family heirlooms this evening." Veronica ran her fingers over the Somerset Necklace as if mocking Marie.

"I could never be disappointed in your father," Marie said. "Presenting me with this necklace is just another way of showing how much he cares for me. Besides, I'm sure I'll have opportunities in the future to wear your family heirloom."

Is it wrong of me to enjoy being so vicious? If the

snarl on Veronica's face is any indication, then yes.

"Mark my words," Veronica threatened, her voice guttural. Marie took a precautionary step backward, just to be safe. "The day you wear a necklace that once belonged to *my mother* will be the day I'm laid in my grave."

Marie let Veronica's venomous warning hang between them for a moment. "Let's not forget that necklace doesn't belong to you, Veronica, so you don't decide who gets to wear it, and when."

Round two of their cat fight ended abruptly when Jonathan stepped onto the terrace.

"There you two are," he said. "Did you step outside to get some fresh air and engage in a little girl-talk?"

In the blink of an eye, Veronica's demeanor flipped. "Daddy, you have perfect timing. I was telling Marie that my girls are upset they can't spend more time with her while she's in town. I had just invited you both to brunch at our house tomorrow."

What the…?!

"That's awfully nice of you and Brian," Jonathan told Veronica. "But, Marie, didn't you say you need to return to New York in the morning?"

Hmm…I intend to have the Somerset Necklace in my possession before the end of the evening. However, if my plan to sway Jonathan fails, then being inside Veronica's home will provide me with a backup plan. Delivering the necklace to Gus might be delayed, but late is always better than never, right?

Marie wrapped her arm around Jonathan's back and switched on the charm. "If you're able to change the time of my flight, I'd be delighted to attend the brunch before I return home. Thank you for the invitation, Veronica.

I'm so happy we've become friends."

****

Toward the end of the evening, Marie invited Jonathan to slow dance with her on the terrace.

"This reminds me of dancing under the stars with you on our first night together," Jonathan whispered into her ear.

"Mm…what a wonderful night that was." Her fingertips toyed with the back of his neck, the spot where the shirt collar met his skin.

Jonathan tightened his hold. "Every night spent with you is wonderful." After a few moments, he said, "You and Veronica weren't really talking about Sunday brunch earlier, were you?"

"No, we weren't."

Jonathan sighed. "I saw the expression on Veronica's face and knew she was on the attack. Do you mind telling me what you were discussing?"

Marie hesitated, to make it appear as if she were reluctant to share the conversation with him. "We were talking about her necklace."

"Let me guess. She couldn't get through the evening without making sure you were aware she'd shamed me into giving in to her."

"You know your daughter all too well."

Jonathan gazed into Marie's eyes as he spoke. "Marie, honestly, I was just trying to keep peace in the family."

Marie gave Jonathan her best pout. "I understand."

"I've made a mess of things. I have the impression you don't care for the necklace I bought you."

"Don't say that, Jonathan. I adore this necklace."

His eyes filled with concern. "But…?"

"I understand she's your daughter and blood is thicker than water, but it doesn't change the fact that you've hurt my feelings."

Jonathan held her close. "I'm sorry, sweetheart. I promise you, I'll make things right."

Marie smiled faintly at her *fait accompli*. Jonathan had, once again, fallen right into her trap.

Chapter 30

Marie

Alone in Jonathan's bedroom, Marie kicked off her shoes and tossed her earrings onto the dresser. Her mind was preoccupied, and she was vaguely aware of Jonathan's presence as he scuttled about on the first floor. She wasn't sure what he was doing, but then neither did she care. He had not "made things right" as he'd promised, and now her alternate plan had fallen to pieces.

Perhaps she'd misinterpreted Jonathan's intentions. She assumed he would speak with Veronica and insist she relinquish the Somerset Necklace to him before the gala ended. Then, alone with Jonathan in his home, Marie would create a way to swap the necklace for the forgery and the most difficult part of her con would be accomplished.

Instead, she stood by with a scowl on her face as the Lamberts said their good-nights and sped away in their sports car with the jewels still clinging to Veronica's neck. Marie was irritated with herself for failing to manipulate Jonathan and annoyed with him for not taking the bait. For the remainder of the evening, she'd barely spoken for fear she'd lash out in anger and regret her words later.

Then, as she unclasped the necklace Jonathan had

given her to mark their first-month anniversary, her dismal mood melted away. She admired the strands of sparkling diamonds and sapphires and was reminded this gift was yet another sign of his deep affection for her. All at once, the source of her frustration became crystal clear. She wasn't upset with Jonathan, the man who proclaimed his love for her, nor was she furious with Veronica, the control freak who couldn't keep her nose out of her father's affairs. When she boiled it all down, Marie was forced to admit she was angry with herself for the crimes she'd plotted against Jonathan and for having tricked him into believing her self-serving lies.

In all her previous jobs, Marie had regarded the men she targeted as nothing more than objects, a necessary means to an end. They in turn treated her as a passing fling to enjoy while their time together lasted. After so many years of being caught up in a constant cycle of brief, meaningless interludes, Marie had trained her heart and mind to expect nothing more from a relationship than for it be short-lived and noncommittal.

Then, she met Jonathan. The fact they'd both taken passes on romance in the past proved to Marie that destiny had intervened to ensure they found each other. Sadly, though, the reality of the situation couldn't be ignored. Marie had dug herself too far into this con to imagine anything other than one of two outcomes: she either hurt Jonathan, or she put Gus in jeopardy. As much as she regretted betraying Jonathan, her allegiance to Gus remained her priority.

Marie became aware of muted voices in the foyer and the sound of the front door closing, then rushed footsteps on the stairs. A moment later, Jonathan entered the bedroom with his hands held behind his back.

"Were you talking with someone just now?" she asked.

"Yes. Brian was at the door."

Marie raised an eyebrow, her curiosity piqued. "Brian? Why was he here?"

"I spoke with him earlier and told him if I didn't soon make things right with you, I'd be banished to the guest room tonight. He understood my predicament and drove over to deliver this." Jonathan revealed the jewelry box he'd been concealing behind his back. He opened the lid and, to Marie's great relief, exposed the Somerset Necklace.

"Oh, Jonathan!" she gasped. "That's the necklace Veronica wore to the gala."

"Yes, it is," Jonathan replied as he placed the necklace on Marie. "I wanted to prove to you I'm a man of my word. A few weeks ago, I promised you could wear this necklace tonight. I know it's late, but the evening isn't over yet."

"You do know you're the most wonderful man in the world, don't you?" Marie hugged and kissed Jonathan, then crossed the room to stand before the cheval dressing mirror. She'd mistakenly assumed the necklace would be more attractive on her than it had been on Veronica. However, her first impression was a lasting one, and she wondered why Gus's buyer was so anxious to purchase such an outdated, garish piece of jewelry. As Jonathan approached her, she invented an apology for her behavior at the gala. "I'm sorry for acting like a child earlier," she said demurely. "I was jealous you'd favored Veronica over me."

Jonathan stood behind her and kissed the side of her neck while his fingers trailed down her back, grasping the zipper on her dress along the way. "You don't owe me any apologies. Besides, the necklace is all yours now."

One corner of Marie's mouth curled ever so slightly. If only Jonathan knew how true his comment was.

Staring at their reflections in the mirror, Marie was mesmerized as she watched Jonathan slowly and methodically seduce her. Every nerve in her body exploded with pleasure as his kisses travelled down her neck. He slid the strap of the gown off her shoulder. She angled her face to the right and spoke softly into his ear. "Perhaps you should put the necklace back in its case for safekeeping."

"I thought you'd want to wear it a while longer." He held her hair up as his lips brushed along the back of her neck. He kissed her other shoulder and guided the strap of the gown down her left arm.

"But, *mon cher*," she pouted enticingly, "I'm tired of being all dressed up."

Jonathan placed his hands onto Marie's hips and slid them forward under the gown's glittery fabric. "You misunderstood me. I didn't say anything about keeping your dress on."

****

When Marie was certain Jonathan had fallen asleep, she disentangled her body from his and inched away, making sure the Somerset Necklace she was still wearing didn't catch on the bedding. As Jonathan mumbled something unintelligible and rolled onto his side, she slipped out from under the covers and slinked across the bedroom. She opened the dressing room door just wide enough to squeeze through the opening. Her movement activated the overhead lights.

Lifting the lid of her suitcase, she opened the same concealed compartment where she'd hidden the Bird Pistol yesterday afternoon. Removing a soft cloth bag, she unfastened the drawstring, held the bag up by its bottom end, and shook out the fake necklace Gus had so expertly crafted. Setting those items on top of the dresser, she attempted to blindly unhook the Somerset Necklace.

The clasp proved to be more difficult to negotiate than she'd anticipated. Its old-fashioned design was tricky and one she wasn't accustomed to handling. She hurried to the full-length mirror affixed to the wall and twisted the necklace around so she could determine how the mechanism worked. After a few failed attempts, the clasp at last released. Tiptoeing back to her suitcase, Marie was unexpectedly consumed with guilt. She'd fretted for weeks over not being able to obtain the necklace. Now that it was in her hands, she questioned whether she could go through with the job.

A month ago, when she and Gus concocted their scheme, she hadn't anticipated falling in love with her target. Since meeting Jonathan, she'd shed the hard-hearted, deceitful persona she hid behind in order to perform the deeds required of an expert con artist. Jonathan had awakened her conscience and made her realize it was time to right her wrongs.

So, what are you going to do? Follow your heart and sacrifice the job in deference to the man you love, or stick with the plan out of loyalty to Gus?

Marie had lingered in the dressing room long enough for her absence to be noticed. "Marie? Are you all right?" Jonathan's groggy voice called out.

"Yes, I'm fine," she replied. Time had run out and

she had to make a choice. She guided the Somerset Necklace into the empty cloth pouch with great care, tightened the drawstring closure, and secured the bag inside the secret luggage compartment. She returned to the bedroom where she placed the fake necklace inside the jewelry box sitting on Jonathan's dresser. She hated herself for taking advantage of Jonathan, but the deed was done. From now on, she'd block out all thoughts of the Somerset Necklace.

She slid under the covers and snuggled up against him. "Go back to sleep, *mon cher*."

"Mm…" Jonathan groaned. Within seconds, he was breathing soundly again.

Marie lay awake most of the night and watched Jonathan while he slept. She needed to cherish every remaining moment with him. Tomorrow, after they said farewell, she'd never see him again.

Chapter 31

Marie

Marie set her running shoes and mini backpack on the floor as she sat next to Jonathan on the piano bench. "You're playing awfully early this morning," she said.

"Just taking advantage of some free time while I have it." Jonathan nudged Marie closer and kissed her cheek. "Where are you off to?"

"I'm going for a short run before we leave for Veronica and Brian's. Last night's meal wasn't the healthiest, and I'm expecting brunch to be more of the same. A run will justify my fall from grace this weekend."

"I envision an extra-long workout session today myself. I'd join you on your run, but I'm needed at the club in half an hour."

"That's okay. I don't mind running alone." In truth, Marie's run was merely an excuse to rendezvous with Roberto and hand off the Somerset Necklace. She pecked a kiss on Jonathan's lips, then slid her arms through the straps of her backpack.

Jonathan partially unzipped the main compartment. "What do you have in here?"

Marie jumped away from Jonathan as though he were coming at her with a branding iron.

"Jonathan, please, you'll make everything fall out,"

she reprimanded. "I just packed a water bottle and my cell phone." *…and the Somerset Necklace I stole from you.*

"Are you sure you wouldn't rather use the equipment in my exercise room? It's supposed to start raining soon."

"Thanks for the offer but, rain or shine, I'd rather run in the fresh air. Besides, I won't be going far."

Outside, Marie sat on a wooden bench positioned near the front door while she slipped on her running shoes. She then removed the phone from her backpack and placed a call to Roberto.

"I'll be at the coffee shop in ten minutes." She didn't need to say anything more. All the details had been discussed during their call earlier that morning while Jonathan was showering.

"I'm already waiting for you," Roberto replied.

****

Marie slowed her pace as she approached the coffee shop. Through a side window, she spotted Roberto. He nodded his head to acknowledge her and rose from the table. After entering the store, Marie located the hallway leading to the restrooms. Checking the ladies' room to make sure it was unoccupied, she stepped inside. A visibly agitated Roberto followed her.

"It's ten o'clock," he said tersely. "We were supposed to meet an hour ago."

Marie scolded him in a near-whisper as she locked the door. "Keep your voice down. I told you I'd call by nine o'clock, not meet you at nine. Why are you so anxious?"

"I could be halfway to New York by now if you hadn't spent the morning screwing your rich boyfriend."

Roberto was standing so close to Marie, a few drops of his spittle landed on her face.

"What is up with you?" Marie grimaced with disgust as she grabbed a paper towel and wiped her cheek dry. "It's Sunday. You'll get into the city in no time." Tossing the paper towel, she set her backpack on the platform intended as a baby changing station and removed the pouch that held the Somerset Necklace. "Here's the necklace. Tell Gus I'm sorry for inconveniencing him."

Roberto slid the pouch into the inside pocket of his jacket. "When are you going back to New York?"

Marie stepped over to the sink to wash her hands. "In a few hours. I'm having brunch with my target's family first, then I'll fly back by chartered plane this afternoon."

"But the job is over," he said. "Why are you staying around?"

Because I need to cling to my every remaining moment with Jonathan. She dried her hands and sidestepped the truth. "Just keeping up appearances so my 'rich boyfriend' doesn't suspect anything."

Roberto grabbed Marie by the shoulders and forced her to face him. "Don't be blinded by your feelings for this man. While you're misleading him, don't be so sure he isn't tricking you."

Marie glared at Roberto. Where did he get off insulting her ability to be in control of her job? Hadn't they worked together long enough for him to realize she had Jonathan eating out of her hand?

"Don't worry about me," she snapped as she shrugged away his hand. "I know what I'm doing." She unlocked and opened the door a crack to make sure the coast was clear. "Deliver the necklace to Gus at the shop and tell him I'll see him tonight when I get back to the city."

****

The SUV idled in front of the Lambert's home as Jonathan and Marie stood under an umbrella and said their good-byes in the pouring rain.

"Are you certain you'll be free to join me in Connecticut later this week for my grandson's birthday celebration?"

"Yes, I'll be there." *Liar, liar, pants on fire!* The reality was, as soon as the proceeds from the sales of the Woodward treasures were deposited into her offshore accounts, Marie would be off to the Caribbean. She'd be celebrating a reunion with her own family while the Woodwards gathered for little Oliver's birthday. All at once, her long-anticipated dream of being rejoined with her family was overshadowed by her intense desire to remain with Jonathan.

Jonathan kissed Marie and told her tenderly, "I love you with all my heart."

"I love you, too, Jonathan." The sentiment flowed from Marie's lips with passion and sincerity while, at the same time, her heart ripped in half. Despite Jonathan's plans for their future, once she climbed into the SUV, their relationship would be over. As Jonathan drew her close, she cherished what she assumed was their final embrace.

****

Marie was not in the mood to flirt with the pilots during her flight home that afternoon. The moment she'd been dreading had arrived. Her affair with Jonathan was history, and the heartache was greater than she'd imagined. As she wiped the constant stream of tears from her cheeks, she used the time to examine who she was and, more importantly, the type of person she wanted to be from that moment forward. She couldn't undo the many offenses she'd committed since adopting the persona of Marie Lacroix; those crimes would remain secrets she'd take to her grave. However, she could choose to conduct herself with integrity going forward.

At once, Marie made the snap decision to put the past behind her and return to being the decent person she'd ignored for the past eleven years, the woman she was itching to be once again. Her conscience would not allow her to inflict any further wrongdoing against a man who vowed his love for her and included her in his dreams for the future. To her dismay, she couldn't stop the sale of the Somerset Necklace as the jewels were already in the hands of Gus's black-market buyer. However, she could stop the half-completed con involving the Singing Bird Pistols.

Jacqueline would be irritated that she'd devoted so much time and effort to a job that ultimately reaped no reward, but she'd get over it. Gus, on the other hand, would be furious. Marie would need to be her most convincing to make him understand why she was no longer willing to finish this job which she'd intended to be her swan song anyway.

Her decision wasn't made lightly. Throughout the plane ride, Marie weighed the pros and cons. By the time the plane touched down in New York, she was convinced she was doing the right thing. After a quick stop at her apartment, she'd go to Gus and persuade him to inform his buyer that the deal with the Singing Bird Pistols had been called off.

Chapter 32

Marie

Marie let herself into the antique shop and secured the lock from the inside. The space was dark and eerily quiet.

"Gus?" she called out. "Where are you?"

Gus's barely audible response rose from his cavernous workshop. "Down here."

Marie descended the staircase and found Gus surrounded by open cardboard boxes, many filled with items he'd displayed on his shelves and workbench for as far back as she could remember. "What are you doing?"

"Getting ready to move," he told her. "I'm leaving behind the tools Christopher needs to keep the business open. Everything else is either going with me or being pitched."

"You're not keeping your autographed baseball from the 2009 championship game?" She'd removed the relic enclosed in its plastic display case from the box sitting on the workbench.

"Be careful with that," Gus warned her sharply. "Of course, I'm keeping that baseball, but it needs to be bubble wrapped before I seal up the box."

Marie carefully replaced the baseball and apologized. "Sorry."

With the sale of the Somerset jewels behind them, Marie imagined Gus would have welcomed her with open arms and a glass of champagne. She had not expected to find him in a grumpy mood, boxing up his belongings as if he were a dictator fleeing his overthrown country. Last night, Roberto had been out of sorts. Today, Gus was having his turn. If something unfortunate had occurred while she was out of town, why wasn't Gus sharing the news with her?

"Did you finalize the sale of the Somerset jewelry to the client's satisfaction?"

"Yes," Gus said sharply, as though she were interrupting his concentration on matters of more importance. "The money's in the safe. I'll start laundering it in the morning."

Marie and Gus had previously calculated their take of the $2 million sale. After giving the rest of the crew a cut for the parts they played in pulling off the deal, she and Gus would walk away with $950,000 each. They'd hold some back in cash. The rest would be funneled through the antique store and their various other semi-legitimate businesses before being wired to their offshore accounts.

Marie took a deep breath and considered how to broach the subject of the Singing Bird Pistols. Alone in her apartment, she'd rehearsed her speech and had arrived at the antique shop convinced she was doing what was best, but the sight of Gus boxing up his belongings laid a serious guilt trip on her. Gus had been planning this move to the Caribbean for years and his dream was finally coming true. Her announcement would not sit well with him, especially when he was already in a sour mood. She hoped to soften the blow with a little help from Max's Deli. Gus's response, however, lacked the enthusiasm he'd shown the last time she brought him a pastrami on rye.

"Can you take a break? I stopped at Max's on my way over."

Gus glanced at her over his shoulder as he leaned two picture frames against the workbench. "Set it down. I'll eat when I get around to it."

Marie placed the paper tote bag on a stool and unpacked the take-out containers.

"Where's Jacqueline? I thought she was meeting us here."

"Right now, Jacqueline should be boarding a plane headed for Santa Martina," he said while tossing a broken screwdriver into the trash.

"She's going home?" Marie asked with alarm.

"Well, since Santa Martina is where she lives..." Gus responded testily, leaving the remainder of his sentence hanging in the air. He pried open a flattened shipping box and began folding its flaps together to ready it for packing.

Marie immediately assumed the worst. "Why? Did something happen to my father? Oh, God! It's not my nonna, is it?"

"Don't worry. Dominic and your grandmother are fine." With the box fully assembled, he began to fill it with books he had stacked on the workbench. "Jacqueline called her boss this morning to ask for more time off work. Since she's already been gone for three weeks, he wasn't too pleased with her request. He told her if she doesn't show up for her shift tomorrow, she could look for employment elsewhere. Maybe you should have considered the position you were putting your sister in before you let this job drag on for so long."

"Oh, so it's all my fault we're still working this con?" Marie replied defensively, her voice raised a notch. "You have a part in this too, you know. If you'd turned over the fake Bird Pistols to me sooner than last Friday—"

"Don't try to spin this," he growled, pointing an accusatory finger at Marie. "You've gone soft on this Woodward guy. You could have wrapped up this job by now if you'd wanted to. Roberto told me you already have one of the Bird Pistols."

"I do," Marie confirmed. What she left unsaid was that she intended to return the Singing Bird Pistol she'd taken from Jonathan as soon as she figured out a stealthy way to do so.

Gus continued packing the stack of books while he barked out his demands. "Then you'll just have to swap out the other pistol yourself, and make sure the job's done by this time tomorrow."

"Are you serious? You expect me to just march into Patrick Woodward's home pretending to be Kelsey Adams?" Marie's goal was to manipulate the conversation in such a way as to convince Gus the logical decision was to call off the Bird Pistol job all together. Getting Gus to come to this conclusion himself was much more advantageous than announcing she'd decided on her own to cancel the con for no other reason than that she'd fallen in love with her target.

"Why not? You look enough like Jacqueline to dupe anyone into believing you're her. Just put on a dark wig and lose the blue contacts."

"Come on, Gus. It's going to take more than just looking the part to convince Patrick Woodward I'm the same person. Maybe we should face the fact that this job *is* taking too long. Like you taught me, the longer the job takes, the riskier—"

"Damn it!" Gus shouted as he kicked the chair sitting beside him. The chair fell over and hit the tiled floor with a loud crash.

"What the hell, Gus?" Marie exclaimed, startled by his angry outburst.

Gus pounded his fist on the workbench. "No more excuses and no more delays! You don't understand the situation we're in."

An unfamiliar voice coming from the stairs behind Marie suddenly chimed in. "Whoa-ho-ho," the stranger chuckled. "Looks like we might have to step in and separate you two."

Marie's eyes locked on Gus, his alarmed expression echoing her own. They swiveled around to find three men descending the staircase, all well-groomed in dark suits and dress shirts, their muscular physiques defined by the trim cut of their jackets.

Gus grabbed a hammer from his workbench and raised it defensively. "How did you get in here?"

"Put the hammer down," the man in the center, who appeared to be the group's spokesperson, ordered. His smile was friendly, but his eyes told a different story. "We're just here to have a nice little chat with you." Then, to his associates, he commanded, "Frisk them."

Thug #1, the burly yet smaller of the man's two companions, approached Marie with a menacing sneer and shoved her face forward against the cold cement wall. She fought the urge to thrust her elbow into his throat as he groped her body in search of hidden weapons. Craning her neck to glimpse across the room, she observed Gus being given the same pat-down by Thug #2.

After being deemed harmless, Marie was released. She spun around to face their intruders.

"Who are you?" she asked the group's leader.

"Whoa, hold up," the head honcho responded, his speech laden with a thick Brooklyn accent. "One question at a time." He sauntered over to Gus's workbench and, perusing the take-out containers, selected a dill pickle. "How'd we get in? Some guy named Roberto was nice enough to unlock the door for us." He paused to crunch into the pickle, his finger catching a stream of juice that trickled down his chin. "You wanna know who we are? We work for the man who's purchasing the Singing Bird Pistols from you."

"Why are you here?" Marie wasn't sure what she would accomplish by pummeling him with questions, but at least she was buying herself some time to assess their situation.

"Ah! Finally, you ask the most important question." The man leaned his back against the workbench as he spoke. "My employer is getting restless. You see, he plans to present these Singing Bird Pistols to his daughter at her sixteenth birthday party which is in just a few days. He expected to have the goods by now, so he sent me and my friends to find out why you, Gus Ferguson, haven't made the delivery yet. Now, from the argument you two were just having, I take it you're still missing half the package because *somebody's* got a case of cold feet." He sighed regretfully and shook his head. "I'm here to tell you, my employer ain't gonna be happy when I call him with this status update. He might ask me to…oh, let's call it *demonstrate*…just how serious he takes his business transactions." He chomped another bite, and said, "Thanks for the pickle, by the way."

Marie stole a moment to scrutinize the other two men who were standing like sentries at the bottom of the stairs. Thug #1, his arms folded defiantly across his chest, squinted at Marie with eyes she imagined had witnessed their fair share of unsavory *demonstrations*. Thug #2, who was taller and beefier than his companions, stood with his hands clasped in front of him and maintained a blank facial expression which, Marie was convinced, reflected the level of activity in his brain. She assumed he was there for his brute force, not for his intellectual counsel.

"Demonstrate how?" Gus asked, his voice strained with tension.

Head Honcho shoved the last of the pickle into his mouth and licked his fingers. "Well, for example," he replied, smacking his lips as he chewed and talked at the same time, "I'm guessing an old building like this probably has some real faulty wiring. Just the kinda thing that could make the place go up in flames overnight. That'd be a real shame, wouldn't it?"

Marie seized the opportunity to negotiate. "Wait! Nothing that drastic needs to happen. I'm sure we can work this out."

"Far as I'm concerned, pretty lady, there ain't nothing to work out," the man snapped in response. "My employer ain't gonna disappoint his daughter, so you got no choice but to make good on your end of the bargain. And, believe me, I can make it so you two have a lot worse things to worry about than a burned down building." He unbuttoned his suit jacket and edged one side back far enough to expose the holster he had strapped to his shoulders.

Marie exchanged horrified glances with Gus. How could this deal have gone so terribly awry? For years, they'd carried out their jobs without a hitch. When she picked up the fake Bird Pistols just two days ago, Gus gave her no indication their buyer had upped the deadline. Something had changed since Friday, something that would explain why Gus was so irritable.

"Gus," Marie said through gritted teeth, "what have you done?"

"I'm sorry, doll," Gus began, his eyes begging forgiveness. "I made a mistake. The deal was all set. Then, out of the blue, I was contacted by another interested buyer who offered two million more. All I saw were dollar signs. My first buyer wouldn't match the new offer, so I reneged on my deal with him and agreed to sell to the new guy without investigating who I was doing business with. Everything was fine until the new buyer called again and demanded that we close the deal right away. When I explained we needed another week, he threatened me. If we didn't deliver the pistols in the next few days, he said he'd make it so we'd never be able to work again. I'm sorry. I never meant to put us in danger."

Marie couldn't be mad at Gus for making a bad decision; she'd made plenty of them herself. Stealing the Singing Bird Pistols was her idea in the first place, and they wouldn't be in this dire situation right now if she hadn't also been blinded by dollar signs. She could only hope, by negotiating and meeting the buyer's demands, they would all reach a mutually satisfying outcome.

"Well, Gus, my friend," Head Honcho commented, "it sounds like you've learned a lesson. But that don't change matters on my end. My friends and I ain't leaving without the items we were sent here to collect, so I'd suggest you start thinking real hard about how you two are gonna resolve this situation."

Marie took a deep breath and prayed the offer she was about to make would appease their intruders. "Listen, there's no reason this needs to get ugly. I already have one of the Singing Bird Pistols there in my bag. Take it as a good will offering and give me a few days to deliver the second one."

The man smirked. "Now that's the kinda positive attitude that gets the job done. Where's your bag?"

"There, on the workbench," Marie said as she pointed to her purse. "The Bird Pistol is inside a wooden box."

He rummaged through Marie's purse, removed the box containing the Bird Pistol, and set it on the workbench. Lifting the lid, he grasped the Bird Pistol with his fingertips and wound the mechanism to trigger the device until the bird shot from the end of the barrel. "Ain't that cute?" he chuckled with amusement. Replacing the Bird Pistol inside the box, he announced his decision.

"Ms. Lacroix, is it?" Head Honcho asked. Marie nodded her head in confirmation. "Okay, Ms. Lacroix. You got until three o'clock Wednesday afternoon to deliver the second Bird Pistol. My pal, Jimmy, will stay with you that whole time." He strolled over to Gus and placed his arm around Gus's shoulder. "While you're doing what you gotta do, me and Chuey are gonna hang out here and keep an eye on our new friend, Gus." He patted Gus's cheek with his free hand. "Now, looking at Chuey, you can tell he's big enough to do some serious damage, and dumb enough to do whatever I tell him. I suggest you take that as a warning, Ms. Lacroix. Should you try to trick us, or if you don't deliver the goods by the deadline, there's no telling what I might have Chuey do. You get my drift?"

"Yes, I do." Marie's eyes darted back and forth between Gus and Head Honcho, her heart pounding in her chest as the gravity of the task she faced came crushing down on her.

"Good." Head Honcho nodded his head toward Marie, and commanded, "Jimmy, get her outta here. Now!"

Jimmy crossed the room, grabbed Marie by the arm, and dragged her toward the staircase before she had time to process what was happening.

"Wait!" Marie shouted at Jimmy. "I need my bag." Jimmy was close enough to the workbench to snatch Marie's purse. In a moment of clarity, Marie considered what else she'd need to complete the job. "That's not all. Gus, where is Jacqueline's phone? And the key to her rental car?"

"They're right here." Shrugging off Head Honcho's arm, Gus grabbed the items from the workbench and handed them to Marie. "The car's parked in the alley behind the store."

Hesitant at first, Marie took the risk of hugging Gus and kissing him on the cheek. "Don't worry. I promise you I'll get us out of this mess."

With the phone and car fob clutched in her hand, Marie stumbled to keep pace with Jimmy as they climbed the stairs. She caught one last frightened glimpse of Gus before Jimmy slammed the stairwell door closed in her face.

Chapter 33

Marie

As Marie fashioned the wig of long, dark hair to resemble the style Jacqueline wore, she stared at her image in the bathroom mirror and recognized for the first time in more than a decade the person she used to be. She'd been so busy for so many years hiding under a false identity in her legitimate career during the day and creating different personas to run her illegal scams at night that, until that moment, she never stopped to consider how much she'd sacrificed. She was exhausted from so often changing aliases and pretending to be someone she wasn't and consumed with regret over all the wrongdoings she'd committed. She couldn't wait to toss every wig, hair extension, and pair of contact lenses and false eyelashes into the dumpster, escape Manhattan, and leave those regrettable memories behind forever.

Marie marveled, as she'd done a thousand times in the past, at how identical her appearance was to her twin's. *So, if you'll be convincing enough to pull the wool over Patrick Woodward's eyes, why are you so nervous?* The answer was obvious. Finishing this job by stepping in for her twin seemed feasible—until she remembered Jacqueline's comment that recently Patrick was all about kicking his relationship with Kelsey up a notch. Marie worried she might find herself in an uncomfortable situation with the young Dr. Woodward. She'd come to terms years ago with the idea of using her body when necessary to get the job done, but she drew the line on becoming intimate with the son of the man she loved.

"Oh, what a tangled web you've weaved," she mumbled to herself.

Jimmy, her now ever-present companion, eyed her suspiciously from the edge of the bed just a few feet away. "What d'you say?"

"Nothing." Marie opened the vanity drawer and tossed her cosmetics into a travel pouch. "I'm talking to myself."

Jimmy rose from the bed. "Come on. It's time to leave."

Marie slammed the vanity drawer closed, entered the bedroom, and tossed her cosmetics into the small suitcase she'd filled with sufficient clothing for the next few days. Testing how malleable Jimmy could be, she told him, "Zip up my bag, and let's get out of here." Leaving him behind to do her bidding, she grinned with the satisfaction of knowing he'd followed her orders without a question or a smart remark.

With Jimmy behind the wheel, Marie took advantage of their travel time to Old Greenwich to outline her plan for the next couple of days. As they crossed the state line into Connecticut, she suddenly identified one aspect with which she'd need Jimmy's assistance.

"Jimmy," she said with a start, "you need to give me a refresher lesson in driving."

"When?" Jimmy took his eyes off the road long enough to glance at Marie. "Now?"

"No, not on the highway, but maybe we can locate an empty parking lot when we get into the suburbs. I have a valid license. I just haven't driven in, well, a while."

"Why the sudden urge to drive?" he asked suspiciously.

"If my first plan doesn't work out and I need to deal with the man I'm conning in person, he'll expect me to drive to his house in this car just as my sister did." As an afterthought, she added, "Don't worry. I'm not foolish enough to divert your attention so I can make a slick escape."

"You're pretty good at reading minds."

"Yes, I am, and I'll advise you not to forget that," Marie warned.

As they neared Old Greenwich, Jimmy spotted a shopping center just off the highway. In an empty section of the parking lot, he exchanged seats with Marie. She maneuvered the car up and down the aisles and in and out of parking spaces until she was comfortable being behind the wheel again. Merging into traffic, she drove the final miles of their journey to the hotel where Jacqueline had taken up residence—not exactly the water-damaged condo Patrick had been duped into believing Kelsey owned.

"A hotel this large should be able to accommodate you without having a reservation," Marie commented as they stepped out of the car.

Jimmy snorted. "Just because I'm being nice doesn't mean I'm gonna let you out of my sight."

Marie stared at him blankly for a few seconds. Her eyebrows shot up when she got the gist of his meaning. "You don't think you're staying in the same room with me, do you?"

"Well, that's kinda what 'not letting you out of my sight' means." Leaning into the car, he removed their bags from the back seat.

"Listen," Marie said, her eyes narrowed, her voice threatening, "I've cooperated with every one of your demands so far, but I will *not* agree to share a hotel room with you!"

Jimmy stepped closer until their noses were touching. "You got no choice in the matter," he said emphatically.

Marie stood her ground until she envisioned Gus holed up in the basement of the antique shop with Chuey. "Fine," she spat out. "Just keep your distance and stay out of my way." She grabbed her bag from his hand and stormed into the hotel with Jimmy following close behind.

Because she'd often visited her twin for consultations and progress updates, Marie was familiar with the hotel and had her own key to Jacqueline's room. "The good news is, we have separate living and bedroom areas," she remarked when they entered the room. "The loveseat converts into a small bed."

Jimmy glanced at the sofa. Shrugging, he said, "I've slept in worse places."

Jacqueline's phone chimed. Marie sat on the loveseat and fished the cell phone from her purse.

Jimmy rushed over to her. "Who's calling?"

Marie opened the messaging center on the phone. "It's not a call. This is my sister's phone. She's gotten a text from Patrick Woodward. He wants to know when he can see her. I mean, see Kelsey." Marie scrolled through Patrick and Kelsey's text history to get a feel for the tone they used when speaking with each other. Her thumbs dashed across the keyboard as she typed her response.

"Let me see the text before you send it," Jimmy ordered.

Marie tsked and rolled her eyes. "Fine." She finished typing and held the phone up to Jimmy's face.

Jimmy read the text message out loud. "*Hi, Patrick! My flight from Ohio arrives tomorrow late afternoon. I'll call you when I land. Miss you!*"

"Satisfied?" Marie asked cynically.

Jimmy sneered, then plopped himself into the chair adjacent to the loveseat. He turned on the TV and scrolled through the channel listings.

The phone chimed again. Marie read Patrick's gushy response, rolled her eyes, and tossed the phone into her purse. Glancing over at Jimmy, she asked, "So, what shall we do for dinner?"

****

Later that evening, Marie reviewed the notes she'd taken during Jacqueline's nightly debriefs regarding her portion of the Singing Bird Pistol con. Marie had jotted down numerous tidbits about Patrick Woodward's background, his habits, his personality, his favorite liquor—pieces of information that would be exceptionally helpful should she need to deal with him in person. She'd also included facts about his son and the nanny, the floorplan of his house, and his relationship with Kelsey. She had no idea what had compelled her to be so detailed, but she thanked her lucky stars that at the time she'd followed her instincts.

On the last page, Marie had noted the details Jacqueline relayed about the location of Patrick's Singing Bird Pistol and the cabinet in which the relic was encased:

*SBP in P's study – off foyer, bottom of front staircase
*Locked inside curio cabinet, corner of room
*Key to curio in late wife's desk
*Jac's search of desk = no key found
*Security code?

Marie stared blankly at the floor and visualized her tactics for the next day. Jacqueline had told her that on Mondays Patrick's son and his nanny were typically away from the house from early morning until lunch. Marie would enter Patrick's home during that time and conduct her own reconnaissance as soon as she was certain the house was vacant.

Keys! Where is the set of house keys Patrick lent his girlfriend, Kelsey? Marie phoned Jacqueline, but the call went right to voicemail. Assuming the phone was still in airplane mode, Marie didn't bother to leave a message.

"What are you doing?" Jimmy asked. He was standing in the bedroom doorway as Marie yanked open and slammed shut every drawer in the room.

"I'm searching for a set of keys," she replied, moving on to the closet. "I know my sister, and I know she would have left them somewhere in this room for me to find." Suddenly, the answer dawned on her. "The safe!" she exclaimed. Rushing into the living room, she opened the door of the credenza. Inside sat the safe, closed and securely locked.

"Ha!" Jimmy chortled as he crouched down beside her. "Without the combination, looks like you're screwed."

Marie raised a condescending eyebrow. "Like I said before, I know how my sister thinks." The first couple of codes she entered—Jacqueline's and her birthdate, the year they were born—were losers. Then, she punched in 0-2-1-4, the date of Valentine's Day. The safe beeped and the door clicked open. *Yes! Thank you, Jacqueline, for being a die-hard romantic!* The contents were exactly what Marie had expected to find—the keys to Patrick's home sitting atop a folded piece of paper. Marie smiled at Jimmy, smugness covering her face, as she reached in and removed the note.

S –

Sorry I can't stay any longer. I hope Gus explained. These are the keys to Patrick's home. The security code is 3627.

Use the door at the back of the house next to the terrace. The entrance is secluded by a covered porch & the neighboring homes are far enough away that you'll have little chance of anyone seeing you. Also, avoid the outside security cameras by staying in the shadows close to the house. Good luck!

J

PS. This one got way too personal for both of us, so I'm done. Please don't ask for my help ever again.

"Don't worry, Jac," Marie mumbled to herself. "I won't need to."

Chapter 34

Marie

Early Monday morning, Jimmy drove the rental car past Patrick's address, then circled around and parked alongside the curb a few houses down the street. From her position in the passenger seat, Marie kept a watchful eye on the home. First, Patrick backed his SUV out of the garage and drove off. Half an hour later, the nanny left in her own car with the little boy in tow. Marie remained in place for ten minutes to make sure no one returned unexpectedly. Believing the coast was clear, she exited the rental car and casually strolled down the sidewalk. Jimmy drove to a public park two streets away where he waited for her to rejoin him.

Marie slipped her hands into a pair of latex gloves. Entering the house through the backdoor as Jacqueline had instructed, she punched in the code to disable the home security system and crossed through several rooms and the foyer before locating Patrick's study. She identified the Singing Bird Pistol inside the curio cabinet, then searched Catherine Woodward's secretary for the key and passcode. Jacqueline hadn't been successful in her covert, middle-of-the-night examination of the desk, but then, she didn't have Marie's knowledge of antique furniture designed specifically to conceal secret compartments.

The secretary desk was old, mid-eighteenth century by Marie's estimation, and similar in design to Jonathan's library desk with its many hidden cubby holes. She proceeded to disassemble the nooks and pigeonholes at the back of the secretary, exposing one section after the other until the entire desktop was torn apart, but to no avail. Either Patrick lied to Kelsey about where he kept the key to the curio, or he'd moved the key to another hiding place in the past few days.

If I were Patrick, Marie speculated while she patched the secretary back together, *where would I hide a small object I didn't want anyone to find, especially a young child?* She began with the upper shelves of the bookcases and worked her way down but discovered no false book spines, hidden panels, nor knickknacks with hollow insides. She ran her hand under all the furniture and lamps. Lastly, she searched through Patrick's desk. Neither the key nor a written security code was anywhere to be found.

Frustrated, Marie slammed her fist on Patrick's desk, upsetting the photo of Patrick and his deceased wife posing in front of a European cathedral. She caught the frame in her gloved hands just as the picture was about to topple off Patrick's desk. "Damn me and damn my damned temper!" she cursed under her breath. The last thing she needed was to leave behind a damaged photo frame as evidence an intruder had been in the house. Then, she remembered every cloud has a silver lining.

Marie wanted to avoid a face-to-face encounter with Patrick at all costs but meeting him in person was now inevitable. In contrast to the professional images she'd seen of him on the internet, the photo in her hand gave

Marie a view of Patrick's tall, lanky physique in a natural setting. She took in all aspects of his features and was struck with melancholy when she recognized the similarities between father and son. Patrick had inherited Jonathan's warm brown eyes and square jawline, and they both had a dimple in their cheeks when they smiled.

As Marie replaced the photo on the desktop, she detected a noise in another part of the house. She cracked open the door leading to the foyer and listened. Voices. A woman's stern tone, a child's high-pitched whining. The nanny and son had returned home sooner than anticipated.

Marie opened the door a little wider to better hear the quarrel taking place in the back of the house. Their voices were muffled as the sound failed to carry well through the rooms, but Marie understood the little boy to be pitching a temper tantrum. She picked out the word "upstairs" in the nanny's disciplinary tone, after which their speech became more indistinct. A few seconds later, she identified the boy's whining again followed by the nanny's commands for him to go to his room, but this time their voices carried down the front staircase from the second floor.

Get out of the house NOW!

Leaving the door to the study ajar just as she'd found it, Marie rushed through the rooms, peeking around every corner before crossing to the next. She stepped outside and breathed a huge sigh of relief as she quietly closed the back door behind her. She slinked along the back of the house to the side yard, then through the shrubs to the neighbor's property. When she was safely far enough away from Patrick's house, she strolled to the park and located the rental car. Within minutes, she and

Jimmy were driving back to the hotel where Marie spent the afternoon working out her next plan of action.

****

"No!" Jimmy shouted. "That's *not* happening!"

"For the tenth time," Marie said through gritted teeth, "if you don't let me go alone, my entire scheme will fail."

"And for the tenth time, I don't trust you."

Marie and Jimmy were arguing over Marie's backup plan. She insisted on flying solo when she returned to the Woodward home that evening. Patrick Woodward, she reasoned, would expect his friend, Kelsey, to park her car in one of his empty garage bays as she'd done in the past. Jimmy disagreed. He insisted on accompanying her. Although she wouldn't admit it, Marie understood his concern. He reported to a badass and was not willing to take the blame if she were making up this scenario in order to give him the slip.

Marie was close to lunging at Jimmy's throat when her father's words echoed in her head: *You catch more flies with honey than vinegar.* "Look, if I wanted to trick you, I'd have done so by now. All I want is to finish this job tonight so your employer gets the product he wants, Gus and I get the payment he owes us, and everyone goes away happy." While Jimmy stared at the floor between them, Marie's intuition told her she had him hooked. "I promise to be back to the hotel by midnight."

"Okay, fine," Jimmy conceded. From his tone, Marie inferred he was not pleased, but understood he had to give her a degree of freedom to play out the con. "But I won't think twice about calling my boss if you're not back here exactly by midnight. I've seen him do some crazy-ass stuff when he gets mad, so there's no telling what'll happen if you start pushing his buttons."

"All right, I hear you!" Marie was under enough pressure without being reminded of the peril she'd created for Gus. Like a fool, she spat out, "Before I leave, I'm going to use the bathroom. Can I close the door, or don't you trust me enough to give me some privacy while I take a piss?"

Her insolence was not well-received. As she stepped toward the bathroom, Jimmy grabbed her upper arm and yanked her toward him. Marie attempted to pull away, but his grip was too strong. "I'd suggest you change your attitude," he snarled, "or I will find a way to make your life miserable."

Marie was trained in self-defense, but she'd be no match against Jimmy if the grasp he had on her arm was an indication of his strength. "Sorry," she said meekly. "I'm just tense about finishing this job, and I'm taking it out on you. I promise to be more cooperative from now on."

True to form, she could look Jimmy square in the eye without giving away the fact she was lying.

Chapter 35

Marie

Marie drove the car into Patrick's garage, shifted into *Park*, and shut off the ignition. With her hands clutching the steering wheel, she closed her eyes and mentally prepared for the task she was about to undertake. In her mind, she reviewed the details she'd gotten from Jacqueline one final time, then ticked off the list of what she planned to accomplish while inside Patrick's home. When she stepped out of the car, she was transformed into Kelsey Adams, happy to be back with her boyfriend after their long weekend apart.

Using Jacqueline's cell phone, Marie had spoken with Patrick earlier that evening to give him her ETA. He must have been watching for her. She'd no sooner gotten out of the car when he flung open the door leading into the house. Taking a deep breath, Marie put on her smiley face. It was show time.

"Hi!" she said with a wave of her hand. "Miss me?"

"More than you know," Patrick admitted, and he wasn't kidding. As soon as Marie stepped from the garage into the mud room, he slammed the door closed behind her and pinned her against the wall. Before she could stop him, his arms were around her waist and his mouth was covering hers.

Well, I can't say Jacqueline didn't forewarn me.

Gently ending their embrace, she said, "Patrick, as much as I appreciate the affectionate welcome home, you should probably stay away from me for a while. The man sitting next to me on the plane had a terrible cold, and now I feel like I'm coming down with the same thing."

"You don't need to worry about me," Patrick said, wrapping his arms around her again. "I was exposed to so many viruses during my hospital rotations, my immune system is ironclad. Besides, I'm so happy to see you, I'm willing to take my chances."

With his eyes closed, Patrick couldn't see the wince on Marie's face as his lips primed for another landing. She'd been opposed to having physical contact with Jonathan's son before; now that she'd met Patrick, her resolve was that much stronger. His mannerisms as well as his appearance were so similar to Jonathan's, even the idea of kissing him made Marie's skin crawl.

"Patrick, please," she said, wriggling out of his arms, "not tonight. I promise, I'll make it up to you in a few days."

Clearly disheartened, Patrick took a step back. "I'm sorry you're not well." He held the back of his hand to her forehead and cheeks. "You don't feel warm. I think you're just tired from the flight."

"Maybe. I'll see how I feel after a good night's sleep."

Frowning, Patrick cocked his head. "Your voice sounds odd. Different, I mean."

Marie was quick to use her bogus illness as the reason the timbre of her voice was different from her twin's. "It's this thing I'm coming down with. My voice always gets deeper when I'm sick." She coughed into the crook of her elbow for effect.

"Come on in and relax," Patrick said as he led the way to the kitchen. To Marie's relief, he appeared to have fallen for her phony excuses. "Do you want something to eat? We have leftover lasagna." He opened the refrigerator and handed her a bottle of water. "Drink some water. You need to keep yourself hydrated."

"I'm not hungry, but I will take the water. Thanks." She cracked the lid, took a long swig, and forced herself to relax.

"You've had a long day. Come, sit with me and unwind."

Marie joined Patrick in a cozy sitting area by the corner fireplace and the windows that overlooked the backyard. In the few minutes she'd spent with him, Marie noticed how similar Patrick's attentive, easy-going personality was to Jonathan's. She imagined he had a wonderful bedside manner with his patients.

"You're right," Marie commented. She made herself comfortable in one of the easy chairs. "I am tired. My weekend was rather busy." Finally, she'd made a truthful statement.

"Tell me about your trip. Did your father's birthday party go well?"

They conversed for a while as Marie recanted a tall tale of the visit with her fictitious family in Ohio and the birthday party that had never taken place. The more Marie got to know Patrick, the more she liked him. And just like the guilt trip she'd laid on herself over stealing Jonathan's treasures, being with Patrick for the sole purpose of swapping out the second Bird Pistol reminded her of the horrible person she'd become.

"I'm glad to have you back," Patrick told her. He

leaned forward and took her hand in his. "You'll be around this week for Oliver's birthday, won't you?"

Marie lowered her eyes, unable to meet his gaze as she knowingly continued the lie. "Where else would I be?" *In the Caribbean, that's where.*

"Good. I can't wait for you to meet my family."

"I'm really excited to meet them." *Oh, Patrick...If you only knew how well-acquainted I already am with the Woodward clan, your father in particular.*

"They'll take to you right away, especially my nieces. My sister and her family plan to arrive later in the week, but you'll get to meet my father much sooner."

Marie's heart leapt into her throat. "Why is that?" *Please don't say Jonathan is in the next room waiting to be invited in to join us.*

"Louise's sister flew in from Florida for a surprise visit, so I gave her the rest of the week off. Since I'm taking vacation myself beginning tomorrow afternoon, I didn't need her to care for Oliver anyway, but I do have surgeries scheduled in the morning which put me in a bind. I asked my father to help out, and he agreed to nanny-sit Oliver tomorrow while I'm at the hospital. He chartered a plane and is flying in as we speak."

The hairs on Marie's arms bristled. If she were present when Jonathan arrived, she had no doubt he would recognize her in a split second despite the dark hair, brown eyes, and absence of a French accent. She needed to leave immediately. However, at the same time, she couldn't ruin what might be her only chance to snatch the Singing Bird Pistol.

"J—" Marie started to call Jonathan by his first name but caught herself. "Your father is on his way here right now?"

"Sure is. He should be here within the hour." Patrick was obviously enthused to introduce Kelsey to his father. Marie, not wanting to raise his suspicions, pretended to be just as thrilled.

"What a nice surprise!" *So, how am I going to get myself out of this mess?* "I also have news. The repair work on my condo is done. I can go back to living in my own home again."

Although Patrick's voice sounded happy, the undeniable disappointment on his face betrayed him. "That's great. They finished the job sooner than you expected."

"Yes, I was stunned when I got the call today from the project manager. It's move-in ready, so I can pack up my things and clear out of your spare bedroom." Marie strolled into the kitchen with Patrick right behind her.

"What's the rush? I told you before, your invitation to stay here is open-ended."

As Marie set her empty water bottle on the kitchen island, Patrick stepped close and wrapped his arms around her. Marie clenched her teeth and allowed him to plant a few kisses on the side of her neck.

"I know you did, and I appreciate your generosity. But you can understand I'd be more comfortable in my own place." When his hands roamed to parts of her body where they were not welcome, she pledged to wring Jacqueline's neck for not mentioning Patrick had been getting quite this handsy with her. Disentangling herself from his embrace, she said, "Patrick, I told you I'm not in the mood."

"Sorry. I forgot you're not feeling well."

Marie sympathized with Patrick's hangdog face, but that didn't mean she would give in to his desires. She retrieved her purse from the kitchen island and announced, "I'm going up to the bedroom to pack my suitcase."

"May I join you?"

"Of course." At the bottom of the staircase, she swiveled around to face Patrick. "Oh, I almost forgot to mention. I told my Grammy about your antique collection, and she was fascinated by the Singing Bird Pistol. I promised I'd text her a video of you demonstrating how the mechanism works. Is that okay with you?"

"Sure. Anything to please your Grammy."

"Oh, Patrick, you're the best," Marie gushed. "Can we record the video now? If we don't, I'm afraid I'll forget."

"Now's as good a time as any," Patrick said with a shrug of his shoulders.

Marie was certain that, armed with the fake Bird Pistol in the purse slung over her shoulder, she'd create an opportunity to switch the trinkets as soon as Patrick's demonstration was complete. However, her perfect plan came to a crashing halt when the sound of piercing screams sent Patrick racing up the stairs to Oliver's bedroom with Marie right behind him.

"Patrick, what's wrong?" Marie was chilled to the bone as she observed the little boy's terrorized behavior from the bedroom doorway.

"Oliver's having another night terror," Patrick explained. "It may take me a while to calm him and get him back to sleep."

Tears stung Marie's eyes as she was drawn in by the tenderness Patrick displayed for his son. Then, her mind reeled back to her own urgent situation. Jonathan would arrive soon, and she had much to accomplish in a short period of time. She blinked away her tears and scurried to the far end of the hallway, where a quick identification of her sister's clothing confirmed she was in the bedroom Jacqueline, as Kelsey, had occupied. She dragged Jacqueline's suitcase from the closet and threw it onto the bench at the foot of the bed.

Jacqueline, a fanatic about order and neatness, would be furious at the haphazard way Marie was tossing her clothing into the suitcase, but at that moment Marie couldn't have cared less. In the bathroom, she located Jacqueline's cosmetic bag and filled it with the items she found in the shower and the vanity drawers. She glanced around to ensure she hadn't left anything behind, then tossed in the cosmetic bag and zippered the suitcase.

Marie's frantic pace was prompted more by anger than urgency. Although she sympathized with Oliver's bouts of night terrors, she was upset over the timing of his latest attack. Had his sleep not been interrupted, she would right now have the Singing Bird Pistol in her possession. Instead, with time closing in on her, she was under enormous pressure to switch the Bird Pistols and be gone from Patrick's house before Jonathan arrived.

Patrick entered the bedroom as she was lifting the suitcase off the bench. His gaze bounced from the empty closet to the suitcase then up to Marie's eyes. Marie cursed herself for allowing his forlorn expression to crush her heart. She'd always treated her targets with indifference. What was it about these Woodward men that sparked so many damned emotions in her?

"How is Oliver?" she asked.

"He's asleep again, at least for the time being. He's been a real handful lately. Louise cut their activities short this morning because of his disruptive behavior. In fact, she told me he'd had her so distracted she forgot to set the security system when they left the house."

Marie wanted to tell Patrick she'd personally overheard his son's tantrum that morning, and that Louise hadn't neglected to set the house security when she left. She herself had disabled the system when she illegally broke in. Instead, she smiled sympathetically, and said, "Be patient with Oliver. He's just going through a difficult stage."

"I sure hope that's all it is," Patrick replied with a heavy sigh. He rested his hands on his hips and glanced down at the suitcase. "I see you're all packed and ready to leave. Is there anything I can say to change your mind?"

"Patrick, I'm sorry. I just need to be in my own home again."

"I understand," he said mournfully. "I'll carry your bag to the car for you."

"Thank you."

As they neared the staircase, Patrick asked, "Do you still want a demonstration of the Singing Bird Pistol before you leave?"

"Oh, yes, thanks for reminding me!" she said, as though creating an opportunity to snatch the Bird Pistol before she left wasn't foremost on her mind. But—fingers crossed—would she have enough time to do so before Jonathan arrived?

"Your Grammy will get a real kick out of this video." Just then, Patrick's cell phone chimed.

Marie held her breath. *Please, please, PLEASE let the text be from anyone other than Jonathan.* "Is that the hospital trying to reach you?"

"No, it's my father. He's only a few miles away. His driver said they should be here in about five minutes."

Marie pinched her lips and fisted her hands to control the angry outburst that was about to escape her mouth. Why did she have the odd sensation Jonathan had timed his arrival to purposely interfere with her plan? With her opening to swap out the Bird Pistols diminishing and her likelihood of coming face-to-face with Jonathan increasing, she used the frustration and panic building up inside her to her advantage. "Oh, my goodness! What time is it?" she asked frantically.

Patrick glanced at the screen of his cell phone. "It's a quarter to nine. Why?"

"I'm such an idiot," she exclaimed as she rushed down the staircase. "I'm supposed to meet the project manager at my condo at nine o'clock for a final inspection. I need to leave right now."

Patrick was close behind her. "This late in the evening? Why can't he do the inspection in the morning?"

"I know it sounds odd," Marie explained. She was making up the story off the top of her head as she raced through the first floor, not caring how unbelievable it was. "He agreed to meet me tonight as a favor because my flight got in so late, and my schedule tomorrow is incredibly busy."

"I want to at least introduce you to my father before you leave. Can you call the man and say you'll be a few minutes late?"

"No, I can't." Entering the garage, she was thankful Jonathan's car was not already parked in the drive. She popped open the trunk for Patrick to place her suitcase inside. "He wasn't happy about us getting together this late to begin with. I'll just have to meet your father another time."

Patrick slammed the trunk closed and grasped Marie by her shoulders. "Kelsey, I won't let you leave until you calm down. You're too nervous to drive right now."

Marie took in a deep breath. "I'm fine. Really." Over Patrick's shoulder, she noticed a set of headlights emerge from the darkness at the end of the street. "Tell your father I'm sorry I missed him." She rounded the back fender, opened the car door, and threw her purse across the seat.

"Call or text me later so I know you got home safely," Patrick insisted. Pretending she didn't hear his request, Marie closed the door and breathed a sigh of exasperation.

The large SUV passed Marie's car as she drove down the street. At the corner, she threw the car into *Park* and adjusted the rearview mirror until it captured the front of Patrick's house. She watched Jonathan emerge from the SUV and greet his son with a fatherly hug. The scene reminded her that, having botched what was most likely her last chance to obtain the Singing Bird Pistol, she'd ruined the possibility of reuniting with her own father at any time in the near future.

Marie rested her forehead on the steering wheel, took a deep breath, and told herself not to give up hope. With the deadline still more than a day away, time was on her side. Shifting the car into *Drive*, she rounded the corner and headed in the direction of the hotel. If necessary, she'd stay up all night inventing another plan to deliver the second Bird Pistol by Wednesday afternoon. Having given Gus her solemn promise, she had no other option.

****

When Marie returned to the hotel room, she found Jimmy, as usual, lounging in the chair and flipping through the TV channels. He made a jabbing comment about her returning well before her midnight curfew and asked if her mission had been successful. Muttering a response, Marie tossed her handbag onto the bed, then barricaded herself in the bathroom. With her pounding headache getting worse by the minute, she needed medication and solitude, not Jimmy taunting her about the pressure she was under.

Her phone buzzed from inside her purse. She shouted through the door, "Jimmy, check my phone and tell me who's calling."

A few seconds later, he replied. "It's somebody named Jonathan."

Jonathan, you have the worst timing tonight. She groaned, then shouted, "Let it go to voicemail."

"Whatever."

Marie removed her wig, washed her face, and downed a few pain killers, then stumbled to the bed and curled up under the covers. While she waited for the medicine to ease her pain, she buried her face in the pillow and focused on the noisy car chase scene in the TV movie Jimmy was watching. When her headache subsided, she played Jonathan's voicemail message and returned his call. Although she would never again see Jonathan, she needed to continue the farce of their relationship until she completed the con, or else risk the chance of raising his suspicions. As the phone rang, she prepared to be tormented yet again by their contrived relationship which she wanted so badly to be real.

Jonathan was excited to share his news, not realizing

Marie was already aware of the circumstances. He'd been called upon to spend the day with his grandson and had arrived earlier that evening at Patrick's home in Old Greenwich.

"Tomorrow afternoon, Patrick and Oliver are leaving to visit Catherine's parents for a couple of days. When they return, the whole family will be here at Patrick's home to celebrate Oliver's birthday. What are the chances you can ditch work beginning tomorrow and spend the rest of the week in Old Greenwich with me?"

Marie hesitated. She wanted to tell him how much she loved the idea, couldn't imagine anything she'd rather do, but that wasn't her reality. "Oh, Jonathan, it's such short notice. Can I let you know tomorrow?" She hated leading him to believe they'd be together again when, in fact, that phone call would probably be the last conversation they'd ever have.

"Please try your best, sweetheart," he urged, the disappointment clear in his voice. "We've only been apart for two days, and I'm already aching to be with you."

"I promise I'll do whatever I can." She sniffled back tears as she told him, "I long to be with you as well." Marie caught a movement out of the corner of her eye. Jimmy was eavesdropping from the bedroom doorway. "I've got to go for now. We'll talk again tomorrow."

"Sleep tight. I love you."

"I love you, too," she replied before disconnecting the call. She glared at Jimmy's snide expression as she set her phone aside. "Can't you give me even *one moment* of privacy?"

Marie's nerves were further irritated during the wee hours of the morning as Jimmy's snoring mocked her inability to grab even a few minutes of rest. She spent the entire night conjuring up images of Patrick Woodward's home and formulating ideas of how to finagle her way inside again without getting caught. By morning, she still hadn't come up with a plan to steal the Bird Pistol, at least one that didn't involve breaking the glass cabinet, grabbing the pistol, and running like hell.

Chapter 36

Marie

"I have to tell you, pretty lady, I'm beginning to wonder if you can pull this job off." Head Honcho's disapproving voice hissed from Marie's cell phone like a python longing to slither out of the speaker and constrict the last breath of air from her body. "What do I need to do to light a fire under you? Bust out a few windows in your friend Gus's shop? Start a rumor at the police station about what kind of business you two are really operating here?"

After a fitful night with no sleep, Marie could do without the reminder she'd as of yet failed to obtain the Singing Bird Pistol from Patrick Woodward's home. Perched on the edge of the bed with her cell phone in hand, she stared at the screen through squinted eyes and envisioned her hateful tormentor speaking to her from inside Gus's workshop.

"There's no need to do either." Marie's tone was stern. She didn't want to make Gus's situation more precarious, but she was on her last nerve. "I have until three o'clock Wednesday to deliver the goods. That leaves me thirty-two hours to meet your deadline." And to come up with a plan to steal the Bird Pistol. The window was getting shorter, as was her patience.

"Yeah, so, that was the deal yesterday," Head

Honcho announced, the delight in his voice unmistakable. "As of this morning, the deadline has changed."

Marie sprang from the bed as if being shot from a cannon. With every muscle in her body tensed, she demanded further explanation. "What do you mean, it's changed?"

"My employer is losing his patience. He upped the deadline to eight o'clock tomorrow morning."

"No!" Marie shouted in disbelief. She glared at Jimmy who stood before her with his arms crossed and his brow furrowed, his gaze piercing. "He can't do that!"

Head Honcho snickered before replying. "He can, and he has. Eight o'clock tomorrow morning, or there's no telling what awful things might start to happen."

The call was disconnected.

"Son of a bitch!" Marie screamed as she threw her phone onto the top of the bed. With her hands clenched into fists, she paced the floor. Her mind flew in a million directions as she ventured to come up with a new scheme to meet the buyer's demands.

"Looks like the pressure's on," Jimmy goaded.

"Thank you," Marie replied sarcastically. "I can do without your damned gloating."

Jimmy grabbed her by the arm and spat out a warning. "Careful how you talk to me. All I have to do is make just one phone call." He shoved Marie away with such force, she fell backwards onto the bed. His reaction alarmed her and, for once, she was speechless. "I'm gonna take a shower. Don't leave this room."

Marie scowled at Jimmy as he entered the bathroom and slammed the door closed. Her anger, combined with a lack of sleep, awakened her defiant streak. "Nobody tells me what to do," she growled under her breath. She grabbed her room key and, although she doubted Jimmy could hear her over the running water, stormed past the bathroom door and shouted, "I'm going for coffee, and you can't stop me!"

Halfway across the room, she remembered she hadn't yet camouflaged herself as Jacqueline. As she stood in front of the mirror and tucked her blonde hair into the long, dark wig, she questioned why she was bothering to disguise her appearance. Surely no one in the hotel, other than Jimmy, would recognize her one way or the other.

****

The elevator bell dinged, and the doors opened. Entering the lobby, the aroma of fresh-brewed coffee made Marie smile despite her depressingly dismal state of affairs. Sidestepping the others who had ventured from their rooms for an early-morning breakfast, she made her way to the beverage bar and helped herself to a large Colombian brew. Although she usually skipped breakfast, the buffet was calling out to her. She speculated that a little food might settle her burning stomach and stimulate her brain.

While spooning cut fruit into a bowl, her mind was preoccupied with the stupidity of her defiant behavior. When Jimmy found her gone from their room, as he probably had by now, he might just call Head Honcho to report her missing rather than first search the hotel for her. She was about to pitch her food and rush back up to her room when she became aware of the man standing close behind her, practically breathing down her neck.

"Good morning, Marie," he said, almost in a whisper.

The man's voice was familiar, his accent unmistakable. Marie glanced to the floor and confirmed her suspicion. She'd recognize those Italian loafers anywhere.

Bewildered, she attempted to make sense out of the man's reappearance. His presence in a hotel where she was registered as Kelsey Adams was no coincidence. The logical explanation was that he'd been hired by Veronica to follow her brother's girlfriend in Connecticut, just as she'd suspected Veronica had hired him to follow her father's new love interest around Manhattan. What didn't make sense was why the stranger called her *Marie* if he'd been told her name was *Kelsey*, and why he was willing to blow his cover by approaching her.

While these questions were flashing through Marie's mind, the man inched a little closer. "Don't think if you ignore me, I'll go away."

Geez, the guy was a real mind-reader! Marie glanced at him over her shoulder and, playing dumb, said with annoyance, "I'm sorry. You must have me confused with someone else." Done. End of conversation.

The man refused to be dismissed that easily. "No, I'm not mistaken," he insisted. "You are Marie Lacroix, and we need to talk."

****

They sat across from each other at a secluded table in the dining area. Marie sipped her coffee and glared at the man's smug face. How dare he create another issue for her to deal with on top of the stack of problems she was already facing! Her curiosity, however, was piqued. She set her coffee on the table and drummed her fingers against the side of the cup. *What is he up to?*

"I'll start off by introducing myself," the man said. "My name is Lou Biondi. Do you remember me?"

Marie raised an eyebrow. "No. Should I?" she asked condescendingly.

One side of Lou's mouth curled into a sneer. "Maybe the better question is, how do I know *your* face and *your* name?"

Taking out her frustration on her food, Marie fiercely stabbed a piece of honeydew with her fork, then popped the chunk of melon into her mouth. She scowled at Lou while she chewed. Lou glared back at her, apparently displeased with her response—or her lack of one.

"You can give me the silent treatment all you want," he started, "but I know you recognize me from when I was tailing you a couple weeks ago. And, yeah, you were right if you suspected that's what I was up to, which I'm pretty sure you did since you sniffed me out and gave me the slip on more than one occasion."

"Who are you working for?" Marie asked before he droned on any longer with his boring explanation.

"Be patient," Lou insisted. "I'm getting there." He cleared his throat and leaned in, his elbows resting on the table. "You already know I'm from Boston. What you don't know is that I'm a bachelor, and I tend to eat out a lot since I don't have a smokin' hot babe like you to cook dinner for me every night. One of my favorite restaurants is Benvenuto, a place that's owned by Brian and Veronica Lambert. I'm a frequent customer so the Lamberts treat me real nice—comp my drinks, an appetizer now and then—which keeps me going back 'cause, well, I'd be stupid to pass up all the freebies."

Finally, Marie's suspicions were confirmed.

Veronica was indeed the person holding the strings that tied all the pieces together. While attempting to anticipate the direction his story was headed, her attention was drawn past Lou's shoulder to the lobby area behind him where Jimmy suddenly appeared, his hair still wet from the shower. Jimmy's eyes frantically darted around the room. When he spotted Marie, his tense shoulders relaxed. He nodded to her and wandered off in the direction of the breakfast buffet. *Good. One less problem to worry about.* She focused again on Lou.

"Now, the Lamberts are a friendly couple, real chatty. Especially Veronica. She's usually not busy running the place like her husband is, so she'll sometimes keep me company while I'm eating and, boy, can she talk. Mostly about herself, but that's okay. I enjoy hearing about how the other half lives. She can also get real suspicious of anyone who tries to worm their way into her tight little family circle. So, when her father took up with this beautiful young thing from New York, the voice in Veronica's head screamed, 'Gold-digger!' That's when she called me, her handy private eye, and contracted my services. She wasn't too pleased when I informed her I couldn't find anything the least bit sinister about you, past or present."

Marie's annoyance was growing by the second. She wished Lou would just get to the point. "I still don't understand why we're having this conversation," she told him through pursed lips.

"That's 'cause I've only told you half my story." Lou paused, as if letting his response sink in before he continued. At the same time, Jimmy strolled by their table carrying a tray of food. Without saying a word, he took a seat at the empty table next to theirs. "A few days ago, Veronica Lambert called again and asked me to tail her brother's new girlfriend, a woman named Kelsey Adams. You see, she couldn't accept the fact that, right after her father got involved with his new girlfriend, her brother also started dating someone and their relationship was moving way too fast for Veronica's liking. Of course, I accepted the job, but imagine my surprise when I followed the girlfriend from the brother's house to this hotel and got a closer look at her. You may be wearing that wig to disguise yourself, but I sure as hell would never mistake your face—nor that tight body I'd sure love to get my hands on."

Lou's lecherous grin turned Marie's stomach. She'd been about to bite another piece of fruit off her fork. Instead, she dropped the fork and slid the bowl of fruit to the end of the table.

"Still," Lou continued, "I could have been wrong. So, I did a little background research on Kelsey Adams and found out she's a complete fabrication. My first assumption had been correct—Marie Lacroix and Kelsey Adams are one and the same person."

Wrong! If you'd conducted a truly thorough investigation, you'd have discovered my identical twin, not me, was playing the part of Kelsey Adams until just a few days ago. At this point, though, that minor detail isn't worth pointing out. I need to concentrate on squeezing more information out of you to determine exactly what your angle is. Why would you disregard your professional ethics by revealing your client's identity? My intuition tells me you have a scheme of your own in the works, and you need my help to carry it out.

As Lou continued, Marie gathered the information she needed.

"I next asked myself the obvious question: What's your game? I don't know exactly what scam you're trying to pull but, considering that the two men you've targeted are filthy rich, I'm guessing you're running a con that will reap you a pretty sweet reward. Which is why I didn't rat you out to my client, although I could have easily. You see, whatever it is you're planning to steal from Jonathan and Patrick Woodward, you're going to let me in on the action."

"And exactly how am I going to do that?" If Marie correctly anticipated the direction Lou was headed, she might be able to use whatever he had planned to her advantage. During each of her encounters with him, he had demonstrated how vulnerable he was to her beauty and charm. She suspected he was just as gullible as every other man she'd ever manipulated. She just might be able to use Lou as the patsy in his own scheme.

"Patrick Woodward's house is filled with artwork and trinkets, many that are worth hundreds of thousands of dollars. I know this because I've had extensive conversations with his sister who tends to brag about how much money her family spends on their fancy purchases. She told me her brother has an original Duncan Cordray painting hanging above the fireplace in his living room. You're going to steal that painting, find a buyer for it, and hand over the profit to me."

Marie was amazed at how well she'd read Lou's mind. However, what he didn't know was that Marie was devising her own plan in which she could trick Lou into believing she was stealing the Cordray painting for him while he was blindly assisting her in obtaining the Singing Bird Pistol.

"So, I'd be putting myself on the line pro bono?"

Lou reconsidered. "Okay, I'll give you a five percent cut."

"Wow, so generous," she commented sarcastically. "In other words, you're blackmailing me."

"I prefer to think of it as a mutually beneficial business partnership."

Marie stared at him while she worked out a tentative counterplan in her mind. "And if I refuse?"

"Not only will I crush your chances with the Woodwards, I'll also put a bug in the ear of the NYPD about the antique store you visited in the Bronx. That place sure smells to me of money-laundering."

Now, Lou had her attention. Without thinking, Marie cocked her head and raised an eyebrow.

"I thought that might perk you up," he said with a sneer. "I followed you when you went there on Sunday. My gut tells me the owner is selling a lot more out of that store than grandma's old rocking chair." He stared Marie down, so smug with his cheesy grin.

Marie took a few seconds to ponder her options. She stood up from the table and announced how they would proceed. "I need to go back to my room to think this through. Give me an hour."

Lou followed her to the elevators. "Wait a second," he ordered as he stepped in front of her. "Is this your way of agreeing to work with me?"

"Do I have a choice? You've kind of got me between a rock and a hard place."

Secluded in the elevator alcove, Lou's behavior became more brazen. He drew close to Marie until his body was nearly touching hers. "I suppose that's an accurate description, although I'd rather have you between my body and the sheets."

His innuendo made her want to vomit, but she needed to put her repulsion aside. She'd dangle a carrot in front of Lou's nose and lead him along to determine how malleable he could be. She rested her arms on his shoulders and ran her fingertips upward from the nape of his neck, past his hairline, and into his graying hair.

"You never know what might happen after this job is done," she said enticingly. Lou's lustful grin betrayed how much he enjoyed her insinuation and confirmed that he'd passed her test. From that moment on, Marie would be the one in control of their arrangement, blindly manipulating Lou to do her bidding.

Lou placed his arms around her waist and drew her close. He attempted to kiss her, but Marie turned her head just at the right moment. She pressed the elevator button. "There's no time to waste. I need to make some phone calls and work out the details of our job." She attempted to disengage herself from Lou's arms, but he held tight.

"It won't take long," Lou whispered into her ear. "I can ride up in the elevator with you and be in and out of your room in no time."

"That's not such a good idea." Marie attempted to back away, but the more she resisted his advances, the stronger he made his grip. She was about to knee him in the groin when Jimmy appeared from around the corner. With another person standing at such close range, Lou backed away.

"I'll meet you in the lobby in one hour," Marie told Lou with finality. The elevator dinged, the doors opened, and she and Jimmy stepped inside.

"I trust you won't try anything sneaky between now and then," Lou threatened her.

"I wouldn't dream of it," she replied.

He raised his arm and pointed to his wristwatch. "One hour!" The door closed in his face.

Marie and Jimmy stood side by side and gazed straight ahead as if they were strangers.

"Thank you for showing up right in the nick of time."

"I figured you could use my help." Jimmy's voice was stern when he asked, "Why'd you leave the room when I told you not to?"

Marie shrugged her shoulders. "You made me angry. I wanted you to know I won't be bossed around."

"You're lucky I found you or things could have gotten ugly."

"I know," she said, embarrassed to admit her rash judgment. "I made a stupid decision, but my hotheadedness paid off."

"Why? Who was that man?"

"Honestly, he's nothing but a scumbag, but he may have just saved the day."

Chapter 37

Marie

Marie would have preferred to tell Lou Biondi in her most unsavory language precisely what he could do with himself, but she couldn't ignore the consequences he'd threatened if she refused to help him steal the prized Duncan Cordray painting. With her anxiety level rising to an all-time high, she spent the morning working out the details of the most daring scheme she'd ever devised. That afternoon, she entered Patrick Woodward's home, this time as Marie Lacroix, mentally and emotionally prepared to launch the absolute last heist she ever intended to carry out.

In the long run, she honestly owed Lou a huge debt of gratitude. He'd given her a legitimate reason to spend another wonderful, glorious, magnificent day with Jonathan. Although she'd been resigned to never seeing Jonathan again, there they were in the center of Patrick's foyer, locked in an amorous embrace. She hugged Jonathan tightly and committed every detail of the moment to her memory: the light scent of his aftershave, the bristle of his chin against her neck, the strength in his arms as he held her close. The rush of sensations made her as giddy as a child whose strict parents had allowed her to stay up past bedtime.

Thanks, Lou!

"I've never been happier than I am right now," she whispered into Jonathan's ear.

"That makes two of us," he said, kissing her one more time. "I'll carry your suitcase upstairs and show you to our bedroom. After you unpack, we can relax and enjoy the afternoon."

"Your son's home is beautiful," Marie said, following Jonathan across the foyer. She glanced into Patrick's study. Had it been just yesterday when she'd rummaged through the room searching for the key and code to open the curio cabinet? So much had happened since then.

"Thank you. I'll give you a tour after you're settled in." As they climbed the stairs, Jonathan shared some news. "I should tell you we won't be alone for long."

Not again! Marie feared she was about to have a repeat of last night, although this time with Patrick as the surprise guest. Fate couldn't be so cruel as to force her to abort her backup plan. With the short deadline looming over her, she didn't have the luxury of switching gears yet another time.

"Why? Who's joining us?"

"Veronica called," Jonathan informed her. "She, Brian, and the girls will be arriving later this afternoon."

"That's a nice surprise!" Although Marie didn't welcome the prospect of sparring with Veronica, she was relieved to know she wouldn't need to alter her plans with Lou. "Why the change in schedule?"

"Phoebe's tennis team has a match tomorrow with a nearby school. Since they were all going to be here later in the week for Oliver's birthday, they decided to take a few vacation days and come to town early. Here we are."

As Marie followed Jonathan through the doorway,

she imagined he wouldn't be pleased to discover she'd been in the same bedroom last evening with his son. "This is lovely," she said as if she were viewing the room for the first time.

"This bedroom is larger than the others and has its own bathroom. Plus, since it's at the far end of the hall, we'll have more privacy."

"We'll need that," Marie said suggestively, running her fingers down Jonathan's back. She began to unzip her suitcase, but she couldn't relax until she inspected the Duncan Cordray painting. "You know, I think I'll unpack later. I'm much more interested in taking a quick house tour, then just lounging around with you."

"Come." Jonathan held out his hand. "We'll begin in the kitchen."

As he guided Marie through the house, Jonathan pointed out the antique furniture Catherine had acquired with his assistance. When they entered the living room, he asked, "Do you recognize the artist who painted the piece hanging over the mantel?"

"Of course." *Well, hello, Mr. Cordray!* Acting as though she had only a mild interest, Marie nonchalantly stepped up to the fireplace to examine the painting at close range. Many of Cordray's works were too large for one person to handle, but she determined this painting could easily be managed by a man of Lou's height and arm span. "Duncan Cordray is one of my favorite artists."

"He's a favorite among us Woodwards as well. Matter of fact, Veronica and Brian purchased this painting. With the help of the realtor, they had it hung there to surprise Patrick and Catherine when they moved in."

"What a perfect housewarming present!" Marie commented. She ran her fingers along the edge of the canvas searching for the alarm device. Hopefully, Jonathan would have the impression she was merely admiring the work.

"Yes. Veronica has her faults, but she's always been exceptionally intuitive when it comes to gift-giving."

Marie's fingertips touched on the security tag attached to the back of the painting's lower right corner. Her gaze darted around the room until she located the transmitter mounted on the wall nearest to the foyer. A person unfamiliar with these types of security systems might mistake the box for a thermostat control, but Marie recognized it as an anti-theft device. Disconnecting the painting from the security tag would trigger an alert to the wall monitor and set off an alarm at the firm charged with ensuring the safety of Patrick's valuables. Marie sent a silent thank you to Jacqueline for giving her a head's up about the system which, in turn, would give her the advantage over Lou when they carried out their scheme that evening.

More at ease now that she'd investigated the home's security system, Marie joined Jonathan and wrapped her arm around his. "I also like the contrast of a modern work of art with traditional décor."

"Well said. When you meet Patrick, make sure to share your point of view with him. He'll appreciate the compliment." Jonathan took Marie's hand and led her from the room. "Across the foyer is Patrick's study where he keeps a relic I'm sure you'll be interested in seeing."

"What is it?" Marie asked, although she'd already guessed the answer.

"Do you remember when you assisted me last summer in obtaining the Singing Bird Pistol for my daughter-in-law?"

"Of course. That was just a little more than a year ago, wasn't it?"

"Yes," he confirmed, "just before Catherine's birthday." When they entered the study, Jonathan led Marie directly to the curio cabinet. "Like me, Catherine kept her Bird Pistol in a space designed solely for her own enjoyment."

Gazing through the glass at the Singing Bird Pistol she so desperately needed to hand over to Gus's ruthless buyer, Marie squeezed Jonathan's hand and said, "She really was a woman after your own heart." As her eyes scanned the other trinkets displayed in the curio, she was struck with a notion. Jonathan and his daughter-in-law had been extremely close. Catherine may have shared the whereabouts of the key as well as the code needed to open the cabinet with him. Time for a little probing. "Her collection is impressive. Is this figurine of the Madonna a genuine Borchardt?" She leaned down to examine the sculpture at a closer angle.

"You have a good eye. Catherine found that piece while we were on a family holiday in Germany a few years ago."

"It's exquisite! I'd love to examine the work up close, but I imagine the cabinet is locked." Her doleful expression worked its magic, just as she'd planned.

"You're in luck," Jonathan told her. "I happen to know where Patrick keeps the key." He stepped over to Catherine's secretary and opened the lid to the desktop.

Marie grinned. Jonathan was so easy to manipulate. "Do you need my help?" She wandered next to Jonathan, curious to observe how his dismantling of the desk would differ from her own attempts.

"No, I don't think so." His face was scrunched in deep concentration as he spoke. "It's been a while, but I think I remember how this desk comes apart."

At first, Jonathan followed the same process Marie had used during her hunt for the key the previous morning. Eventually, however, he removed a section she hadn't uncovered and exposed the box that contained the key to the curio cabinet.

"Here it is!" Jonathan exclaimed. He inserted the key into the keyhole, then stepped in front of the security pad. Marie discretely angled herself into a position from which she could follow his fingers and memorize the code. However, rather than lifting his finger to the security pad, Jonathan instead crossed his arms over his chest and grunted a bewildered, "Huh."

Marie clenched her jaw. Otherwise, a string of swear words would have bolted out of her mouth like thoroughbreds jumping from the starting gate. "Is something wrong?" she asked calmly.

"The code had been my late wife's birthdate," Jonathan replied as his eyes narrowed and his brow furrowed, "but I'm almost positive Patrick told me he reset the code." He faced Marie. "I hope you don't mind," he said, "but I think we should put this off until Patrick returns home. I'd rather open the curio properly than try to convince the police I'm not a burglar."

Marie forced an understanding smile. "Yes, that would be awkward. In a community such as this, I imagine the police would respond within maybe five minutes?"

Jonathan shrugged his shoulders. "Five to seven,

tops." He took her hand. "Come on, let's have a drink on the terrace while we wait for Veronica, Brian, and the girls to arrive." As he stepped away from the cabinet, Marie stopped him.

"Jonathan, shouldn't you put the key back in the desk?"

"And have to undo those compartments all over again?" he replied with a lopsided grin. "It's easier to leave the key in the cabinet. After all, we're the only people in the house, and I know for a fact I'm not a thief." He gazed intently into Marie's eyes for a moment before asking, "Is there a reason I should be worried about you?"

For the second time in the past few days, Marie had an inkling that Jonathan doubted her credibility. She assured herself she only imagined the accusatory tone in his voice and the glare that caused the corner of his eye to wrinkle with scrutiny for just a second. He couldn't possibly have seen through her charade. She'd been too artful, too precise, too unflinchingly convincing.

Hadn't she?

Chapter 38

Marie

As the minutes ticked past midnight, an eerie stillness settled over Patrick's home. Having slinked away from a sleeping Jonathan, Marie was alert to every creaking floorboard and rattling window as she crept down the front staircase. The sounds, she assured herself, were the normal grunts of the house stretching its muscles, but the faintest noise could be a warning she wasn't the only person awake and wandering about. A random encounter with any of the other house guests would place her in the awkward position of explaining why she was sneaking around the darkened house, fully dressed, in the dead of the night.

Marie entered the bathroom that connected Patrick's study to the first-floor bedroom. She grabbed the bag she'd secreted inside the vanity earlier that day and removed a long-sleeved tee and lounge pants which she slipped on over her sleepwear. Slinging a cross-body satchel over her shoulder, she double-checked its contents to make sure the pouch contained the fake Bird Pistol and the various other items she'd need during her impending rendezvous with Lou Biondi.

When she and Lou met for the second time yesterday morning, she had outlined her plan to assist him in stealing the Duncan Cordray painting from

Patrick Woodward's living room. She informed Lou she'd confirmed that, although Patrick and his son were out of town, Patrick's father would be in the house while they executed their heist. She found no reason to alter the game plan now that Veronica and her family had arrived, nor did she consider their presence important enough to mention. All Lou needed to know was that he should be at the back entrance to Patrick's home at twelve-thirty and to follow Marie's instructions.

After closing the bathroom light, Marie snaked noiselessly through the house. In the mud room, she opened the door leading to the covered porch where Lou was impatiently waiting.

"It's about time you showed up," he grumped while stepping inside.

"We said we'd meet at twelve-thirty," Marie reminded him.

"So, sue me for getting here early." Lou stuffed his hands into the front pouch of his pullover. His body rocked back and forth as his eyes nervously darted around the room.

"You're awfully jittery," she remarked.

"Yeah, sure, I'm nervous," Lou admitted. "I've done plenty of underhanded things in my day, but I've never committed a B and E."

Marie glared at Lou with questioning eyes. This job required precision and expert timing. The last thing she needed was a bungling amateur to screw things up. "Listen, I refuse to put myself in jeopardy. If you don't think you can go through with this job, tell me right now."

Lou removed his hands from the pouch and shook them out. He took a deep breath and said, "I'm good.

Let's do this."

Marie reconsidered how confident she was in Lou's willingness to follow her lead without question. At this point, however, her options were nil. To satisfy Gus's impatient buyer's demands, she had no choice but to keep a close eye on Lou and move forward with her plan.

"I checked out the painting," she informed him. "There's a sensor attached to the back on the bottom right corner. But I have this." She retrieved a small black box, two by three inches in size, from her satchel. With only the moonlight streaming through the window, the room was too dim for Lou to get a good view of the piece as she held it in front of him.

"What is it?" he asked, his suspicious eyes squinting in the darkness.

"This case contains a high-powered magnet. I'll hold it up to the wall monitor to scramble the signal. When you lift the painting and the security tag disconnects, this magnet will prevent the monitor from receiving any communication from the sensor, and the silent alarm won't activate." She closed her hand over the device before Lou realized she was holding nothing more than an empty hide-a-key container.

Lou shook his head. "I don't know. That sounds pretty iffy to me."

"Trust me," Marie reassured Lou, although her claim was totally fabricated. "I've dealt with these systems a dozen times and this work-around has never failed me." When Lou grunted and continued to disagree, Marie worried he'd gotten cold feet. She utilized a surefire way of motivating him. Stepping close, she caressed the back of his neck with her fingertips. "The longer we stall, the less time we'll have to celebrate afterward."

A lewd smile spread across Lou's face. "You're right. Let's stop wasting time."

Marie always got her way with men, one way or another. She allowed Lou the pleasure of squeezing her ass before she shoved him away. From her satchel, she removed two pairs of thin cotton gloves.

"Put these on." She handed Lou one pair while she slid her hands into the other. "Where did you park?"

Lou slipped on the gloves per her command. "Four houses down on this side of the street."

"Perfect," Marie replied.

While working out the details of the job, Marie had convinced Lou she would need his muscle and might (flattery, she'd learned, will get you everywhere) to lift the Duncan Cordray from its mounting, and Lou (his ego shamelessly bursting at the seams) had agreed to lend his assistance. After Lou carried the painting from the house, Marie would wait in the shadows with the stolen painting while Lou retrieved his truck. As he neared the house, Marie would use the grove of trees that ran alongside Patrick's driveway for cover to carry the painting to the truck. She and Lou would then drive off to New York where they would secure a black-market buyer.

That was the plan...as Lou understood it.

Marie dug into her satchel again, this time to retrieve a folded vinyl artist's portfolio case and a small flashlight. "We'll place the painting in this carrier to protect it from damage."

"Oh, yeah, good thinking," Lou decreed with a nod of his head.

"Now, follow me and be quiet," she instructed. "If you need to speak, keep your voice low." Marie tucked the portfolio under her arm and flicked on the flashlight. Keeping the beam low to the floor, she guided Lou through the house. They stole down the back hall, through the kitchen and dining room, and entered the living room. Marie shined the light on the painting above the fireplace. "This is the piece you said you wanted," she announced quietly.

Lou was nearly salivating when he whispered, "Come to papa, you sweet thing."

Marie crossed the room and held her faux magnetic device up to the wall monitor. Playing out her ruse, she watched the monitor for a few seconds, then gave Lou a thumbs up. She illuminated the fireplace mantel with the flashlight while Lou lifted the Cordray off its mount. Marie spent a few more seconds pretending to inspect the wall monitor again for activity before shooting Lou another thumbs up to make him believe the magnet had successfully tricked the signal. Next, she unfolded the portfolio and held it open while Lou slid the painting inside. After closing the zipper, she leaned close to Lou.

"Before we leave, I need to take care of one minor detail," she whispered into his ear. "It will only take a second. Wait for me here."

Lou grabbed her arm. In too loud a voice, he blurted out, "What are you—"

Marie held her finger to Lou's lips to remind him not to speak, then raised the open palm of her other hand, commanding him to stay put. Trusting he'd follow her order, she gingerly ran across the living room and foyer and entered Patrick's study.

Inside the room, she pointed the flashlight at the curio cabinet and the Singing Bird Pistol displayed on the top shelf. The key was still inserted in the cabinet door just where Jonathan had left it. Since the silent alarm had already been activated, Marie was no longer concerned about entering the security code into the keypad. Holding the flashlight with her teeth to keep the cabinet illuminated, she twisted the key in the lock and opened the wood-framed glass door. From her cross-body satchel, she removed a cloth pouch from which she extracted Gus's replica of the Singing Bird Pistol. She exchanged the fake trinket for the genuine piece, dropped the original Bird Pistol into the cloth pouch, and placed the pouch into her satchel. Lastly, she closed and locked the curio door. The switch had taken less than a minute to accomplish.

The job was far from complete, however, and the whole scam could blow up in her face if she didn't handle the next segment carefully. She crossed the foyer and waved her hand as an indication for Lou to follow her. With Lou clutching the portfolio, they hurriedly retraced their steps. Once outside the house, Marie flipped off the flashlight and reminded Lou of what he was to do next.

"Use that grove of trees as cover to get out to the street," she told him, keeping her voice low. "I'll wait for you here by the garage doors. As soon as I see you driving down the street, I'll use those same trees for cover to get out to your truck. Any questions?"

"No, I got it," Lou confirmed with a lecherous grin. Now that the job was almost done, he was back to being the abrasive jerk she'd met over breakfast yesterday morning. "Don't expect to get any sleep tonight." He attempted to kiss her.

Marie backed away, repulsed by his insinuation. "Save it for later," she said.

As soon as Lou was out of sight, Marie leaned the

portfolio against the garage door and ran to the back entrance of the house. Contrary to the directions she'd just given Lou, she had no intention of driving off with him and the stolen Duncan Cordray to a safe place where they would have celebration sex. If the next few minutes played out as she'd planned, Lou would be heading empty-handed back to Boston, Marie would be saying good riddance to Jimmy, and Gus would be resuming the preparations for his move to the Caribbean.

Marie stepped into the seclusion of the covered porch that housed the back door to Patrick's house. "Jimmy?" She called out in a loud whisper.

Jimmy emerged from the shadows where Marie had told him to wait while she completed the first portion of the con. "Did you get the job done?" he asked.

"Yes," Marie replied. Her voice was sharp when she spoke, for she detested the scam she'd been obligated to carry out against Jonathan. She handed the satchel over to Jimmy who'd previously been instructed to drive the rental car directly to Gus's antique store. "Deliver the Bird Pistol inside this bag to your boss and make sure you remind him that not only have I complied with every one of his demands, I also made delivery well before his deadline. Tell him to call me by eight o'clock tomorrow morning to confirm our transaction is complete."

Jimmy snickered under his breath as he slung the sack containing the Bird Pistol onto his shoulder. "I'll be sure to pass on your instructions," he replied cynically.

"Finish the job and get out of here," Marie commanded. "The police will be arriving soon."

She entered the house and locked the door from the inside. As she hurried through the mudroom, she detected the sound of a crowbar being wedged into the doorjamb followed by the splintering of wood as the locks were forced open. Per Marie's instructions, Jimmy had created the illusion that a burglar had used this door to pry his way into Patrick's home.

Marie's internal clock calculated that no more than four minutes had passed since Lou lifted the Cordray painting from its mounting and disconnected the security tag. Jonathan had told her the response time for local police and the security service was five to seven minutes. Completing her final steps as quickly as possible was crucial. To save time, she stripped down to her sleepwear as she hurried through the house. Within seconds, she was back in the bathroom adjoining Patrick's study. While stashing the flashlight, gloves, T-shirt, and pants into the bag she'd left inside the vanity, she ran through the plan one last time to make sure even the smallest detail hadn't been overlooked.

The previous morning, Marie had hit a brick wall. To fulfill their buyer's demands, she believed her only recourse was to shatter the glass front on the curio cabinet, snatch up the Bird Pistol, and hope to escape without being caught red-handed. She was in the process of talking herself into committing this brazen act of thievery when Lou Biondi entered the picture.

While Lou sat across the breakfast table and spelled out his plan to blackmail her, an idea formed in Marie's mind. If she opened the cabinet that housed the Bird Pistol without following the proper procedures, she'd set off the silent alarm. However, if she had Lou remove the Duncan Cordray from its position over the fireplace, he'd breach the security system first. She could then open the curio cabinet and swap the Bird Pistols without causing suspicion. If the security firm detected individual points of compromise, the police would assume the same burglar had also attempted to break into the curio cabinet. To stay in the clear, Marie needed to choreograph each step of her plan with precision to convince everyone, including Jonathan, she was in their bedroom the entire time the robbery was taking place.

Marie despised herself for using Lou in such a devious way, but she eased her conscience by rationalizing that Lou wasn't entirely innocent in this matter. Blackmailing her into committing the robbery was his idea in the first place. Marie had merely helped to facilitate his scheme.

As she switched off the bathroom light, Marie became aware of a disturbance on the street in front of the house. She bounded up the front staircase and scurried down the hallway. Silently entering the bedroom, she tossed her bag under the bed and slid beneath the covers.

"Jonathan! Jonathan, wake up!" she said with alarm as she shook his shoulder. Outside the house, the sound of vehicles careening down the street grew louder, followed by the screeching of brakes. Bright lights flashed against the curtain-clad windows.

Jonathan sat upright. "What's going on?"

"I'm not sure, but I think the police are outside," she replied, making sure to sound fretful and concerned. Muffled sounds rose from the lawn, voices of the authorities communicating through two-way radios, and the pounding of feet running through the yard. Marie pictured Lou flooring it when he noticed the flashing lights coming up fast behind him. She assumed by now he was out of the neighborhood and headed toward Boston.

Jonathan's cell phone rang as he rose from the bed. "It's my son," he announced as he crossed to the window and parted the drapes. "Hello, Patrick...Yes, there's some activity out on the street...You did? What did they say?...How is that possible?...No, we were all in bed...I'm on my way downstairs now. Stay on the phone while I find out what's going on."

Marie eyed Jonathan, scrutinizing his behavior. *Is it my imagination, or is he a little* too *alert for a person who was supposedly sound asleep just moments ago?*

"Patrick received a call from his home security firm," Jonathan told her while heading toward the bedroom door. "We've had a break in. I'm going downstairs to find out what's happening."

"Jonathan, wait! What if the thieves are still in the house?" She left the bed and slipped on her robe.

"That's a chance I'm willing to take." Jonathan opened the door to find Brian and Veronica rushing toward him.

"Oh, you are awake," Brian said. "We wondered if you'd heard the commotion outside."

"Of course." Jonathan held up his cell phone. "I have Patrick on the line. He was contacted by the home security firm. Apparently, we've been burglarized."

"Ohmygod!" Veronica gasped and touched her hand to her chest. "If anything's happened to our girls..." She dashed down the hall to the room Gwen and Phoebe were sharing.

Jonathan brushed past Brian. "I was just on my way downstairs."

Brian was right on Jonathan's heels. "I'll go with you," he announced as the front doorbell rang.

Veronica emerged from the girls' bedroom. "Thank

God!" she said with relief. "They're sleeping right through all this noise. Did I hear the doorbell?"

"Yes," Brian responded. "It's probably the police. Your father and I are going downstairs."

"Well, don't think you're going without me," she huffed.

At the top of the stairs, Jonathan flicked on the foyer lights. He glanced back at Marie. "Come along, Marie," he commanded. "You're just as much a part of this as we are."

Marie preferred to observe the scene play out from the shadows of the upstairs hall. Assuming Jonathan would let her have her way, as he always did, she invented an excuse to remain behind. "Perhaps I should stay close to Gwen and Phoebe in case they wake up."

"That's not necessary," Jonathan replied in a stern voice. "Veronica assured us the girls are fine. I want you with me."

Marie frowned, perplexed by Jonathan's unusually gruff tone. Was he overly concerned for her safety, or was she seeing a different side of his personality for the first time? Either way, she thought it best to succumb to his demands rather than argue the point. She reluctantly joined the trio as they hastened down the staircase. Marie remained near the stairs while the others stepped into the foyer. When Jonathan opened the front door, a whoosh of night air flooded over them. Marie crossed her arms to fend off the chill.

"Good evening, sir," the short, muscular female officer said in greeting. "I'm Officer JoAnn Carter with the Old Greenwich Police Department. Sorry to disturb you at this hour. Are you the homeowner?"

"No, my son is," Jonathan responded. "However,

he's out of town. We're all housesitting until he returns." He held up his cell phone and informed the officer, "I have my son on the phone. He said he was contacted by his home security service about a break-in."

"Yes, sir, your son is correct," Officer Carter confirmed. "There was an attempted robbery at this address. Although we recovered the stolen property, there's no sign of the perpetrator. He must have dropped the goods and run off through the yards when he saw us approaching the house. We've locked down the neighborhood and have several patrol cars scanning the area."

Standing beside the officer was a tall, thin man clad in the home security firm's uniform. "Sir, I'm John Gregorio with Eastern Home Security." He held up an artist's portfolio by its handles. "We assume this is what the thief removed from the house. May we ask you to identify the item?"

Jonathan stepped aside to allow the officers into the foyer. "Certainly. Please, come inside." He accepted the portfolio, unzipped the case, and allowed the front to fall forward.

Pointing at the painting, Veronica said, "Brian, that looks like the Duncan Cordray we bought Patrick as a housewarming gift." She crossed over to the living room and flipped on the track lights to illuminate the fireplace. Above the mantel, where they were accustomed to viewing the Cordray, the space was bare. "Ohmygod! This is unbelievable!" Veronica exclaimed.

Patrick's far-off voice sounded through Jonathan's cell phone. "Dad, what's going on?"

While Jonathan gave Patrick a summary of what had transpired, a second officer stepped into the foyer, a balding, middle-aged man whose shirt buttons were on the verge of losing their battle to hold his uniform closed over his expansive beer belly. His name tag identified him as Officer Charles Wilson.

"The break-in occurred at a back entrance to the house," Wilson informed his partner. "A crowbar was found in the bushes next to the porch. We suspect the burglar used it to pry open the locks." He glanced at Brian. "Who's the homeowner?"

Brian shook his head. "Not me. The house belongs to my wife's brother." He extended his arm to Veronica, and she eased into his embrace.

"The owner is my son," Jonathan told the paunchy officer. "I have him on the phone. He intended to be out of town for a few days, but now he's thinking of returning home tomorrow to deal with this break-in."

Marie lowered her head to conceal the grimace on her face. Her intentions for the next day were to confirm the sale of the Bird Pistols and Gus's release from Head Honcho's clutches early in the morning, then spend the rest of the day enjoying Jonathan's company for the last time. Although she would be breaking all the rules by remaining with her target after the con had ended, she needed to indulge herself just this once. However, if Patrick cut short his visit with Oliver's grandparents, she'd need to make herself scarce shortly after sunrise.

"That may not be necessary," said Officer Wilson, "since we still haven't apprehended the perp. We have several officers on foot and two patrol cars cruising the surrounding neighborhoods, but so far there's been no activity to report," he spoke the next to his partner, "other than that pickup truck that was driving down the street when we arrived on the scene."

Marie's breath caught at the news that Lou hadn't been fast (or perhaps smart) enough to get off the street before the police arrived. She glanced at Jonathan, hoping he hadn't noticed her instinctive reaction, but he appeared to be scrutinizing her every movement this evening. The accusatory stare he shot her from the corner of his eye caused a cold shiver to creep down her spine.

"Did you question the driver?" Carter asked Wilson.

"Yeah," Wilson replied. "Looks like he's clean. He said he was on his way home from a friend's house and got trapped between our cruisers when they came at him from both ends of the street." Wilson chuckled. "I think we scared the shit out of the poor guy. Oops! Sorry, folks. Pardon my French."

"Are you hearing all this, Patrick?" Jonathan said into his cell phone. "Yes, everything seems to be under control…No, don't worry, I'll take care of it for you…Okay, let me know in the morning if you change your mind." After disconnecting the call, Jonathan said to the officer, "My son will probably remain out of town for the next couple of days, so I'll handle this situation in his absence."

Marie assumed the crisis was over. She'd just begun to breathe easier when Jonathan stunned her by presenting the policemen with a proposition. "Officers, I know this is an unusual request, but why don't you bring the man you were just questioning into the house? The one driving the pickup truck, I mean."

"Sir, I don't see what purpose that would serve," Officer Carter responded.

"I was thinking," Jonathan explained, "if we all sit down and talk over coffee, he might relax and remember something that will help in your investigation."

The officers exchanged glances. "I guess that's all right," Wilson said with a shrug. Stepping toward the front door, he said, "I'll bring him in."

This isn't happening! If Lou finds me cozied up inside this house with the Woodwards, it will only take him a second to figure out I stabbed him in the back, and he doesn't strike me as the kind of person who would take such a betrayal lightly. I need to remove myself fast!

"Jonathan," Marie said as she began to climb the staircase, "it's obvious I'm not needed. I'm going up to bed."

In three brisk steps, Jonathan was at her side. "No, Marie." He firmly grasped her arm. "I insist that you stay. The police just may have a few questions for you before this ordeal is over."

Jonathan's comment and his piercing gaze created the same doubt Marie had experienced the previous afternoon when, as they were leaving Patrick's study, Jonathan asked if he needed to worry about her being a thief. Although she was certain she hadn't blown her cover, she thought it better to comply with Jonathan's demands than to give him any reason to distrust her. Besides, she doubted Lou would agree to join them all for a piping hot cup o' joe and some friendly chatter. A moment later, when Lou's belligerent voice grew increasingly louder as he approached the front entrance, she suspected Jonathan had purposely set a trap for her. She cowered in Jonathan's shadow, hoping to render herself invisible.

"I don't know what this is going to accomplish," Lou said. "I already told you, I didn't see anything."

"We just have a few more questions for you," Wilson told Lou. "This won't take long."

Wilson all but shoved Lou ahead of him as they crossed over the threshold. "Okay, folks," the policeman said. "This is the man we found driving down the street shortly after the break-in took place."

Lou, although clearly nervous, stood his ground just inside the foyer and surveyed the faces of the group assembled before him. When his gaze fell upon Veronica and Brian, his jaw dropped.

"Lou Biondi?" Brian said, his brow knitted in confusion. "What are you doing in this neighborhood?"

"Sir, do you know this man?" a stunned Officer Carter asked Brian.

"Yes." Brian spoke hesitantly, as though he were trying to make sense of the situation. "He's, uh, he's a private investigator and a frequent patron at one of our restaurants in Boston."

Veronica couldn't conceal her disgust when she said, "Well, Lou, so much for your contract stating that your surveillance methods are discreet. Apparently, that was a typo."

"Veronica, you didn't!" Brian said through pursed lips as he glared at his wife. "You hired Lou to investigate Pat's friend even though you promised me you wouldn't interfere."

Quick to defend herself, Veronica placed her fists on her hips. "Well, it's a good thing I did. No one's ever stolen something from this house until Patrick invited that Kelsey woman to live here. Don't you think that's more than just a little coincidental? Maybe Lou's investigation—which *YES* I hired him to perform—can provide proof that Patrick's new girlfriend was involved in this break-in."

"Or maybe it won't," Jonathan said as he

approached Lou, "but even the smallest bit of information could help." He extended his arm toward the back of the house. "Why don't we all go into the kitchen and have some coffee?"

"Thanks, but no thanks," Lou replied. Noticing Marie for the first time, his expression changed from surprise to resentment in seconds. "I already told the police I didn't see anything."

"Then what were you doing on my son's street this late at night?" Jonathan probed. "If you've been following her, you must have known his friend, Kelsey, hasn't been here for the past few days."

"Well, I, uh…" Staring at the floor, Lou's eyes darted swiftly back and forth as if he were attempting to concoct a reasonable response. "I kind of lost track of Kelsey Adams, so I thought I'd keep my eye on the house tonight in case I could catch her either coming or going."

"So, you lied to us," Wilson said. "You weren't just casually passing through the neighborhood. You were working a job."

The security agent, Jon Gregorio, had been preoccupied with his cell phone from the time he entered the house. While the others were probing Lou with questions, Gregorio had been sharing whatever image he was watching on his phone with Officer Carter. They had a whispered conversation during which time Carter's eyes wandered back and forth between the screen and Lou Biondi.

"The security firm has been reviewing footage taken of the outside perimeter of the house," Carter announced. "The cameras captured what appears to be an adult male crossing the driveway around the same time as the robbery, and the man's stature and clothing bear a close resemblance to yours." She stared accusingly at Lou.

Lou's entire body stiffened. His eyes filled with fright, as if he'd just stepped off a curb into the path of an oncoming bus. "No!" he replied. "That's impossible. I told you, I've been in my truck the entire night."

"Yes, we know that's what you *told* us," Carter replied, "but you've already proven you're not exactly trustworthy. This footage warrants further investigation." As she moved toward Lou, she commanded, "Wilson, cuff him. We need to take him to the station for questioning."

"How can you be so sure it's a *man* running across the drive?" Lou asked, squirming with resistance as Wilson struggled to fasten the handcuffs. "Maybe what you're looking at is actually a woman." He spoke with a vengeance aimed directly at Marie. "A really tall woman, one who's familiar with this house and thinks she knows how to bypass the security system."

"Officers, are you listening to Lou?" Veronica blurted out. "He may be right. That could have been a woman lurking around outside, and I'd be willing to bet it was that Kelsey person my brother's been seeing."

Brian, clearly embarrassed by his wife's unwarranted conjecture, said, "Veronica, listen to yourself. Will you stop at nothing to destroy this woman's reputation?"

"Your wife isn't as far off the mark as you might think," Lou told Brian. "She not only asked me to conduct a background check on Kelsey Adams, she also hired me to complete one on Marie Lacroix." A smug smile spread across his face as he glanced at Marie.

Marie expected Jonathan to jump to her defense. Instead, he ignored her as though she weren't even in the room. The walls began to close in on Marie as Lou continue to spill his guts.

"I thought both investigations would be cut-and-dried," Lou said, "but they turned out to be pretty juicy. You see, it didn't take long for me to figure out Kelsey Adams isn't a real person. She's actually Marie Lacroix in disguise."

Jesus! Lou thinks that footage will identify him, and he figures that if he's going down, he's taking me with him! If ever I've needed to stand up for myself, that time is now.

Marie glanced around the room and surmised from everyone's facial reactions that not one person was buying Lou's story, not even Veronica. Taking that as an encouraging sign, she shouted, "He's crazy! I've never heard such a ridiculous lie!" She backed away, her heart pounding in her chest.

"She's been working a scam on both Jonathan and Patrick Woodward over the past month," Lou said. "My guess is she's been stealing from them both that whole time, but she obviously botched up the scheme she tried to pull off tonight."

So, is this how my life of crime ends, with some lowlife P.I. blowing my cover? I've charmed my way out of many a tight situation before, but I have a sinking feeling that this time I am totally *screwed!*

Before Marie could refute Lou's claims, Jonathan came to her rescue. Placing his arm around Marie's waist, he said, "Let's put a stop to this nonsense right now. I'm willing to personally vouch for Marie's integrity, and I can assure everyone here that she could not possibly have attempted to steal the Duncan Cordray painting tonight. Marie and I retired to our bedroom at eleven o'clock." As he spoke, Jonathan gazed into Marie's eyes and conveyed a clear message: she was not to disagree with him, nor make the police aware he was telling a bold-faced lie. "Until the police arrived, neither of us had left our bedroom for even a second as we've been...how do I say this politely?" He grinned mischievously. "We've been engaged in some rather intimate activities."

From across the foyer, Brian muttered, "Damn!" under his breath as Veronica rolled her eyes and snapped out an appalled, "Ohmygod, Daddy!"

The niggling sensation that had washed over Marie in the bedroom earlier was back. She was now certain Jonathan had purposely duped her into believing he was asleep when she snuck downstairs to carry out the art theft with Lou. *He knows! He knows I was gone from the bedroom while the crime was being committed. He knows that Lou and I worked in tandem to steal the painting. But why the conspiracy? Why does Jonathan want my complicity in this crime to remain our dirty little secret?* Marie stared at Jonathan, wondering who he had become, for he was no longer the kind, soft-spoken man she'd found so easy to manipulate.

"No!" Lou shouted. "I'm telling the truth! Mister, can't you see you've been duped? This woman is a professional con artist. Don't believe anything she says!"

"I think we've heard enough," Officer Carter said. "Whatever happened here tonight," she told Jonathan, "rest assured we'll do everything we can to find the culprit." She gave Lou a shove, and said, "Wilson, take this man to the station for questioning. I'll follow as soon as I wrap things up here."

"No, wait, I have more to say!" Lou said.

"I'm sure you do," Wilson replied sarcastically as he gripped Lou's arm and forcefully escorted him from the house. Lou's rants carried through the night air until he was securely placed inside the cruiser.

"Daddy, what's going on?" Gwen called from the top of the staircase.

"It's nothing, sweetheart," Brian said calmly. He and Veronica rushed up the stairs to escort their daughter to her bedroom. "Let's all go back to bed. And try not to disturb Phoebe. She has an important tennis match in the morning and needs her sleep."

"I'll be on my way as well," Officer Carter stated. "Sir, you'll need to stop by the station tomorrow so we can take a statement from you for our report."

"I'll be happy to," Jonathan replied. "Thank you, Officer."

"A few things before we leave," Gregorio said to Jonathan. "At Dr. Woodward's, your son's, request, my office is sending out a man to board up the damaged back door. He should be here shortly. Also, and this is concerning, we detected another breach of security inside the house. An unauthorized disconnect occurred in a display cabinet that we need to investigate before the police leave."

"Well, that would have to be the curio cabinet," Jonathan pointed out as he led the officers to Patrick's study. "Follow me."

Alone in the foyer, Marie lowered herself onto the stairs and buried her face in her hands. *Please, Jonathan, please find the room exactly as you and I left it yesterday afternoon.* To her relief, Jonathan and the two officers emerged from the study a few moments later with smiles on their faces.

"Everything appears to be untouched," Jonathan remarked.

"There must have been a malfunction in our system," Gregorio said. "We'll have a technician out in the morning to check the sensors on the cabinet. Please call us if you need anything before then, regardless of the time."

"I will. Thank you." Jonathan bid the officers a good night, then closed and locked the front door. "Well, this turned out to be an eventful evening." He offered Marie his hand to assist her in rising from the step. "Correct me if I'm wrong, but you seem to be especially unnerved by tonight's events." He gazed intently into her eyes. "Is there something you'd like to tell me?"

"I guess I was just overly concerned for our safety," she answered, as though everyone's well-being was foremost in her mind.

Facing each other for a long, tense moment, Marie's eyes begged remorse for her wrongdoings while Jonathan, whose eyes had always twinkled with adoration and desire, now glared at her with disdain.

"You've had a busy night," he said coldly. "Go back to bed."

"And you?"

"I need to make sure the handyman arrives to board over the back door."

"I'd be happy to stay with you," Marie told him sweetly. Her fingertips caressed the nape of his neck, then slid upward to toy with his hair. Although she dreaded his response, she needed to confirm whether she still held Jonathan's trust.

"Don't do that," Jonathan said dismissively. He placed her hand back at her side. "Being together right now is not a good idea. I need time alone to think about us, and to decide where we go from here. Get some sleep. We'll talk in the morning."

Marie's eyes followed Jonathan as he faded into the dark recesses beyond the foyer. A sickness formed in the pit of her stomach. Reason told her the scam she'd carried out with Lou had been failsafe, but her intuition disagreed. Somehow, Jonathan had discovered the details of her plan to steal the painting and had orchestrated the evening's outcome.

Adding to her growing anxiety was the issue of Lou Biondi. Marie was ninety-nine percent sure the cameras had not captured a clear enough image of Lou to tie him without a doubt to the crime, but she wasn't nearly as confident in Lou's ability to keep his lips sealed during the interrogation. If the police managed to worm a confession out of him, Lou would certainly give her up as well. The notion of the police digging into her personal life made her tremble with fear. Her plan all along was to permanently discard the persona of Marie Lacroix soon after the Singing Bird Pistol con was wrapped up. Now she needed to seriously consider ditching the fake identity sometime within the next few hours.

She rushed up the stairs and barricaded herself in the bedroom. Like Jonathan, she would use this time alone to anticipate what situation she might face in the morning, and to plan how she would escape without suspicion.

Chapter 39

Marie

As daylight crept over the window ledge, Marie stared at the bedroom ceiling with bloodshot eyes. She'd lain awake the entire night chastising herself for not running when she had the opportunity. If she'd dashed off with Jimmy to deliver the second Bird Pistol in person, she'd be at the antique shop right now celebrating the completion of the Woodward jobs with Gus and discussing what loose ends needed to be tied up before they permanently traded Manhattan for the Caribbean.

So, why didn't I leave when I had the chance? Marie could invent a dozen reasons, excuses really, but the harsh reality was she'd exercised bad timing and poor judgment. Expertise and cunning were her strong suits, but she'd always harbored the premonition that, one day, her overconfidence would prevent her from recognizing when enough was enough. Like a gambler on a winning streak who believes his luck will never run out, she'd played one game too many and now risked losing it all.

She'd also allowed her emotions to blind her. The upside of being forced to complete the Singing Bird Pistol con was that she'd gained one more day to bask in Jonathan's company. But her craving wasn't satisfied. She'd attempted to turn one day into two and, just like

351

her con job, she was paying the price for pushing the envelope too far.

Around sunrise, voices in the upstairs hall meant the Lamberts were preparing to depart for Phoebe's tennis match. At seven o'clock, Marie heard their car back out of the driveway. The one bright spot in Marie's dismal morning was the relief of not needing to explain her sudden exit to Veronica and her family as well as to Jonathan. As soon as she received the phone call from Head Honcho confirming their transaction was completed to his satisfaction, she planned to make a beeline for the front door.

With her cell phone at arm's reach, Marie couldn't have missed the call, but she checked anyway. Nothing. She got out of bed and shuffled to the bathroom. Two tension-filled, sleepless nights in a row had taken their toll. After washing her face, she squirted drops into her eyes to ease the redness and applied makeup to conceal her dark circles. She dressed, then placed her suitcase on the bench at the foot of the bed and gathered her belongings. Marie was checking her phone again when she detected a light knock at the door.

Jonathan peered into the room. "May I come in?"

"Of course." Her greeting was pleasant, as though their relationship had not taken a dire hit. Regardless of what information Jonathan may or may not have gathered, she couldn't jeopardize her cover, assuming she still had one. Setting down her phone, Marie said, "I missed waking with you next to me this morning. Why didn't you come back to bed last night?"

"We were better off spending the night apart," he said matter-of-factly. Marie longed for the other Jonathan, the one who would have enveloped her in his arms and smothered her with kisses. The man she'd fallen in love with. "You'll be interested to know I spoke with the police a little while ago. They didn't have strong enough evidence to arrest the P.I. they took in for questioning, so he's been released."

Miracles do happen! Although she would have bet against him, in the end Lou proved to have enough common sense to keep his secrets to himself. Having one less problem to fret over was good news indeed, but she still had to face the issue of Jonathan's unnerving behavior.

Keeping in character, Marie replied with just the right degree of indignation. "I hope the police did the right thing. When that man accused me of being a thief, I was convinced he would say or do anything to save himself."

"Surprising, isn't it, the deceitful acts some people are capable of committing?" Jonathan gazed at her with steely eyes that made Marie's blood run cold. He nodded toward her half-packed suitcase. "I take it you're preparing to leave."

Marie dredged up her French grandmother's failing health, the same excuse she'd used when applying for her leave of absence from Willow's. The contrived tale had elicited the sympathy of her co-workers; surely Jonathan would have a similar reaction. She hated to mislead him, but she either continued the deception or she told the truth, and the latter was not a viable option.

"Yes. My grandmother is ill. I'm flying to France with my siblings to be with her. Sorry about leaving on such short notice. I hope you understand." She spoke with her back to him as she continued to pack her suitcase. When they first met, she'd been able to lie to his face. She hadn't craved his admiration then.

A heavy pause, then Jonathan grunted and said, "Well, that would be quite a sad story, if only it were true." He stepped beside her and tossed two boxes into her suitcase. "Whatever country you're fleeing to, you may as well take these with you. I have no use for them."

Once, as a six-year-old still learning to swim, Marie had brazenly jumped into the deep end of a pool and quickly became disoriented. She panicked, fearing she would drown. Eventually she surfaced, gasping for air. She'd never again, in her entire life, experienced such gut-wrenching terror—until now.

She stared at the boxes, the bile churning in her stomach. "What are these?" she somehow managed to ask. Opening the larger of the two, she exposed both Singing Bird Pistols. Her hands trembled as she lifted the lid of the second box and revealed the Somerset Necklace. She didn't need to examine the pieces to know they were all Gus's reproductions. She breathed deeply, attempting to steady her pounding heart. In a last-ditch effort to save herself, she faced Jonathan and innocently said, "Jonathan, these are your precious treasures. They're worth millions. Why are you tossing them around so carelessly?"

Jonathan snickered. "You know perfectly well those are the phony replicas you swapped for the originals. Please, take those pieces of junk with you and save me the trouble of having to pitch them."

Marie frowned in confusion. Each detail of her con had been planned with such care, and she'd been certain she had Jonathan eating out of her hand. What could she possibly have overlooked? She didn't know how, or when, he'd caught on to her, but she refused to believe he was privy to her entire scam. Foolishly, she kept up the pretense.

"*Mon cher*, why would you accuse me of doing something so horrible?"

"Okay," Jonathan said, crossing his arms over his chest, "the act, and the phony accent, stops right now, Marie. Or do you prefer me to call you Siena?"

And there it was—the clincher. Jonathan had spoken her given name, confirmation that he'd gathered more information on her than Siena imagined was possible. *And all along I thought I was being so clever. Well, congratulations, Jonathan. You outdid me. You succeeded in playing the more artful con game.*

Since Jonathan had exposed *who* she was, he certainly knew *what* she was. She was disgraced by his glower of scorn and disenchantment. Ashamed, Siena lowered her head and asked in her normal, unaccented voice, "What gave me away?"

"Well, I finally get to see the real woman behind the mask," Jonathan said, mocking her. "I've been aching to meet the person hiding underneath that fake French façade."

Siena glared at him. "It appears I'm not the only person who's guilty of trickery. Since last evening, I've been with a different Jonathan Woodward than the man I became so intimate with this summer."

"But there lies the difference. While I'm merely exposing another side of my personality, you intentionally duped me into believing you're a person who doesn't truly exist. You do see the distinction, don't you?"

In a burst of anger, she shouted, "Of course I do!"

Siena's entire body shook with rage. But who was

she angrier with, herself or Jonathan? How many times, despite Gus's warnings, had she insisted she had her head on straight and her emotions under control? *Well, Miss Smarty-Pants, it appears you weren't fooling anyone but yourself with those phony assurances.* Still, in her own defense, how could she have resisted Jonathan when he incessantly tempted her with his charm, his sophistication, his passion? Just those damned dimples were enough to make her melt. He'd made her fall in love with him against her will! She wished she'd gone with her instincts and taken a pass when Gus first mentioned the Somerset Necklace. If she had, she might never have found a compelling reason to meet Jonathan face-to-face, and she would have saved herself from suffering through this mortifying humiliation.

"My, my, Siena," Jonathan taunted. "You have a bit of a temper. Marie would never behave so inappropriately."

Siena let out a short laugh. "Hah! You don't even want to know the things I've done that the prim and proper Marie Lacroix would consider *inappropriate.*"

Jonathan sighed as he sat on the edge of the bed. "You're right. I don't want to hear about the things you've done in the past. You know, when I first uncovered your true reason for meeting me, I had a hard time understanding why a woman with your intelligence and beauty would misuse her talents in such an insidious way. I wonder if you'd indulge me and explain what motivated you to get into this—for lack of a better term—*profession* in the first place."

Now that he'd confronted her, Jonathan was again the calm, considerate man Siena had fallen in love with. However, she was a pro at getting people to confide in her and then using their secrets against them. She needed to poke around a bit until she was certain Jonathan wasn't playing that same trick on her. She sat on the bed next to him, keeping a respectful distance between them.

"I do want to come clean with you, Jonathan," she said, attempting to regain his favor. "First, I need to understand how you discovered Marie Lacroix is my alias. Was it something I said, or did, that made you question me?"

"Oh, no, quite the opposite," he assured her. "Your cover was flawless, but I became wary of you during the vetting process."

"You had me vetted?" she blurted out. "Jesus, talk about being blindsided!" She'd considered Jonathan to be a man without a suspicious bone in his body. Unfortunately, she was realizing far too late that underneath his ingenuous personality was a savvy man who guarded himself against people who were inclined to take advantage of him. People like her.

"I'm sorry if you mistook me for being a pushover. When I was a young man, my father taught me to be cautious of vultures who want to sink their claws into our family's wealth. His advice has served me well over the years, particularly in the last few weeks."

Although Siena dreaded learning the results of the investigation, she needed to know exactly how much Jonathan had unearthed about her sordid background. She was too disgraced, however, to make eye contact while he relayed the information. She crossed the room and, leaning against the dresser, stared at herself in the mirror as she urged him to continue.

"Go on. I'm dying to find out what dirt you dug up."

Jonathan took a deep breath. "I received an initial

report just before our weekend on Nantucket, but the results were inconclusive. Prior to eleven years ago, my investigators couldn't find a history of anyone matching the details I'd given them about Marie Lacroix. There were no school records, no relatives in Versailles nor Manhattan, no history of an antique store owned by the Lacroix family. However, I kept an open mind and assumed they just needed to dig a little deeper. You see, I'd already fallen in love with you and wanted more than anything to believe you were genuine. While we were on Nantucket, my mind was filled with plans for our future. Then, a few days later, just before I left for Alaska, I paid a fateful visit to my son."

Siena gazed at Jonathan's reflection in the mirror. What did he mean by *fateful*? Had he encountered Jacqueline while at his son's home, and mistaken her for Marie? Jacqueline had insisted she'd kept her distance from Patrick while his father was in town, but maybe she'd unknowingly slipped up.

"Why?" she asked. "What happened during your visit?"

Standing a few feet behind her, Jonathan held Siena's attention as he explained. "You may not realize how often you use the expression '*pauvre petit*'. I always found your occasional use of French terms to be an endearing reflection of your upbringing, so imagine how surprised I was when my four-year-old grandson uttered those two words. When I asked Oliver how he knew the expression, he proudly informed me he'd learned the phrase from Patrick's new girlfriend, Kelsey.

"Oddly enough, Patrick had just commented on the fact that he and I, at almost the same time, had met two wonderful women who, by our own descriptions, sounded as though they could be the same person. When Oliver used your French saying, I was convinced the similarities were not a mere coincidence. I was horrified to imagine the woman I'd fallen in love with was also seducing my son. And, if she were, to what end?"

Siena stared at her own stunned reflection in the mirror. For all her careful planning, reminding Jacqueline to refrain from using any expressions they'd learned from their mother as young girls had never even crossed her mind. If she weren't so angry with herself, she would have laughed at the irony. She shook her head adamantly. "No, Jonathan. You were wrong."

"Yes, I was, as I soon found out," Jonathan informed her. "Before I left for Alaska, I assigned my investigators a new task: find out everything you can about Kelsey Adams. They presented me with an enlightening report within a few days, one that gave me a bit of solace. You see, unlike my daughter, who hired a third-rate P.I. out of convenience, the firm I have on retainer performs detailed and reliable investigations.

"My team tracked Kelsey to the hotel where she was staying, then on to an antique store in the Bronx. She used a back entrance, a sure sign she hadn't gone there just to shop. A search of the business' registration revealed the owner to be Wendell Ferguson who, it turns out, hadn't always been a sole proprietor. He had co-owned the store with a man named Dominic Ricci until their partnership dissolved eleven years ago, around the same time Marie Lacroix was hired at Willow's Auction House."

Siena wanted to beg Jonathan to stop but, at the same time, she needed to understand how he'd connected her to the con. She crossed the room and sat on the chair by the window to put some distance between them.

"You've come this far. Please, go on."

Jonathan faced Siena. Leaning his back against the dresser, he crossed one foot over the other and continued. "Eleven years ago, a career thief named Dominic Ricci was shot several times by the irate husband of a woman who was, I speculate, the victim of a scam he was running. No charges were filed, no legal action taken and, after being discharged from the hospital, Dominic Ricci vanished into thin air. That left his business partner, Wendell Ferguson—I understand you call him Gus—to operate the antique store minus the man who produced most of the income for their money-laundering business. Oh, right," Jonathan interjected with a snap of his fingers, "I neglected to mention my team and I determined the antique store is a front for Gus's real endeavors.

"Anyway, Dominic had two stunningly beautiful daughters—identical twins named Siena and Jacqueline. The interesting thing is, at about the same time Dominic disappeared with his gunshot wounds, Marie Lacroix materialized out of nowhere and, although she had shorter blonde hair and deep blue eyes, her resemblance to Siena Ricci is unmistakable. Now, is it just me, or do you also find that to be an odd coincidence?"

"Please, Jonathan," Siena said with a tsk, "I can do without the sarcasm."

"Sorry. Do you care to hear my theory? I'm not certain what happened to Dominic and Jacqueline Ricci, but you—Siena—transformed yourself into Marie Lacroix. You got hired at Willow's Auction House so you could have a legitimate job while operating as a con artist on the side, replacing your father as Gus's most reliable source of income. I believe you use your client contacts at Willow's to meet wealthy men and, a few months ago, you chose me as your next target. How am I doing so far?"

Siena refused to be goaded into an admission of guilt. She angled her body away from Jonathan and gazed out the window.

"Well, I guess your silence speaks for itself. So, let's get back to Gus's antique store. While my investigators were surveying the store's activities, they noticed one particular gentleman who always used the back entrance to the shop. They tailed him and caught him pickpocketing a tourist, of all things. The next day, they set up their own sting and snagged him when he attempted to lift one of their wallets. They shoved him into the backseat of their car and did their best to intimidate him, but his lips were tight. However, when $25,000 in cash was dangled in front of his face, he, as the expression goes, sang like a bird. By now, you've figured out I'm talking about Roberto Lopez."

Siena had difficulty believing Jonathan, but his information connected the pieces of the puzzle. After all the opportunities Gus had given Roberto, the weasel had the nerve to rat Gus out.

"That damned bastard!" The curse shot from her mouth with a vengeance. Now she understood why Roberto was so jittery while he assisted her on the Somerset Necklace job, and why he'd admitted the three thugs into the antique shop on Sunday afternoon. She recalled her last conversation with Roberto when he warned Jonathan might be playing a trick on her. Although she'd forever remember Roberto as being a louse, in his defense, she now understood he truly had tried to alert her. If only she hadn't allowed her ego to get in the way, she may have heeded Roberto's warning and seen through the trick Jonathan was pulling on her. She swiveled in the chair to face Jonathan. "And you! You seriously paid Roberto $25,000 to squeal on us?"

"I did, and the payment was worth every penny. In the long run, the investment saved me from losing the Singing Bird Pistols and made me aware of your plan to steal my heirloom necklace. When we discovered what you were up to, I suggested a counter plan. You see, I didn't receive a phone call on Saturday afternoon requiring me to rush off to the club, leaving you alone with easy access to my Singing Bird Pistol. I didn't leave the key in Patrick's curio cabinet yesterday out of laziness. And I didn't get the necklace back from Veronica after the gala just to make you happy. Everything I did was designed to make the thefts easier for you. I was intent on speeding up the process and ending this sham of yours as quickly as possible."

"Is that why you were in such a dour mood when I returned from the spa on Saturday afternoon?"

"Yes," Jonathan admitted. "While you and Veronica were off pampering yourselves, the full depth of your scheme was revealed to me. That was when I made the decision to proceed with my own ruse against you."

How could she have been bamboozled so easily? Siena had always considered her keen judgment of character to be a gift and attributed her natural instincts as the reason she was always able to stay ahead of the game. Unfortunately, her love for Jonathan combined with her smug overconfidence turned out to be her downfall.

"Now, let's get back to my counter plan. My

investigators wouldn't support my idea, but they put me in touch with a former colleague of theirs who will do anything for a buck and has some rather unsavory connections. I hired this man to contact Gus and express interest in the Singing Bird Pistols. Gus pretended to be ignorant of the pieces until my man offered more than his current buyer was willing to pay. Of course, Gus couldn't let a few million dollars more slip through his fingers. My associate then hired three reformed gang members he's acquainted with to burst into the antique shop and force you to steal Patrick's Bird Pistol by eight o'clock Wednesday morning. Our ruse was going along smoothly until yesterday afternoon when the man assigned to stick with you, I think he calls himself Jeremy—"

"Jimmy," Siena corrected.

"Sorry, Jimmy, told us he learned Veronica had hired an investigator of her own, and the P.I. had approached you about stealing the Duncan Cordray painting. I had to do some side-stepping but, with Jimmy feeding us your every move, I was able to revise my plan and bring an end to this fiasco."

Siena's anger exploded. She bolted out of the chair and confronted Jonathan head-on. "Since Sunday, I have been frantically trying to diffuse a situation I was afraid could turn very bad very quickly, and all the while you were just playing a game with me?"

"Let me explain." Jonathan attempted to place his hands onto Siena's shoulders, but she slapped them away.

"Don't!" She stormed to the window and spoke angrily. "I adored you, Jonathan. How could you have deceived me like this?"

Jonathan lashed back, his voice raised. "You have a lot of nerve accusing *me* of being underhanded. Let me remind you that you attempted to con me out of millions of dollars. From my point of view, you were long past due to receive a dose of your own medicine."

Until then, Siena had a flawless track record, but Jonathan had proved to be her ruin. He was right. She deserved to be the victim for once, to experience the rug being yanked out from under her. The faces of the men she'd preyed on over the years flashed through her mind, filling her soul with remorse. She lowered herself into the easy chair and spoke from her heart.

"Earlier, you asked me to help you understand why I became a con artist. I'd like to explain myself, if I may."

"Yes, please do," he replied. "I need to understand why the woman I fell in love with is a conniving thief."

Siena lowered her head, her eyes all but closed as she gathered her thoughts. When she was ready to speak, she gazed up at Jonathan for a moment before her eyes drifted off to the far corner of the room, conjuring up a past she seldom recalled and events of which she never spoke.

"I was just a couple of years out of college, determined to become the youngest vice president in my company's history, when my father was nearly shot to death. As you know, he survived the attack, but one of the bullets damaged his spine and left him a paraplegic." Her voice caught. She wiped away a tear. "The man who assaulted him was outraged when he learned my father was still alive. He was well-connected to some seriously bad people who threatened my father while he was still in the hospital. My father couldn't stay in New York. He'd never know when or where another attempt would be made on his life.

"Gus made the decision to hide my father on an island in the Caribbean as soon as he was well enough to travel. My Grandmother Ricci joined him, as did my sister. Since Jacqueline is a nurse, she became our father's primary caregiver. She got a part-time job at a local clinic, but her income wasn't enough to pay for their living expenses *and* my father's medical needs.

"Gus and I stayed in New York and did what we could to support them financially. I worked my ass off to earn a promotion, but my bump in salary didn't come close to covering the increase in my expenses. I needed to make big money, and I needed to make it fast. Even though I'd vowed never to join my father's business, of all the options I considered, becoming a con artist was the most logical solution. Plus, it would be easy for me."

"Easy?" Jonathan questioned. "Weren't you afraid of the peril you'd put yourself in, especially after what happened to your father?"

"You don't understand. Conning people is a lifestyle I grew up with. It's second nature to me. Plus, I'm a risk-taker and, I'll admit, I got a thrill from the danger I'd sometimes find myself in. And the money I made was damned lucrative. While my job at Willow's covered my living expenses, the money I made from my nighttime ventures supported my family and left me a little to invest for myself. However, over this past year, I was considering calling it quits. When Gus approached me about stealing your heirloom necklace, I had pretty much decided that job would be my last. Then, the opportunity to sell the pair of Singing Bird Pistols came along, and...well, how could I pass up a job with a multi-million-dollar profit? My decision to take the Bird

Pistols from you and Patrick was motivated by greed, pure and simple.

"Gus found a buyer and I enlisted my sister's help to swindle your son while I worked the con on you. Everything was running according to plan…until I fell in love with you. What dumb luck, huh? The target I select for my final job ends up being the man of my dreams. I desperately wanted to be with you, but there was no way our relationship could survive my seedy history. The best solution for us both was for Marie Lacroix to simply disappear. But first, I needed to stop the plan to steal the Singing Bird Pistol from your son."

Jonathan interrupted her. "Stop right there. You'd changed your mind about stealing Patrick's Bird Pistol? When did you make that decision?"

"During the plane ride back to New York on Sunday. My heart and my conscience teamed up and forced me to face the horrible person I'd become. I couldn't stop the sale of the necklace. That transaction had already taken place. But I still had time to prevent Jacqueline from stealing your son's Bird Pistol. I also intended to return the Bird Pistol I'd taken from your library, although I hadn't yet figured out how."

"My God," Jonathan mumbled as if to himself. "If only I'd known…"

"There was no way you could have known. I was about to share my change of plans with Gus when the goons you hired showed up and started slinging their intimidating threats at us. I had no other recourse but to complete the con as agreed. Now, after three days of living in fear and conspiring with a stranger to steal a valuable painting from your son's home, I find out you were the person pulling the strings all along. Am I pissed about being tricked? Yes! But I'm also relieved to have this awful ordeal behind us. I owe everyone, especially you, an apology for allowing my greed to get us into this mess in the first place."

"Oh, I think you owe me more than an apology," Jonathan informed her. "Although I didn't lose the Singing Bird Pistols, I am minus one diamond and sapphire necklace which carried a value of around $1 million."

"Jonathan, I'm so sorry. I wish I'd never agreed to the Somerset Necklace job in the first place." She hesitated to ask but needed to understand Jonathan's intentions. "Will you report the theft to the police?"

Jonathan stared at the carpet and massaged the back of his neck. Gazing up at Siena, he said, "I'm still on the fence about the necklace. You see, although you committed a crime, you also did me a favor."

Siena frowned. "What do you mean?"

"Let's face it, that necklace was downright ugly. My grandfather was the only person impressed by it. My grandmother never wanted it, which was the reason she passed it on to my wife. Patricia considered it garish and only wore it on occasion out of respect for my grandparents. Veronica insisted on wearing it to the gala simply to prevent you from having it. I'm also well aware Gwendolyn will sell it in a heartbeat if I hand it down to her. So, in the long run, you've done me a favor by taking it off my hands. However, by doing so, you made a handsome profit on a necklace that wasn't yours to sell."

Siena jumped in to bargain her way out of what could turn into a ruinous situation. "Can we negotiate? I'll give you my profit from the jewelry sale in exchange for your promise to forgive both the theft of your necklace and my botched attempt to take the Singing Bird Pistols." *And the fact I deceived you? Can I dare ask you to forgive me in your heart as well?*

Jonathan smiled warily. "Excuse me for suspecting you of planning to flee the country before living up to your end of the bargain. Where is the money?"

"In the safe at Gus's shop." Siena stared into Jonathan's contemplative eyes, nervously waiting for his decision.

"Fine. I agree to your terms. Finish packing your bag. I have a car waiting out front to drive you to the antique shop where my investigators will meet you. You can hand off the money to them. After that, we'll be done."

"Thank you, Jonathan," she said timidly. She stepped past him and packed the remainder of her clothing in the suitcase. Although she was relieved to have dodged any criminal charges, knowing she'd lost Jonathan's respect was a deeply crushing blow. She kept her back to him and hoped he didn't notice the tears she was wiping from her face.

"Just for the record, you didn't need to negotiate your freedom. Overnight, I'd decided to suggest the same arrangement. It's odd. You should be arrested and justly punished, but I can't stand the thought of you being treated like a criminal, even though that's exactly what you are." In little more than a whisper, he added, "Maybe I still love you more than I'm willing to admit."

Siena zippered her suitcase, then gazed sincerely into Jonathan's eyes. "You know, I'm honestly relieved you found out who I really am. I may have dyed my hair and used a fake name to conceal my identity, but there was nothing phony about the person I was behind the façade. The woman you fell in love with wasn't Marie Lacroix. She's Siena Ricci." She stepped closer and gently touched his cheek. "Jonathan, I'm convinced destiny brought us together. You can't tell me you don't believe that in your heart as well."

Jonathan opened his mouth as if to speak, then abruptly closed it. Siena understood. What was the point of saying anything more? Their relationship was over. He lowered his head, but not before she spotted that familiar flicker of desire in his eyes.

"I'll carry your bag out to the car for you," he said.

As they descended the staircase, she asked about Patrick. "What will you tell your son about Kelsey?"

"Patrick is already aware of who Kelsey really is," Jonathan confessed. "When I arrived here the other night, I told him everything. He was incredulous and his ego's a bit scarred, but he'll get over her. Patrick's heart serves him well with his patients, but in his personal life he needs to be more discerning. As Veronica has reminded him many times, he's too gullible for his own good."

Funny. Until last night, Siena would have used those exact words to described Jonathan. In the end, the only truly gullible person in this charade was her.

As they approached the SUV, the driver took the suitcase from Jonathan and secured it in the vehicle's storage area. Jonathan faced Siena. "So, this is our final good-bye," he said. She'd never seen such sadness in his eyes.

Siena impulsively threw her arms around Jonathan's neck, refusing to callously toss away everything they'd meant to each other. "I'm so sorry," she said, her voice choked with emotion. "I love you, Jonathan. Please forgive me for all the horrible things I've done."

Jonathan enveloped her in his arms. "I will always remember you as the woman who excited me in more ways than I'd ever thought possible. I couldn't have stopped myself from falling in love with you even if I'd wanted to."

Siena boldly kissed Jonathan one last time. When his arms tightened around her and he made that familiar moan deep in his throat, she understood the demise of their relationship was as poignant for him as it was for her. Wiping the tears from her face, she stepped away from him and took her seat in the SUV. Before closing the door, she shared with him the sentiment she'd forever hold dearest in her heart.

"At least I can say, for a few brief weeks, I was the luckiest girl in the world. Good-bye, Jonathan."

Chapter 40

Jonathan
Ten Months Later

Jonathan stared blankly at the screen of his laptop. He should have been reading the essays of the students who had applied for next year's Patricia Woodward Memorial Scholarship, but instead he was thinking about the bike ride he'd taken with Siena Ricci on Nantucket last summer. After nearly a year, he still couldn't erase Siena from his heart. He put on a good show in front of family and friends, but not having her by his side was a void he found impossible to fill. Memories of Siena haunted him during the day and her image filled his dreams every night.

Brenda, Jonathan's personal assistant, entered the library and roused him from his daydreams. "Jonathan, while I was preparing your travel bag, I found this package inside one of the compartments."

Jonathan perched his reading glasses on top of his head. "I haven't used that bag for several months." He examined the small leather box tied up in a white satin ribbon and bow. "I have no idea what's in this box."

"Well, I'll leave you to figure it out while I speak with the property manager about your rental on Maui. Let me know when you've solved the mystery."

"I will. Thanks, Brenda."

Turning the box over, Jonathan noticed the imprinted Willow's Auction House logo. Bewildered, he untied the ribbon and pried open the lid. Inside the box was an antique pocket watch and fob. He smiled as a vision of his Grandfather Woodward's watch, similar in design and always worn in Granddad's vest pocket, came to mind. Jonathan hadn't relished those memories for a long time.

He wedged out a small card that was tucked into the lid. Lowering his reading glasses, Jonathan smiled as he read the note written inside.

My dearest Jonathan,

On our first morning together, you shared a fond memory of your grandfather. I hope this pocket watch keeps his spirit alive in your heart, and may it also remind you of the many precious moments that belong only to us. Like the time kept by this watch, mon cher, my love for you is eternal.

Marie

Jonathan removed the watch to examine it more closely. He recalled the magical first night spent with the woman he'd known then as Marie Lacroix and their conversation over breakfast the following morning. Her eagerness to engage him in a discussion about his family's jewelry was Jonathan's first inkling that she may have been more interested in his assets than she was in him. At the time, he ignored the nagging voice in the back of his mind. She was everything he desired, and he wanted to believe she was perfect.

He'd like to say he'd regard the watch as a token of a brief and bittersweet love affair he'd enjoyed while it lasted, but that would be a lie. Despite her depraved history and laundry list of transgressions, Jonathan still ached to wake with Siena beside him every morning, to enjoy the pleasure of her company every day, and to spend every night with her in his arms.

Siena's sentimental note was a wake-up call. Throughout his entire life, Jonathan had let nothing stop him from getting what he wanted, so why was he hesitating now? The family vacation in Hawaii would give him time to think through his emotions, but as soon as they returned from the trip, he was determined to mend his broken heart once and for all.

****

Siena

Three Weeks Later

Siena's day had been productive. During the evening's live auction, she'd gained the confidence of two new clients by securing their winning bids. None of her clients had expressed interest in the final item on the agenda, so she was done for the day. Although grateful for the downtime, she abhorred the idea of spending another lonely evening sipping cheap wine and watching mindless TV in the dreary emptiness of her tiny apartment.

Her world had changed drastically since she'd botched the Woodward job. Gus had handed over the business to his apprentices, packed up his belongings, and departed for the beauty of the Caribbean and a reunion with his lifelong friend, Dominic. Siena, who hadn't seen her father and Grandmother Ricci since their hasty departure from New York eleven years earlier, joined them for an emotional three-week visit. Siena clung to her father and grandmother and sobbed with regret over the years of lost time they'd never regain.

During her stay, Siena investigated opportunities for

Rosemary Kubli

employment, even entertained the idea of opening her own business. In the end, she had the good sense to refrain from making such a life-altering decision while her emotions were in upheaval. Her dream of reuniting with her family no longer held the same appeal when her heart was with a man who lived over a thousand miles away. She told her loved ones she belonged in New York, not the Caribbean, and needed to return home to sort out the mess she'd made of her life.

The good news was, with Gus stepping in to help with Dominic's care, Jacqueline was able to work full-time at the clinic. Despite her substantial salary increase, Jacqueline still needed to pull money out of the local bank account Siena had set up to help with their living expenses. "Do so sparingly, Jac," Siena had warned her sister. "That's all that's left of the money I profited from my con jobs. There won't be any deposits going into the account from now on."

Back in Manhattan, Siena resumed her guise as Marie Lacroix and returned to Willow's until she decided what her next step should be. Pouring herself into her job, along with extended workouts at the fitness center, helped her deal with the overwhelming sense of self-loathing which could easily consume her if she didn't keep her emotions in check. For a while, she spent too much time beating herself up over her shameful history and for essentially throwing away more than a decade of the prime years of her life. She doubted she'd ever stop lamenting the what-could-have-beens.

For the sake of her own mental health, she swept her past under the rug and concentrated on the person she wanted to be going forward. She socialized more often and dabbled in cooking and interior decorating. She'd even, at long last, purchased an area rug to cover her bare bedroom floor. Following Jonathan's example of giving back to the community, she volunteered on the weekends at a local homeless shelter. It was a start. At least she was learning to like herself again.

Her goal was to get through one day without wishing she could return home to find Jonathan waiting for her with outstretched arms.

The auctioneer's assistants were preparing the final item for the bidding block. Siena assumed she was done for the night and was gathering her paperwork when Caitlin, one of the interns she was mentoring, approached her.

"Marie, there's a gentleman on Line 3 who needs your help with the next auction."

"Okay." Although she didn't mind bidding for the client, she hated being unprepared. "Is he registered for the auction?"

"Yes. He intended to be here but had a last-minute change of plans. He asked for you specifically. Said you've helped him in the past."

Well, nothing like working under pressure. "Do you know the client's name?" Siena asked while she paged through the catalogue to familiarize herself with the item being offered in the final auction.

"No. Sorry."

"That's all right. You said he's on Line 3?"

"Yep. Oh, and here's his paddle. Thanks, Marie."

"Sure, no problem." Siena thumbed through the catalogue until she arrived at the correct page. She froze when she eyed the larger-than-life photo of the item coming up for bid. The client had requested her assistance to acquire a 4-carat diamond ring belonging to the estate of Marilyn Dohar, a mid-twentieth century Washington D.C. socialite. The ring itself wasn't an issue, but the design triggered an unwanted memory of selecting an engagement ring with Jonathan's granddaughters during their weekend on Nantucket last summer. "Of all the rotten luck," she mumbled under her breath. She searched for Caitlin–*Please assign the client to another of the phone bidders!*–but the auctioneer had already begun his introduction. *Great.* Siena cleared her throat, lifted the phone's receiver, and punched the button for Line 3.

"Hello, this is Marie Lacroix. Who am I speaking with?" A few seconds passed without a response. Had Caitlin been misinformed about which line the caller was on? Or had the client changed his mind? "Hello, are you on the line?"

After a brief pause, the client said, "Hello, Siena. How have you been?"

Siena opened her mouth to speak, but no words came out. She shook her head, hoping to regain her senses. For a second, she could have sworn the man's voice sounded like...

"Jonathan? Is it really you?"

"Yes, it's really me. I'm sorry to ask for your help at the last minute, but it's imperative I obtain this ring. You and I were such a good team in the past, I'm banking on your willingness to pair up with me one more time."

A flush, brought on by her mounting anger, began in Siena's chest and was making its way up her neck and onto her face. How dare Jonathan request her assistance with this item! The ring was certainly not something he'd purchase as a gift for any of the females in his family, and he'd never expressed interest in jewelry for the investment value. Therefore, she surmised, he was about to become engaged to another woman. Talk about pouring salt into an open wound! *Calm down, Siena. He's nothing more than a client who needs your expert assistance.* She took a sip of water and swallowed her pride.

"I'm happy to help you, of course. What is your maximum bid?"

"The sky's the limit."

Imagining the phone receiver was Jonathan's neck, Siena squeezed the handle with all her strength. *Get over it, Siena. Don't let your emotions interfere with business.*

"Bidding started at ten thousand with minimum increments of five thousand." She raised her paddle. "I've bid $25,000 on your behalf." Her advice would have been to not bid any higher than forty thousand, but since Jonathan had given her *carte blanche*, well…Lifting her paddle a second time, she informed him, "I just raised your bid to thirty-five thousand."

"Offer fifty and let's see if anyone outbids me," he instructed.

"You're the boss." As the auctioneer was attempting to raise the bid above $40,000, Siena held up her paddle and called out, "Fifty-five thousand!"

The auctioneer glanced at her with questioning eyes. Was she serious? She smiled and nodded her head. *Yes, the bid is legit.*

"I believe I told you to bid fifty thousand, not fifty-*five*," Jonathan reminded her. He sounded amused, as though he realized she'd taken him for a ride.

"Oh, sorry," she replied flippantly. "I must have misunderstood you."

"I'm offered $55,000 for this exquisite diamond

ring," the auctioneer announced. "Do I hear sixty? Sixty thousand? Fifty-five going once…going twice…Sold to Bidder 1076 for $55,000."

"Congratulations, Jonathan. You offered the winning bid. The ring is yours." She hoped the woman who'd be wearing the 4-carat cluster of diamonds was spectacular, or Jonathan had just wasted a ton of money. *Well, if I can't have the man, at least I've earned myself a nice commission.* "I assume you want the ring shipped to your home address?"

"No, I'll take care of collecting it myself. I'm standing near you, in the back of the gallery."

"You're where?" Siena asked as she swiveled around in her chair. With so many people blocking her view, she needed to step around her station before she caught sight of him. Jonathan smiled and waved a greeting. "Then, why…"

Jonathan chuckled. "Meet me in the lobby in fifteen minutes and I'll explain."

Siena slammed the phone down so hard she was sure she'd broken it. *Damn! Now here comes Stephanie, the office gossip monger, to ask if everything's all right.* "Yes, everything's fine, Steph." She smiled (unconvincingly), picked up her belongings, and stormed out of the gallery.

Following a quick stop at her cubicle to drop off her notebooks and grab her jacket and purse, she was heading straight home to drown her sorrows in the bottle of wine she'd opened last night. Jonathan could wait in the lobby until he was blue in the face for all she cared. After a while, he'd get the hint she wasn't interested in joining him for a stroll down memory lane. He'd be free to rush back to Burgess to surprise his lady friend with her huge rock and a proposal of marriage. With each glass of wine, Siena would toast to their happiness.

Yeah, right.

Have fun playing nice-nice with Veronica, new Mrs. Jonathan Woodward. But wait! Maybe Veronica was gaining a stepmother who was a bigger bitch than herself. Now, that notion made Siena laugh out loud.

As the elevator descended to the main floor, Siena changed her game plan. *Screw it.* She couldn't live with herself unless she gave Jonathan a piece of her mind. But she'd be civil about it. She wouldn't dare create a scene at her place of employment. As she exited the elevator and rounded the corner, she found Jonathan waiting in the lobby.

"Jonathan, what a nice surprise." She acted as though they'd never been anything more than mere acquaintances. Meanwhile, just being near him again sent her heart racing.

Jonathan's smile grew wider with each step she took toward him. "Marie, it's wonderful to see you." At least he had the courtesy to refrain from using her real name in front of her co-workers.

Jonathan placed his hand on her arm and kissed her cheek. Siena breathed in his scent, and—*uh-oh!* —her passion was immediately aroused. *Seriously, Siena. You didn't expect that to happen?* Still, her desires were torn. Which did she want more—to throw her arms around his neck or to slap him across his face?

A few people were still milling about the lobby. "Let's duck into an alcove so we can have some privacy," Siena suggested, leading the way to a more secluded area.

"I guess I don't need to ask how you've been,"

Jonathan said. "If it's possible, you're more stunning now than the last time I saw you."

"Cut the sweet talk, Jonathan! You have a lot of nerve coming here and asking for my help to purchase that ring. Wasn't it enough for you to break my heart once? What possessed you to show up at the gallery tonight and rub my face into the fact that you've found someone else to share your life with? Meanwhile, I can't even enjoy myself on a date because I spend the entire evening comparing every man I go out with to you. If it's revenge you're after, congratulations. You've succeeded." She hadn't meant to speak with such bitterness, but once again her temper had taken control. *Well, the words are out of my mouth now and I can't take them back.* "There. I've said it. Whoever this woman is, she'd better be amazing, or she doesn't deserve to be with you. And she'd damned well better be worth the price you just overpaid for her engagement ring."

Is that a glimmer of amusement in Jonathan's eyes? Did he just chuckle?!

"This is the second time I've seen that feistiness of yours, and I have to admit I rather like it. And you are correct. I do intend to present this ring to the most captivating woman in the world, the woman I love with all my heart. If you'd bid a million dollars, she'd be worth every penny."

Siena's jaw dropped. Why was Jonathan being so cruel? The man she loved had never displayed this vindictive side of his personality. Perhaps she was just now seeing the real Jonathan Woodward. If so, she had no interest in continuing their conversation.

"Well, I'm glad we had this time to catch up," she told him politely. "I hope your perfect woman appreciates how lucky she is to have snatched up the most perfect man in the world, and I wish the best of everything for you both." As she imagined Jonathan spending the rest of his life with someone other than herself, Siena's heart broke. Tears spilled from her eyes before she could stop them. "Sorry, I didn't mean to go all weepy on you."

Jonathan stepped closer and brushed her damp cheeks with his fingertips. "Don't be embarrassed. You just confirmed what I hoped was true. You still love me every bit as much as I love you."

Siena gazed questioningly into his eyes. Had she understood him correctly? "Jonathan, have you gone mad?"

"No," he said with a smile. "I can assure you, I'm as sane as I've ever been."

"But, how can you say you love me when you know about all the horrible things I've done?"

"I honestly don't care about your past. All I know is that, since last summer, I've been miserable without you. So, I finally came to a decision. I'm willing to forget about the indiscretions you committed as Marie Lacroix in exchange for the pleasure of spending every day for the rest of my life with Siena Ricci. Please tell me you feel the same way," he said, grinning and showing off those adorable dimples that always made her knees go soft, "or I just spent a ton of money on an engagement ring for no good reason."

"So, the woman you purchased the ring for is…" She didn't finish her sentence for fear of being presumptuous.

"Is you, of course." Jonathan removed the jewelry box from the pocket of his sport coat. He opened the lid and said, "I considered romantically whisking you off to Paris and proposing at the foot of the Eiffel Tower but, sorry, I just couldn't wait that long for your answer." He slid the ring from its satin cushion and dropped the box back inside his pocket. Holding the ring before her, he took her hand in his, dropped to one knee, and gazed imploringly into her eyes. "So, right here, in the cold marble lobby of Willow's Auction House, I surrender my will to destiny and my heart to your keeping. Siena, I love you with every fiber of my being. Will you marry me?"

Siena wanted to jump in the air, wanted to shout with joy, but she was too overcome with emotion to speak. She barely managed to nod her head and eke out, "Yes!"

Jonathan stood, raised her trembling left hand, and slipped the ring onto her finger. Siena wrapped her arms around Jonathan's neck and kissed him over and over again. She clung to him for fear that, if she let go, she'd wake from yet another dream and find she was hugging her pillow again instead of Jonathan. "I can't believe this is happening," she whispered into his ear.

"You have no idea how relieved I am," Jonathan admitted. "I was convinced you'd tell me to get lost after the way I treated you the last time we were together."

"I don't want to think about our last few days together nor speak of them ever again."

"Neither do I."

Their lips met again, and they savored a long, passionate kiss. Only then was Siena secure enough to step back and admire the glistening cluster of diamonds that adorned her ring finger. Now that she'd had time to settle down to earth, she questioned how Jonathan could be so trusting when their previous association was built on fraud and deceit.

"Jonathan, considering my history, aren't you concerned I'll sell this ring for a profit and vanish into thin air? I mean, that's basically what I'd planned to do to you a year ago. What makes you think I'm not still involved in that same type of illicit activity?"

Jonathan raised an eyebrow as a shrewd grin appeared on his face. "What makes you think I've changed my ways? We wouldn't be here right now if I weren't certain you've kept your nose clean since the last time we were together."

"But how would you—" Siena suddenly got it. "Oh. You put your investigators back on the job, is that it?"

"I wasn't about to make the same mistake twice."

Part of her was insulted he'd had her comings and goings monitored, but she couldn't blame him for being cautious. "And how will you explain me to your family? They'll wonder why I changed my name and lost my accent."

"Actually, that's water under the bridge. I told them all about you and my intention to win you back while we were on a family vacation a few weeks ago."

Siena considered the conversations that must have taken place, and the perhaps unpleasant discussions that were still to be held when she arrived in Burgess. "Aren't they opposed to you marrying a woman whose past is so tainted?"

Jonathan gave her a lop-sided grin. "Well, I may have romanticized your history a bit as I pled my case to them. What they don't know won't hurt them." Jonathan took her hand. "Come on, let's get out of here. My driver is parked out front. I have a hotel suite reserved for the night. Tomorrow, we'll fly home to Burgess."

Home. The idea of being with Jonathan and calling his home her own made Siena happier than she'd ever been. However, she did have a life in New York she couldn't simply walk away from. As they exited through the front doors, she said, "Jonathan, I will need to take care of a few *minor* details before I leave New York, like turning in my resignation at Willow's and cleaning out my apartment."

"You can take care of Willow's tomorrow, but your apartment will need to wait. We're flying to Italy on Sunday. I've rented a villa for us in Tuscany."

Siena gazed at Jonathan with wide, unblinking eyes. What mystical powers did he possess to always know what made her happy? "That's the region where my grandmother was born. I've always dreamed of visiting Tuscany."

Jonathan smiled sheepishly. "I figured as much." When Siena cocked her head in confusion, he told her, "Remember, I had you vetted. I probably know more about you than you know about yourself."

She didn't care any longer about the investigations, nor the reason why Jonathan had needed to conduct them. This moment began their new life together, a future that would not be bogged down by the ghosts from her past.

"Did you know I'm named after the city in Tuscany where my grandmother was born?"

Jonathan laughed. "Now *that's* something I did not know about you."

"How long will we be in Italy?"

"We have the villa for a month, but we can remain in Europe if you'd like. Maybe travel around, stay through the summer."

"I don't care where we go, as long as we're together."

The driver greeted them and opened the back door of their town car.

"Will you miss Manhattan?" Jonathan asked.

Before stepping into the car, Siena took in the city where she'd lived her entire life—the bright lights, the exhaust fumes, the constant din of voices and car horns and music blaring from rolled-down car windows, the streets crowded with residents hurrying past tourists frantically snapping photos. She recalled the painful memories of her parents' volatile marriage, her mother's depression and desertion of her family, her father's near-fatal attack, and her unsavory years working as a con artist. She'd wanted to escape the big city chaos and leave her past behind for a long time. At last, her dream was coming true.

She gazed into Jonathan's adoring eyes and told herself that, yes, she truly was experiencing a fairy tale ending. Not only did she have the chance to begin a new life, she would be doing so with the man she loved. Tomorrow and every day going forward, she'd fulfill the fantasy she created on their first morning together. She'd wake with Jonathan by her side and view every day spent in his company as a gift to treasure.

"New York will always be a part of me, but my heart hasn't belonged here for a long time. I'm more than ready to make a fresh start." Smiling tenderly, she caressed Jonathan's cheek and said, "Let's go home."

A word about the author...

Rosemary Kubli was born and raised in Northeast Ohio where she and her husband currently reside. When not travelling, on land to visit family and friends and on sea to any destination a cruise ship will take her, she can be found with her nose in a book or obsessing over the latest binge-worthy TV series. *Gullible* is her debut novel. rosemarykubli.com

Thank you for purchasing
this publication of The Wild Rose Press, Inc.

For questions or more information
contact us at
info@thewildrosepress.com.

The Wild Rose Press, Inc.
www.thewildrosepress.com